BOOK ONE

CREATURES

OF

CHAOS

BOOK ONE

CREATURES OF CHAOS

USA TODAY BESTSELLING AUTHOR

JULIE HALL

Creatures of Chaos (Book 1)

Published by Julie Hall LLC

www.JulieHallAuthor.com

Developmental Editing by Wendy Higgins. Line Editing by Lee Burton. Proofreading by Janelle Leonard. Cover Designs by Maria Spada and K.D. Ritchie. Cover Typography by Christian Bentulan. Interior artwork by Damián Sanchez, Sasha Lee Coleman, Irene Barboni, Camille Lou Illustration, and Lyubov Podgorysheva.

ISBN (paperback): 978-1-954510-18-0

ISBN (hardcover): 978-1-954510-19-7

ISBN (signed special edition hardcover): 978-1-954510-17-3

Awards

Gold Medal Winner / *Creatures of Chaos*
2025 Illumination Awards

Finalist, Paranormal & Supernatural / *Forging Darkness*
2022 Realm Awards

Audiobook Finalist / *Stealing Embers*
2022 Realm Awards

Winner, Speculative Fiction / *Stealing Embers*
2021 ACFW Carol Awards

Gold Medal Winner / *Stealing Embers*
2021 Illumination Awards

Finalist, Paranormal & Supernatural / *Stealing Embers*
2021 Realm Awards

Finalist, Young Adult / *Stealing Embers*
2021 Realm Awards

Finalist, Readers' Choice / *Stealing Embers*
2021 Realm Awards

Parable Award Finalist / *Huntress*
2021 Realm Awards

Young Adult Finalist / *Stealing Embers*
2020 The Wishing Shelf Book Awards

Finalist, Speculative Fiction / *Huntress*
2018 ACFW Carol Awards

Young Adult Book of the Year / *Huntress*
2018 Christian Indie Awards

Gold Medal Winner / *Huntress*
2018 Illumination Awards

First Place Winner, Religion / *Huntress*
2018 IndieReader Discovery Awards

Christian Fiction Finalist / *Huntress*
2018 Next Generation Indie Book Awards

Alliance Award (Reader's Choice) / *Warfare*
2018 Realm Makers Awards

Parable Award Finalist / *Logan*
2018 Realm Makers Awards

Gold Medal Winner / *Huntress*
2017 The Wishing Shelf Book Awards

Best Debut Author / *Julie Hall*

2017 Ozarks Indie Book Festival

Best Inspirational Novel / *Huntress*
2017 Ozarks Indie Book Festival

Second Place Winner / *Huntress*
2017 ReadFree.ly Indie Book of the Year

First Place Winner / *Huntress*
2012 Women of Faith Writing Contest

***USA TODAY* Bestselling Author**
August 17, 2017 & June 21, 2018

I NEVER WOULD HAVE ENTERED the tunnels if I'd known what was going to happen. But that's the thing about making stupid decisions, they never seem that way at the time.

The faelight torches that illuminate the underground passageways crisscrossing beneath Nightlark Academy are only just bright enough to keep me from face-planting into the rough stone walls. I move as quickly as I can in the low light; the echoes of the rocks crunching beneath my shoes the only sound as I shuffle-run down the long corridors.

I can't be late to my next class. Last week Mr. Sullivan threatened to fail me if I show up late again, and if that happens I'll be forced to take summer classes to graduate. That's *not* an option. I've endured the torture that is Nightlark Academy for four excruciating years. I'm not spending a single day longer here than I have to.

Rounding a corner, I skid to a halt. The tunnel ahead is completely dark. Since faelight is eternal, it doesn't extinguish on its own. Someone had to have removed the torches or used magic to douse the flame.

My breathing sounds unnaturally loud in the stillness. I strain my ears, trying to pick up a hint of movement or the faintest whisper. The passageways are indisputably creepy, and the darkness makes them even more so, but normal Nightlark students wouldn't be as on guard as I am right now.

But normal students have magic. I do not.

The underground tunnels that connect the academy's outer buildings and the main castle might technically be a shortcut, but they aren't popular. They're dark, dank, and dusty, the three D's that usually keep students topside, but that's not what keeps me taking the long way between classes each day. No, I've done my best to avoid the tunnels since freshman year because I'd been jumped in them too many times to feel safe down here anymore.

A beat passes as I try to make up my mind: turn back or keep going? The only thing worse than racing through pitch-black corridors alone would be finding out too late that I'm *not* actually alone.

My classmates might not get physical out in the open academy hallways, but what happens in the tunnels stays in the tunnels. But even so, I chanced it today because I was running super late to Elemental Chemistry and was left with no choice. Since there are only a few precious minutes before the period starts, I assumed any other student traversing the tunnels would be long gone by now.

It seemed like an educated risk at the time, but as the hair begins to rise on my arms I start to regret my decision. I may not have the natural instincts of a shifter, but what instincts I do have are suddenly screaming at me.

"Run, little bunny," a taunting voice whispers from the yawning abyss in front of me.

Jules.

Fear hits me like a tidal wave, flooding my veins with equal parts fire and ice. I know that voice. I know what's coming.

I twist to flee, but before I take my first step it's already too late. My back foot sinks into the solid ground, trapping me in the confined space with a psychopath. I yank at my leg that's buried halfway up to my knee in a solid twelve inches of dirt and stone.

The crazy wolf shifter must be using her magic to keep the ground sealed around my foot.

A chorus of eerie detached chuckles floats toward me as I continue to tug.

Oh no. She's not alone.

I double my efforts, struggling in vain because I know that even if I manage to free myself she'll just use her earth magic again to sink my other foot into the ground. But I don't give up. I'm many things, but a quitter isn't one of them. That's probably one of the reasons the wolf shifter won't leave me alone. As an alpha female in her pack, her natural instinct is to dominate. She wants to see me broken, in body and spirit. But that will never happen. I'll never give her the satisfaction of breaking my spirit.

The crunch of loose gravel reaches my ears and I look up to see Jules and two of her minions appear from the darkness, smiling maniacally. They're all dressed similarly in camo cargo pants, sneakers, and tight crop tops that just touch the waist of their pants. It looks like they're trying too hard to look both fashionable yet tough. I'm not impressed.

Jules has been a thorn in my side for years. All because I punched her in the nose for picking on a small fae girl in our first year of elementary school. She's had it out for me ever since, but it wasn't until she came into her powers roughly nine years ago—and I didn't—that the real trouble started. It was worth it though, because the small fae girl, Ensley, and her dragon shifter twin brother, Becks, have been my ride-or-die besties ever since.

Realizing I've run out of time, I straighten to my full height, which isn't much and even shorter with one leg sunk into the ground, and I face them head-on.

"What have we here?" Jules asks, flipping a chunk of her wavy brown and gray-streaked hair over her shoulder.

"Looks like a whole lotta nothing to me," Dina, her friend-slash-lackey answers, and Jules and the other redheaded wolf shifter, Freya, laugh.

I don't bother asking what they want, because I already know. To see me bleed.

Clenching my jaw, I size them up. If magic wasn't in the picture I'd have a chance, even against all three of them. Creatures like Jules who have strong magic tend to be poor fighters, relying on their magic to protect them. But Jules' earth magic, however untrained she is, is still powerful. Dina's and Freya's less so, but *some* magic still trumps *no* magic.

If only my father's shifter strength or my mother's fae magic would finally manifest in me. I'd even welcome some distant ancestor's creepy vampire powers if it meant I could face off with these girls on an equal footing, but here I am, almost eighteen and well past the age creature powers emerge and still not presenting even the smallest spark of magic.

Familiar resentment at my magical impotence rises in my gut like bile burning my esophagus, but like always I choke it down. It won't do me any good to rage against something I have no power to change. At least that's what my parents always tell me before reminding me how strong I am even without magic, but in times like this physical strength will only get me so far.

Jules steps closer but stays out of reach. I squeeze my fists in frustration. If she'd only come a few feet closer so I could nail her in the face with a left cross. A hit in the right spot could put her down, but they know what I can do with my fists, so all three shifters stay out of range.

Jules lifts her hand and a stone the size of my fist floats into the air in front of her. Dina and Freya follow suit, the rocks they chose only slightly smaller than Jules'.

Showy. If they want to throw rocks at me, they could just use their hands.

"So, Locklyn," Jules starts, a wicked gleam in her dark predatory eyes. "Looks like we have you at a disadvantage. If you'd like to beg me to let you go, I'll consider having mercy on you."

I glare at Jules. "I'll never beg you for anything."

Jules' grin widens, taking on a sinister twist. "I was hoping you'd say that."

With a flick of her wrist she shoots the stone at me. I try to dodge it but can only move so far because of my trapped foot. The projectile smashes into my shoulder, knocking me back against the rough stone wall. A burst of pain radiates down my arm as stone dust rains on me from above.

Dina's and Freya's stones fly at me next. They don't have the same heat Jules' did, but I can't dodge both at the same time and one nails me high on my forehead, right at the hairline. I feel the trickle of blood as it slides down the side of my face before I register the pain.

Jules high fives Freya and I glare at all three of them, baring my teeth in an empty threat. I hope now that they've seen me bleed, it will be the end of it, but it's not. They take turns pelting me with a half-dozen more rocks. I manage to protect my head, but I'm going to be a patchwork of bruises tomorrow.

When three stones come at me at once, I twist away as far as I'm able, hunching over to protect my head. As soon as my back is to them they start in on me with their fists and feet. I fight back, swinging wildly, even connecting a few times, but with my foot sunk into the ground I'm off kilter and can't land a solid blow. That doesn't stop me fighting like a hellcat though. The three of them only double their efforts because of it and I slip out of fight mode and into survival.

I take a hit to my mouth and then spit a glob of blood onto the ground right before a fist plows into my gut. The impact steals my breath and sends me crashing to my hands and knees. My foot finally loosens from its dirt prison, but at this point it doesn't even matter. I'm too beat down to move, let alone fight them off. I grit my teeth and brace myself for the next blow, but my tormentors switch from physical to verbal abuse.

"You should have been put down ages ago," Jules sneers.

"Yeah," Freya agrees. "You're just a magicless freak with hardly any friends."

Low blow on both accounts, but I don't so much as flinch. I'll never let anyone know how deeply their taunts cut.

They can watch me bleed, but they'll never see me cry.

I look up and get a little bit of satisfaction when I notice Freya's eye is swollen and Jules has a small cut on her cheekbone. Looks like I landed a few hits after all. Too bad wolf shifters heal quickly, and the evidence will probably be gone in an hour.

"She should be shipped off to Slinker Island with the rest of the defectives," Dina adds. I don't see any injuries, but there are dirt smudges all over her top and pants, and half her dark ponytail has fallen out.

Slinker Island is just a myth, the place where creatures with little or no magic are said to be sent. In reality, it's not much more than a gruesome fairy tale parents tell their children to scare them into taking their magic skills and abilities seriously. I know, because if it were real, I would have been sent there already. But even though the place may not be real, the insult is.

Most creatures come into their magic at around eight or nine, before puberty starts. There are rare instances where a kid reaches ten or eleven before presenting their magic, but creature powers always manifest well before their teen years.

Always. Without exception. *Except me.*

Freya is right. I'm a freak and no one knows why. The excuse the doctors gave us was that my magic was just too weak to detect, but that's not it. I'd be able to feel it if I had even a touch of magic. I know in my heart it's just not there.

I glare up at the trio as I catch my breath and then spit another blood loogie, making sure to aim for Jules' white sneakers, but the projectile falls short.

Jules sneers at me. "You're disgusting. And worse than that, you're a nobody. You should do everyone a favor and just stay where you are right now, down in the dirt by our feet."

She flicks a hand, and filth and small stones splatter me. Laughing, she turns and walks away, Dina and Freya following in her wake.

With shaky knees, I push to my feet, wiping at a trickle of blood running from my busted lip down my chin. My t-shirt and jeans are covered with grime and blood, and there's a tear in the fabric over my knee. I don't even bother to check my hair. I'm sure it looks just as bad as the rest of me.

I'm a mess. I can't walk back into class like this.

Sighing, I tip my head back against the stone wall, taking a moment to rest and slowly move all my limbs to make sure nothing is broken. My ankle tweaks a little when I put pressure on it, but I don't think it's serious.

I'm so tired of this. What I wouldn't give to go up against each one of them one-on-one without magic. I'd show them what it feels like to be me every single day of my life.

Vulnerable. Weak. Outmatched.

"Locklyn!" My name echoes off the tunnels and my body locks up before I register who's calling for me. When I do, the fear leaks out of me, but shame takes its place, and for a moment I consider hiding from him. But it wouldn't make a difference. Becks would find me, he always does.

It's a few heartbeats and then Becks is standing in front of me, his green eyes wild as he takes me in, checking me from head to toe. "What happened?"

"Nothing." It's obviously a lie.

His gaze fills with compassion, and I have to look away. That's not the emotion I want to see shining in his eyes when he looks at me.

He shrugs out of his dark overshirt and clutches it in his hand, leaving him in just a tight-fitting tee. Stepping closer, he uses the shirt to gently wipe the blood from my forehead and cheek. His body heat brushes up against me in the chilly tunnel, making me want to burrow into his chest, but I suppose being a dragon shifter he can't help how hot he runs.

"Where else are you hurt?"

"I'm fine," I say in a small voice, and I am. I'll have bruises, but bruises heal.

He murmurs my name, and on instinct I tip my head back and gaze up at him. Like it has so many times before, my stomach drops to my toes as I gulp in his perfection.

Perfect jawline. Perfect high cheekbones. Perfect straight nose. Perfect green eyes. Perfect honey-gold hair that falls perfectly on his perfect brow.

My gaze dips down to his perfect mouth and I bite down on my bottom lip, wincing because the lip has already endured enough abuse today.

Don't stare at his lips, you idiot.

My body screams at me for it, but I gently push Becks' hands away and step around him, putting a safe distance between us. He stuffs the corner of his shirt, now stained with my blood, into the back of his pants, and like the good friend he is, he does me a solid and pretends not to notice how I was practically drooling over him. It's an unwritten rule that friend-zoned besties shouldn't ogle each other, but it's one that I can't seem to help breaking. Especially in the last year.

"Who was it?" he demands, a hard note in his voice, and I know without a doubt if I confess the truth he'll do something drastic.

That's the thing between Becks and me, we'd do anything for each other. The problem is that even though I was the one to protect his sister all those years ago, they have been fighting my battles practically ever since. Our friendship isn't balanced. It hasn't been since their powers came in and mine didn't. It didn't used to bug me, but it does now.

I shake my head. "It doesn't matter."

Any remaining softness on his face disappears. He's probably imagining charring whoever did this to me, which admittedly makes me go a little mushy inside, but I push those feelings aside.

"Locklyn." He says my name like a warning and takes a step forward, crowding me, but I hold up a hand to stop him.

I gentle my next words, wanting him to know I appreciate his concern, but also that I'm firm on the point. "I have to start dealing with this type of stuff on my own."

He shoves the hair off his forehead as he studies me, the inner battle shining from his eyes. I know he wants to respect my desires, but it's in his nature to protect what he considers his. And as his friend, I fall into that category.

He releases a frustrated sigh. "We'll talk about this more later. We've got to find Ens. She's looking for you too."

I give him a questioning look and he shrugs. "When you didn't show up to class we got worried."

Closing my eyes, I let out a groan that has nothing to do with the aches and pains in my body. Forget being tardy to Elemental Chemistry, I'm going to miss a solid half of the period, or more. It's going to take some major begging and pleading to keep Mr. Sullivan from failing me. Or maybe I can convince him I was violently ill or something to get a pass this time?

Opening my eyes, I fix my gaze back on Becks. "How did you know I didn't show up to class? You're not in that one with me."

"Ens came and got me. She's checking the closets and bathrooms."

I nod. That makes sense. I've been known to hide in a bathroom a time or two before. I'm lucky to have friends like them.

Fortifying myself, I start making my way slowly down the passageway. Now that Becks is with me I'm no longer concerned about the dark sections of the tunnel. No one in their right mind would mess with Becks. He's the most powerful dragon shifter in our generation. I don't get four steps before he notices I'm favoring my right ankle and he scoops me up. I consider demanding that he put me down, I can still walk, but I know he won't listen to me anyway, so I sit stiffly in his arms, fighting against the urge to melt against him with every step.

When we reach the door that leads to the first floor of the castle and he finally sets me on my feet, I try to ignore the way my heart rate spikes when I slide down the front of his body, or how his heat lingers on my skin when he turns away from me to peek through a crack in the door, but it's hard. Taking a steadying breath while his back is to me, I tell my body to cut it out and focus on all my aches and pains rather than the warm fuzzies.

Becks looks over his shoulder at me. "The coast is clear. Everyone's in class."

"I've got to clean myself up," I tell Becks, and he nods, opening the door so I can go in front of him.

We walk down the hallway in silence, footsteps echoing off the dark-stained wood floors and locker-lined stone walls of the gothic revival interior. Nightlark Academy is a strange mix of old and new. The main building we're walking through is a castle-like structure built in the mid-1800s that used to be the home of a wealthy landowner back in the day. But the school also includes several auxiliary buildings spread out around the perimeter of a three-acre quad. Even though none of the additional structures are as old as the main building, they were all built at different times throughout the last hundred years and their exteriors mirror the intricately carved stone castle. Even the gym and sports center next to the castle has a steep gabled roof and external buttresses. The interiors of most of the outbuildings have been modernized, but not much of the main castle structure has been changed except for the addition of lockers and bathrooms and contemporary furniture.

When we reach the girls' bathroom, Becks tells me he's going to wait outside for me before I shove through the door. I breathe a sigh of relief when I find the bathroom is also empty.

Thank the Creator.

When I look in the mirror a moment later the feeling of relief vanishes. Calling myself a mess is an understatement. My hair looks like it hasn't been brushed in a month and is covered in so much stone dust it's now whitish gray instead of auburn. My lower lip is cracked and swollen; dried blood is smeared over my chin from when Becks tried to clean me up in the tunnel. A bruise is already starting to form on my cheekbone and there's some blood caked along my hairline where I was struck with a stone. My clothes are in as rough of shape as the rest of me.

No wonder Becks had shot me so many half-panicked glances. I look like I've been run over. I can't go to classes like this.

The door bangs open, and I bolt into a stall, slamming and locking the door behind me. I hold my breath as the clicks of heels on the stone floor gets closer.

Please don't be Jules again, I silently plead. *I've had enough of that hag today.*

"Locklyn? Where are you?"

The air rushes from my lungs in relief. Ensley. Of course. Becks wouldn't have let anyone in the bathroom with me other than his fae twin sister.

"Over here," I say, but don't leave the stall. Now that I know what I look like, I don't really want anyone else to see me like this.

She walks over, stopping on the other side of the metal door. "Are you going to come out?" she asks when I don't immediately emerge.

"I'd rather not."

"Why?" I can hear her tapping her foot and imagine she's standing impatiently on the other side of the door with her arms crossed.

"Let's just say I'm not that pretty right now," I say, thinking of the bruises and blood.

She chuckles. "I beg to differ. You're adorable."

I scrunch my nose. No seventeen-year-old girl wants to be referred to as adorable. Adorable is what you call stuffed animals or kittens, not a datable female.

"I didn't mean it that way," I say grumpily.

"I know," she says with another chuckle. "But will you please just come on out so I can get a look at the damage?"

Oh great, Becks already told her.

Unlocking the stall door, I let it swing open. Ensley's large green eyes bulge when she sees me. She stops tapping her studded high heeled boot and just stares. Unlike me, she's perfectly put together. Her waist-length blonde hair hangs loose and long down her back, streaked with glamoured purple highlights today. The off-the-shoulder graphic tee she's wearing under her cropped black leather jacket is as white as it was this morning, and her rocker chic jeans are only purposefully ripped in all the right spots. I, on the other hand, look like I need to be taken outside and hosed off.

"What happened?" she asks as I stride past her toward the sink.

I cup my hands under a stream of cool water and splash my face rather than answer her. A paper towel appears next to me, and I mumble thanks as I blot my face dry, wiping the smear of blood off my chin then dabbing my busted lip. When I'm done, I toss the soiled towel in the trash and look at myself in the mirror again. It's better, but not much.

"Okay, spill. Who was it this time?" Ensley asks as she watches me. "Leo and his cronies?"

When I don't answer her, she goes back to guessing.

"Lilith and her wannabe flower power group?" she says, naming one of the fae cliques I've had a run-in with a time or two before. I still don't react.

"Jules and her brainwashed followers?"

My gaze shifts to hers in the mirror and she sighs.

"Just please don't tell Becks who it was," I whisper so that he won't be able to hear me if he's still outside.

She presses her lips together in a firm line but nods her agreement. We both know how Becks can get. It's not that we're protecting Jules. It's that we're looking out for Becks. Ever since he was named dragon heir last year he's been under a microscope by not only their parents, but the whole dragon council as well.

He doesn't open up about it much but living up to their expectations as the future House of Dragon heir weighs heavily on him. He's not allowed to be a teenager like the rest of us because he's destined for so much more.

Turning me toward her, Ensley pinches my chin between her fingers and turns my face back and forth, checking out my fat lip and bruised cheekbone. She lets out a low whistle and then releases me. "They sure did do a number on you this time."

A fresh wave of anger against Jules and her friends rolls through me. I snatch a paper towel from the dispenser, wet it, and start scrubbing the dried blood from my hairline that I missed before. When I'm done, my face is blood-free, but the bruising and swelling is all the more obvious.

"Come here," she says, wiggling her fingers. "I can at least help you get through the rest of the day." White fae magic glows from her hands as she prepares to glamour some of my face so my injuries aren't as obvious.

"Yes, please," I say with a clap, smiling broadly, but then wince when the movement makes the cut on my lip split open and start oozing again.

Ensley waits for me to dab the drops away, then places her hands on either side of my face, an inch away from my skin. The light emanating from them brightens and I close my eyes, enjoying the warmth coming from her palms as she weaves her magic.

Ensley's glamour is top notch, probably because she takes after her father, a fae known worldwide for pioneering beauty products imbued with traces of fae glamour. Even though Ensley and Becks are twins, they're different creature species. Just as Ensley takes after her father, Becks takes after his powerful dragon shifter mother. Together, both parents help run B&A Beauty, a lucrative beauty company that they founded together when the twins were babies.

Ensley's done in less than a minute, and when she drops her hands I swivel toward the mirror to take in her handiwork. Fae magic is amazing. The bruise on my cheekbone is hardly noticeable, and despite the way my busted lip throbs, my mouth looks full and lush and totally kissable—not that there's anyone who'd kiss me. Almost eighteen and never been kissed is just super depressing.

I turn my face one way and then the other, marveling at how smooth and radiant my skin is. For once the freckles smattering over the bridge of my nose and high on my cheekbones add interest to my face rather than make me look like a child. My hair is still a mess, but just as I think it Ens slaps a hairbrush in my hand, and I get to work shaking out the stone dust and brushing the strands straight. When I'm done I turn my head this way and that, checking for any bits hiding in my auburn mane that I might have missed.

"You're the best, you know that?" I say as I hand her brush back, giving her a quick hug.

When I let her go, Ensley rolls her eyes. "Of course I do."

Leaning forward, I squint at my reflection. "Did you make my eyes bigger?"

She shrugs. "Maybe. But the glamour will wear off before tomorrow, so who really cares." She gives me a once over. "We're going to have to do something about this too," she says, gesturing to the rest of my body. She shrugs out of her leather jacket and hands it to me. "Your shirt is dark so it's hiding the bloodstains, but those jeans won't do."

I glance down at the rip in the knee and the blood splatters. "I have a pair of leggings in my gym locker."

"Good. If we go now we can get you cleaned up enough to make next period."

She hefts her bag on her shoulder and starts for the exit.

"Wait. You don't have to come with me. Just because I'm missing class doesn't mean you have to."

"It's okay," she says with a shrug. "Mr. Sullivan loves me."

That may be true, but that won't stop him from marking her down for skipping most of his class. But Ensley doesn't really care about school. Besides being a natural genius, she knows that after high school she'll start working at her family's beauty business without having to further her education. That is assuming her band doesn't suddenly get discovered. So as long as she doesn't flunk out completely, she's golden either way. That's the only reason I'm not itching with too much guilt over her ditching class to help me.

"I wish I could say the same. He said he was going to fail me if I was tardy to his class again."

Ensley waves her hand in the air like she's brushing the problem away. "Don't worry about that. I'll tell him later I found you heaving your guts out into a toilet. He can't fail you for being sick."

I shoot her a thankful smile, knowing that if I tried to feed him that story he'd never believe me, but that he won't even question Ensley. Some of the tension leaves my shoulders knowing that issue is going to be taken care of. I'd rather not graduate than be forced into summer school.

When we leave the bathroom, Becks isn't there anymore and Ensley explains she forced him to go back to his class already. She comes with me to the gym and helps me look semi-put together in time to make my next class. I make it through the rest of the day with minimal stares thanks to Ensley's glamour. But as the day drags on I can't let go of what happened to me. I grow more and more agitated the longer I think about it, and like boiling water trapped in a kettle, I need to let off some steam. And there's only one way I know how to do that.

Two

I'VE BEEN WAILING on the punching bag for so long that my knuckles have gone numb. I grit my teeth as sweat drips down my temples, the cadence of my fists hitting the leather bag over and over again doing little to soothe the angry beast inside. The short hairs around my face stick to my cheeks and forehead and I'm breathing like I've just finished a marathon. But I don't stop.

It's been four days since Jules and her crew cornered me in the tunnels. The bruises are fading, and the swelling has gone down, but I'm no closer to figuring out how to get her and the rest of the school bullies off my back than I was the moment I walked myself into her trap that day.

I've been coming to the gym every day after school to blow off steam, which is my go-to activity when things get overwhelming. Besides it being cathartic to punch something that isn't going to punch back, some messed-up corner of my brain thinks I can fight my way out of any predicament. That if I just hit hard enough I won't be what I am anymore.

The only magicless creature on the face of the planet.

"Whoa there." Strong hands steady the weathered bag, keeping it from swinging every time my fist connects.

I keep my eyes on my target, refusing to look at Becks. I don't need to look at him to know what I'll see in his gaze: pity. I don't want anything from him, least of all his pity.

Okay, that's a lie. There are *some* things I want from Becks, but nothing he's willing to give me, so obsessing over what will never be is only a waste of time.

Mind you, I say that, yet here I am doing my best to beat a hole in a weathered punching bag as if that will change anything about my situation.

Becks lets me take out my aggression on the punching bag for several more minutes, waiting until he sees the strain of the workout in my flagging muscles before saying anything. He knows me well enough to know when to push me, and when to let me be.

"Wanna talk about it?" he asks.

My arms are about as strong as wet noodles at this point, so he isn't straining in the least to keep the bag still. How annoying.

"What do you think?" I snap back between punches, instantly regretting my tone. My anger isn't directed at Becks, he's just the closest target.

He frowns, flipping the lock of honey-gold hair that's fallen on his forehead away. My traitorous eyes track the movement of his hair as it flops back onto his brow rather than focus on my target, and my hand grazes off the worn leather. My momentum takes me forward and I lose my footing, tripping slightly, and Becks reaches out and stabilizes me.

His hands feel like brands on my biceps and cause a jolt of delicious awareness to shoot throughout my body. I quickly right myself and pull out of his grasp, hoping he thinks the reddening of my cheeks is from exertion alone.

"Sorry," I say with a sigh as I step away from the bag. "You didn't deserve that. It's just been a week."

I don't look up as I busy myself with removing my hand wraps. When I'm done, I open and close my hands, my fingers stiff from clenching them into fists for so long.

"Did something else happen this week?" Becks asks, his voice taking on a dark note. I glance at him, instantly seeing the tension in his face and shoulders.

I shake my head. "Nothing's happened," I answer honestly. "It's just . . ." I let the sentence drop.

How do I explain that things have changed? With Becks, I want to be so much more than what we are. I don't want to be just his charity case, his loser friend who needs to be rescued on the regular. No, with Becks I want to be his everything.

Becks' muscles relax and his eyes soften. "Anything I can do to help?"

I give him a small, hopefully convincing smile. "No. I'm fine."

He follows me over to my duffle and waits while I change shoes and wipe the sweat from my face with a hand towel.

"How did you know I'd be here?" I ask, finally in a better headspace to talk. The workout seems to have done its job helping me burn off my excess rage and frustration. It didn't hurt that I pictured Jules' and her cronies' faces on the bag as I punched away.

Becks gives me a look. "Where else would you be?"

"I'm not that predictable. Am I?"

A deep laugh rumbles in Becks' chest, making goose bumps pop out on my arms. "Do you really want me to answer that?"

I roll my eyes. "Okay, fine. I'm that predictable."

Becks chuckles. "Want a ride home?" he asks, knowing I walked here because I don't have a car.

"Sure."

Not having a car isn't usually much of an issue for me. The two places I'm at the most, Nightlark and Peet's Gym, are within walking distance to my home. And then when I'm out with Becks or Ensley, they just drive. But sometimes it's nice to not have to hike back after a long workout.

Picking up my bag, we head toward the exit. Becks throws a casual arm over my shoulder as we walk, completely oblivious to how his nearness affects me. I bite my lower lip and force my body to stay loose.

"Locklyn," someone calls, and I glance back at Peet, the owner of Peet's Gym. "Gideon can't make it tomorrow to teach his class. Any chance you can fill in for him?"

Tomorrow's Friday, and as much as I wish I could say I had a life and couldn't fill in for Gideon at a moment's notice, that just isn't true. My only friends are Becks and Ensley. Friday night, Becks attends dragon council meetings, and Ensley practices with her band. Tomorrow night is pathetically wide open.

"Yeah, I can be here. Level 2's, right?" I ask and Peet nods. That won't be so bad. Level 2's are still young enough that they haven't developed their magic. It doesn't matter that I'm one of the most advanced fighters who comes to Peet's gym and can lay out guys twice my size in a fair fight. Once the students learn that I don't have magic, I lose their respect and trying to teach them is useless.

A relieved smile breaks out on Peet's face. "Thanks, Locklyn. You're a life saver."

I manage to force a smile and wave before Becks and I shove through the doors into the late afternoon dying sunlight. The early spring air has a bite to it, but I don't mind because it feels good against my overheated skin.

"Come on, I'll buy you dinner before taking you home," Becks says, leading me away from where his car is parked and down the sidewalk instead. "Food always cheers you up."

He's not wrong, but I'm a gross mess after my workout. My compression leggings and white tank are damp in embarrassing places, and my hair atop my head is a knotted mess. No self-respecting creature would be caught publicly looking like I am with the next dragon heir.

I open my mouth to give him some excuse, but at the thought of food my stomach growls loudly.

Becks looks down at my belly where my white tank is plastered against my skin and then back up at my face with an amused grin. "I'll take that as a yes," he says, and because I'm a pushover when it comes to Becks, I mumble, "Sure," and follow his lead, like a good little puppy.

Sometimes I wonder if that's how Becks sees me, as a cute little helpless puppy that follows him around and needs his protection. He might enjoy my company, but I know we aren't on equal footing, and that chafes.

I know I'm selling myself short. I have redeeming qualities. I'm funny, a great listener, sharp-witted, and the most loyal friend you'll ever find. But I'm on a roll feeling bad for and about myself today and don't have the energy to pull myself out of my funk, so I think I'll just chill here for a bit longer.

Becks has his phone out and is typing a message to someone. He hits send and jams the device back in his pocket. I don't have any clue who he was messaging, and I don't ask him. Becks may be one of my only friends, but I'm not the same for him. He's charismatic, charming, ridiculously hot, and an heir. Meaning he's practically beating creatures off with a stick who would die to be his friend, or more.

He looks up at me. "Sloan's?"

Sloan's is a local hangout and I know it will be packed with Nightlark students. The last thing I want is to see more of my fellow peers, but since I can never seem to say "no" to Becks, especially recently, I hold back a groan and nod. If he notices an iota of reluctance in me, he ignores it.

"Sweet. I already told Ensley to meet us there." He rubs his stomach causing his shirt to come up a little, showing a sliver of his chiseled flat abs. "I've been craving one of their shakes all day."

I look away quickly, my face reddening.

A bell over the door jingles when we enter Sloan's a few minutes later. Several heads turn our way and Becks waves at some shifters he knows as we take a seat in one of the only available places, a booth that is regrettably in the middle of the diner.

I shift uncomfortably in the vinyl seat, self-conscious about being the center of attention and wishing more than ever I would have taken a few minutes to shower after my workout. Reaching into my bag, I pull out a zip-up hoodie and throw it on over my tank.

A waitress heads over and takes our order, and almost immediately after she leaves I see someone approaching us out of the corner of my eye. When I look over, Vesper, a pretty vampire a year younger than us, moves to stand next to Becks. Her skirt is as short as her top is low and I notice Becks give her a quick once-over before trailing his eyes to her face.

I don't blame him. Heck, I couldn't help but look either, but that doesn't stop an ugly emotion from churning in my gut. Although I've never had an altercation with this vampire, I have the sudden urge to dump one of Sloan's famous chocolate shakes over her head.

Vesper slowly twirls a piece of her glossy brown hair around her index finger as she stares at my best friend with heavily lidded eyes. "Hey, Becks, I saw you play last weekend. That goal you made at the end of the game was epic."

Becks is the captain of Nightlark's vodenball team. The sport, which is played with a ball you can kick but also move with your powers, is seen as the ultimate measure of athleticism and magical abilities. It's the most exclusive sport at our school. Tryouts every year are cutthroat, but making the team guarantees you a certain level of clout. If he wasn't already popular for being the dragon heir, leading the school's vodenball team to victory throughout the last season would have pushed him to the top of the social ladder. I know Becks loves the sport, but I think he's ready to be done for the year. Their regular season is technically over, but they still have some post season practices and scrimmages over the next several weeks.

Becks smiles back at her, but Vesper doesn't know him well enough to realize the gesture is false. "Thanks, Vesper. Glad you could make it out. Having support really means a lot to the whole team."

She leans in closer, so her chest is eye level with Becks' face. "Well, I'm not really there to see the other players, if you know what I mean."

Yes, Vesper. He knows what you mean. We all know what you mean.

Becks sits back in his seat, keeping his eyes dutifully on her face, but his smile looks more like a grimace now.

"Yo, Ves, shove off," Ensley says as she comes up behind the leggy brunette. She nudges her out of the way so she can slide into the booth next to Becks. Ensley's golden blonde hair is streaked with red-glamoured highlights today. I dig the vibe.

Becks releases an audible sigh of relief as Ensley takes up the space between him and the pushy cheerleader.

"I was just—" Vesper starts.

"Yes, yes. You were just throwing yourself at Becks but let me save you the time and let you know he's not interested. Now shoo," Ensley says, and waves Vesper away.

Ensley's my hero.

Vesper sputters and shoots Becks a look, probably expecting him to step in and defend her, but he just shrugs.

With a huff, Vesper spins and stomps away in her three-inch heels, rejoining her friends on the other side of the restaurant.

I hold a fist up and Ensley bumps it with her own.

"The vultures just keep getting bolder," Ensley says.

She's not wrong. Becks has always been undeniably attractive. He never even went through an awkward phase. But since his power registered off the charts and he was named the dragon heir, girls have stopped trying to be subtle about their attempts to get his attention.

"But really, Becks," Ensley continues. "You need to learn to beat them away yourself. I won't always be here to do your dirty work."

"Hey, it's not like I'm encouraging them."

"You're not discouraging them either though," she says, shooting him a knowing look.

"What's that supposed to mean?" he asks, a pleat between his brows.

Ensley rolls her eyes.

The waitress interrupts our conversation by dropping off our food and taking Ensley's order, but then Becks starts it up again when she leaves. "You know no matter what I do they'll keep coming. Besides, why do you care anyway?"

Ensley's gaze flicks to me but is back on Becks so quickly I don't think he notices. I still hold my breath until the conversation moves along. I've never told a soul about my true feelings for Becks, but Ensley is sharp. She's caught me staring at him when he wasn't looking more than once, and she definitely picks up that I get uncharacteristically quiet whenever the subject of Becks' love life comes up, so I know she suspects. Which is a particular brand of awkward since she's also his sister.

"I care because your inability to turn off your smolder subjects me to the drudges of our high school society. Cheerleaders." Ensley fakes a shiver. "Yuck."

Becks chuckles as he munches on a fry.

"Why not just pick one already and be done with it. Then your girlfriend can act as your shield so I won't have to."

I'm taking a sip of my soda as Ensley suggests Becks gets a girl-friend, and I start choking. Both their heads turn toward me. Becks looks alarmed, but Ensley's gaze is knowing.

"Hey, you all right?" Becks asks as I try to control the hacking. He reaches his hand across the table, maybe to place it over mine, but then stops himself and pulls back.

I clear my throat, my voice sounding a little froggy when I say, "Yeah, just went down the wrong tube."

"So, how about it, Becks? Pick one in the lot and put us all out of our misery."

Becks takes his gaze off me to scowl at his twin, and I shoot her a glare of my own.

"I'm not going to get a girlfriend just because you don't like all the attention I get."

That's right, Becks. You tell her.

"Besides, my mate will be picked for me in a few years, so what's the point of dating now?"

My stomach sours at the reminder. Becks' life-mate will literally be decided for him. They'll pick a female with a crazy amount of magic from a high creature house, probably another shifter, but if the female is powerful enough maybe not, and that will be that. With a powerful life-mate, he'll one day be named ruler of the entire House of Dragon and live happily, or unhappily, ever after. But either way he'll never be mine.

"That's another great reason to get a girlfriend now," Ensley says. "Might as well live it up while you can."

"We've been over this before," Becks says, his head down as he pretends to find his food especially interesting. "It's not fair to the girl." And then he says more quietly. "And it's not fair to me."

Becks puts on a good face for his family, but Ensley and I know the truth. He doesn't want to be the heir to the House of Dragon. But he doesn't have a say in it either way. The dragon heir is always the most powerful dragon shifter of his generation. We always knew Becks was powerful, but it was still a surprise to all of us last year when he was named heir.

Ensley releases a low whistle, focusing on something over my shoulder. "Who is that?" she asks, her gaze lit with interest.

Becks lifts his head. His eyes narrow as he tracks someone behind me.

Lifting up and twisting in my seat, I look for what's captured their attention. It takes me all of a half second to figure it out.

The guy who just entered the diner strides toward the to-go counter, his steps eating up the distance quickly. There's more than one set of eyes on him as he leans his tanned forearms on the diner bar, waiting to place an order.

He's wearing a gray t-shirt under his unbuttoned collared shirt that's pushed up to his elbows. His dark hair, almost black, curls out from under the front of the knit cap seated on the crown of his head. I can't really tell the exact color of his eyes from this distance, but I assume because of his overall coloring that they're dark as well. Dark washed jeans and black skate shoes complete his look.

He drums his fingers against the cheap laminate and glances around the restaurant, his mouth curving into a knowing smile when he catches Vesper and her group of female vipers checking him out. He dips his chin in acknowledgment that he caught them staring and then his gaze brushes past the lot of them.

I should probably look away when his face swings toward me, but I don't. What do I care if he catches me staring? I'm not mooning over him like the other girls are. At most my gaze is inquisitive, so I don't have anything to hide. But besides all that, I'm expecting new guy's gaze to skip right over me anyway. I'm invisible to most creatures.

It's not that I think I'm ugly. Under the right circumstances I would even consider myself cute, but as a shortie with red tinted brown hair that might be considered auburn on a good day, light brown eyes, freckles, and no discernible magic, it's not like I'm stopping traffic on the regular.

As expected, new guy's gaze passes over me, but then unexpectedly tracks back.

Shoot. He's looking right at me.

When our gazes connect, I tell myself to look away, but I can't. His eyes narrow and a small crease forms between his eyebrows.

I was wrong. His eyes are blue. A light gray-blue, not dark at all.

He tilts his head like he's confused by me, but then his upper lip peels back and I get the distinct impression that something about me angers him.

That breaks my trance immediately.

Whatever. I prefer blonds anyway.

I turn back to my friends, plopping back down in my seat. "Vampire?"

There are three main creatures most of the population falls into: shifters, fae, or vampires. When it's not completely obvious which creature someone is, my friends and I like to make a guessing game out of it.

"Naw. I don't see any fangs. My money is on fae," Ensley says.

"That's just wishful thinking," I say with a chuckle. Unveiled interest shines in my friend's eyes. Most vampires only let their fangs descend when they are feeding. Ensley just likes the idea of the hot new guy being a fae like her.

Ensley tears her gaze from new guy. "Wishful thinking that's probably wasted since it's not me he's staring a hole through right now." She gives me a mischievous wink and Becks' frown deepens.

He's still staring?

It's physically hard to keep from sneaking another peek.

"Snake shifter for sure," Becks says.

I scrunch my nose. He knows I'm not overly fond of snakes. All the slithering gives me the creeps. And some snake shifters can fork their tongues without fully shifting and do oscillating tongue-flicks to taste the air, picking up on a creature's pheromones to detect if they're scared, excited, or even turned-on. It's just . . . yuck. Not to mention invasive.

I think about the look on new guy's face, how it went from inquisitive to something closer to loathing and it makes me mad. I don't need that kind of judgment from a veritable stranger. I get that enough from my schoolmates.

"I change my vote. I'm with Becks. Definitely snake shifter. He has that sketchy slimy vibe about him."

Ensley's eyes grow wide, but I don't know why. It's not like what I said is that scandalous. I've said *way* worse about Vesper and her friends.

"Sketchy slimy vibe, huh?" comes a deep voice from right over my shoulder. "I need to work harder on my resting face if that's what I'm giving off."

Squeezing my eyes shut, I pray for the ground to swallow me whole, but I'm not that lucky.

When I open my eyes again, the guy is standing next to our table, but thankfully he's no longer looking at me.

"Becks, right?" he says to my dragon shifter friend, who raises his eyebrows in surprise.

"Yeah, that's me."

"Cool. I'm starting at Nightlark Academy on Monday. My Uncle Drake told me to look for you. Said you could show me the ropes. I'm Talon."

"Drake Brayden?" Becks asks, and Talon nods. "Yeah, I know him. He's on the dragon council. Welcome." There's no genuine warmth in Becks' words.

"Thanks, man." Talon has a to-go bag clutched in one hand, but holds out his other fist to Becks, who reluctantly taps it with his own.

Interesting.

Becks is nothing if not diplomatic. He knows how to turn the charm on like a light switch, but he's not trying very hard right now. I wonder if Talon notices Becks' hesitation. If so, he doesn't act like it.

"What brings you to Everton?" Becks asks.

"My parents have a work assignment overseas, so they shipped me off to my uncle's for the rest of the academic year."

I frown. That sucks. He looks too old to be anything but a senior like us. Starting a new school well into the second semester of your last year has to be hard.

As if on cue, a group of girls pass behind Talon, giggling loudly. Talon shoots them a lopsided smirk before turning back to our table.

Pfft. I take it back. He's going to be just fine.

"So, I'll see you around then," he says to Becks, basically ignoring Ensley and me.

Ensley doesn't seem to mind the snub, she's too busy drinking him up with her eyes. But I mind. It's just rude.

Becks nods. "Yeah, sure."

Talon turns to leave, but his gaze flicks to me right before he does.

"Later, Freckles," he says under his breath as he passes.

Suddenly, something coils around my ankle and starts to slither its way up my leg. With a squawk I jump out of the booth, furiously patting my leg to brush off whatever creepy crawly is trying to scale me, but there's nothing there.

My friends, as well as diners in the booths around us, stare at me in shock. Deep chuckles reach me, and when I look over Talon is standing at the diner entrance, his smirk telling me everything I need to know. That was his little trick he played on me.

I scowl at his smile, and then he shoves through the door and is gone.

Three

"LOCKLYN, SWEETHEART, IS THAT YOU?" my mom calls from another room as soon as I shut the front door behind me.

My parents and I live in an apartment above the rare books and antique shop they run. It's not a large home like Becks and Ensley's, but it's the only one I've known, and I love it. It's cozy and filled with memorabilia from my childhood. The clay sculpture of a dragon I made in art class when I was eight, framed photographs of my parents and me on family vacations, my favorite signed collection of fairy tales. And since my mother is a fae there are plants everywhere.

I drop my backpack in the foyer, keeping my gym bag hefted on my shoulder as I enter the living room, where my mom stands on a bookcase ladder thumbing through a giant leather-bound tome. Our living room is part-library, part-greenhouse, and is hands down my favorite room in our home.

"Hey, Mom," I say, stopping to say hi before dumping my gym bag in my room and jumping into the shower.

"Sweetie," she says, a smile breaking out on her face as she shuts the book and re-shelves. "We missed you for dinner tonight."

"Oh shoot, I'm sorry. I got caught up at Peet's and then Becks stopped by and asked if I wanted to grab something with him. Ensley met up with us. I should have called to give you a heads-up. I hope you weren't worried."

I have a phone, I just rarely use it. Just another way I'm totally different than every other teen I know. It didn't even cross my mind to pull it out to call my parents.

Gah, I'm an awful daughter.

Turning from me, she climbs the short distance down the ladder to the floor and waves off my concerns. "No, of course that's fine. We figured that's probably what happened. Besides . . ." She leans in and lowers her voice, casting a look toward the kitchen where I can hear my dad cleaning up from their dinner. "Your father cooked tonight, so you dodged a bullet."

My parents are well aware that I have trouble making friends, so they've always been extra supportive of my relationships with Becks and Ensley. They'd never give me a hard time about hanging out with either of them. Any time I'm not with Becks or Ensley, I'm with my parents, so we get a really good amount of family time.

"I heard that!" my father calls from the other room. "You said the vegetable stew was delicious."

"Oh, honey, it was," my mom calls back, but she looks at me with wide eyes and shakes her head, letting me know the truth. For added effect she sticks her tongue out and squeezes her eyes shut, making a gagging face. Unfortunately for her that's the moment my dad walks into the room.

"Zia," my dad says, his face stricken. "But you love root vegetables."

"Oh, babe. I do. It's just the combination of all that cinnamon with the heavy cumin was . . ." Her nose scrunches as she searches for the right word or phrase. "Perhaps just a little too adventurous for me."

Dad's shoulders sag in defeat. My dad is six-foot four and burly with dark brown hair and eyes, and a short beard. It doesn't stretch anyone's imagination to know that he's a bear shifter. My mom, in contrast, is petite like me but an inch shorter at five foot two. She has a mane of glorious red hair that I would have killed to inherit, and bright green eyes. Likewise, her delicate elvish features and slightly pointed ears are a dead giveaway that she's fae. They're a picture-perfect example of opposites attract. My mom, like most fae, is a vegetarian. My dad, like most shifters, is not, and when it's his night to cook he always tries really hard to come up with dishes she'll enjoy—but usually fails.

My mom goes on her tiptoes to press a kiss to the corner of my dad's mouth, and his face softens. "Don't worry, babe. I didn't marry you for your culinary skills."

"I know exactly why you married me," my dad says suggestively as he wraps my mom in his arms and pulls her close. She giggles when he buries his face in her neck, and the sounds coming from my dad makes me think he's kissing her.

It's my turn to gag. "Come on, you guys, seriously? There's a child present."

My mom only giggles more, and my dad informs me I should leave if I don't want to be scarred for life. I make a show of covering my eyes as I leave the room and then head toward my small bedroom.

My parents are disgusting, but in the best way possible.

My heart's a little wistful as I drop my gym bag and head to the bathroom to shower. My parents may look like an odd match, but they couldn't be more perfect for each other. Someday I want what they have.

An image of me wrapped up in Becks' arms like my mom was in my dad's pops in my head, and I don't immediately swat it away. I close my eyes, imagining what it would feel like to be held by him. To be kissed by him. Both take a little stretch of my imagination because I've never even held a guy's hand before, let alone been kissed. My lack of romantic experience isn't a secret. It's obvious to everyone who knows me I come up short in that department. But even so, I know being in Becks' arms, having him look at me like I'm the only girl in the world, would be as close to divine as a creature can reach on this side of heaven.

THE BELL above the door of my parents' store, Belcourt Books and Antiques, jingles, letting me know a customer has entered. Sighing, I close the textbook in front of me. My parents don't typically ask me to work in the store for them, but my dad is meeting with an antique dealer about a two-thousand-year-old fae artifact that was just discovered at a site in the Dark Forest, and my mom is checking in on my grandma who lives a couple hours away.

I don't mind stepping in to help. It's not like I have anything better happening on a Saturday afternoon. *Sadly.* But I was just getting into a groove with my Classic Mythology homework, so I'm a little salty to have been interrupted.

Giving myself a mental slap, I plaster on a pleasant smile and look up to greet the customer. The smile freezes on my face when I see the tall, dark-haired male dressed down in a t-shirt and joggers walking toward me, his head bent as he reads a piece of paper in his hand.

Talon.

I can't say I'd given him more than a passing thought over the last two days, but now that he's here, in my parents' shop, my heart starts a weird cadence. I know I don't like him because of the trick he played on me at the diner, but what I'm still uncertain about is just how much.

He reaches the counter and then finally looks up and his eyes flare.

Yeah, buddy. I'm just as surprised to see you.

It's not like Talon looks like any of our usual clientele, older male and female creatures with deep pockets. You won't find our wares pawned at flea markets or secondhand stores. Our antiques are legit and carry a price tag to match them.

Talon recovers from the surprise of seeing me and leans forward against the counter, giving me a lazy smile I've no doubt works on lots of other girls. What he doesn't realize is that I'm not like any of those other girls.

"Freckles," he says, the tone of his voice causing a warm sensation low in my gut that irritates me.

"Can I help you?" I say, but my tone and eyes are actually saying, "Why are you here and what do you want?"

Talon ignores my sassiness, a smile growing on his face. "So you work in an antique shop," he says rather than answer my question.

"Not really."

He lifts his eyebrows and glances around the shop before looking back at me. "Could have fooled me."

"My parents own the store. I only fill in for them occasionally."

I don't know why, but I spot interest in his eyes. "That's cool," he says, and it seems genuine, but I'm so used to being treated poorly that in the back of my mind I assume there's some angle.

I also haven't forgotten the look he gave me when we first locked eyes at Sloan's. I couldn't put my finger on the emotion behind his hard eyes in that moment, but I know the look wasn't friendly.

I shrug. "I guess. So . . . did you need something?"

Our shop isn't the type of store someone would come into to browse, so if Talon found his way here, there must be a specific reason. Either that or he's lost.

"That depends," he says with a lopsided grin. He rests even more of his weight on the counter, bringing himself a few inches closer to me. "Can I trust you?"

Umm . . . what? What a weird question.

"Yes?"

"You don't sound sure."

"I don't really know what you're asking me," I admit.

"Hmm," is all he says, his eyes turning intense as his gaze brushes over me. Well, not exactly over me, but more like the space around me. A small pleat appears between his brows, displaying his frustration. Over what though, I have no idea.

Once again I wonder what kind of creature he is. I'm still leaning toward vampire, because he made me believe something was crawling up my leg at the diner. Vampires are forbidden from using compulsion except under very monitored circumstances, but that doesn't mean some of them don't bend or break the rules from time to time.

It's possible he used air magic to make it feel like there was something slithering up my leg. There are a number of different airborne shifters, like birds and dragons, with that kind of magic. And fae is still an option as well. He's not wearing a knit cap today; his dark hair is shorter on the sides and longer on top, which makes the rounded tops of his ears easy to see, but many years of breeding within species has made it so there are as many fae with rounded ears as pointed. I'm not sure what kind of fae magic he could have used to create that illusion, but fae are notoriously sneaky, so I'm not ready to rule them out yet either.

Talon clears his throat, the intensity in his gaze melting away as quickly as it came upon him as his mouth hitches back up in a grin. "I think you're safe enough," he declares, and I don't know what that's supposed to mean either. "I'm looking for Shadow Striker."

"What's that?" I cock my head. Not many of our items have official names like that. I was expecting him to ask about a twelfth century armoire or a handcrafted fae rug from the Dark Forest or something of the like. The name he gave me doesn't sound like an antique, it sounds like an artifact. Or a really cool name for a fantasy villain.

"Well, that's up for interpretation," he says. "And it also depends."

"Depends on what?"

"If you believe the Ancients."

The Ancients are a set of legends, stories if you will, that were passed down from generation to generation until they were written and compiled a couple thousand years ago. A singular story within the compiled Ancients is referred to as an Ancient. The stories that make up the Ancients range from cautionary tales to information on objects said to be imbued with magic beyond what we know today by the great Creator of all. Every so often something will be found, like a scroll or unearthed cave drawing, that somewhat validates one of the Ancients. Or at least validates that some portion of a particular Ancient is based on fact. There are lots of creatures who have faith that the Ancients, and the fabled Creator who weaved them, are true.

I am not one of those creatures.

Talon stares at me, drumming his fingers against the wood counter as he waits for my answer.

"Who's to say if the stories are true or not?" I say, noncommittally.

Talon jerks his head, flipping a clump of hair that fell on his forehead back and drawing my eyes to his thick locks. A spark of attraction ignites in my gut, surprising me. I might prefer blonds, but there's something about Talon I grudgingly find alluring. He's a little taller than Becks, but not as broad. His arms highlighted in his black t-shirt are heavily muscled, and from the way his shirt fits I can tell his stomach is flat as well.

I have a habit of comparing every guy I meet to Becks. It's admittedly a bad habit, but not one I'm working on breaking. But Talon's bronze skin, wavy dark hair, and gray-blue eyes are just so different from Becks' light features that his attractiveness takes me a little off guard.

"If you believe in the old legends, it's an object of unparalleled power that was forged in the lakes of Hell and given by a demon to the first Vampire King to aid him in his bloody campaign to rule over all creatures." Talon's eyes darken and his voice takes on a serious undertone. "You see Shadow Striker wasn't just a fancy-looking weapon. It was a dagger that gave its wielder unimaginable power."

Okay, now he has my attention. A way for someone to gain power. Yeah, I'm here for that. I'm not particularly well-versed in the Ancients, but like most creatures I know some of them. This one, however, is new to me.

"Gave powers?" I prompt.

He nods. "The legend says that once activated, the wielder of Shadow Striker can take another creature's power by drawing their blood with it."

"It steals powers from murdered creatures?"

"I never said that you had to kill to take powers, just draw blood."

"So it steals powers from the living?" That's diabolical. A creature is nothing without their magic—I would know.

Talon shrugs. "It's been debated whether the dagger steals the magic from creatures or just gives the wielder similar powers. But the Ancient about Shadow Striker says it made the first Vampire King the strongest creature that ever lived."

"So he succeeded in ruling over all the creatures?"

"No." Talon shakes his head and I get distracted by his dark strands again but snap out of it quickly.

Blond. You like blonds, Locklyn.

"During the final battle, the one that would have made him conqueror of all, he was betrayed."

"By whom?" I lean forward. I may not believe the Ancients are true, but it's a compelling story.

"His one true love."

I suck in a small breath, conflicted a little because it's obvious the Vampire King is the villain in the story, but to be betrayed by your one true love would be devastating.

"He fell in love with his best friend. They'd grown up together, trained together, and when he started his campaign for domination she was there fighting by his side."

My heart tweaks because this part of the story reminds me of Becks and me. How could it not? We practically grew up together, would do anything for each other, and always have each other's backs.

Talon continues, oblivious to my inner turmoil. "If the dagger is only used a handful of times there are no ill effects, but the Vampire King didn't hold himself back and eventually the powers he acquired started to warp him into someone his love didn't recognize. Some of the stories even say his quest started out as noble, that he wanted to free the oppressed, but at some point the dagger's powers started to warp him until he no longer cared about anything but gaining more power, and he turned into something greedy and ugly."

"Well, what did he expect accepting a gift from a demon?" I say with a shrug.

"The Vampire King was deceived by the demon and wasn't told the dangers of wielding Shadow Striker. He knew the dagger came from evil origins, but he believed he could use it for good without falling prey to its lure."

"Typical overconfident dude." I roll my eyes. *Males. Am I right?*

Talon smiles, but the expression starts to flatline as he continues the story. "So the vampire's one true love knew that the male she fell in love with was gone, even though he wasn't technically dead. The one caveat of Shadow Striker was that if anyone willingly sacrificed themselves for the wielder, the power he or she had gathered would be stripped from them. She knew this loophole because he'd confided in her about it, and so she baited him into a fight. The dagger had so warped his judgment that he became enraged and fought her. She willingly stepped into the path of his blade, sacrificing herself so that he would be restored to his former self, which he was the moment the steel pierced her skin."

"What happened to them?"

"She died in his arms and the Vampire King, realizing what he'd done, was filled with remorse and dread. He vanished into the Harshlands, never to be seen or heard from again. Or that's how the story goes."

I stare at Talon with my mouth hanging open. That is the worst ending to a story I've ever heard.

"But . . ." Talon says, and I hang on his next words, waiting for more of the tale because I don't want to believe it ended that tragically. I was, after all, a closet romantic. Before my eyes his mannerisms change from intense to blasé, and he says with a shrug: "If you don't believe the legends, then it's just a really old and cool dagger worth a good deal of coin. Would make a wicked gift for my father's birthday. He's somewhat of a collector of Ancient artifacts."

Wow, what a letdown.

I deflate, only realizing now that I'm leaned halfway over the counter and into Talon's space. Clearing my throat, I shift back. "Do you have any idea what the dagger is supposed to look like?"

"It's a black flamed-bladed dagger that's said to be made of damasked steel, so the metal will have a wavy pattern on it. It won't be more than a foot in length, with an etched black onyx hilt."

"Damasked steel? Hmm. You don't see that every day," I muse.

"It's truly one of a kind." Reaching into his pocket, he pulls out a folded piece of paper and hands it to me. It's a rough sketch of a dagger, exactly how he described it.

"What are the etchings on the hilt?" I squint to see them, but the sketch isn't detailed enough to make out any words.

The side of Talon's mouth kicks up. "I could tell you, but then I'd have to kill you."

I roll my eyes and hand the paper back to him. "I can tell you we don't have anything like that in the store. But let me check our inventory."

Reaching under the counter, I pull out the store laptop, booting it up quickly and opening the inventory software. We own a small warehouse where we store items if there's not enough space in the shop, or while we're waiting to get pieces appraised or cleaned before sale. My parents catalog every item they bring in, so if we have it, or had it in the past, it will be in the database.

I try looking for "Shadow Striker" first, and unsurprisingly it doesn't come up. I look through our weapons categories next, searching for an item that matches the description Talon gave me. This is a little more tedious because I have to pull up pictures one by one. Talon waits on the other side of the counter while I hunt for the artifact, silent but tapping his finger anxiously against the wood.

While I search through the weapons, my mind starts to wander. What high school senior tracks down Ancient artifacts in his spare time? I've never once had a classmate push through the doors to our shop, excluding Becks and Ensley if they were looking for me.

Talon is shaping up to be an enigma, one that I have the wild suspicion has unfathomable depths. I have this weird compulsion to scratch beneath the surface to see what he's hiding, but that impulse scares and confuses me. I've only just met the guy. And sure, he's the only person around my age besides Becks and Ensley who's made it through a whole conversation without ridiculing me, but my interest in him is still unnerving.

I'm acutely aware of Talon's gaze as my fingers fly over the keyboard. I think he's using the time to study me, but I refuse to glance up and check. After I've spent a good ten minutes searching for Shadow Striker, I finally look up.

"I'm sorry, but we don't have anything like that in our inventory."

Talon's face falls and his shoulders hunch, giving me an idea of how badly he was hoping we'd have the artifact.

He forces a smile. "Okay. Thanks for checking."

I feel compelled to offer him something, even if it's a longshot. "I can ask my parents about it. They might have seen it before or know someone who has." The look on his face has me instantly nervous that I'm giving him false hope. "But keep in mind an artifact like this, assuming it's a real object and not just an allegorical object in an old myth, would be difficult to find," I say, backtracking quickly. "It could be literally anywhere. The chances of you finding it somewhere in Everton are probably pretty low."

His smile is no longer forced, and I'd be lying if I said it didn't make my cheeks warm.

Blast my fair skin.

"I had a tip it was floating around the area. Any information you manage to dig up would be helpful, but can you be discreet about it?"

"Why?"

He runs a hand through his dark locks and then rubs the back of his neck. "There are a few other interested parties looking for it as well. It's important I'm the first person to find it."

Umm, okay. That sounds ominous.

Talon leans forward, his eyes darken and his voice quieting and dropping an octave as if we'd be overheard by someone else when there's no one in the store but the two of us. "But seriously, any information you get, even if it's a weak lead or sounds weird, I'd like to know."

His deliciously spicy scent wraps around me and I have to swallow to wet my suddenly dry throat. This guy really knows how to turn on the charm. Maybe I should tell him to tone it down a bit. He's wasting his efforts on me.

"What's your number?"

"What?" I practically squeak. He wants my number? No one in the history of ever has asked for my digits.

"Your number," he repeats. "I'll message you, so you have my number to get a hold of me if you find anything."

Right. That makes more sense. He doesn't want my number to socialize. He just wants to make sure I know how to track him down if I find the mysterious Shadow Striker.

I pull out my phone, intending just to ask him for his number, but for some unknown reason when he holds out his hand and wiggles his fingers for me to drop my phone into his palm, I hand it right over.

He gets a gleam in his eye as he punches in his number and then saves it to my contacts. And before I realize what he's doing he shoots himself a text, his phone beeping in his pocket when it goes through.

"So I can get in touch with you. You know, in an emergency."

"Right. An artifact emergency," I say as I shake my head, unsure how I feel about him having my number.

He shrugs as if to say, "it could happen," when we both know it won't.

Talon raps his knuckles against the counter and then pushes back away from it. "Thanks for helping me out today," he says as he walks backward a few steps.

"Sure," I say, even though I didn't really help him at all.

He jerks his chin in a quick nod and then spins, taking long strides toward the front door. With his hand wrapped around the handle, he pauses, glancing over his shoulder and giving me another slow once over. His gaze takes on the now-familiar intent look and a hint of frustration pulls his features. I'm convinced more than ever that when he stares at me like this he's looking for something specific but keeps coming up empty. When his eyes connect with mine, my stomach bottoms out.

Oh, girl, you are in trouble.

The problem is that I don't want trouble. I have enough of it on my own, so I don't need to go looking for more. My gut tells me there's something dangerous about Talon. It may be an irrational feeling, but it's there nonetheless, and if there's anything I can trust it's my instincts.

I decide then and there it's best to stay away from him. That probably won't be an issue, because come Monday I'm sure he'll hear of my magicless status and start ignoring me like most everyone else at Nightlark Academy does, so it's a moot point. No need to give him a second thought after he walks out that door.

Talon shakes his head, his crooked smile looking almost self-deprecating, but who the heck knows why.

"See you on Monday, Locklyn," he says, and then pushes through the door, the little bell chiming as he leaves. It isn't until well after the door shuts behind him that I remember I never told him my name.

Four

MY WHOLE, "I'm not going to give Talon a second thought," thing has not been working out for me. Since the day he visited the store he's carved out a small space for himself in my mind that is starting to feel permanent. But in fairness, it's mostly because I can't get Shadow Striker out of my head.

I believe most of the Ancients are harmless myths at best, and completely fabricated stories to keep creatures in line at worst. But even so, for the rest of the weekend I can't stop myself from circling back to the idea that there could be an object in existence that gives powers. It would be no surprise to anyone that a magic-less creature like me would be intrigued by that concept, but the fact that I can't seem to let it go disturbs me a little.

When my parents and I sat down for dinner the evening Talon dropped by our shop, I mentioned Shadow Striker to them, but they wore puzzled expressions. My mother, who's more familiar with the Ancients than my father, said it sounded vaguely familiar, but she couldn't provide me with any details. I explained to them that a potential customer had stopped by looking for the artifact and gave them the description Talon provided me of the weapon. They said they'd put in some inquiries with antique dealers they frequently worked with, and that was the end of that conversation.

That should have been enough for me, but it wasn't.

After tossing and turning in bed for several hours that night, I finally gave up on sleep and took to the internet for information. One would think a story about a Vampire King trying to take over the world would be one of the more popular Ancients, but it was just the opposite. My parents' lack of knowledge of the tale, and hours of searching the internet and coming up practically empty, proved that point. By the time the sun crested the horizon the next morning, all I had to show for my sleepless night was bits and pieces of the story Talon already told me, which only piqued my interest more and made me wonder just how he knew it in its entirety when the Ancient was so obscure.

I spent a good chunk of Sunday sourcing books from our collection that could potentially have some information on the tale, and then poring over them late into the night. I told myself this new obsession was just because I wanted to assuage my own curiosity, but deep inside I knew it was more than that. Talon might have played it off like he didn't really believe the Ancients, but I could tell he did. And his belief that there was at least a kernel of truth in the story of Shadow Striker created a spark inside me as well.

What if there was something out there that could give me magic, could make me powerful? My life would change in so many ways.

Hours of research on Sunday only led to one possible and very shaky lead. In a copy of *The Ancients as History*, I uncovered a vague reference to some of the Ancients having been sealed away and struck from history because their tale, and the knowledge it provided, was considered too dangerous to pass along. The books from our collection were old enough to be considered collector's editions, but if it were true that some Ancients were purposefully concealed, then perhaps the tale of Shadow Striker and the Vampire King were part of that purge. Frustrated and unfulfilled

I'd flopped into bed only a few hours before I'd have to get up again, dreading the next day.

When I wake on Monday morning, bleary-eyed and foggy, I trudge through my morning classes with my head down, looking forward to lunch when I can meet up with Ensley and maybe even Becks.

Becks is popular, so he doesn't always sit with us at lunch. His status as the dragon heir gives him a lot of clout at this school, but it's more than that. Becks is the kind of creature who others are attracted to without even knowing why. And it goes beyond his good looks. He has natural charisma that can't be taught.

Honestly, my friendship with Becks is probably the only reason I'm not bullied on the regular. There are only a small handful of classmates like Jules who take the time to try to beat me down. Usually I'm just ignored, which works out fine for me. I walk through the halls invisible to most of the students at Nightlark Academy. Of course, I'm not actually invisible. If I had the power to render myself unseen that might be cool, but the truth is the other students see me, they just pretend they don't. Perhaps some of them have been pretending for so long I have disappeared to them. Their minds completely dismiss me the moment I enter their field of vision.

It's hard at times, but if my choices are to be invisible or bullied, I suppose I'm glad it's the former.

I slide into my usual seat at the round table in the corner, keeping my back to the walls so I face out toward the rest of the space. Students eat lunch in the covered interior central courtyard in the middle of the main castle structure. The courtyard used to be open-air but was glassed in at some point. Despite how busy it always is, it's my favorite place in Nightlark Academy. The ground is worn gray cobblestones, and there's a smattering of fruit trees that circle a working fountain in the middle of the space. The four walls that enclose the courtyard have some of the most intricate stonework of anywhere in the building, telling me this must have been a special place for the original owner as well or he wouldn't have bothered making it so ornate. The courtyard is the most social space in the school, and although I'm never part of any of the drama, I still like being able to watch it.

I'm only starting to unpack my lunch when Ensley plops down next to me, her tray loaded with fresh fruits, vegetables, and nuts. She scowls at my chicken sandwich but doesn't say anything. She's a hardcore vegetarian—most fae are—and even though she's given up the fight to get me to stop eating meat, she still turns her nose up at my dietary choices.

Becks sits down next to her a few seconds later with a double cheeseburger and meatball sub on his tray.

"Hey, Locklyn," he says with a nod. "How was your weekend?"

"Boring," I say, but when I glance over at him I immediately know something is wrong. He's smiling, but it doesn't reach his eyes. I know him well enough to recognize when he's stressed.

"Seriously, Becks?" Eyeing his tray with disgust, Ensley gets up and moves to the empty seat on the other side of me. "Yuck," she says, and then pinches her nose. "I can still smell that minced flesh from here."

Becks laughs and picks up his sub. "This school is filled with meat eaters. I'm sure it's not just my food you're smelling." He takes a big bite and chews.

"You know you don't actually need to eat a living being in order to live. You can get all the nutrients you need from other foods—foods that don't require murdering something."

Becks finishes his bite and wipes his mouth with the back of his hand. "Come on, Ensley. I'm a natural predator. They'd take away my dragon card if I stopped eating meat."

Ensley rolls her eyes. "Or you could stand up for something and actually change something about our world."

I know Becks has zero motivation to change what he eats. This isn't the first argument he and Ensley have gotten into about it.

I'm pretty sure he secretly chooses to eat hamburgers and steaks in front of her just to set her off.

Becks shrugs. "Dad got over it for Mom," he reminds her, which only makes her madder.

I let my gaze drift over the courtyard as Becks and Ensley continue to argue over his lunch.

A group of fae are using their magic to make oranges grow from one of the fruit trees in the center of the rectangular space. A small food fight has broken out at a table to the left, and I catch Ms. Teller, my literary teacher, making a beeline across the court-yard to stop them. I smile, thinking of the food fight the shifters started last week. It ended when a couple of otter shifters acciden-tally doused a vampire at the table next to them with a cupful of red soda.

As I continue to scan, I catch Talon sitting on a table on the opposite side of the courtyard, his butt on the wood surface and his feet planted on a chair instead of the floor. There's a ring of admirers around him. Mostly female.

The smile slips from my face.

I can't believe I thought for even a second that it would be hard for him to adjust to a new school.

"So what are we thinking now?" Ensley asks as she follows my line of sight over to Talon and his groupies. I hadn't even noticed they'd stopped arguing. "Dragon shifter?"

Becks glances over at Talon and then shakes his head. "He wasn't at the council meeting with his uncle on Friday. If Talon was a dragon shifter, he would have been there."

Just because his uncle is a dragon shifter doesn't mean he is as well. It's not uncommon for creatures to marry outside their species or sub-species—my parents are a prime example of that, as are Becks' and Ensley's—and when that happens their biological children only inherit one of the creature traits. Or in my case, neither. It's rare, but occasionally a recessive gene from an ancestor flares and the child turns out to be a completely different species than even both parents. So if one of Talon's parents isn't a dragon shifter, he could be a different type of shifter, or even a fae or vampire.

I narrow my eyes at Talon as he throws his head back and laughs at something Vesper says, their interaction making me even more annoyed that I couldn't keep him out of my thoughts all weekend. Not to mention I feel silly for handing my phone over to him so easily. I played into his hands as willingly as Vesper is right now, and having anything in common with that vapid vampire makes me feel a certain type of way.

"I'm sticking with snake shifter until proven otherwise."

I noticed later in the weekend that Talon put himself in my phone as, Not-A-Snake-Shifter-Talon. I thought it was kind of funny at the time, but now it just irritates me. I need to get off the subject of Talon. Between his visit and my unnerving obsession over Shadow Striker, I've already wasted enough brain space on him.

"How was the council meeting, by the way?" I ask Becks, more to change the subject than anything else. Only dragon shifters are allowed to attend their meetings, but from what Becks has told us about their weekly gatherings, they sound incredibly boring.

A dark shadow seems to cross Becks' face. "Fine," he says, but he won't meet my gaze.

I open my mouth to question him about it when a sheet of lime green paper is slapped on the table in front of us and I jerk.

"What do you think, Becks?" Leo says as he grins down at us. "You gonna step up and show everyone at this school why you're such a big deal?"

I lift my lip in a silent snarl and lean away from Leo. He falls into the small minority of students who choose to bully me rather than ignore me. I hate him. As far as I'm concerned, the only thing he's good for is reminding me why I'm thankful I'm invisible to most of the kids in our school.

Becks barely looks at the green sheet of paper. "What are you talking about?" he asks, shooting Leo a glare the hyena shifter is ignorant to. No one would ever accuse Leo of being the sharpest.

I lean forward to see the paper. There's not much on the sheet besides printed blood splatters with a series of numbers that look like they could be coordinates, and what might be an emblem or insignia—a circle divided into four sections with a smaller ring in the middle and a cross going through the central ring. Each of the sections has a symbol in it, but I don't care enough to study it.

"What, you haven't heard?" Leo says in mock surprise. "The word is Chaos is starting up in a week. The prize is supposed to be something of epic proportions. There are whispers it's like nothing anyone has ever seen before. Nothing mundane like cash or a new ride. Something really valuable. Something powerful."

Ensley barks out a short laugh. "Chaos. Are you serious? Do you think that story is going to trick anyone into attending one of your lame parties?"

Leo shoots her a nasty look. "This isn't my party."

"Yet you're passing out flyers you made. Sure seems like it's your party."

"No," Leo says again, getting angry. "Someone sent these to me. They're paying me a hundred bucks to pass them out."

"Who?" Ensley presses.

"No one knows who runs Chaos," Leo says, shooting Ensley another glare before turning back to Becks.

"Chaos is nothing more than an urban legend," Becks scoffs, and then digs back into his food, a clear verbal sign he's done talking with Leo. Unsurprisingly, Leo doesn't pick up on the hint and instead pulls out a chair next to Becks and plops down into it.

"It's not a legend. It's real," Leo says defensively. "My second cousin swears he was a competitor in the last one. That's how he lost his eye."

Every student at Nightlark Academy, former and current, has heard about Chaos. It's some sort of underground competition that happens every ten or fifteen years or so. No one knows who the organizers are, but the prizes are always said to be life-changing. And they'd have to be, because the trials themselves, a series of five events, are dangerous enough to take a life. The rumor is that during the last Chaos two of the competitors failed to escape one of the trials and died, and then their deaths were covered up as a double suicide. But the thing is, Chaos has always just been a rumor, no more than an unsubstantiated legend passed down over the years.

Becks snorts. "Vanguard lost his eye in Mr. Smalls' shop class six years ago."

Leo's face starts to redden in anger.

"You're just scared you won't be able to win," he accuses Becks, who doesn't even dignify that with a response.

When it's clear Becks isn't going to engage with him, Leo turns on me.

"How about you, gimps," he says, smirking. "It might be entertaining watching you get smashed during one of the trials. At least that way you'll be good for something."

I clench my fists under the table, but as humiliating as it is, Leo isn't wrong. If Chaos were real, I probably wouldn't last a single event. As a magicless creature, the only chance I'd stand would be having a good chance I'd get myself killed participating in the events that are specifically supposed to test the strength of your powers.

Ensley chucks a tomato at Leo. It hits him in the chest, splattering over his orange t-shirt.

"Hey," he says as he flicks wet seeds off him.

"Get out of here," Ensley says. "No one at this table wants to be in your space."

Becks tries to hand the flyer back to Leo, but he won't take it.

"Keep it," Leo says. "You might change your mind."

Rolling his eyes, Becks crumples the flyer. With a twist of his wrist he sends a spark at the balled-up paper, and it goes up in flames, not even so much as singeing his skin because as a dragon shifter he's fireproof.

"Whatever," Leo says, shoving out of his chair. "You'll see this is the real deal and wish you'd taken me seriously."

"How about you hold your breath waiting for that," Ensley suggests with a smirk.

Leo flips her the bird and then ambles off to the next table. He slaps another ominous flyer down, but they look more receptive to Leo's bull than we were.

Ensley surprises me when she says, "You don't think it could actually be happening, do you?"

I look over at her, my eyebrows hiked. She's one of the most cynical creatures I know. Out of the three of us she's the last I would expect to take this seriously.

"Naw," Becks says. "I don't think it's true. He's just trying to get classmates to come to some party he's throwing."

Truth be told, I'm a little surprised Becks isn't taking it more seriously. If Chaos were real, he'd probably be able to win the whole thing.

"If it were true, would you enter?" I ask, curious.

Becks chuckles, but the sound is brittle. "You think I'd be allowed to participate in something like that? The house owns me now. I can't do anything without the council's approval."

Ensley and I exchange a look. He's never spoken out about the House of Dragon like that before. And even if his words weren't inflammatory, there's no missing the bitterness in his voice. Something is definitely up with him. Something happened at that meeting, and I want to know what, but I also want to respect Becks' privacy. I expect he'll tell me when he's ready. There are very few secrets between the three of us.

"Freckles, I was disappointed I didn't hear from you. I did nothing else this weekend but sit by my phone and wait for you to call me." Talon's voice runs over my skin like hot coals, searing everywhere it touches.

I glance over to find him standing directly over my shoulder. I didn't hear him approach, which is unnerving because part of me is always watching my back.

Talon grabs an empty chair from the table next to us, spins it around, and then wedges it between me and Becks. His eyes never leave my face as he sits down, his legs wide on either side of the chair as he rests his arms on the back and encroaches on my space.

I can feel Ensley's gaze on me. Becks scowls from the other side of Talon as he scooches his chair away to reclaim his own space.

If I were to glance up and scan the courtyard, I'd bet I'd find a good number of the students staring at us. Becks, who's as charismatic as he is attractive and powerful, has always drawn attention. It's clear Talon has a similar effect. Having both of their attention right now isn't going to do me any favors later. Some of the girls are going to be threatened by that and want to take me down a few pegs. I'm going to have to be on guard for the rest of the day.

Fantastic.

"Yeah, Locklyn," Ensley says as she elbows me in the side. My face heats as I realize they were all waiting for me to say something. "Why didn't you call our new friend, Talon?" Her voice is heavy with sarcasm, and I know I'm going to get it from her the moment he leaves.

I didn't tell her or Becks about Talon's visit to the shop this weekend. I considered it but didn't want to deal with any questions about it from either of them. But now I wish I had because Talon makes it sound like it was something that it wasn't.

"I have a very hard time believing that was the only thing you did this weekend," I say, letting my gaze purposefully shift to where Vesper is standing, glaring at us from the other side of the courtyard.

"Oh, but it was," he says, sounding nothing but sincere. "Nothing would have made me happier than to hear your sweet voice on the other end of the line."

Ensley digs her elbow into my side again, prompting me to respond.

"I'm sure." I give myself credit for containing an eye roll.

Talon leans in, his voice becoming intimate, and my body heats involuntarily. "You broke my heart a little when you didn't call me."

Ensley starts choking, and Becks releases a low growl; the smell of smoke tickles my nose. A telltale sign he's pissed off.

A hint of a smile appears on Talon's face, letting me know he enjoys stirring the pot.

Okay, enough of this. Becks' scowl is starting to look murderous, and I'm going to have bruises peppered along my ribs from Ensley digging her elbow into me every time Talon opens his mouth.

I lean away from Talon, putting some respectable distance between the two of us. This seems to please Becks because the smoke clears. Ensley, on the other hand, continues to nudge me closer to the dark-haired troublemaker.

"My parents said they'd put out some feelers for the artifact you came into the store looking for. I gave them your number so they can get in touch with you if they find anything," I say, letting my friends know that Talon is full of it and that the only reason he wanted me to call is about an antique he's searching for, and simultaneously letting Talon know that any further information about the whereabouts of Shadow Striker won't be coming from me.

"He came into the store?" Becks asks, looking a million times more relaxed than he did a minute ago.

"Yeah," I answer, before Talon can open his mouth and spin it to sound more salacious than it actually was. "He's looking for a particular artifact. A present for his father, I believe."

"What are you looking for?" Becks asks.

"Something incredibly rare," Talon says, his gaze still on me. The intensity in the gray-blue depths makes me want to squirm in my chair, but I keep myself in check. Something tells me that letting Talon know he's affecting me would be a bad idea.

"There are lots of places to look for antiques around Everton," Becks says.

"I know. But I think Freckles here might have exactly what I'm looking for."

The scent of smoke permeates the air again.

Talon is specifically baiting Becks. I don't know why, but it's starting to piss me off.

"I don't have anything you're looking for," I say, adding a touch of ice to my words.

"Don't be so sure of that," Talon challenges, leaning forward to recapture some of the space I'd put between us. "You have more to offer than anyone realizes."

Talon hasn't looked away from me since he sat down, and it suddenly doesn't feel like we're talking about looking for Shadow Striker anymore.

The bell rings, signaling the end of lunch. I've barely touched my food, but I'm not hungry anymore.

Someone calls Talon's name, and he raises a hand in their direction, signaling he heard them without breaking eye contact with me.

Chairs scrape against the stone floor and trays clank as students stack them by the door on the way to their next class, but I can't seem to look away from Talon, at least not until a hand lands on my bicep. When I glance up, Becks is standing next to me. His hand is warm on my arm, and my insides go melty.

"Come on, Locklyn. I'll walk you to class."

I smile up at him, thankful for the rescue even though I'm confused about why I even needed it.

"See ya around, Freckles," Talon says. I'm no longer looking at him; my eyes are on Becks. But I hear him push out of his chair and walk away.

No one bothers us as Becks and I walk to my next class, but it's hard to ignore the stares and whispers. Ensley has class on the other side of campus or I'm sure she'd be in my ear right now, asking me all about what went down when Talon came into the shop this weekend, wanting to know if I learned anything interesting about him. But I don't want to talk about Talon, so I was relieved she didn't have time to give me the third degree. The look she shot me before heading in the opposite direction let me know I'd only bought myself some time, not escaped her inquisition altogether.

"You headed to Peet's Gym after classes today?" Becks asks, avoiding the topic of Talon as well.

"Probably. My parents don't need my help at the shop, and I don't have much homework. I could use a quick workout." *To work off some of this extra energy*, I think, but don't say.

I feel weird and a bit jittery after the lunch interaction with Talon. Like I have a bunch of extra emotions I don't want or need. Perhaps I can shake them off by pummeling a bag with my hands and feet. It's worked in the past.

"Cool. I might come with," Becks says just as we arrive at my class.

I glance at his biceps as they strain against the confines of his t-shirt. Those muscles aren't just for show. I know, because sometimes he comes with me to the gym to spar or work out on his own. He's a beast in and out of the ring. And I'm not even talking about his dragon form.

I let my gaze drift down his arm and over the bit of his tattoo that peeks out from under his sleeve. In my mind's eye I can see the entirety of the ferocious inked dragon that wraps around his bicep and curls onto his shoulder, but in a t-shirt only flashes of its hind legs and tail are visible. He got the tattoo last year after he was named dragon heir. I remember how my stomach flipped the first time he showed it to me. The ink gave him a bit of an edge that only heightened his appeal. I was surprised though because he'd never shown interest in being inked. When I asked him why he got it he said that he needed a permanent reminder of how his life had changed.

I drag my focus from his tattoo down to his hands. He's amazing with his fists. As I stare at his hands like a weirdo, my mind drifts to what else they are good for, and I flush.

"You okay?" Becks asks. "You're turning red."

Kill me now.

I swallow, wetting my suddenly dry throat. "Yeah, sorry. I just remembered I have a quiz in Creature History today I forgot to study for."

That answer doesn't explain my sudden redness at all, but Becks nods like it does. "Sucks."

"Yeah." And it does. I really do have a quiz I forgot to study for in my search for Shadow Striker information this weekend. So unless the questions are about obscure Ancients that no one seems to know about, I really am screwed.

"Hey, Becks, did you transfer into our class?" Sutton, a cute blonde fae with a pixie cut asks as she chews on a piece of gum. The look in her eyes is nothing short of hopeful.

An easy smile lifts the corners of her mouth when he glances over at her. A frown pulls at my features from losing his attention. I don't have anything personal against Sutton. She's never been overly aggressive toward me. We've probably never said more than a handful of words to each other. She's definitely part of the student population that ignores my existence, and so that makes her A-okay in my book, but just the way Becks smiles down on her now instead of me makes me prickle.

"Hey, Sutton. Naw, I was just keeping my bud, Locklyn, company on the way to her class. I'd better head out before I'm late to my next class."

"Oh," she says, her pretty face falling and her lower lip jutting out in a small pout.

"See ya," he says to her, and then holds his fist out for me to tap, our usual goodbye gesture.

I hold back a sigh. I'm so far in the friend zone I can't even see the end of it.

After I tap his fist, he turns and walks down the hall toward his class on the other side of the building. I stay outside the classroom, watching him leave, a forlorn ache in my chest.

The moment after Becks rounds the corner, I'm hit in the back of the head with what is probably a crumpled piece of paper.

I sigh. The reprieve Becks offered was nice, but it's over.

Five

"YOU STILL INTERESTED in coming with me to the gym?" I ask Becks, who's leaned up against the locker next to mine as I unload the books I don't need.

He shakes his head. "Something came up with the council. I have to shoot over there right now. Sorry."

"No worries," I say, trying to cover my disappointment.

Becks has a far-off look in his eyes when I shut my locker and turn to him. I'm about to ask him if everything is okay when Shawn, a fellow dragon shifter and one of his vodenball teammates, comes up from behind him and slaps a hand on his shoulder.

"Hey, Becks. Heard the council is looking for your match. You'd better get whatever fun there is to be had right away before you're shackled to some chick."

Becks swivels his head to glare at Shawn, but Shawn doesn't even see because he's already moved past us to join a group of guys exiting the school.

"What's he talking about?" I ask, anxiety crawling up my chest to lodge in my throat.

Becks won't meet my gaze, his eyes unfocused as he runs his tongue over his top row of teeth.

"Becks?" I prod around the knot of unease.

He releases a sigh and finally looks at me. "The council decided it would be beneficial for me to be mated after I graduate."

My heart stops, the blood freezing in my veins, chilling me to the core. It takes a solid five seconds before I can respond.

"What? They want to mate you? You're just barely eighteen. Usually heirs aren't matched—let alone mated—until their mid-twenties."

"Yeah, well—" He grabs the back of his neck, rubbing it as he grinds his teeth. "They decided otherwise."

"But . . . why?"

Panic wells in my chest and spills over like a boiling pot of tar, scalding my insides and making it hard to breathe.

I always knew Becks wasn't for me. Even before he was named heir I knew he was destined to marry someone powerful and would never be mine. I told myself so many times that I was just thankful and content with our friendship, but as the reality of Becks being pledged to another female stares me in the face, I know I've been lying to myself the whole time.

I'm not okay with just being his friend, and I don't think I ever will be.

Hunching over so we're closer in height, he gently grabs my shoulders and turns me toward him. "Don't worry about it, okay? Nothing will change between us. I promise."

Not even Becks' warm touch can thaw me now. I am ice. Hard. Cold. Incapable of feelings.

"Change nothing?" Is he delusional? "Becks, having a life-mate is going to change *everything*. Not just between you and me, but in all aspects of your life. Nothing will ever be the same again."

Becks straightens, putting distance between us. "I know that!" he snaps, taking me aback. Becks hardly ever raises his voice, least of all to me. "They said that it could just be a mating in name at first. At least until next fall. So even if I'm matched, I'll have the rest of the summer."

He runs a hand through his hair; the strands stick up at all different angles. There's a wild look in his eyes he's trying hard to contain, and it's in that moment I realize that the lie that nothing will change is what Becks is telling himself to hold himself together.

Does the thought of Becks being matched, let alone mated, to another female unleash an almost debilitating sense of panic within me? Yes, of course it does. But even if it feels like I'm cracking apart, this is happening to Becks, not me. If I'm panicking, Becks has to be doing a million times worse. He doesn't need a friend who's freaking out on him right now, he needs a rock, someone calm and solid who will tell him everything is going to be okay, even when it obviously isn't.

I move closer to Becks, placing a light hand on his forearm for comfort. The muscles beneath his skin are tight and bunched, as if he is getting ready to hit something, but then he starts to relax beneath my grip.

Shifters are a touchy-feeling bunch, especially dragon shifters, who see physical touch as a way to offer heat to another. According to Becks, it's comforting and seen as a way to care for one another, so although physical contact is a little awkward for me, I don't shy away from it now because I know it soothes my friend.

"You're right. It's going to be okay," I say, my voice leveling out and calm. "It's still mid-semester, so you have months before graduation." Really only two, but I don't point that out. "And who knows, maybe the council will change their mind and give you another couple years like you expected. Nothing is set in stone right now."

"Right, exactly," Becks says, some of the crazed look leaving his eyes. "Maybe they will change their minds."

Now that some of the shock has worn off, his comments about not having control of his life and his bitterness against the council earlier today make crystal clear sense now.

"Is there any way to get out of this?" I ask gently, hoping there might be some sort of loophole to help him prolong the inevitable, or maybe get out of his situation altogether. Arranged matings of any sort are almost unheard of nowadays, but as the dragon heir, Becks has to play by a whole different set of rules than the rest of us. If only being the dragon heir was something Becks had a choice in. It's a role he never wanted, but it's not one he's in a position to abdicate.

He shakes his head. "Not that I know of, but I can do some poking around."

"Would your parents be able to help?"

Becks stiffens up again. "They won't be any help," is all he says, and I get the impression I shouldn't push for why.

"Okay. Well, you have me and Ens. We can both search for anything about council rules that might help." Even as I say it I know it's a hollow offer. The House of Dragon is notoriously private. Becks is open with me about most things, but never that.

"Please don't say anything to Ens," he asks. "She doesn't know yet."

That surprises me. As close as Becks and I are, Ensley is his sister. But I agree, not wanting to upset him any further.

Becks looks relieved and changes the subject, trying to lighten the mood and pretend he's fine, but there's tension in his shoulders and splashed across his face. There has to be a way to get my friend out of this situation. I may not be privy to the inner working of their council, but that doesn't mean I'll give up.

THOUGHTS OF BECKS and his situation swirl in my mind, distracting me from anything else, and so my workout that afternoon is sloppy at best. I almost sprain my ankle sparring with one of the other teachers when I lose my footing. Then I forget to put the clip on the barbell, and when I start lifting, a fifty-pound weight drops off the end of the bar in the middle of my bench press, narrowly missing the foot of a burly wolverine shifter as he passes by. He chews me out for a solid three minutes before moving on. Sweaty and defeated, I give up after that and grab a quick shower in the locker room.

The rest of the week doesn't go much better. I hardly see Becks —he doesn't sit with Ensley and me during lunch—and the few times I catch him between classes or after school he seemed distracted or in a rush. After the first few days I can't help thinking he's avoiding me, regretful that I know about his impending life-mating. On that note, Ensley notices I'm off as well and repeatedly asks me what's wrong, but I wave off her concerns the best I can, not feeling like it's my place to tell her Becks' secret when he specifically asked me not to.

I don't have any further one-on-one interactions with Talon the rest of the week either, which I'm not sad about. But even though we never speak, I do catch him staring at me a couple of times from across the courtyard or in the hall as we pass one another. More often than not, the expression on his face is the same, like I'm a puzzle he can't quite solve. But whenever he catches me staring back he throws on a lazy smile or gives me a suggestive wink that makes my face heat, so I look away.

"So, I had an idea," Ensley says, wrenching me out of my own thoughts as we head to the parking lot so she can give me a ride home.

"What's your idea?" I ask, managing to sound way more interested than I actually am.

"Before I tell you, you have to say yes."

"Yeah, that's not how it works," I say on a laugh.

"It does this time." The grin on her face is slightly maniacal. The creepy smile along with the multicolored streaks in her hair today makes her look a touch like a deranged clown.

I shoot her a side-eye look.

"Just promise. Please," she says, drawing out the last word. There's a wild glint in her eyes that tells me she's up to something.

"I promise that I'll seriously consider whatever you are about to say before immediately saying 'no.'" That's as much as I'm willing to budge. I've known Ensley long enough to know she has a knack for getting me in trouble.

She juts out her lower lip and tips her head down in an impression of a puppy dog pout. "Come on, Locklyn. When was the last time I steered you wrong?"

I snort. "Do you really want me to answer that?" I say, thinking of how just last month she convinced me to skip third period with her to buy the newest version of her phone before they sold out, *promising* me we wouldn't get caught. Technically, she was right. *She* didn't get caught. *I* did. Dean Faust saw me rushing across campus in the middle of a period when I was trying to sneak back. I got a lecture, a call to my parents, and two weeks of weekend detention where they made me scrub the toilets in the boys' bathroom. I still shudder just thinking about what was crusted on that porcelain.

"At least admit your life would be boring without me."

"That, I can agree with." If nothing else, Ensley does keep things exciting.

"Fine," she says on a huff, realizing she's not going to get me to blindly agree with whatever scheme she's cooking up. "But at least hear me out."

"I said I would." *Oh boy, this is going to be good.*

We stop in front of Ensley's shiny silver sports car and I turn to face her, letting her know she has my attention.

"We should go to the Chaos party this—"

"Nope," I say, my head shaking before she can get the rest of the sentence out, let alone plead her case.

"Locklyn," Ensley whines, "you promised you'd hear me out."

I fold my arms over my chest, giving her the stink eye.

Chaos is all anyone at Nightlark Academy seems to be able to talk about. I don't for a second think it's real, let alone starting this weekend, but the school is divided. Half the students believe Chaos is actually happening, and the other half don't but are still excited for the kickoff party taking place on Saturday. Either way, whatever is going to go down this weekend is sure to be epic, and I want no part of it. I've never been to a real rager before and have less than zero interest in breaking that longstanding tradition.

"We weren't invited," I say, hoping to throw her off, but she just rolls her eyes.

"Lock, everyone was invited. That's what an open invite means."

Shoot. Good point.

I run my tongue over my bottom lip, trying to think up another plausible excuse that might detour my pushy friend. The gleam in her eyes tells me that's going to be hard. It looks like she's already set her mind on attending, and once Ensley makes up her mind it's near impossible to change it.

"Come on. Becks said he would go," she says, a knowing half-smile curling the corners of her mouth.

That does the job and spikes my interest, but I play it off, not wanting to let Ensley know. "Well, whatever. Becks goes to parties all the time."

"But he said he'd go *with* us to this one."

Okay, that's new. Becks has never offered to go to a party with me before. Probably because I've always been really vocal about how I'd rather get a tooth pulled than be forced to hang out with our peers from Nightlark outside of school, but it's always secretly bugged me he never at least asked.

"He did?" I say, nibbling a bit on the bait she dangled before me.

She nods. "This is too big to miss, and Becks knows you aren't much for parties and would feel more comfortable attending if the both of us were close by."

Translation: she guilted him into it by saying that I wouldn't go unless he went with us.

My friend is a devious little she-devil sometimes.

A tiny voice whispers in my head that I might not get very many more opportunities to hang out with Becks, but I shake my head. No way am I going to put Becks out like that. I know he enjoys spending time with me, but a party is so not my scene. I'd just ruin it for him if he wants to go.

An image of Becks at a party, with Vesper or one of the other powerful females in our school pawing at him, rises in my mind, making my stomach sour.

"No. I don't want to go."

It doesn't matter what Ensley says. I am not going to that party.

Six

"I CAN'T BELIEVE you convinced me to do this," I say, pulling down the hem of the borrowed skirt I'm wearing. If it's this short on me, it has to barely cover Ensley's butt. I wrap my arms around myself, trying to ignore how chilly the early spring night is. It would be unusual for this time of year, but I wouldn't be overly surprised to see a flake or two of snow hovering in the air. At least the off-the-shoulder white shirt I'm wearing, also borrowed, covers my arms and stomach. It's probably a crop top on Ensley.

Parking on the edge of Woodwinds Forest, we head into the woods and start tromping around trees and through soggy leaves to get to Deepseat Caverns. After ten minutes of walking, we still aren't there. My foot sinks into the mud and makes a suction sound when I pull it free. *Yuck.* Thank the Creator Ensley let me wear my sturdy black combat boots. She said it made my outfit look edgy, but really I was just glad they were comfortable, made for walking, and laced up my calves.

Using her flashlight app, Ensley holds her phone up in front of her to light the way for us. We aren't the only students sludging through the forest in search of a good time. Whispers and the occasional laugh ring out all around us as students converge on the party destination.

Ensley flashes me a toothy smile. "You'll thank me someday. I'm sure of it."

"Don't count on it," I grumble.

Ensley isn't just a sneaky she-devil, she's a manipulative little witch as well. She somehow talked me into coming to this party when I was dead set against it. I don't even really know how she did it. I said no about a million times yet still found myself at her house getting ready for the event of the year I wanted nothing to do with. Maybe she's part-vampire and used compulsion on me?

Okay, that couldn't actually happen. Fae can't use compulsion, but still, the way she mind-tricked me into coming still makes me wonder.

Deepseat Caverns is a network of underground caves and tunnels just outside Everton that's filled with stalactites and stalagmites, mirror pools, columns, and flowstone. It's a tourist attraction during the day but closes after dark. I came here once with my parents when I was ten, and I remember being entranced by the eerie beauty of the caverns.

Fellow partygoers, familiar and unfamiliar alike, materialize from the dense forest the closer we get to the cavern's entrance.

"Yo, Ens, you made it," someone calls to our left, and when I look over, Konan, one of Ensley's bandmates, is jogging toward us.

Ensley and I are close, but just like Becks she has interests outside our friendship. I don't have much interaction with her bandmates, but when it happens they're never overly friendly, but always polite.

The news of this party has really spread like wildfire if Konan is here. He plays bass in Ensley's punk rock band and is two years older than us and attends Everton Community College. When he reaches us he loops an arm over Ensley's shoulder and tugs her into his side. Ensley punches him lightly in the stomach but doesn't move out of his embrace.

Konan is tall with light brown skin and a trendy fro-hawk. Ensley looks equally edgy with the purple and blue strips weaved into the rows of braids on the side of her head. Both of them dressed in black biker jackets and chunky boots, they look good together, but according to her it will never happen between them. She said she views him like a brother, but from the fire in his eyes as he smiles down at her I'm not sure he's on the same page. I don't blame him though. Ensley is gorgeous, with an amazing personality and talented to boot. She's a catch, and he won't be the first to find her irresistible.

"So, what do you think?" he asks. "Just a regular rager, or is this really the start of Chaos?"

I scoff and Konan looks over at me for the first time.

"Seems like you have an opinion," he says good-naturedly.

I shrug. "I just think the idea that Chaos is even real at all is a little far-fetched."

"You're probably right, but wouldn't it be sweet if it was?"

I make a noncommittal sound. The truth is I don't really care either way. I'm only here because Ensley worked some fae voodoo on me.

"Where's the rest of the group?" Ensley asks, meaning her fellow bandmates.

"Inside already," Konan answers. "At least I think. I was running late. I got a message from them when they arrived but haven't heard from them since. Must be having too much fun to stop and check their phones."

Almost to the entrance of the caverns, the crowd around us has grown. I recognize some of the teens as we're all bottlenecked through a narrow ravine, but not all. There must be more than just Nightlark Academy students invited to this party. I look for Becks, but don't see him anywhere. I was surprised I didn't see him back at his house before we left, but Ensley said he was headed to the party straight after practice.

Anxiety starts to churn in my gut. I don't love big groups.

Some might think there's safety in numbers, but I don't. More creatures just means more opportunities for chaos to ensue. And if something goes down tonight, I'll only have my fists and feet to protect myself.

When we come around the corner, the entrance to Deepseat Caverns yawns before us. At least thirty feet high and wide, the stalactites that hang down from the ceiling and stalagmites that jut up from the ground make it look like a macabre open mouth, waiting to swallow us whole.

Apprehension slides down my spine like an ice cube. There's no light coming from the caverns, and the moment someone passes through the barrier it looks like they disappear. As we come closer I make out a barely discernible transparent barrier covering the opening. It's just a slight iridescent shimmer. Some sort of magic I'm not familiar with, probably to block out the noise and sights of the party raging from within the cavern's belly, but it only makes my unease grow. I like to know what I'm getting myself into before I leap.

Ensley notices my steps slowing. "You okay?"

I glance over at her and Konan, both their faces completely free of worry and filled with anticipation for a fun night out. It makes me sad how different I am from even my best friend.

How did I get this way? I don't want to be like this, scared of my own shadow. I want to be fearless and bold, to take life with both hands and direct it rather than let it drag me around. I want to change, but to do that I have to start somewhere. This feels like as good of a time to start as any.

I straighten my spine. "Yeah, I'm good."

Ensley's face splits into a huge grin. "You're going to have a great time, just wait."

I force a smile as I nod my agreement. Even so, I squeeze my eyes shut as we pass through the barrier, my body tense as if preparing for a blow, which in a sense is exactly what happens, because when we step into the cavern my eardrums are immediately assaulted with blaring dance music. I crack open my eyelids to find the world painted in red strobe lights and bodies flashing in and out of view all around us. Under the macabre lighting the cavern has become even more sinister—a veritable hellscape.

I'm not the only one shocked. "Wow!" Ensley shouts, her eyes wide and mouth open as she takes everything in. "This is wicked," she says, a grin replacing her gaping mouth.

I do my best not to stumble as we walk down a wide tunnel that will open up into a larger cavern. At least that's what I remember from the last time I visited here as a child. When we reach the open space, the sound has a little more room to disperse so the music isn't as deafening. The red strobe lights also seem to be contained to the tunnel. Although the scene in front of us is different, it's no less intimidating.

There must be several hundred bodies crammed into a circular cavern only a bit larger than our school gymnasium. The light is still dim, and colors flash intermittently, making it hard to identify anyone. The domed ceiling of the space is a solid eighty feet in the air, another random tidbit I remembered from our visit, but some of the stalactites almost reach the floor on the sides. The ground in this cavern is smooth, if not level, from years and years of feet trampling over it, and there's a large rock with a flat top jutting up in the middle of the space.

Konan, Ensley, and I start to skirt the crowd. Half of the attendees are dancing in the middle of the cavern; the rest are dispersed in smaller groups, drinking and talking. There's a fair number of couples making out as well, but I avert my gaze quickly, feeling like a voyeur if I stare for too long. We almost reach the other side of the space before stopping next to a thick cluster of stalagmites.

"I'll see where the others are," Konan says as he pulls out his phone. His brow furrows as his fingers slide over the screen, and a moment later he sighs. "Well, at least now I know why I haven't heard from anyone."

"What do you mean?" Ensley asks.

He jerks his head toward the entrance. "That barrier back there isn't just dampening the noise and lights. It shut off our electronics as well."

"What? No way." Ensley yanks her phone out of her back pocket, checking it. I can tell from the look on her face that Konan was right, but I don't bother reaching for my phone. I left it in Ensley's car because it would have been bulky in my skirt pocket.

"That's sketch," Ensley says with a frown and my heart drops. How are we going to find Becks in this crowd?

Konan shrugs. "If Chaos is going down, it makes sense they don't want any digital information leaking. The trials are supposed to be dangerous. The authorities would shut it down in an instant."

He has a point, and for the first time I actually consider whether this whole Chaos thing could be real, but then I shake off the thought. No way. It's just too unbelievable. But the lack of communication with the outside or even the ability to take photos or record the party fills me with unease. Someone went to a lot of trouble to make sure we were cut off and wouldn't have any physical proof of what goes down this evening.

"Hey, there you are!" someone calls, and then a moment later the rest of Ensley's bandmates, Canin, Holland, and Sol, descend on us.

"We would have called you—" Holland, a black-haired cheetah shifter starts.

"But your phones aren't working," Konan finishes for her.

"This is wild, isn't it?" Sol asks. He's a short fae a year younger than Ensley and me, with green spiky hair that sticks up all around his head like a porcupine. According to her, he plays the drums like he has a vendetta against them, which I guess is a good thing.

I press back into the shadows as Ensley laughs and catches up with her bandmates. Crossing my arms, I lean against a large stalagmite that connected with a stalactite to form a pillar, wishing I'd stuck to my guns and avoided this whole event altogether. Becks is nowhere to be seen and the flashing lights are starting to give me a headache.

As I wait in the shadows, a strange awareness brushes over me, pebbling my skin, and when I glance to the side I realize I'm not the only person taking refuge in the darkness.

Slowly, a figure steps forward, his body shape and features becoming recognizable in the darkness.

"Freckles," he says, his familiar tone washing over me. "I didn't expect to see you here."

Seven

TALON'S deep voice sinks past skin and bones, embedding itself in my core. When an involuntary shiver passes through me I tell myself I'm just chilled from the damp cavern air.

"What are you doing here?" I ask, and he quirks his mouth into a lopsided smile.

What a stupid question. In the short time he's been at Nightlark, Talon's already one of the most popular guys at school, so of course if there's a big party he's going to be there.

"I suppose the same as you. Attending the party of the century," he says, but his tone is mocking as his gaze travels past me and slides over the mass of partygoers holed up in the cavern. "Dancing. Drinking. Debauchery. The trifecta of teenage rebellion." He sighs, looking suddenly weary, like this whole thing is tedious and he'd rather be anywhere but here tonight.

"Right. The trifecta. I guess I'd have to experience it at least once before graduation."

Talon's brows wing and he tilts his head. "Don't tell me this is your first party?"

"First and last, if I can help it."

"Ah, well, don't let my jaded soul taint the experience for you."

I shake my head. "It won't. This just isn't my scene. My idea of a fun time is a night in bingeing my favorite show with a pint of cookie dough ice cream."

As soon as the words are out of my mouth I want to face-palm myself. *Why did I say that?* Could I have made myself sound any more pathetic?

The corners of Talon's mouth curve up. He's probably trying not to laugh at me. So of course I continue to word vomit and make it worse.

"I mean, that's not all I like to do. Hanging out with friends is cool too. But I don't really get invited to parties, so it's not like my *thing* or whatever.

Stop talking, Locklyn. Please stop talking. But I can't seem to keep my mouth closed. The words keep spewing, each sentence worse than the last.

"It's just that you get judged for everything at Nightlark. What you say, what you do, what you wear, even what friends you hang out with. We all sort each other into different categories just to try to figure out where we belong. It's exhausting, and I don't see the point to subjecting myself to all that after hours as well."

Groan. Would the ground please open up and swallow me whole . . .

I glance around, wondering why he's even lurking in the shadows with me right now. Surely there's someone else he'd rather be talking to. Probably someone leggier and a lot less awkward.

"I get that," Talon says, and I make myself look back at him. "No one likes feeling judged. But it will get better. High school isn't forever, and it's rough for a lot of us."

"You seem to be sailing through pretty easily." I'm not trying to be a jerk, it's just true. He's only been at Nightlark Academy a couple of weeks, but he's certainly not hurting for friends.

"You'd be surprised."

I take a moment to study Talon as his gaze moves past me to scan the crowd. He looks off tonight. Not aesthetically speaking. His ripped jeans and black t-shirt are simple enough, but the darkness of his clothes combined with his black hair makes his muted blue eyes pop. There's something different about his demeanor tonight. He might be dressed the part, but he doesn't seem like a high schooler out for a good time. There's an unusual edginess in the way he's holding himself; his muscles are tense and rigid, and his hands are curled into fists. It feels like he's here for a purpose that has nothing to do with teenage rebellion or chasing a high. The intense look in his eyes makes me think he's searching for someone, or something.

"Looking for someone in particular?" I ask, and he jerks his attention back to me, his gaze dark.

He shoves his hands in his pockets as he shakes his head. "No. Just staying alert."

I shoot him a look. *Staying alert.* That's a weird thing to say. I'm about to comment on it when Talon changes the subject.

"You look amazing," he says, his shoulders relaxing and an easy smile melting on his face, but I can't help but feel like he just slipped on a costume to hide some of his truth from me.

He looks me over from head to toe and back up again, a spark of appreciation in his eyes. I fidget, uncomfortable with his regard.

"Don't you agree?" Talon asks, his gaze still locked with mine, so I think he's talking to me until I sense a presence at my back.

When I glance over my shoulder, Becks is standing there, fists clenched and muscles bunched as he glares daggers at Talon.

"What are you doing here?" Becks asks the same question I'd presented to Talon, but Becks doesn't mean *here* at Deepseat Caverns like I did, he means *here* as in talking to me. On a different day I might be pleased by the note of possessiveness, but instead the darkness in Becks' voice turns my stomach sour.

I step to the side so I can keep an eye on both Becks and Talon. There's something going on between them that feels a little dangerous, but I can't for the life of me fathom why. They hardly know each other, and as far as I can tell I've had more interaction with Talon than Becks has, so it doesn't make sense that Becks looks like he's one wrong comment away from throwing down.

"I'm just enjoying the festivities and keeping Freckles company," Talon says, his smile growing when Becks' eyes narrow. "I saw you talking to Vesper when I first came in. She certainly is . . ." Talon pauses, looking like he's mulling over how to describe Vesper, finally landing on " . . . persistent."

At the mention of Vesper and Becks, any lingering hint of excitement I had for this evening disappears. Becks opens his mouth to respond when the music is cut and the crowd roars in displeasure.

"That's weird," I start, but then the lights disappear as well, plunging the cave into total and utter darkness.

There's a beat of silence and then pandemonium erupts. Some creatures, like certain shifters and vampires, have varying degrees of night vision, but the rest of us are blinded. Screams echo off the cavern walls and feet pound against the stone ground as partygoers start racing toward the exit. Someone slams into me, and I get the wind knocked out of me when I hit the ground. A booted foot stomps on my leg before I can regain my footing, and a sharp burst of pain explodes on my thigh.

"Locklyn!" Becks shouts.

"Over here," I croak as I scooch toward the perimeter of the cavern, searching for the wall so I don't get trampled.

"Keep your head down," Becks calls out, and then a plume of fire shoots from his hands into the air, hovering in the space above my head long enough for him to spot me from half a dozen feet away.

It goes dark again, but before I know it, arms wrap around me, and I'm hauled to my feet. Becks walks me backward until my back bumps up against the cavern wall. The coolness of the stone behind me seeps through my clothes, giving me chills.

"Are you okay?" he asks, his voice rising above the din of panic.

He has me boxed in between two immovable forces: his body

in front and the stone behind. I only realize my hands are on his chest when I register the furious cadence of his heartbeat. No doubt it matches my own. Under normal circumstances I'd be self-conscious about our closeness, but in the darkness his presence makes me feel safe, protected.

"Yeah, I'm fine," I say, breathless. I'm probably going to have a boot-shaped bruise on my thigh tomorrow, but I don't think anything is broken.

"You sure you're not hurt?" It's too dark for me to see his face clearly, but the touch of panic in his voice rings loud and clear.

Without waiting for my response, his hands start to roam from my shoulders down my arms and the sides of my body as he checks for . . . what? Maybe broken bones? I know his touch is innocent, but the caress of his hands over my body feels criminally good, and my words stick in my throat. Despite the madness around us, my limbs go languid as I sway toward Becks.

Becks' hands suddenly stop on my hips and tighten. "Lock-lyn?" he asks, his voice filled with uncertainty. His face is so close his breath feathers across my forehead and a thrill runs through me when I think of how near his mouth is to my own.

I have to swallow to wet my suddenly dry throat before answering, and even then my voice is no louder than a whisper. "I'm not hurt."

In the distance, someone yells that the exit is blocked and then pinpricks of faelight start to illuminate the space behind Becks. His face is still shrouded in shadows, but between the low light and his night vision, I have no doubt he can see me clearly now.

"Locklyn," he whispers again, and skims a hand up my rib cage and over my shoulder to land on my neck, his fingers gentle as he brushes them back and forth over the sensitive skin. My lids get heavy, and I have to battle to keep my eyes open.

Becks has never held me like this. He's never touched me the way he is now, and the assault on my senses causes the flimsy shield around my emotions to shatter. My feelings for him that I usually stuff way down deep balloon in my chest. I know they're probably broadcasting across my face, but the moment is too raw for me to hide them.

Part of me realizes this is a completely inappropriate time for us to be having a moment. The bedlam in the cavern hasn't subdued. Party goers shriek and race back and forth looking for a way out, but I'm so focused on Becks that the craziness surrounding us might as well be a million miles away. A bomb could fall on us in this instant and I'd hardly notice.

I inch the hand that I have pressed up against his chest higher and he stops breathing, his muscles tensing impossibly tighter.

What's gotten into me? I've never been this bold with Becks before, but deep inside I'm both out of control and completely calm. Like this is where we've been heading all along, but we just needed a little push to get here.

Becks may never be my future, but in this moment it feels like he's mine and I'm not letting it pass without claiming him.

The faelight shining behind Becks is just bright enough to make out the curve of his jaw, the arch of his cheekbone, and a flash of his green eyes. He's drifted toward me and now his lips are only inches from my own. I tip my head back, sliding my hand even higher so that I'm cupping his jaw, his scruff deliciously rough under my fingertips.

Becks' breathing is as ragged as mine. His hand clutching my hip curves to my lower spine and he draws me closer, while his other hand slides from my neck to the back of my head. The gentle tugs on the strands as he buries his fingers in my hair send bolts of electricity through me.

As more fae use their magic to light the cavern, the crowd finally starts to calm. The murmurs behind Becks seem more confused than panicked now—but who cares? Becks and I are in our own glass bubble, separate from the rest of the world. This couldn't feel more right, and it's a toss-up about whether I want this moment to last forever, or rush toward the precipice we're about to fall over.

Becks' mouth is now so close I can almost feel the warmth of his lips, almost taste their sweetness. I have to bite back the whimper that's lodged in my throat. I've never wanted anything more than to feel their softness against mine and experience my first kiss. To know that the two of us fit together like puzzle pieces, despite what the dragon council, the students at Nightlark Academy, or anyone else may think.

I start to go up on my toes, too impatient to wait for him to come to me, when a loud boom rocks the cavern, eliciting another round of screams.

A bright light flashes behind Becks and he twists to see what's going on. He shoves me behind him as he pulls away. Everything in me protests and I want to weep over the moment that was just stolen from us.

The cavern has gone eerily quiet. I peek around Becks' giant body to see what's going on. The rock formation in the middle of the cavern is lit with a column of silvery light, as if it has a spotlight directed at it. Standing atop the stone is a figure robed in red. Parts of my brain are still a little muddled, so it takes me a second to really absorb the strangeness of the situation.

Is this some kind of prank?

Becks glances over at me with a frown when I slide out from behind him to get a better look at the spectacle. I know he wants me to stay put, but I don't need his protection.

As if under a spell, the crowd is transfixed on the figure, staying still and silent. I sneak a quick glance around, catching Ensley and her band members not far away, but Talon is nowhere to be seen. I have a momentary twinge of worry for him before my thoughts are interrupted by a booming voice.

"Welcome to Chaos," the figure atop the stone outcrop says. His voice is all gravel and grit as it booms throughout the space, his words lingering in the air even after the echoes fade.

Becks and I glance at each other, our faces mirror images of shock as audible gasps and excited *whoops* reverberate throughout the crowd.

I guess this is really happening. I'll never say I haven't been wrong before.

The figure, who sounds male but whose body shape is undistinguishable under the red robes, waits until it's silent again before speaking. "Your attendance tonight is considered your acceptance as Chaos spectators. The barrier you passed through upon entering the caverns isn't just to block out the sound and lights of this evening's festivities." He pauses again and every creature in the crowd hangs on his next words. "It also prevents you from discussing Chaos with anyone who isn't here this evening. Just like tonight, your devices won't work at any of the participating events either."

I suck in a gasp and look up at Becks, whose mouth is flattened into a grim line. That sounds like some sort of vampire compulsion magic to me, which is very illegal.

"A magical gag? Is that even possible?"

"I've never heard of anything like that before," he says, but what he doesn't say is that it's not possible.

The robed figure turns slowly, taking in the entirety of the crowd surrounding him. When he's pointed in our direction, his hood is so low over his face it conceals his features entirely. I'm sure that's not accidental.

"You may have heard rumors of Chaos and its trials, but I can assure you, you don't know the truth. Chaos is bigger than any of you can imagine, and older than you would believe. Its secrets have been taken to the grave more than once."

Dramatic much?

"I am your game master, one of only a few individuals tasked with keeping Chaos and its traditions alive. My identity will remain unknown for the duration of Chaos. I may be your next-door neighbor, I may be someone you pass on the street, but you'll never know because secrecy is of the utmost importance. Without it, Chaos wouldn't exist."

A low murmur starts in the crowd as everyone begins to really absorb that this is happening. The game master ignores the commotion and keeps talking.

"Tonight, you will take part in Chaos history. Each one of you will have the opportunity to compete, but beware . . . once you identify yourself as a competitor, there's no backing out." Of course there's no way to tell with his hood pulled so low, but the game master is pointed in my direction when he speaks his next words, and even without seeing his eyes, I can't help but feel he's speaking directly to me. "The first Chaos trial begins this evening. The four others will take place over the coming weeks but be assured these trials aren't for the weak or faint of heart. They are fraught with life-threatening dangers and intended for only the strongest among you. Once you enter Chaos, there's no way to self-eliminate and no guarantee of safety, so don't make this decision lightly."

What was a low murmur before has turned into a full-blown commotion. The energy in the crowd is a strange mixture of fear and excitement. Becks must feel it too, because he tries to step in front of me once again, but I skirt him and scurry over to Ensley, tugging on her hand to let her know I'm there.

She looks at me with wide eyes. "Can you believe this is happening?"

I shake my head. "Not really."

I feel, rather than see, Becks come up behind me. He steps close enough that his body heat buffers up against me, but he stops short of touching me. I'd be lying if I said I wasn't disappointed.

"Who would be stupid enough to enter this thing?" he asks, his low voice rumbling behind me.

Ensley and I both shake our heads and shrug, but a sense of foreboding takes over me, and goose bumps pebble my skin. I rub my hands over my arms to chase them away.

Becks leans forward. His chest brushes my back, and his breath tickles the hairs next to my ear. "Cold?"

Heat flashes through my body as I'm brought back to what happened, or rather what almost happened when the lights were doused a few minutes before. If only we'd had a few more moments . . .

I notice Ensley eyeing me, so I clear my throat, forcing those thoughts from my mind. "No. I'm fine."

Becks makes a sound in the back of his throat that shouldn't be attractive but still sends a shiver down my spine. I take a tiny step forward, needing some space or I might burst into flames at any moment.

"Finally, the prize," the game master announces, raising his voice to be heard over the commotion. "It is truly one of a kind. A priceless piece of our history that creatures have fought and died for over the centuries." The robed figure falls silent once again.

I have to keep from rolling my eyes. He certainly likes his dramatic pauses.

"An artifact once thought lost to time but recently re-discovered, its fabled powers have the potential to change the course of history itself," he says, and then raises his arms.

A boom sounds throughout the cavern, then a three-dimensional image appears in the air over his head. I take a step forward, not quite believing my eyes as a hologram of Shadow Striker rotates slowly in front of me.

Eight

I ONLY HAD one look at the picture Talon showed me, but Shadow Striker is branded in my mind: wavy blade, worn, with etchings on the onyx hilt. I don't care if the game master says the blade is Santa Claus' staff, I know that's Shadow Striker.

I start scanning the crowd for Talon, but don't see him anywhere. It's like he vanished the moment the lights were doused, but I know he's around here somewhere.

Did he know this was going to happen? That Shadow Striker would be the Chaos prize? And how did someone get their hands on it anyway?

I don't know the answers to any of those questions, but I know with certainty that Talon's going to be entering Chaos.

The game master continues to talk up Shadow Striker, calling it the Blade of Power, a priceless one-of-a-kind dagger. But what he doesn't mention is the dagger's most important feature, the ability to grant the wielder unimaginable power. But from the buzz that circulates the crowd, it seems like he doesn't need to sell the prize because there will be entrants just for the glory. Whoever wins Chaos will be a legend.

I start to drift away from Ensley and Becks, looking for Talon. Looking for answers.

The game master drones on about Chaos' trials as I search, checking the shadows for Talon's dark figure. I'm only half listening to him but I pick up that the first trial starts in fifteen minutes, and that anyone willing to enter the competition needs to cross the start line in the back of the cavern. After announcing that there are cameras hidden in the caverns and tunnels so everyone can watch the event, with a dramatic flourish he disappears the same way he appeared, in a cloud of smoke.

When the smoke clears, the hologram of Shadow Striker has disappeared, but in its place is a large digital clock, counting down from fifteen minutes. Screens start to roll down from the cavern ceiling, which must be how the spectators will watch the trial.

A collective gasp rises from the crowd when part of the cavern wall disappears to reveal a large tunnel. Partygoers start to back away from the tunnel, and through a break in the crowd I spot a yellow beam of light shooting across the ground. The starting line the game master spoke of.

"What are you doing over here?" Becks says, coming up beside me.

"I'm just looking for . . . someone." I don't want to admit I'm looking for Talon, but from the tightening in Becks' shoulders I can tell he already knows.

He gives me a curt nod and then lets his gaze travel over the crowd. There's something about the way he looks when his gaze settles back on me that causes the knot of unease to start to unfurl in my gut.

"Locklyn, about what almost happened earlier when the lights went out," he starts, and the pained look on his face turns my unease into full-blown concern. "I'm sorry if . . ." He rubs the back of his neck, clearly uncomfortable, and looks at the ground. "What I mean to say is you know I'm going to be betrothed to someone else soon and all that."

Don't say it, Becks. Please don't say it. I hold my breath, as if that will do something to keep the next words from coming out of his mouth.

"I just don't want to mess up our friendship for something that can never happen, you know?"

My heart cracks.

Becks has never laid out the facts so bluntly before. Did he say, *Nothing romantic can ever happen between us because I have to be with a powerful female and you're magicless*? No, not in those exact words, but he might as well have because we both know that's what he meant.

"You understand, don't you?" he asks when I remain silent. "With everything that's happening right now, I just can't lose you as a friend. You're too important to me."

I think he intends for me to find comfort in those words, but each one felt like a dagger to my heart.

We'd been so close to that line. A few more millimeters and we would have stepped over it and things would have changed between us. I'm sure of it. But we didn't close that distance and now Becks is pulling away from me, putting up a friend barrier higher and thicker than it was before.

Heaviness settles in the air between us.

"Locklyn?" Becks asks, his voice full of uncertainty, but when I look into his eyes it's clear he's desperate for me to agree with him. His fear of losing me is so palpable I can almost reach out and touch it. Seeing him so distressed softens something inside me, because at the end of the day all I want is for Becks to be happy.

"Yeah, sure. I totally understand." The words taste false in my mouth, but I force a smile on my face that wobbles a bit. Becks is so relieved he doesn't seem to notice.

"Okay. Great. Glad we got that cleared up." His smile is large and genuine, and another crack fissures my heart. He lays a hand on my bicep, and I flinch a little, not liking how much I enjoy the heat of his palm seeping through to my skin. "Wanna get out of here?"

"Sure." I don't care what we do anymore. A deep melancholy has settled in my chest, and my desire to find Talon has drained right out of me as well.

"Me too. Let's let all these idiots battle it out and go grab a shake at Sloan's instead."

"Okay."

"I'll go see if Ensley wants to come with or stick around."

"Alright." Apparently all I was capable of in the moment were one-word answers.

Becks gives me a long look, his eyes a muddled mix of sadness and concern. I force a wooden smile that I'm sure isn't convincing at all. With a sigh, Becks turns and weaves through the crowd until he reaches his sister. My eyes are locked on him, but my mind drifts to Shadow Striker. Like a bird stuck in a tar pit, I can't free myself from my obsession over the magical blade.

Righteous anger rises inside me.

This isn't fair. My lack of magic isn't something I can change.

But what if it is? my mind whispers.

What if Shadow Striker really can give powers? And if by some miracle if I could win Chaos, then I'd become worthy of Becks. We'd be free to explore what could be between us because if I were powerful the dragon council couldn't deny we'd make a good match.

I think back to our moment together, to Becks' hands on me, to the hungry look in his eyes when his gaze dropped to my mouth, the desperate way he whispered my name as his breath softly brushed over my lips. My mouth starts to tingle at the thought, and I bring a hand up to touch my lips, finding them sensitive.

I glance over at the tunnel that was revealed when the game master disappeared, and my feet take me toward the starting line. Some creatures have already crossed the yellow beam of light and are just waiting for the trial to begin. The competitors are a mixture of males and females. Some of the faces are familiar to me, but not all.

Moving closer to the start line my mind easily supplies an image of what it would be like if I had magic. Becks smiling down at me as we walk down the academy hallways together, hand-in-hand. Stolen kisses in between classes. Date nights at Sloan's as jealous females glare daggers at me, but not being concerned at all by their anger because I'm powerful enough to defend myself.

I want it so badly I start to shake. There's just one thing standing in the way, and Chaos is offering a way to smash through that obstacle. How can I not at least try?

When I glance over at the hovering clock, it's ticking down with only thirty seconds remaining. Once the timer runs out, the chance to enter Chaos, the chance to someday claim Shadow Striker, will be gone.

I take another step forward, stopping with the toes of my boots only inches from the yellow beam. All it will take is one more small step. One more small step can put me on a course to change my life. On a course to bring me what I've always wanted. And I'm not just thinking about Becks anymore—although that's certainly the biggest motivator—but gaining respect as a creature.

"Locklyn!" Someone shouts my name, and I glance over my shoulder to see Becks' surprised face as he jogs toward me.

There are only mere seconds on the clock, and I know if Becks reaches me he'll convince me not to do this, so before he can stop me I lift my foot and take one tiny step over the line.

Nine

AN ALARM SOUNDS, signaling that the clock has run out. I spin around. Becks stands opposite me, his eyes wide and his mouth moving, but I can't hear anything he's saying. In fact, I can't hear anything happening beyond the line I just crossed.

Lifting my hand, I move it toward Becks but hit an invisible barrier. It's smooth, like a sheet of glass, hard and impenetrable, preventing me from walking back over the line I just crossed.

Bony fingers of fear drag down my spine.

What have I done?

"Not to sound like a broken record, but I didn't expect to see you here, Freckles."

Talon's voice is as much a comfort right now as it is unnerving. Becks' gaze flicks over my shoulder to where Talon stands, and then hardens to granite. When I turn to Talon, I catch him wiggle his fingers at Becks, a full grin splitting his face.

Becks slaps his hand against the barrier, and shouts something at Talon neither one of us can hear.

"Don't provoke him," I say, crossing my arms over my chest as Talon's gaze shifts to me.

"Who, me?" he says innocently, like that wasn't just what he was doing. I shoot him a look that only makes him chuckle. "Too bad time just ran out. It certainly looks like he wants to be over here."

Becks paces back and forth in front of the line, tendrils of smoke coming off of him. If he doesn't chill, he's going to shift. Unable to hold his gaze, which is heavy with a mix of anger and betrayal, I turn away from him.

"Becks never would have entered. He's too controlled to do something so reckless."

Talon tilts his head, his blue-gray gaze assessing. "You really think so?"

"I don't just think so, I know so." He'd said as much the day we found out about Chaos. That he'd never get approval from the dragon council to enter, and I know he'd never go against their wishes.

"Hmm. If you say so." But Talon doesn't look convinced.

I don't want to talk about Becks anymore. I know he's going to be furious with me for entering, and it's not even as if I'm going to be able to explain it to him. But that was a problem for *future Locklyn*. The problem for *current Locklyn* is how I'm going to make it through this competition unscathed.

"So I guess we know where Shadow Striker is," I say to Talon as I scan the other competitors, doing my best to put Becks out of my mind and ignore the pit of terror swirling in my gut.

The hairs on the back of my neck raise when I spot Jules huddled with some of the other competitors on the other side of the tunnel, glaring at me. The growing pit inside me widens and stretches, threatening to pull me under. I snap my gaze back to Talon in time to catch a shadow sweep across his face, darkening his eyes before it clears.

"Indeed," he says, a muscle jumping in his jaw at the reminder of the artifact he's been hunting.

I tilt my head as I regard him. "The artifact must be really important to your father for you to go to all this trouble," I prod.

"You have no idea," he says, and then forces his features to relax, but the smile that stretches his lips looks fake. "But I think your entry into Chaos is far more interesting than mine. Tell me, was my story of the Vampire King so engaging it sparked a chord of interest in you? Are you hoping to use Shadow Striker's powers for yourself?"

My stomach dips. He said it jokingly, but there's a glint of something in Talon's eyes that tells me he's serious. He wants to know what provoked me to enter this dangerous game and he's already brushed too close to the truth for my comfort.

"I won't deny that the Ancient was captivating, but I'm less interested in Shadow Striker's fabled powers and more interested in the price it will fetch." I shrug. "That artifact could pay for all my university tuition, otherwise I'll have to postpone going to college after graduation."

It was the most believable explanation I could think up on the spot. Better he believe anything than the truth.

The way Talon regards me makes me think he's not buying it, but he doesn't press.

"I'll be open to talking about selling Shadow Striker to you once I win it," I say with a sweet smile.

Talon's gaze warms, a true smile fitting his mouth. He inclines his head to me. "That would be very generous of you."

"Not very generous," I say. "I'm planning on charging you double for the trouble."

"I wouldn't expect anything less," he says and then rubs his mouth like he's trying to keep his smile from growing.

A loud horn sounds, startling all the competitors. The levity I found moments ago with Talon is wiped away as the game master appears at the entrance of the tunnel. When I look back over my shoulder, Becks' gaze is fastened on the figure as well. There is a deep groove between his brows and his fists are clenched.

I have the sudden urge to throw myself into his arms, but even if it were possible to step back over the barrier, I wouldn't. The only chance Becks and I have is for me to not only make it through the Chaos trials, but to make it through them as the victor.

I'm not delusional enough to believe I have a good chance, or even a small chance of winning Chaos. The truth is my chances of beating out the other competitors are minuscule at best. And I also don't know if I can even get powers from Shadow Striker. There's a high probability that the story Talon told me is just that, a story, and that Shadow Striker is just what it was presented to be, a very old weapon. But what I do know for sure is that I can't just sit back and let Becks be mated to some faceless female he doesn't even have affection for.

So yeah, the odds aren't in my favor, but I don't care. I'm fighting for this anyway. I'm fighting for Becks, and I'm fighting for me.

"You'll have exactly one hour to make it through the maze, find a gold coin with the Chaos symbol on it, and then make your way out of the labyrinth," the game master announces. "If you are late exiting the tunnels, you will be disqualified. If you cannot find the coin, you will be disqualified. Those are the only rules."

Those are the only rules? He said nothing about sabotaging or interfering with other competitors.

I covertly glance around at the fae, shifters, and vampires nearest me, and can tell I'm not the only one who picked up on the game master's omission. Competitors are blatantly sizing each other up, some with looks of glee, others with trepidation.

I try not to let emotion show on my face, knowing that showing fear will just paint a bigger target on my back, but then my gaze connects with Jules. The smile on her face is nothing short of sinister. She's too far away for me to hear anything, but her lips start moving, mouthing the words, "You're dead."

A ball of lead drops to the bottom of my stomach, and I glance back at Becks for comfort, but when there's only concern and anxiety splashed across his face, I only feel worse.

"You've got this," Talon whispers in my ear, and I jolt, looking at him in surprise.

His gray eyes spark as he stares back at me. In direct contrast to Becks, he looks so sure and confident that it helps me shove some of the noise from my mind. "Creatures underestimate you. Use that," he says, and then straightens, focusing on the game master, who tells us the first trial will officially start in sixty seconds, and then disappears in a cloud of smoke.

Dramatic.

Creatures underestimate you. Use that. I mull over Talon's words, looking for the confidence I so desperately need right now. What if he's right and I could turn my biggest weakness into my greatest strength? Someone like that could be unstoppable.

The barrier between the competitors and audience drops, and cheers and shouts from the creatures in the cavern behind us slam into me.

"Locklyn," Becks roars, shattering the small amount of peace I'd managed to wrap around me. His voice sounds shredded and frantic to the extent that something inside me wants to soothe his pain.

I start to turn toward Becks, but Talon grabs my arm, staying my movements. He doesn't say a word, but slowly shakes his head, giving me a look that tells me to ignore Becks, but I can't. Yanking away from Talon, I sprint over to him.

"Come back," Becks begs.

There's a slight shimmer in the air between us, letting me know the barrier is still there.

"I can't. You heard what the game master said. Once you enter the competition, there's no backing out."

"It hasn't started yet," Becks says. "You can still back out."

I don't know whether or not that's technically true, but either way I'm torn. Do I try to step back over the barrier and return to Becks, return to how life has always been? Or do I take a chance and maybe my life will change in ways I can't even imagine now?

One choice is safe. One is dangerous.

"Locklyn," Becks murmurs my name and holds out his hand. "Come back to me."

Ten. Nine.

A countdown starts, the numbers ringing clearly through the air, making the crowd in the cavern go crazy.

I stare at his outstretched hand while the countdown ticks down, my heart beating hard enough to bruise my ribs.

Seven. Six.

"Nothing has to change," Becks says, a touch of desperation in his voice. "We can forget this night ever happened and everything will go back to the way it's always been."

Those words make up my mind for me. I don't want things to stay as they are with Becks. I can't go back now. I won't go back. I want more.

Three. Two.

I've sat back long enough and let things happen to and around me, seemingly powerless to change my circumstances. At my core that isn't who I am. I'm a fighter. It's time I acted like it again.

One . . .

"I'm sorry," I say, and then take off after the other competitors, disappearing into the pitch-black tunnel.

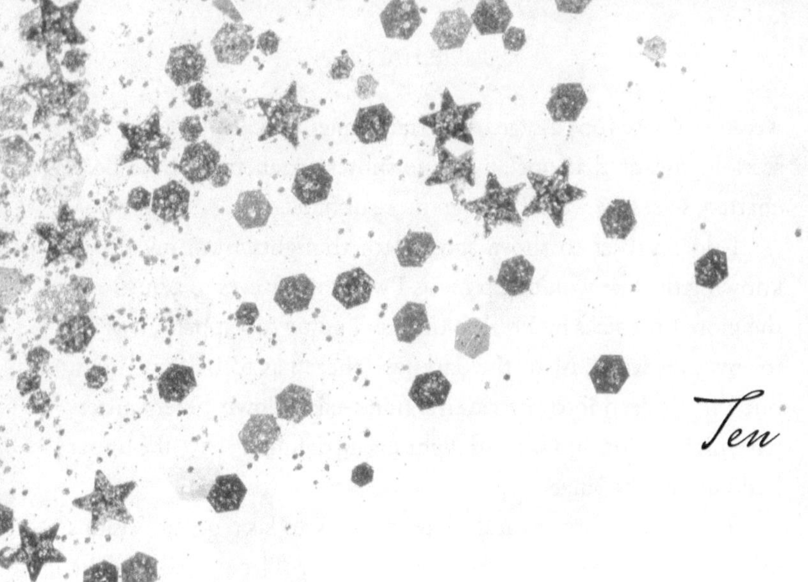

Ten

I DON'T KNOW the meaning of true terror until the starting horn blares for the Chaos trial and I plunge headfirst into the darkness. It isn't long before any light from the main caverns disappears and I'm completely blind, stumbling over the uneven, rocky ground, listening to the shuffling feet and shouted curses of my fellow competitors as they rush in front of me.

Finding the tunnel wall, I make slow progress into the abyss, my muscles tense and senses stretched as I move forward, listening for a potential attack. I haven't forgotten Jules' mouthed words before the trial began. It feels like at any moment I'll be struck down.

I don't have a plan for how to make it through this first trial. The only things I know about the tunnels are what I'd learned when I came to Deepseat Caverns with my parents years before, which isn't much. And the factoids that do come back to me now are wholly unhelpful and only scare me more. Like the guide's warning not to wander from the group because there are over a hundred miles of tunnels that crisscross and zigzag beneath the earth. They cautioned us that getting lost in the labyrinth wouldn't only be frightening, but also potentially life-threatening. Collapses were common in some of the tunnels, and so they weren't all safe for passage. And the danger of collapses in certain sections meant that not all of the subterranean paths have been charted, so rescue would be even more difficult.

I do my best to shove those dark thoughts from my mind, knowing the fear won't help me as I wait for my eyes to adjust, but the more time ticks by I realize that isn't going to happen. In order for my eyes to adjust to the darkness, there has to be some light, but I'm so deep into the caverns none exists down here. Shifters with night vision and fae with light magic definitely have the upper hand in this challenge.

The tunnel narrows and I have to duck to keep going. Visions of being swallowed by a giant rock monster fill my head, spiking my blood pressure. I never thought I was claustrophobic, but the confined space in the tunnel, along with my blindness, are becoming too much for me. I slow my footsteps, wanting to turn around or sink to the ground and curl into a ball, but I force myself to keep moving forward, even if it is at a snail's pace.

Eventually I reach a junction. Using my hands as guides I figure out that there are three separate paths I can take. I've fallen so far behind the rest of the competitors that I can only hear faint echoes of voices up ahead, but I have no idea which of the offshoots they're coming from. And even if I did know, that wouldn't mean it's the right one. None of us have any context for where these Chaos coins are hidden or how to make it out of the maze of tunnels.

Indecision freezes my limbs, making it feel like I'm encased in a block of ice, unable to move in one direction or the other. The guide's warnings slither through the cracks in my mental shields, reminding me of the consequences of getting lost in the vast underground labyrinth.

I close my eyes. If I don't pull myself together I'm not only going to get disqualified from Chaos before it barely starts, but I truly will get lost in these tunnels. I take two slow breaths through my nose and let them out slowly through my mouth.

You've got this. Creatures underestimate you. Use that. Talon's whispered words ring in my head and I latch on to them, letting them wash over me and finding strength in them and myself. With one more calming breath, I snap my eyes open, newfound determination flowing through my veins.

I've got this.

The air around me stirs, gently moving through the tunnels as if the caverns are breathing. I reach out, feeling the chilly bite of the air, woodenly moving in front of the next tunnel and the last, testing the temperature of each. The first tunnel is the coldest, and the last the warmest, at least relatively speaking since all the air is cold.

My goal is to find a coin and make it to the surface. The only weapon at my disposal right now is logic, and I know hot air rises and cold air sinks, so I make the decision to go down the third tunnel where the air is slightly warmer. With my hand still trailing along the wall, I pick up my speed, practically jogging in the dark. It's not more than a minute before I hear the echoes of voices coming from somewhere in front of me. Sweet relief floods my system. I don't know if I picked the tunnel that will take me to the surface, but at least I'm not down here alone.

The farther I travel, the more I'm able to pick up little details here and there as well, telling me there's a light source of some sort ahead. After a couple of twists and turns the tunnel lets out into a round cavern. Little pinpricks of blue and green light dot the ceiling like constellations, casting a soft glow over the space. And in the center of the cavern is a crystalline pool, the surface as smooth and still as glass.

"I'm telling you there's one right in the middle," a female to my left says, pointing to the center of the pool. "Right there."

I crane my neck to see what they are talking about and catch a glint of gold. A Chaos coin.

"I'm going to get it," she says, and starts forward, but as soon as her foot lands in the water a scaled beast the size of a full-grown crocodile emerges from under the sand at the bottom of the pool. It snaps its jaws at the girl, who immediately shifts into a parrot and starts flying around the cavern, squawking her head off. The beast submerges back into the pool, disinterested in taking chase.

It takes the girl several minutes to calm down. Finally landing next to her friend, she shifts back into her creature form. She has a small cut on her calf. It's probably only an inch long and barely bleeding, but she bursts into hysterics, talking about how her blood is going to draw the beast out of the water again for it to eat her.

I would have found the whole thing humorous if I wasn't so shocked. How is anyone supposed to get the Chaos coin with a water monster guarding it?

The pair ignore me, or don't even notice I'm there, I'm not sure which, but I stay quiet as the girl's friend tries to calm her, letting her know she's safe and assuring her that the sharp-toothed beast isn't going to crawl out of the water to eat her. But the parrot shifter isn't having any of it and eventually bolts from the cavern. Her friend follows, leaving me alone in the dim space with just the shallow pool and water beast to keep me company.

Making sure I'm not within snapping distance of the beast's jaws, I grab a stone about the size of my fist and lob it into the water. The beast stirs once again, splashing and flashing its jagged teeth at me, but then it just slides below the water when it realizes it was only a stone. The monster doesn't seem interested in stalking prey outside the waters, so that's at least something.

I stare at the coin in the middle of the pool. Even in the relative darkness the gold shines, almost glowing. I take a tentative step forward, the tips of my shoes only inches from the shoreline, and contemplate what to do next. I could abandon the coin like the two others had, hoping I can find another before the time runs out. That's what every other competitor who'd passed through this cavern decided to do, not deeming the coin worth the trouble of the water beast that guards it. But considering I'm so far behind everyone else, the other coins have probably been picked over. This may be my one and only chance to retrieve one.

I huff, putting my hands on my hips. There has to be a way to get that coin or it wouldn't have been placed there . . . right?

Casting a glance around me for something, anything I can use to get that coin, I notice a long stick propped up against the side of the cave.

That's weird. I expect rocks and sand beneath my feet. Even the glowworms lighting this cave aren't out of place, but what's a piece of wood doing in an underground cavern? Did someone bring a walking stick down here?

Being cautious not to set foot in the water, I carefully, but quickly, skirt the pond until I reach the stick. It comes to just above my waist and is a little thicker than my thumb. I bring it closer to my face, noticing etchings running up and down the shaft, but it's too dark to make them out. Also weird.

I'm wasting time looking at this random piece of engraved wood, but I can't shake the thought that there's something important about it. Like it was placed in this cavern on purpose. Or *for* a purpose.

At the very least I can use it to test the shoreline. Maybe there's a spot to enter the pool where the beast won't attack. Turning, I position the stick over the waters and then slowly drop the end. I'm expecting the water beast to snap at it the moment it breaches the surface, but that's not what happens at all. The moment the stick enters the water, the shaft vibrates, making small waves in the pool. There's a muffled shriek and the water beast appears from under the sand, but rather than clamping its jaws around the wood, it shoots to the opposite side of the pool, thrashing back and forth in obvious anger or distress.

More of the beast is visible than before and I notice it's shaped like a large fish, with a pair of small dorsal fins along its spine and two powerful pectoral fins like a shark. I don't see any legs, but its head looks like a crocodile and its entire body is covered in thick scales like a reptile.

A shudder starts in my chest and runs down my limbs. It's super ugly and extra terrifying. I've never seen anything like it before, and I'm probably going to be having nightmares about it for the rest of my life.

I glance down at the seemingly harmless piece of wood in my hand, knowing it's not actually a stick at all. It has to be some sort of device that's activated by the water. Yes, it has a rough bark-like exterior, but that's probably just camouflage to throw off the Chaos competitors. In all honesty, I don't really know what I'm holding, but it's clearly keeping the water beast at bay and that's really all I care about.

The beast breaches the surface on the other side of the pool to release another furious shriek that sounds between a bird caw and lion roar. I'm not sure how long this stick-like rod is going to keep the monster away, so I quickly pull off my boots and wade into the pool, gasping as freezing water hits my bare legs. It takes me no time to reach the center, but the water is far deeper than I realize, coming to my chin.

I start to shiver, my limbs aching from the frigid water, and my fingers start to lose feeling. The coin is right at my feet, but I'm going to have to dunk under to grab it. Taking a deep breath and squeezing the rod as best I can with numb hands, I dive down, snatch the coin from the pool floor, and then quickly resurface.

Water trickles down my face and I brush a chunk of wet hair out of my eyes and look down at the golden object in my hand. The Chaos coin has the same emblem stamped on it as was on the flyer, a circle divided into four sections with symbols in each and an inner circle with a cross.

I clench my fist around the treasure and start back toward the water's edge. The beast thrashes in agitation and shrieks behind me, running my nerves completely raw. I pick up speed, wanting nothing more than to be out of the icy water and safely planted on solid ground. The water is up to my thighs when I trip over a large rock and pitch forward. I have the sense to keep my hand around the gold coin, but I drop the rod when I put a hand out to catch myself.

The beast lets out another horrible shriek and then it falls silent. I freeze, looking over my shoulder but not spotting the monster anywhere.

My heart beats frantically, pushing blood through my veins quickly enough to make me forget about the cold. I have to get out of this pool immediately or I'm not going to make it out of this trial alive. I'm not so far from the pool's edge, but far enough that if the beast attacks I won't make it in time.

Reaching down, I search the pool's floor for the rod I dropped, knowing it's the only thing that will keep it at bay. Sand and rocks shift through my hands, but I can't find it in the murky waters.

There's a splash behind me, and when I look over my shoulder a wide mouth full of serrated teeth are coming straight at me.

No way am I dying like this. A late-night snack for a cavern monster.

I bound forward, the water slowing my steps as I sprint for the edge of the pool. Part of me knows it's useless, but my fighting spirit refuses to give up.

I don't have to look behind me to know that the water beast has almost reached me. I already feel its phantom teeth clamping down on my flesh, tearing into skin and muscle and crunching through bone.

The edge of the pool is only feet away, but it might as well be a mile.

With my heart racing, my foot snags on another rock and I plunge forward, landing face-first in the water just as the beast lunges and snaps its jaws in the air where I was standing. Its body comes crashing down next to me and I'm doused by a wave of icy water. Jerking out of the way of a second snap, I scramble to my feet as the monster thrashes in the shallow waters to chase me.

It's only two large steps to the pool's edge. But just as I'm about to take the final step out of the pool, the beast throws its body sideways, bashing into my knees and knocking me over. When it rolls over me I lose my breath as I'm crushed beneath its weight.

While it struggles to right itself, I drag myself to my feet, hacking up water. I fling myself out of the pool and onto the rocky ground, shuffling as far away from the edge as possible.

The beast releases another rage-filled shriek and thrashes its tail, slapping the water in anger, but doesn't try to reach me now that I'm out of the pool. After its temper tantrum subsides, it maneuvers itself into deeper waters then submerges.

I stay lying on the ground, gasping for air. It's only when the waves and ripples disappear, leaving the surface of the pool as smooth as glass, that I close my eyes and sigh a breath of relief. Taking deep, even breaths, I will my blood pressure to return to normal.

After a while, feeling starts to return to my numb limbs and I notice my hand aches. Opening my eyes, I look down to find my fingers still clenched around the Chaos coin.

Unbelievable. I can't believe I held on to it.

A wholly inappropriate laugh burst from my lips, and I struggle to a sitting position. The unhinged sound bounces off the walls of the cavern. It's a solid minute before I regain my wits and push to my feet—waterlogged, dirty, exhausted, but otherwise unharmed.

After wringing out my hair and putting my boots back on, I store the coin in my skirt pocket and slog to the cavern's exit, following the same path the girls before me did.

Eleven

I KEEP to the edges of the tunnels and caverns as I make my way through the maze, looking for the exit while doing my best to stay unnoticed by the other competitors I come across. And for the most part it works, which is perfect, because I pass more than one fight along the way. Competitors who haven't been able to locate a coin attack others who have, hoping to steal their bounty.

It turns out Talon was right: being underestimated isn't such a bad thing. Anyone who notices me creeping by immediately dismisses me, which is fine by me. I don't need to be getting into any fights with creatures that have magic.

I'm cold. I'm wet. I'm tired. I just want to find the way out of this abyss and be done with it.

The air around me has warmed considerably, which gives me hope I'm nearing an exit. After a few steps a breeze brushes against my damp skin, carrying the scent of rotting leaves and grass. It's not a particularly pleasant smell, but it's a welcome one.

When I reach a fork in the tunnels, a handful of competitors are in front of me, one of which is a fae holding a ball of faelight in the air in front of them to light the way. I hang back while they argue about which way to go, waiting until they make their decision and clear the area before deciding for myself.

"You look like a drowned rat shifter," a familiar voice says behind me, and my blood runs cold.

I twist to see a single set of glowing eyes in the darkness. Wolf's eyes.

Jules takes several steps forward, her eyes reflecting the faelight behind me as she nears, even as the rest of her is concealed by the darkness. But I'd know her voice and the look in her psychopathic eyes anywhere.

When she materializes in the low light, she looks a little worse for wear, a dirt smudge high on one cheek and a shallow cut on one forearm, but not nearly as bad as I'm sure I do. With my damp and ripped clothes, a messy head full of tangles and bits of sand and dirt, I probably look worse than a rat shifter right now, so I'm not even offended by her comment. It's just truth.

"I didn't think you could get any more pathetic looking, but I guess I was wrong," she sneers, her upper lip curling back in disgust.

Good. Maybe she'll be too grossed out to get close to me and pass right on by.

But I'm not that lucky and Jules stops directly in front of me, only an arm's length away. Without thinking, I move my hand over my pocket where the Chaos coin is nestled, and she doesn't miss the motion. Her eyes spark with interest and my stomach drops.

"What are you protecting in that pocket of yours?" she asks, a sinister smile curling the corners of her lips.

I keep my mouth shut, knowing that any denials that I'm hiding something will make it that much more obvious than I am. Instead I just drop my hand away from my pocket, doing my best not to look guilty.

Jules' gaze runs over me slowly; it feels like slugs passing over my skin.

"Well, well, well. Is it possible you actually snagged a coin? I wouldn't have believed it, but you look like you've had a rough evening. Like you fell into one of the Chaos traps. How fortunate for me."

She reaches forward like she's going to dig through my pocket, and I twist away. Her smile widens and there's a feverish gleam in her eye that reminds me of a rabid dog.

The tunnel starts to dim, and I realize with a sinking feeling that the group I was waiting on to pick a tunnel is finally moving on, taking with them their faelight and possible protection.

A few days ago, all I wanted was to have the opportunity to fight Jules one-on-one, but not like this. Not when I'm already exhausted and stuck in a dark tunnel with a shifter who has excellent night vision and earth powers.

Spinning, I take off toward the fork in the tunnels, veering left without really knowing where I'm going but hoping to see faelight from the group in front of me soon. I need to get away from Jules or else something very bad is going to happen. Her chuckles follow me as I run. I must have picked the wrong tunnel because there's no faelight and the temperature drops.

The tunnel cants to the left, but I don't realize it because the light is so poor, and I clip the wall with my shoulder and stumble. Before I can right myself, a hand dives into my hair. My head gets wrenched back painfully and I fall to the unforgiving ground. Sharp rocks cut into my palms right before I'm jerked to my feet by my hair and then slammed back against the tunnel's arched stone wall hard enough to knock the wind out of me.

"Pathetic as always," Jules says. I can't make out her features in the darkness, but she's close enough that her breath skids across my face.

Coughing, I try to catch my breath as I swing out wildly, but blinded as I am I only barely connect with some soft part of her body. I swing again, aiming for what I think is her face, and my fist slams into something fleshy but hard. I think maybe her cheek, but Jules is a tough wolf shifter, and before I can follow up with an uppercut to her chin she clamps a hand around my throat. I go wild, clawing and punching whatever I can reach.

Jules cusses and tries to stop my attacks, but like a cornered animal I throw everything I have at her, unleashing in an explosion of pent-up anger and frustration. But Jules has magic and night vision and I don't, so she still has the upper hand. Grabbing my arm, she slams it against the wall behind me. The rocks instantly swallow my palm and fingers, tethering me to the tunnel.

I scream in frustration and try to yank away from the wall, but I'm not strong enough to break free from the rocks she reformed around my hand. While I'm distracted trying to free myself, she shoves her hand into my pocket and pulls out the gold Chaos coin.

"No," I yell, trying to snatch it back, but she easily dodges. "That's mine."

"It's mine now." I can't see her in the darkness, but I hear her walking away, chuckling under her breath.

Like a fast-working venom, fear paralyzes me. She's going to leave me alone and trapped down here. There's more at stake here than failing out of the first Chaos trial. No one else has come down this tunnel. I'm all alone.

I tug on my trapped hand, but it doesn't budge. I don't have anything to chisel through solid rock. If I can't free myself, who is going to find me?

"Don't do this, Jules," I call after her retreating footsteps. "I could die down here."

"Here's hoping." Her voice sounds very far away, or maybe that's just my mind playing tricks on me.

For the second time in one evening my life is on the line, but trying to appeal to Jules' compassion is useless. She doesn't have any.

Think, Locklyn, think, I command as I force thoughts of my body rotting and decomposing in this labyrinth from my mind.

My imprisoned hand starts to go numb. I crouch down as far as I can, but with one arm stretched above me and the other reaching down, I can't quite reach the tunnel floor to search for a rock to use to break apart the stone encasing my hand. I strain hard enough that my shoulder could pop out of joint any minute. As much as that would suck, it would give me the couple of extra inches I need to reach the ground, so I don't stop pulling.

When I stop to catch my breath, the air around me has gone eerily still. A sense that I'm not alone crawls over me and I slowly straighten, trying in vain to see something, anything, through the absolute darkness.

Trepidation skates down my spine like bony fingers rubbing over my skin, giving me chills.

Someone's here. I know they are.

"Hello?" I call into the abyss. My voice echoes down the tunnel walls.

I hold my breath, straining my ears to pick up on sound, but it's as silent as a tomb.

"Looks like you could use a hand . . . literally," says a familiar deep voice, and the air I trapped in my lungs comes out in a rush.

"Talon. You scared me half to death," I say, laying a palm over my beating heart.

There's a soft click and then light shines from Talon's direction. I think it's faelight at first, but then realize it's just a small keychain flashlight.

He flashes the light in my face and I shield my eyes.

"You do look a little worse for wear, but I wouldn't go as far as to say half dead."

I wait until he points the thin beam of light out of my eyes before answering. "That's just because you don't know the night I've had."

"Need some help?"

"Yes." I'm hoping Talon has earth magic and can easily undo Jules' handiwork, but instead of using powers, he searches the ground until he finds a rock about twice the size of his fist and palms it. I get a little nervous when he lines it up with my trapped hand.

"You're going to crush my hand with that if you're not careful."

Talon's gaze tracks from the wall to my face. "Do you trust me?" he asks, the shadow of a wicked smile curling the corners of my mouth.

"Not really," I say, unsure if that's a lie or not.

He chuckles, unoffended. "Probably smart, but unfortunately for you, you don't really have a choice right now."

He's not wrong. And if it's between a smashed hand and being stuck down here until I die of thirst, some broken bones are the better option.

Taking a deep breath, I look away, fortifying myself. "Okay, just do it."

Talon cracks the rock against the stone wall, and I brace myself, expecting a bolt of pain to hit me, but it doesn't come. Instead I hear the sound of rocks cascading to the ground. It takes a few hits, but finally enough of the tunnel wall is chipped away that I can squeeze my hand out.

My fingers are stiff and cold, but other than that I'm no worse for wear. I clench and unclench my fist, working the blood back into my hand. I don't know how he managed that without hurting me, but I'm glad for it.

"Thank you," I say, looking up at Talon, and he nods.

"We should get going. Time is running out."

"Right. Chaos," I say, a deep melancholy falling over me when I remember Jules stole my hard-earned Chaos coin. The chances of finding another before time runs out are less than zero. It's only the first trial and I've already failed.

Falling into step beside Talon, I heave a defeated sigh as we make our way back up the tunnel to the fork.

"So, the brutish wolf shifter took your Chaos coin?" Talon asks, almost casually.

I glance over at him; the faint light from the mini flashlight illuminates his mouth and part of his cheeks but leaves the rest of his face mostly shadowed.

"How did you know?" I ask, a note of suspicion creeping into my voice. Had Talon been hiding in the shadows the whole time? Could he have stopped Jules' attack but chose not to?

His eyes glow silver, reminding me of the way Jules' eyes reflect light in the darkness, but not quite the same. "I overheard her bragging to someone about it."

Right. That makes sense. "That sounds like her," I admit, my shoulders sagging.

"Where did you find a coin?" he asks.

"The first cavern after the tunnels. The one with the shallow pool and the water monster."

He tilts his head, but I can't see his face clearly enough to read his expression.

"How did you manage that?"

I shrug even though he probably can't see the motion. "There was a device camouflaged as a stick in the cavern. When I put it in the water, it kept the beast at bay. I think through some sort of vibration, or maybe even a high-pitched sound I couldn't hear. I waded into the pool and got it." It was an oversimplification of what really happened, but I didn't feel the need to tell Talon I'd almost been eaten alive.

"Brave," he says, and I scoff. "Seriously. Once I saw that a Leviathan was guarding that coin, I passed right on by." *Leviathan? Is that what that monster was?* I make a mental note to look it up later. "It takes intelligence to find a workaround like that."

Or just dumb luck. But I find I like Talon's compliments, so I don't contradict him.

"Well, it doesn't matter now. That coin is long gone. I guess Becks was right. I shouldn't have bothered entering at all. All I got for it were some near-death experiences."

We reach the fork in the tunnels, and I turn to go down the right one, but when Talon doesn't follow I stop and turn back toward him. The flashlight is pointed right at me, but he angles it down when I lift a hand to shade my eyes.

"Let's go," I say, but Talon just stands there, staring at me.

He stays silent long enough that I start to shift under his regard. Finally, he reaches into his pocket and pulls something out. He takes my hand, and a zing of awareness travels up my arm. Flipping my hand over, he presses something into my palm. I look down and gasp.

A Chaos coin.

"I can't take this," I say, and try to give it back to him.

What are you doing? my mind screams at me. *Of course you can take it. Close your fingers around that treasure and run for the exit.*

"Don't worry about it," he says, and then puts his hands in his pockets and something jingles. I don't miss that it sounds like loose coins knocking against each other.

My eyes widen. "You have more than one coin?"

From the sounds of it, he has several.

He shoots me a sly smile. "The less coins available, the less competitors going through to the next round."

He's right, but my mind is spinning on the fact he was able to collect multiple coins. I almost died getting just one, and from what I could tell going through the tunnels and passing other competitors is that none of the coins were just lying there, waiting for someone to pick up. You had to work for them.

I look back at Talon with new eyes. Who *is* he?

"Why are you giving this to me?"

He's silent for a moment before answering. "You earned your coin. No one should take that away from you."

Talon's explanation is simple, but it resonates with me.

I close my hand around the coin, fresh hope swelling in my chest. "Let's get out of here."

Talon nods in the direction of the tunnel. "You go. I'll be there in a second."

"But time's running out. You said so yourself."

"Don't worry about it. There's just something else I have to do. I'll be right behind you."

I don't understand what he could possibly still need to do, maybe he's going to collect more coins, but I get distracted when I hear voices coming from behind Talon. I don't want another run-in with any other competitor if I can help it.

"Take this." Talon holds the small flashlight out for me.

"Don't you need it?" I ask, but still take the small light.

"Naw. Don't worry about me. I can see pretty well in the dark," he says even as he's backing up into the shadows. "See you out there."

The voices are getting louder, and so with a last look in Talon's direction, I take off. The flashlight is a huge help. It allows me to run through the tunnel, which slopes up until it ends in a large cavern. Moonlight shines down through an opening in the cavern's ceiling and a small handful of competitors are scaling the wall to reach the hole. It looks like a fairly easy climb, which may be the only easy part of this whole exhausting and terrifying night.

Rushing to the wall, I start to climb. Good thing I'm not afraid of heights. Voices filter through along with the moonlight, and it's clear there's a celebration going on somewhere up on solid ground above.

Even though the climb isn't difficult, my muscles shake from fatigue and adrenaline, making it harder than it should be. Rather than looking up to track how much farther I have, I keep my eyes on the wall right above me and search for the next handhold until I reach the opening. Before I heave myself up and through it, I have to deposit my Chaos coin into a carved slot on the wall. After, I hear my name being announced above, letting everyone know I've passed the first trial. A cheer sounds, but I'm hardly paying attention as I muscle my way out of the cavern and collapse on the ground.

I CAN'T MAKE out the stars through the tree branches above me. I'm lying on the soggy ground for less than a minute before Becks is there, reaching for me and helping me to my feet. Uncontrollable shudders rack my frame, violent enough to make my teeth chatter as I come down from the adrenaline rush.

Becks crushes me against his chest, and I soak in his warmth.

I did it, I think to myself. Sure, I probably wouldn't be standing here if Talon hadn't helped me out, but I'd still made it through the first trial when other competitors hadn't.

A bubble of pride starts to swell in my chest until Becks' voice shattered it. "What were you thinking?" he snaps as he pulls away, his face reflecting a storm of emotions, all of them bad. "You could have been killed."

The warmth that had started to permeate my body immediately flees. I take a step back, wrapping my arms around myself.

Granted, what I did was rash, but the last thing I need right now is for Becks to throw it in my face.

"Come on," he says as he grabs my hand and starts to tug me through the crowd surrounding the hole I just climbed out of. "We need to figure out who is in charge of this and get you out of this mess."

Wait. What?

"Becks, stop." I plant my feet, but he's so strong it takes him a few beats to realize that he's dragging me behind him.

When he stops and turns back, I really look at him. His hair is disheveled like he's run his hands through it again and again, and his mouth is pinched into a straight line. As we stand there his gaze bounces over my face and then down my body, like he's looking for injuries. Admittedly, I'm a mess, but I'm relatively unharmed and in one piece, but there's a savage gleam in Becks' eyes that makes me think he's just barely holding on. I've never seen my friend like this before. Almost as if he's spooked. Or unhinged. Or both.

"You heard the rules," I say gently, knowing he's so close to snapping. "There's no way to withdraw from the competition now. I have to see it through."

Becks shakes his head. "No, there must be—"

"I don't want to pull out of Chaos," I say firmly, stunning him into silence that then hangs between us, thick and uncomfortable.

"Locklyn, you can't be serious." The lines of concern on his face slowly morph into something else. Something darker and ugly. "It was just dumb luck you made it through this trial alive. You'll never make it through the rest of them, and I won't be there to save you."

The words hit me like daggers to the heart, and I flinch. There are certain realities about me that I've accepted, one being my magical weakness compared to other creatures. But Becks had never treated me as less than . . . until now.

Becks must have seen me flinch because he starts to backtrack. "I didn't mean it like that. You know I think you're capable, it's just that this is different. Competitors are going to get hurt before this is all said and done. Some already have. It was agony watching —" His voice breaks and he looks away, running an agitated hand through his hair before pinning me with a stare that sends shockwaves through me with its intensity. "Please don't ask me to sit back and watch you go through these trials."

The screens that rolled down from the cavern's ceiling . . .

I'd completely forgotten the trial was being broadcasted. How much had he seen? The cameras couldn't have shown everyone at once. Did he see what happened with Jules in the tunnel? I didn't think so or he'd really be losing it.

I don't know what to do. Part of me is seriously hurt by Becks' lack of confidence in me. In a few short sentences he validated every insecurity I've ever felt about myself. But I can clearly see that watching me battle through the first trial has cost him. The price is written all over his face. I might have been the one who was physically challenged in those caverns and tunnels, but the trial took a toll on Becks as well.

I open my mouth, to say what I'm not yet sure, when I'm tackled by Ensley. She bounces up and down, taking me along for the ride.

"That was seriously epic," she squeals before releasing me. "I mean, I can't believe you actually entered Chaos. We are going to have some serious words about what you were thinking, but oh my garsh, when you dropped the rod that was keeping that scaly beast away and it came swimming toward you, I thought my heart was going to explode."

I wince, realizing that Becks must have seen that as well. No wonder he'd lost it.

"Yeah, that was wicked," Konan says from behind Ensley. The rest of her bandmates, Canin, Holland, and Sol are behind him, and they look at me with respect in their eyes. It's a look I'm not used to being directed at me, and I'd be lying if I said it doesn't feel good.

"Awesome job, Locklyn," someone calls, and when I look over a classmate waves at me before moving on.

This is going to take some getting used to.

Becks' frown deepens, but I turn away from him and toward Ensley's beaming face instead. At least one of my friends is proud of me, but then her smile dims. "What do you think the next trial is going to be?" she asks, and my stomach hollows.

I don't want to think about that. I'd rather ride the high of making it through the first round as long as possible.

"Who knows?" I say, trying to make my voice sound light rather than weighed down with worry.

A buzzer goes off and is trailed by a chorus of cheers and disappointed groans and I realize that must be the end of the time limit, meaning I'd made it out just in time. Did Talon?

I crane my neck to search for him through the mass of creatures still surrounding the hole, but it's useless. It's too dark and there are too many bodies. I hope he made it out in time. I'd feel awful if he failed because he helped me. But something in my mind whispers maybe it won't be the worst thing if he's disqualified. He's going to be a hard competitor to beat, and my desire for Shadow Striker has only grown since I stepped over that glowing yellow line.

"Let's get out of here," Becks says, and we all agree.

There's already a steady stream of party goers headed back to their cars. I don't know exactly where we are in Woodwind Forest, but Becks and Ensley seem to know where they are going. I follow along, each step harder than the last as exhaustion pulls at me, making my legs feel like they are made of lead. I don't even want to know what time it is. With any luck my parents are in bed asleep and come morning will have no idea what time I crept back into the apartment.

As we trek back to the cars, I receive a few more congratulations along the way. Becks is leading our small group and I watch his back as we jostle our way through the horde of creatures around us. The set of his shoulders is rigid, and I can't help feeling like he's purposefully not looking at me, but maybe that's for the best, because I don't know what to say to him to make things better between us. I can't tell him the real reason I entered was to win Shadow Striker so that we'd have a chance to be together. I'm not ready to face that truth with him, and I don't have any other explanation that he'll accept.

The trees have just started to thin when I finally recognize the terrain, but my attention catches on a figure up ahead and off to the side. When I swing my gaze back in that direction, it collides with Talon's, and sticks.

Leaned up against the trunk of a tree, he's half in the shadows. A touch of relief trickles through me that he made it out in time. I would have felt guilty if he hadn't. Bodies pass between us as I slow to hold his gaze, but it somehow feels like it's just the two of us. The moment stretches, testing the boundaries of time.

We don't break eye contact until I'm about to pass him, and then a hint of a smile lifts his mouth, and he gives me a small nod, respect shining from his eyes. I return the gesture and then the moment breaks as I'm swept away with the crowd. When I'm in my bed no more than an hour later, tossing and turning as I fight to fall asleep, it's the memory of Talon's face that lingers in my mind as I finally succumb to fitful rest.

Thirteen

MONDAY COMES like it does every week, but today isn't like any other Monday I've had before because today I'm no longer invisible.

The changes seem subtle at first: a girl gives me a tentative smile when she passes me as I'm switching books out in my locker, the guy I sit next to in my Creature History class acknowledges me with a nod when I slide into my seat, but as the day wears on it's obvious something has changed.

"Is something wrong with what I'm wearing?" I ask Ensley as I sit down next to her at lunch.

Tilting her head, she looks me up and down, taking in my off-the-shoulder graphic tee and ripped jeans. I fidget under her regard, sure there's something different or wrong with how I look today.

Ensley shrugs. "No. You look cute. Why?"

I sneak a covert look over my shoulder and notice several sets of eyes pointed in our direction. "I guess it's not a big deal, but it's just that classmates have been . . . noticing me." I feel silly once the words leave my mouth.

Ensley's brows hike and she scans the tables around the court-yard, probably not seeing anything out of the usual. I've almost convinced myself it's all in my head when she turns back to me and says, "I think you're right."

I lower my voice, irrationally worried we'll be overheard. "What do you think is going on?"

She leans back in her seat, a thoughtful expression on her face. "I think it's because you entered Chaos and made it through the first round. That took guts, Lock. Creatures noticed."

"You really think so?"

She nods and I take another look around, noticing that the majority of the stares in my direction are neutral, which is better than openly hostile, but it seems like the students at Nightlark are still making their mind up about me or how they feel about me being a Chaos competitor. I'm not naive enough to think that something couldn't push the consensus in a negative direction, so for now the extra attention isn't good or bad. It just is.

Ensley moves closer, lowering her voice. "We never did talk about why you entered in the first place," she says, letting the statement hang in the air between us.

I knew my friends were going to grill me over Chaos, but even after a couple of days I still haven't figured out how to answer the question about why I entered without revealing my feelings for Becks.

Becks' face immediately fills my mind. I haven't seen him at all today, and he's noticeably absent from lunch. Is he avoiding me? Maybe. I know he was upset at me for entering Chaos, and I'd been too chicken to reach out to him over the weekend. I'd hoped having some time to cool off would put him in a calmer headspace.

"It was a spur of the moment decision," I say, hoping the kernel of truth in that statement shines through.

Ensley barks out a laugh. "You're kidding, right?"

I shrug. It's not *not* true. "It just felt like something I had to do," I answer vaguely, and Ensley studies my face. "Why?"

"You know that answer isn't going to be enough for Becks. He moped around the rest of the weekend. He's really bent out of shape over the whole thing."

"He'll get over it." *At least I hope.*

"I don't know. He doesn't get like this often. He's concerned about you. I think he's seriously in his head about it."

A spike of guilt shoots through me because I'm not the only thing Becks is concerned about right now. I don't doubt he's worried about me; it's Becks' nature to be protective, and when I'm competing in Chaos all he can do is stand back and watch. But how much of his energy is wrapped up in his impending arranged life-mating? And as far as I can tell, Ensley is still in the dark. I don't want to betray Becks' trust, but he needs all the support he can get from those closest to him. His parents might not be fighting back against the life-mating, but I know that his sister will be on his side.

"Ensley," I start. "Has Becks mentioned—"

The chair next to me is pulled out, the legs scraping against the stone floor with a cringy screech. I look over and Leo flops his lanky body into the seat. Pulling back my upper lip, I lean away from him.

"Gimpy, you surprised me," Leo says with a smile that shows too many teeth, so it comes across disturbing rather than friendly.

"Beat it," Ensley says.

Leo holds up his hands in surrender. "Hey now, don't kill the messenger."

"What do you mean?" I ask before Ensley can come to my defense again. I may despise Leo, but I need to start sticking up for myself in small ways if I'm going to take back my power.

Leo digs into his backpack, pulls out a small black rectangular device, and places it on the table in front of me.

"Chaos tracker," he says by way of explanation. "All the competitors are getting one. You're supposed to keep it on you at all times."

I pick up the device. It's thicker than my phone, but smaller in overall size. "What is it for?" I ask, turning it over in my hand. There don't seem to be any buttons or a screen.

"Just the messenger, remember?" he says, and then shoves out of the seat once again. "Good luck during the next trial," he says, leaving, but the wolfish grin on his face tells me luck isn't what he wishes me.

"Can I see?" Ensley asks, and I hand it over. She turns it over like I did, but finally hands it back with a shrug.

The bell rings and I give my lunch a forlorn glance. I never even touched any of it, and my stomach grumbles to show its displeasure. After saying goodbye to Ensley, I drop the tracker in my bag and shove half a peanut butter and jelly in my mouth on the way to the garbage. After I dump the rest of my meal, I look up and catch the back of Becks as he slips out of the courtyard through a side door.

He was here?

My class is in the other direction, but I know the longer I put off talking with my best friend the harder it will be. This isn't going to be an easy conversation between the two of us, but it's necessary.

Going against the flow of traffic, I dodge bodies all the way to the other side of the courtyard and slip through the same door I saw Becks take. It dumps me into a stairwell that goes all the way up to the turreted top floor of the academy. It takes me a couple of minutes to scale the winding staircase, but when I reach the landing Becks is there, looking over the quad.

He doesn't turn when I walk up behind him, but his shoulders tense, letting me know he's aware I'm here.

"Don't you have class right now?" Becks asks, his voice weary.

"Don't you?"

He turns his head when I rest my forearms on the stone ledge beside him. His eyes are a dull green today and there are dark smudges underneath them. He regards me warily, and it makes my heart twist. Becks has never looked at me like this before. He's guarded, and I don't know how to fix that.

"How did you know it was me?" I ask, and he shrugs.

"I always know when you're around," he says by way of an explanation, and something about that makes me warm.

"So . . ." I say, not sure how to start the conversation.

Becks, picking up on the tone in my voice, tenses up again, and I frown. Becks and I have always been a refuge for each other, but that's changed. I don't know if that's because of Chaos, or because we brushed up against a line this weekend that best friends aren't supposed to cross.

At a loss for words, I finally settle on, "Are you okay?"

"Am I okay?" he says, his eyebrows raising. "Isn't that what I should be asking you?"

"I'm fine. You saw me after the trial. A few bumps and bruises never slowed me down before. I'm pretty tough."

Becks frowns and his eyes darken as his gaze sweeps over me, almost as if he's seeing injuries that aren't there, but when he reaches my face the green hue brightens and my stomach bottoms out. What happened between us in that cavern wasn't my imagination. There's something brewing between us, I know it.

"I've been hurt worse in the ring," I say, my voice soft to soothe his roughness.

"This is different," he says, and takes a half step closer.

His hand twitches and he fists it, making the muscles in his forearm jump. I can't help but wonder if he's stopping himself from reaching for me. I wouldn't have to stretch more than a foot to place my hand on his chest, but I hold back as well. Even if our years of friendship weren't deterring us, his arranged mating hangs like an impenetrable barrier in the air between us.

"Why haven't you told Ensley about the life-mating?" I ask, breaking the spell that's enthralled us both.

Becks twists away from me to survey the school grounds once again. His jaw clenches as his hands grip the stone ledge, his knuckles white with the amount of pressure he's exerting. I half expect the weathered rock to crumble beneath his grip.

Conversation between us suddenly feels like a minefield, and I hate it.

"She's going to find out sooner or later," I say gently, thinking of how I found out about it in the hallway from another student. It's actually amazing she hasn't caught wind of it already.

Becks sighs and hangs his head. "I know, it's just if she doesn't know, then it won't . . ."

"Be real?"

He nods.

"Ensley might be able to help you with your parents. And if not, she can still help look for a loophole."

Another sigh. "There is no loophole, Lock."

I refuse to believe that. I'm already working on one, but I'm not about to tell him about my Chaos contingency plan.

"We'll get you out of this," I say, my voice filled with conviction, and when Becks looks at me his gaze is a mix of hope and despair that rips a hole in my chest.

When Becks hurts, I hurt too.

"Please pull out of the competition," he says, surprising me with the abrupt change in subject.

"What?"

"I can't protect you in Chaos," he says, his head dropping forward.

Reaching out, I lay a hand on Becks' shoulder, and he tilts his head to look at me. There's rawness in his gaze.

"I need to learn to live without your protection," I say.

I'd be lying if I said dropping out hadn't crossed my mind more than once since the trial. Becks is right about Chaos being dangerous, but the lure of Shadow Striker and all it can potentially give me are too strong to ignore, so I shake my head.

"Why do you have to do this?" he asks, his gaze penetrating, and I almost say, "*For us.*"

"I've already told you. You just don't like my answer."

"You don't need to prove that you're capable of defending yourself."

"If that were true, you wouldn't be so worried about me."

Becks shoves away from the ledge, pacing away from me and then back again. "The thought of watching you in those trials makes me feel like I'm going crazy," he confesses, plowing his hands in his hair.

I hate that I'm causing him this stress, but I believe it might all be worth it in the end.

"All right. Then don't," I say, a heaviness settling in my chest. It will be hard to face the trials without Becks there, but maybe it's for the best. "You don't have to watch. You should skip them."

He stops pacing and stares at me, utter defeat scrolling over his face. "I could never leave you to face them alone. No matter what, Locklyn, I'll always be there for you. To the depths of hell or the heights of the heavens. It's you and me against the world. Always."

Oh, my poor little heart. If I wasn't already full-on crushing on Becks, that statement would have pushed me over the edge.

"Becks," I whisper, stepping toward him, and then I'm in his arms. This isn't a passion-charged embrace like the one in the cavern. This is an embrace of comfort.

"I'm going to be okay," I say into his chest, and only notice a little how wonderful he smells and feels.

Becks' arms tighten around me, but I don't mind the extra pressure.

"I hope so," he says, and a small shudder runs through his body.

"Are we going to be okay?" I ask, my voice small.

Becks heaves a sigh. "Yes, of course."

I start to wiggle out of Becks' arms because the platonic feelings of comfort are starting to morph into something decidedly not platonic, and he lets me go.

"I'm sorry I was so cold after the trial. You just really scared me.

You in Chaos on top of everything else going on right now is just messing with my head."

"I understand." And I really do. If I were in his shoes, it would kill me to see him in danger as well.

"Come on," he says, throwing an arm over my shoulder and tugging me back toward the stairs. "We've got to get you to class so you don't flunk out and are forced into summer school."

"Summer school?" I give an exaggerated shudder. "Never. Who really needs a high school diploma?"

Becks chuckles. "Don't worry. I won't let anything bad like that happen to you."

I smile up at him because I truly believe him.

WITH BECKS and Shadow Striker still on my mind, my feet take me to the Emporium. I'm no longer looking for confirmation that Shadow Striker is real, I know that it is, but what I want to know are details on how to harness the dagger's magic. I don't want to end up like the Vampire King, going mad from corrupted powers. I also want to know if Shadow Striker steals the powers, leaving creatures magicless, or just copies their gifts somehow and then gives them to its wielder. As much as I crave magic, I don't think I could ever purposefully steal someone else's abilities in order to gain them. Talon seemed unsure of that part of the legend and I'm hoping to uncover a few more details. I don't want to risk my life to get Shadow Striker only to find out that I can never actually use it.

I stand in front of the spired building that houses everything from novelty items for tourist to centuries-old artifacts. My parents often purchase items from the owner and our family friend, Mr. Brone, a shifter who sources some of his more valuable objects from estate sales and overseas brokers. He came into town about five or six years ago, taking over the Emporium from the previous owner. Rather than being competitors, he and my parents frequently send business back and forth. It's common for him to reach out to my mom and dad to get appraisals on items or offer to sell things to them at a discount. I wouldn't consider him a super close family friend, but he's certainly been a steady fixture in my life for several years.

I'm here today because I don't know another place in Everton that has as well stocked of a collector's library as he does. Ours is probably second best, but since I couldn't find what I'm looking for in our book collection, I'm hoping Mr. Brone can help me out.

The giant wood doors squeak loudly as I push through them. Mr. Brone is sitting behind the front counter when I enter, his salt and pepper hair slicked back, and his black-rimmed glasses are perched on the end of his nose as he inspects some papers. Mr. Brone is a hawk shifter, and I always thought his nose reminded me of a sharp beak. He lifts his head and spots me, his dark eyes brightening as his mouth stretches into a smile.

"Locklyn," he says, and then rounds his desk to greet me. "To what do I owe this surprise visit? Are you here for something for your parents?"

"No," I say, shaking my head. "I'm not here for my parents. I was actually hoping you might let me have a look around your library."

He cocks his head, his eyebrows rising over the rims of his dark frames. "Is that so? It's been some time since you've last lost yourself in the dusty depths of my library."

He's not wrong. I used to spend countless hours up there reading through some of the weathered leather-bound books. My favorites were fairy tales that took me far away from my reality. But when I got old enough to help my parents with the store, at some point I realized life wasn't and would never be a fairy tale, and so reading them just made me sad.

"I know. I'm sorry I haven't visited more. I need to do some research for school," I lie, instantly feeling horrible about it.

He waves me off. "No worries about that. I remember what it's like to be young. The world is fresh and exciting. Enjoy these years. They'll be some of the best of your life."

If these years are supposed to be the best of my life, I'm in serious trouble. Rather than contradict Mr. Brone, I smile politely.

"You know the way up to the library. My knees aren't what they used to be, so I hope you don't fault me for not walking you up."

Mr. Brone is only a few years older than my parents and relatively fit. I'd wager money that he could zip up and down those stairs with no problem, and even if he couldn't, he could shift and fly up there. But I don't blame him for not wanting to make the six-flight trek up to the top of the Emporium.

"Of course not. Thanks, Mr. Brone," I say with a half-smile as he moves back behind the desk and grabs a key.

"Oh please, we've known each other too long for you not to call me Kerrim," he says as he hands me the keys.

I nod and thank him, and then turn toward the stairs. As I make my way up to the library my thoughts shift from Becks to Shadow Striker. The "what-ifs" haunt me, sticking to me like wet sand. Irritating and impossible to get rid of.

The door to the Emporium library is unassuming and small. If I were an average sized creature I'd have to duck as I walk through the frame, but as I'm on the shorter side I don't need to worry about bumping my head. The entrance, however, is completely at odds with the cavernous room beyond it.

I slide the key in the lock, open the door, and immediately suck in a large breath of dust-filled air, relishing the smell of leather and parchment. A feeling of familiarity, home, settles over me as I take in the two-story room of floor-to-ceiling bookshelves. A stained-glass window on the opposite side of the space lets in rose and purple tinted light, and sconces of white faelight ring the space.

After setting my backpack down on one of the two long rectangular tables in the center of the room, I walk to a familiar shelf to trail my fingers over some of my old favorites: *The Tale of Twin Foxes, The Ogre and the Princess, The Saga of the Doomed Siren Pirate*. All fairy tales I'd escaped into. And I didn't just read the stories, I devoured them, becoming part of them the same as they became part of me. For the short time I immersed myself in their tales I didn't just read about the princess who fell in love with an ogre who turned out to be a cursed fae prince, I *became* her. I sailed crystalline seas with siren pirates and rescued a merman from certain death. I became a cunning fox shifter and fooled a greedy dragon king out of his riches. I lived a hundred different lives in this library and wished each time that I'd magically fall into a story and never escape.

But that's not how life works, and every time I closed a cracked and aged spine I had to return to reality and a life where I was spurned and shunned for my lack of magic, judged based not on who I was but on what I couldn't do. Some days life felt unbearable, and even though I'm blessed to have parents who love me and two good friends who stand by my side, there are days that still just doesn't feel like enough, days where I'd give anything to be someone else, to walk in different shoes. But books could only take me so far, and eventually reading the tales of adventures I would never live started to make me depressed. And so I stopped.

I haven't been to the Emporium library to read for pleasure in over two years. A twinge of nostalgia spikes in my chest at the smell of the parchment and papyrus of the aged books in Mr. Brone's collection, and along with it comes the urge to search the fiction section for what new books he's acquired. But that's not why I'm here today, so I turn away from the temptation and travel farther into the room, where I know he keeps his oldest and most rare tomes.

Three hours later, the light coming in from the stained-glass windows has almost completely disappeared and I have to squint to read the faded page in front of me. My neck aches and my butt has gone numb from the harsh wooden chair. Worst of all, I've come up completely empty and feel utterly defeated.

What if Shadow Striker doesn't hold any power and I entered Chaos for no reason? My stomach bottoms out, because if that's true, not only will I remain powerless, it means I have no idea how to help Becks.

Frustrated, I shut the book, a first century edition of the Ancients that should probably be in a museum rather than the Emporium's unkempt library, and slouch back into the uncomfortable wooden chair. I would have preferred to sit in one of the padded armchairs sprinkled throughout the room, but for my research the single table in the middle of the space was best.

I shove away from the table to get some feeling back into my butt and legs when my gaze snags on a volume in the legal section of the library. I can confidently say it's a small bookshelf I've never given more than a cursory glance, but the gold lettering against the black leather binding that spells out *Dragon Shifter Law* gets my heart pumping a little faster.

From the condition of the binding and crisp white pages I can tell immediately it's not an old book. It was probably printed sometime in the last twenty years. It seems like an odd edition to have here. It's true that different creature species, and dragon shifters in particular, have their own set of rules and laws for their clans, but because of the secretive nature of the content not much is available for public consumption. It's considered proprietary information, and truth be told I'm not even sure it's legal for Mr. Brone to have this book. Perhaps a desperate dragon shifter traded it to Mr. Brone for extra money? If the local dragon shifter clan knew it was here, they'd surely demand its return.

I shouldn't even be looking at it, but after pulling it from the shelf I flip it open to the table of contents, scanning until I land on

"Mating Rules and Rituals." With shaky hands, I turn to the pages, skimming quickly.

At first it only talks about how each shifter has to go before the council to get approval before declaring a mate. That's common knowledge and for the most part just a formality. I've never heard of a mating being rejected, but as I keep looking I finally come across what I'm searching for, the section on the dragon heir.

I only get through the first sentence before the door creaks open. I slam the book shut, sliding it across the table toward the piles of other books I'd already searched for information on Shadow Striker.

"Ah, Locklyn dear, you are still here," Mr. Brone says as he walks toward me. "I closed the Emporium fifteen minutes ago."

"It's that late already?" I ask, digging for my phone in my bag.

Sure enough, when I pull it out it shows it's a quarter past eight, and I've missed calls and texts from both my parents. Typing out a quick note with my thumbs, I send them an apology and let them know where I am and that I'll be home soon.

"Are you done with these?" Mr. Brone asks when I look up, pointing to the messy stacks of books spread across the table.

"Oh yeah, I'm sorry. Let me put them away," I say, snatching up a small pile and shoving the *Dragon Shifter Law* book on the bottom. I'm not willing to take the chance that if I ask Mr. Brone to borrow it he might just take it away from me.

For the next few minutes Mr. Brone and I return the books to their spots on the shelves in silence. With his back turned, I slip the dragon shifter book into my backpack, a knot of unease forming in my gut, but I assuage my guilt by reminding myself it's for a good cause. Besides, I'll return it when I'm done, and Mr. Brone will probably never even know it was missing. I have to have a look at this book though. How am I supposed to help Becks out of his arranged marriage if I don't understand dragon shifter law?

After Mr. Brone and I clean up the mess I made over the last several hours, I follow him out of the library and down the winding staircase to the ground floor.

"I hope you found what you were looking for," he says conversationally, and I think about the contraband I have hidden in my bag.

"Actually, no. I was looking for some information on an Ancient, but I'm starting to think it's a lost cause."

"Research for one of your classes, right?" he asks, and rather than contradicting him I just nod. That's easier than explaining my new obsession with Shadow Striker.

"I heard about a specific story, but I'm starting to doubt it's even actually an Ancient. I can't find any information about it anywhere."

"Hmm," he says as we reach the ground floor and head toward the entrance so Mr. Brone can unlock it for me to leave. "What's the story? I've done my fair share of studying the Ancients over the years. Call it a hobby, if you will. I may be able to point you in the right direction."

I wave, unconvinced Mr. Brone will know anything when no one else has. "It's really obscure."

"Well, now you have to tell me," he says with an easy smile. "Try me."

We pause in front of the door. "Have you heard of the tale of Shadow Striker and the Vampire King?"

Mr. Brone's smile dims. "That certainly is an obscure tale. Where did you hear about that particular Ancient?"

"A customer who came into the shop asking about Shadow Striker," I answer honestly, the chance that he may actually know of the tale making my tongue looser. "I'd never heard about it before then."

Mr. Brone looks thoughtful. "Interesting," he says. "Not many are aware of that Ancient. It's a sordid tale of a corrupted soul and a weapon that never should have been forged. I suggest you see if you can switch the topic of your class assignment. There's not much information available about the tale, and even less truth. If you continue to chase after it, you won't be the first to find yourself left frustrated and empty-handed."

What a weird way to put it.

Rather than dampening my curiosity, Mr. Brone's warning only ramps it up. It's clear he knows more about Shadow Striker and the tale of the Vampire King than he's letting on.

"That may be true, but I find it a really interesting subject, so I'm not sure I'm ready to drop it just yet. Do you happen to have any books that mention it? Maybe I missed something when I was upstairs."

Mr. Brone shakes his head. "No, and you're not likely to find one either."

My insides deflate. "Why not?"

"It's one of the stricken Ancients, removed from the original canon. Most of the information we have on that tale is hearsay passed down from creature to creature."

"Yet you've heard about it," I say, pressing him.

He crosses his arms over his chest, seemingly uncomfortable with this conversation, but I can't let it go now. He's the first creature I've talked to who knows something about the tale besides Talon. "Was there something in particular you wanted to know?" he asks. "I may have the answer, but I'm not sure if your teacher will count me as a credible source for your project."

"Oh, I'm sure they will," I say, waving off that concern. It won't matter if my teacher thinks he's a credible source, because I'm not actually researching Shadow Striker for a project. "From what I know, the blade gives its wielder other creature's powers. I wanted to know if the blade stole powers from creatures or not. And if it really did corrupt the Vampire King."

He studies me. His gaze turning shrewd. "Who's to say? It's only a story," he says with a shrug, and frustration bubbles in my gut.

I'm about to thank him for letting me use his library and leave when he says, "But . . ." and I straighten my spine, hoping for a more definitive answer. ". . . if the dagger truly exists, from what I've gathered about the tale, I think it's entirely possible the blade doesn't steal powers but rather replicates them. Shadow Striker need only draw blood to work its magic, so if it's not taking a life, then I would assume it's not actually taking powers either. My theory is that when the blade soaks up the blood it's learning the creature's magic to replicate it. But of course that's just my opinion."

That makes sense to me, but is it enough to risk if Shadow Striker were actually in my hands?

"And as far as the poor Vampire King, the tale does suggest that he underwent some sort of change. There's more evidence that backs up the theory that his quest started nobly, but it's debatable whether it was Shadow Striker that poisoned his mind, or if it was something far simpler. I would think that any being with that much power would be susceptible to corruption. Don't you agree?"

I nod. He makes a good point.

I thank him for the information and his time, and he has to remind me another time to call him by his first name.

"Kerrim, right," I say, the name sounding weird on my tongue.

"Don't be a stranger, Locklyn. And good luck with that project. I hope you get a good grade."

I smile, and with a final wave leave to head home. I may not have found exactly what I was looking for by coming to the Emporium, but between the *Dragon Shifter Law* book hidden in my bag, and Mr. Brone's theories on Shadow Striker, I'm certainly not leaving hopeless or empty-handed.

Fourteen

IT'S HOPELESS.

I stare at the page in front of me, my eyes dry from reading the same few lines over and over and over again.

The dragon heir's life-mate will be chosen by the council. In order to be considered a viable female, the dragon heir's life-mate's magic level should match or surpass that of the dragon heir himself. Once mated, the dragon heir will take up the mantle of the head of the dragon clans as dragon king until such time the next dragon heir is declared and comes of age.

The only positive part of everything I read in the *Dragon Shifter Law* book was that the law didn't explicitly state that the dragon heirs had to be mated to be a dragon shifter. It seems magic trumps species, and as long as the female promised to Becks is powerful enough, it won't matter if she is fae, vampire, or another type of shifter. But no matter how many times I read through the pages about the laws surrounding the dragon heir, unless the dragon council changes their mind I can't find one single thing that gives me hope Becks can somehow get out of his arranged life-mating.

In fact, now that I know more about the laws surrounding the dragon heir, I realize just how tightly bound Becks is. He did a decent job downplaying just how little control he has over the rest of his life this past year, but that bud of hope I had before I dove into dragon shifter law had long since withered and died.

I snap the book shut, pounding my fist on the cover for good measure. Do I want Becks to be free to choose his own life-mate for selfish reasons? *Sure.* But this isn't even about me anymore. Besides any romantic feelings I've developed for Becks over the years, he is first and foremost one of my best friends. Now that I understand just how trapped he is, my heart cries out for him. It isn't fair that he has to give up so much for a title and role he never even wanted to begin with.

The search for Becks' life-mate won't be contained to our school alone. Becks isn't just the dragon heir of Everton, he's *the* dragon heir and will someday become *the* dragon king. Any female on the planet of marriageable age is going to be considered, but that doesn't stop me from thinking about the most powerful females at our school as potentials for Becks.

Unfortunately, my nemesis Jules would probably make that list of potentials. She might be as dumb as a pile of rocks, but she's a powerful wolf shifter and power seems to be the only thing dragon shifters value. Vega, a particularly strong fae whose small stature hides the fact that she's a magical powerhouse, would be another prospect for him. I haven't had much interaction with her over the years, but now I instantly hate her.

Another possibility would be Sienna, the vampire whose soul is as black as her raven hair. I've tried my best to steer clear of Sienna over the years because she always gives off an unhinged vibe. She's the type of girl I'd expect to hide desiccated animal carcasses under her bed and keep pin-filled voodoo dolls of her ex-boyfriends in her closet. I cringe to think of Becks being tied to someone like that for the rest of his life, and then circle back to where I started, with the realization that short of a miracle where I come into my powers overnight, I'll never be able to be in Becks' life how I truly want to be.

Unless I can win Shadow Striker.

If these are the thoughts going through my head, what must it be like for Becks right now? He must be driving himself half mad with the possibilities of how this life-mating can go wrong for him.

Okay, so the laws are a dead end, but there has to be another way. I'm not giving up on going after Shadow Striker in order to become powerful enough to be in the contention for Becks, but I'm also not willing to risk Becks' future on a longshot.

Think, Locklyn. Think.

But it's late and my brain doesn't want to cooperate.

There's a buzz and I pick up my phone to check it, but the screen is dark. *That's weird.* With the phone still in my hand, I hear the buzz again and realize it's coming from my bag. Digging around in the pack, my fingers brush over the smooth surface of the Chaos tracker just as it starts to vibrate.

My heart rate stumbles as I pull it out and find the screen lit with words and numbers. A date, a time, an address, and numbers that I'm assuming are coordinates. It must be for the next trial, which according to the information will happen on Thursday, three days from now.

My stomach drops. That's so soon.

Twisting in my chair to face my computer, I type the coordinates into a search. A part of town I don't venture into very often pops up, but I recognize where it is because my parents' warehouse isn't far from there. It's an industrial area that isn't known to be the safest. Even though our warehouse is on a slightly safer street, my father doesn't ever let my mom venture there alone.

Grabbing my phone, I type out a group message letting Becks and Ensley know about the message. Becks' reply comes instantly. "Okay. I'll be there." Ensley's comes a few minutes later and with lots of crying emojis. Apparently her band has a gig that night so she won't be able to make it. She says she's going to see if they can get a replacement for her, but I know they won't be able to because she not only sings lead vocals but also plays the bass, so I tell her not to worry about it. Becks chimes in with, "Don't worry. I've got her." I know he doesn't mean anything deep by that, but it still makes my heart beat a little faster.

I don't sleep much the following days. If I'm not trying to keep my nerves tamped down about Chaos, I'm stressing about Becks' arranged life-mating. Fortunately, Becks finally confides in Ensley, and when she finds out she's livid at the council and goes directly to her parents to give them hell for backing them. Unfortunately, with or without their parents' approval, the council is going forward with their plans to mate Becks off in the next half year.

Before I know it, it's the evening of the second trial. Becks picks me up in his truck and we drive to the warehouse district in silence. My knee bounces up and down the whole way until Becks reaches over and sets his hand on it, settling me and offering silent comfort.

Cars line the usually desolate streets as we look for parking. It doesn't take long to find a spot, but it's several blocks from the coordinates. The strain of what's to come is all over Becks' face when we get out of the truck and start the short walk to the warehouse. We're not alone as we walk, but our quiet somberness is at odds with the party atmosphere around us. It's not until we're about to push through the doors to the warehouse when Becks stops me, pulling me to the side.

He turns me toward him with warm hands on my biceps. "Are you sure about this?"

I want to shake my head because now that I'm about to enter another Chaos trial my nerves are wreaking havoc on me, but I know that if I give Becks any indication that I'm not one hundred percent confident in my decision, I'll be over his shoulder as he sprints me away in less than two seconds flat. So I force a smile that I hope isn't wobbly.

"Yeah. I've got this," I say with false confidence.

He searches my gaze, and I'm pretty sure he reads the truth in my eyes, but he gives a resigned nod.

"Okay, let's do this, then."

I like the way he included himself in that statement, like we were really doing this together.

My knees are a little shaky as we approach the door, but I force steel into my spine. The same shimmer that covered the mouth of the cavern blankets the industrial warehouse as well. I don't let myself pause as I walk through the magical barrier and push open the doors. Just like at the Chaos party, I'm assaulted by noise and lights the moment we enter the space.

Bass thumps in my chest, and it takes my eyes a moment to adjust to the flashing lights, but when they do I focus in on two square cages set in the middle of a ring of bleachers. Half the stands are already full of spectators, and some of the Chaos competitors, blocking a clear view of the cages, but as we near I note that they are roughly the size of a sparring ring, which is somewhat comforting since the sparring ring at Peet's Gym is practically my second home. But unlike the ring I'm used to, the floor is rough concrete and the bars along the cage are lined with two-inch metal spikes, making it so that if someone slams into them they'll get seriously hurt.

Becks shifts closer, putting a protective hand on the small of my back, and I have to stop myself from melting into him. When I glance over, his face is leached of color and his eyes are wide as they run over the cages. It doesn't take a genius to realize I'm going to have to get in one of those at least once tonight.

Someone shouts Becks' name and we both turn, spotting some of his fellow dragon shifters mid-way up the bleachers waving us over. Taking my hand, Becks leads me to where they're sitting, letting go to greet some of them with fist bumps and high fives. I sit down on the cool metal bleacher a few feet away from where Becks is catching up with the shifters, my eyes on the spiked steel bars of the cages below.

"You're Locklyn, right?" comes a voice next to me, and I look over to see a girl I recognize from Nightlark but never had any interaction with. I think she might be a year or two younger than me and a shifter of some sort.

"Yeah," I say with a nod, having to raise my voice over the EDM music pumping through the cavernous space.

A smile curves her mouth that lights up her bright hazel eyes. Her skin is a beautiful rich brown color, and her hair falls down her back in hundreds of small teal and black braids. I don't know why she's talking to me right now, but I'm instantly wary.

"Wicked, I'm Shayla," she says, and holds out her hand for me to shake.

"Nice to meet you," I say lamely because I'm not sure what else to say.

"I was watching you during the last trial. You're really brave," she says, surprising me.

"Oh. Um. Thanks?"

Her smile widens and a dimple pops out in one cheek. "My boyfriend, Owen, entered the contest too but couldn't find a coin in time." She looks over and points out one of the beefy dragon shifters talking to Becks. He has shaggy brown hair and blue eyes. He's nice looking, but next to Becks he's just average. But that's how most everyone looks next to Becks.

Even Talon? my mind whispers, and I tell it to shut up.

"It was nerve racking watching him. I'm not sorry he was disqualified. I'm sure Becks was a mess as well."

"Oh. But Becks isn't . . . I mean he and I aren't—"

She holds up her hands, a stricken look on her face. "Oh yeah, I know that. I just meant that everyone knows you guys are close, so it was probably hard for him to watch."

"Right. Yeah, he didn't love it."

I glance over at Becks to find him staring back at me, his gaze moving between me and Shayla questioningly. I give him a small smile to let him know that everything is okay.

"You guys have been friends a long time, right?" Shayla asks, cutting off the silent communication between me and Becks.

When I look back at her she looks sincere, but I don't know if she's fishing for information or just making conversation.

"Since first grade," I confirm.

Shayla leans in. "Is it true—" she starts, but then just like back at the caverns the lights and music cut suddenly.

Unlike last time, hysteria doesn't hit the crowd because they know what's coming, but an excited buzz fills the space. Someone sits down next to me as faelights start appearing around the room.

"It's just me," Becks says in my ear, and goose bumps break out on my arms as his breath washes over my neck. He scoots over until his hip is pressed up against mine.

A spotlight appears in the space between the cages, illuminating the red-robed game master. His hood is once again hanging low over his face, hiding his identity.

"Tonight's trial will pit competitor against competitor in a hand-to-hand battle," he says, not wasting any time getting to the point.

A roar goes up from the crowd and Becks tenses next to me. I keep it together, at least on the outside. I knew this was coming the moment I laid eyes on those cages, and I remind myself that I know my way around a ring.

The game master goes on to explain how two battles, one in each cage, will be going on simultaneously. Each of the fights will last ten minutes, or until one of the competitors is unconscious. There's no tapping out. We're required to fight through broken bones or any other injuries that don't knock us out. We'll fight multiple times until we are ranked, and the bottom third of the competitors will be eliminated.

My chances of making it through this trial are going to depend on who I'm up against. Even without magic I'm confident I can beat some of the competitors in a hand-to-hand fight. I just have to hope that luck is on my side this evening.

"The overall winner of the battles will be given an advantage in the next trial," the game master says, and an excited murmur moves throughout the crowd. But I almost laugh out loud. Forget an advantage, I'm just hoping to make it through to the next round, preferably in one piece.

After that announcement, the game master calls the competitors forward and I stand to join the others, but Becks catches my wrist, stopping me before I can step away from him.

"You know how to fight. Use all your skills to protect yourself," he says.

"I will."

Rather than letting go, Becks just squeezes tighter. "Lock, this won't be like sparring at Peet's. This isn't going to be a fair fight. They're going to play dirty. You need to too." Becks' piercing green eyes stay locked on mine for another few seconds, before I gently tug against his hold.

I nod to let him know I heard him and then turn to leave. I size up the other competitors as I make my way to the front, noting there are probably around sixty of us left. We're told to head to the back of the warehouse to get ready, and I follow the group to two separate rooms in the back that are acting as makeshift locker rooms. Unfortunately, they haven't segregated the genders, only split us in half.

I don't see Talon in the room I'm ushered into, which means he must be in the other one. I do see a few other familiar faces I wish I hadn't, one of whom being Jules, who eyes me with a look of disdain. I avert my gaze and try to mind my own business. I know Jules isn't much of a fighter, but her powers render me almost useless every time we go up against each other. To win I'm going to need to be smarter and faster than my opponents.

At the back of the room is a bin of clothes, only shorts for the guys and shorts and sports bras for the girls. Without having to be told, the competitors dive in and look for their sizes. I wait until the crowd has thinned before searching for something to wear.

"Looking for a body bag?" comes Jules' voice behind me.

With my back still to her, I give a shake of my head. "I'm

looking for a straitjacket for you. Sorry to say I don't see your size though." I straighten with a small pair of shorts and a sports bra in my hand and come face-to-face with her.

"You're going to get murdered out there," she says with glee.

I shrug, trying to look nonchalant, when in reality that's a very real possibility. All it will take is one spike to the head and I'll be a goner for sure. "I'm not worried," I lie, but she sees right through me, her smile oily and bloated with confidence.

"This is going to be awesome," she says with a laugh, and then walks off.

Guys are changing in the middle of the room without any regard for their nakedness, but some of the girls have constructed a privacy screen in the back corner. I go and wait, keeping my gaze firmly off all the flashes of skin around me, and then change quickly when it's my turn. I'd be self-conscious about the amount of skin I have exposed after I emerge from behind the screen if I didn't have bigger things to stress about.

It's not another five minutes before I hear the game master's voice again, announcing the first two competitors to battle. I take a deep breath when they announce Talon and another name I don't recognize. Cheers sound as I assume Talon and his opponent emerge from the other room. I don't know what type of fighter Talon is, but I imagine he isn't feeling any of the trepidation I am right now.

The game master quiets everyone down and then announces the second pair. Jules' name is announced first, and I'm in the middle of thinking that it sucks for whoever is paired against her when my name is called as well.

The blood in my veins turns to ice and my body locks up.

"Get up," the girl next to me says. "You have to get out there."

She practically hauls me from my seat and shoves me out the door to where Jules is waiting with a smile on her face. I walk woodenly next to her toward one of the cages, my eyes finding

Talon's halfway there and holding. He's staring at me with a frown, and his eyes filled with concern.

I bite my lip, ordering myself to suck it up. Jules has magic, but that's it. I've always thought even without magic I had a chance to take Jules down. I just have to be smart about it.

The game master offers a few more words to pump up the crowd. I'm only a handful of feet from him at this point and I still can't see his face. I realize it's because he's using magic to shadow his features. Talon edges toward the robed figure but suddenly stops, almost as if he can't get any closer, and I wonder if the game master is magically shielded. He sure is taking keeping his identity secret seriously.

When the game master finishes talking, the doors to the cages swing open. We're told to take off our shoes and enter the cage, which we do, and then the door clangs shut behind us.

"And there's one more thing," the game master says, and then goes over to Talon's cage and pushes a button I didn't notice was there. Talon and his opponent jolt and then they turn to the game master with matching frowns. When the game master pushes the button on our cage, Jules flinches as well, but I don't know why. I don't feel a thing.

Finally, the game master resumes his position between the fighting cages. "These matches will take place without the use of magic. May the best creature win."

My breath catches. With just one sentence my nightmare has turned into a wish granted: me and Jules in a one-on-one where she can't use her magic.

I turn toward Jules, and we start to circle each other, waiting for the countdown to begin. She's trying to keep it together, but I see the panic leaking into her. She's twitchy and the maniacal smile she wore just moments ago has morphed into a frown.

This is going to be fun.

A countdown from ten starts and I suddenly catch Becks' face in the crowd. He's moved to the front of the bleachers, his body tense and rigid as he stares back at me as the rest of the crowd goes wild.

Becks gives me a nod and a slow smile breaks over my face. *I've got this.*

A loud beep fills the air when the timer reaches zero and I snap my attention to Jules, who's shifting her weight back and forth on the other side of the cage, looking unsure of what to do, concern clearly shining from her eyes.

I jump into action. Reaching Jules quickly, I land the first blow with a jab right to the center of her face. My fist connects with her nose and her head snaps back. Blood immediately starts pouring from her now crooked nose, filling me with satisfaction. That hit was a long time coming, but it knocks Jules out of her funk, and she rushes me with a rage-filled scream.

It's immediately clear Jules doesn't have any real fighting skills, which is what happens when you get lazy and rely too heavily on your magic, but what she lacks in form she makes up for in pure unfiltered fury.

I duck her sloppy punches easily and practically dance around her as she comes at me with pinwheeled arms. The crowd starts screaming, which distracts me for a moment, and Jules lands her first hit, an open-handed slap to my cheek that leaves a sting. There's a small reaction from the crowd, but I'm assuming most of them are focused on whatever is going on over in Talon's cage, which is probably far more entertaining than watching me evade Jules' untrained attacks.

Landing a hit seems to give Jules some confidence. She starts trash talking me again, but her barbs don't find purchase. Little does she know I'm just wearing her out, biding my time, and it isn't long before she starts lagging.

A roar sounds from the spectators, but I learned my lesson the first time and it's Jules whose focus slips with the ruckus. I take the opportunity to kick out, landing a roundhouse kick to her face, which causes her to do a half-spin before hitting the concrete below us.

I should really follow up that hit with another, but instead I sneak a glance at the cage next to us to see how Talon's doing, which from the looks of it is well. Talon is hunched over his downed opponent, delivering a series of brutal punches as the crowd goes crazy. Once again, the distraction costs me and I don't even see Jules coming until she tackles me to the ground.

She has the upper hand and manages to get a couple of shots into my ribs before I buck her off. We grapple on the ground while I hear the crowd chanting, "Girl fight," over and over again.

I'm not used to matches in front of this big of a crowd and the distraction is hindering my performance. I force myself to shut out the noise and concentrate on Jules so that I don't end up knocked out, or worse.

The crowd erupts, and Talon gets declared the winner of his fight, but I'm finally focused on what I should be—my own match —so I only vaguely register the sound.

Jules manages to squirm out of my hold and we both pop to our feet. Sweat runs in rivulets down the sides of her face. Her nose is crooked, and her mouth and chin are covered in blood. One of her eyes is also swollen shut, but I'm hardly winded. Besides the slight sting on my cheek and a little tenderness around my ribs, I feel great.

With a shout of fury, Jules barrels at me, dropping her shoulder to catch me in the gut, but I twist out of the way and her momentum takes her past me, right toward the spiked bars. Without thinking, I reach out and grab what I can to keep her from face-planting into the spikes, and with a fistful of her pony-tail and one strap of her sports bra, I yank her off course. She stumbles, falling and rolling into the bars. She screams and pulls away. When she stands, six puncture wounds dot her shoulder and arm, weeping blood, but she's lucky it wasn't her face.

Jules snarls at me, looking extra grotesque with the blood

covering her face and teeth from her other injuries. "I'm going to rip you to shreds," she yells, but at this point the threat is laughable.

She's out of gas, so it's time to end this.

At the gym, we're not specifically taught how to knock an opponent out, because it's considered unsportsmanlike, but I know a hit to the temple or middle of the chin are the best options.

I come at Jules, not worrying about broadcasting my moves in the slightest anymore. I swing wide to build up power, hitting her in the temple with a cross, and then immediately follow up with an uppercut blow to her chin, nailing both vulnerable spots one after the other. I'm not leaving anything up to chance.

Jules' body folds like an accordion to the floor. Blood still drips from her nose as she lies on the gray concrete, out cold.

Fifteen

I **WON**. And it feels amazing.

The moment I let my guard down, sound comes rushing at me. Whistles and shouts pierce my eardrums. Some are even chanting my name.

I blink, looking around in shock. I was so far in the zone I blocked out the world around me, and now that I've let it back in the sensory overload is overwhelming. Or maybe I'm just experiencing the effects of the crash after the adrenaline rush.

I don't know, but whatever the reason, I'm disoriented until I find Becks in the crowd. He's standing only a few feet on the other side of the spiked bars.

"Are you okay?" he asks, his voice elevated to be heard over the crowd behind him.

"Yeah, I'm good," I call back.

He lets out a breath, and the lines of tension on his face soften. "Good," is all he says, but I sense there's something more behind that word.

I'm announced as the winner, and then the game master immediately reminds the crowd that all of the fighters will participate in at least one more fight to determine who the winner is and the competitors who will be eliminated. I'm not happy I'm going to have to fight again, but now that I know I'll be on an even playing field with my opponents, I'm not as stressed.

Someone has to go into the cage to drag Jules out, and then they try to revive her, but I don't stay to watch as I make my way back to the temporary locker rooms. My body starts to feel heavy. I'm definitely experiencing a crash from the adrenaline rush.

"That was some impressive fighting back there," Talon says as he falls into step with me. I guess he stayed to watch the end of my fight when his was over.

His hairline is slicked with sweat and there's a small bruise high on his cheekbone, but he's grinning down at me as if he doesn't have a care in the world. In fact, if anything it looks like the fight invigorated him.

"I've been taking self-defense and kickboxing lessons since I was eight."

He nods. "It shows. Maybe I should stop by your gym, and you can give me some pointers."

I shoot him a look. That sounded like a pick-up line, and despite myself I do what I didn't have the nerve to do before and let my gaze covertly slide down his sweat-slicked chest. My stomach bottoms out and my mouth goes dry. I knew Talon was muscular, but I wasn't prepared for the stack of abs so cut I could wash clothes on them, or how appealing the indents on either side of his hip bones are. I follow those indents with my eyes until they disappear beneath his shorts and then quickly look away, feeling even more blood rush to my already reddened cheeks.

Pull it together, Locklyn. You see shirtless guys at the gym all the time. So he's cut . . . who cares?

I clear my throat, hoping it wasn't overly obvious I just checked him out. "Clearly you don't need any pointers," I say with a pointed glance behind us at his opponent, who still hasn't regained consciousness.

"You can always learn more," he says with a shrug, not seeming to react to my ogling. Thank the Creator for that.

We reach the locker rooms and I turn toward my door.

"Good luck with your next round," Talon says. "But it doesn't look like you're going to need it."

I snort a laugh. "You too," I say, and then push through the door.

My next match I'm paired up against Kiaro, a bald six-foot snake shifter who won't stop staring at my chest and rubbing his thumb over his bottom lip as we stand across from each other, waiting for the fight to begin.

A thread of unease slithers through my body as I size him up. I've sparred against plenty of guys larger than me, but I don't know Kiaro's skill level. I have to just hope he is as untrained as Jules.

The countdown begins and then the buzzer goes off. Kiaro immediately rushes me, reaching out with his arms to do who knows what, but I deftly duck under his reach and bounce to the other side of the cage. The way the dude has been looking at me and how he just tried to pull me into some sort of embrace makes me not want to get within arm's length of him, which is a problem because I'll need to get close to land a punch.

"Oh, I see. You're shy," he says with a lecherous grin.

Barf.

His tongue comes out to lick his bottom lip and it's forked at the end. Not forked like it would be if he'd partially shifted, but forked as if he had his tongue cut that way on purpose.

I don't respond to his taunts, but instead take note of his movements as he comes at me again. This time he doesn't bother trying to pull me in, but swings out with his left fist, which lets me know that's his dominant hand. I easily dodge his second attack and scamper away from him.

The crowd boos, but I block them out. I'm not going to be pressured to attack until I know more about him. Until I'm ready.

We dance around the cage for several more minutes and Kiaro gets increasingly frustrated with me. His movements become more aggressive, and I finally get an opening when he takes a wide swing at me. Rather than ducking away like he expects, I move closer, surprising him, and then deliver a quick jab to his cheek followed by an uppercut to his chin, and then quickly spin away before he has a chance to retaliate.

With murder in his gaze, Kiaro lifts his arm and wipes a trickle of blood away from the corner of his mouth with the back of his hand. Several feet apart, we stand and stare at each other; both of our guards are up.

Kiaro thought this was going to be an easy win for him, but now he knows better. It's about to be a real fight now.

Without warning, Kiaro juts forward, his fist on a collision course with my nose. Even without the use of his magic he's insanely fast, but I manage to shift so that his blow grazes my cheek rather than smashes my nose. It wasn't a solid hit, but my cheek still throbs. That one's going to form a nice bruise.

Over the next several minutes Kiaro and I trade blows. I don't take any serious hits, but unfortunately neither does he. After five more minutes of fighting, we're running out of time and neither one of us has the clear upper hand. I'm covered in a fine layer of sweat, my mind working hard to catalog his weaknesses, but finding it difficult to come up with any. He's proving to be a much more challenging opponent than Jules. He's not wearing out as fast as she did, and on top of that it's clear he knows a little about boxing and hand-to-hand combat. His moves aren't as precise or as polished as mine, but each of his hits has more power and his reach is a lot longer.

If Kiaro has one weakness, it's that he doesn't know how to use his legs in a fight and relies solely on his upper body. As a result, I end up relying heavily on my kicks to keep him at a distance. I don't want his fists anywhere near my face. If he gets in one good shot it will be all over for me.

As the seconds tick by I can feel myself flagging. Kiaro comes at me, and I screw up and don't duck away from him quickly enough, giving him an opening to snatch me from behind, which he immediately takes advantage of, putting me in a chokehold.

His forearm presses down on my windpipe, trying to cut off air, but I don't panic. I know how to get out of a chokehold, I've done it a million times before. I'm about to initiate a movement to break his hold, but I'm thrown when Kiaro bends down and licks the side of my face.

"If I promise to make this quick, will you make it up to me later?" he whispers in my ear.

Revulsion sloshes in my gut and it takes effort to keep the contents of my stomach from making an appearance.

A furious roar comes from the crowd. My gaze flicks up in time to see Becks trying to rush the cage, but he's being held back by four guys. He manages to shake one off, but only makes it a step before he's pulled back again.

Kiaro tightens his grip, and pulling his shoulders back he picks me up.

I curse myself for not breaking free of the chokehold immediately. It's so much harder to escape this position without my feet on the ground.

With effort, I push Becks and everything but Kiaro from my mind. I can't afford these distractions. Curling my legs toward my chest, I kick out and buck, which throws Kiaro off balance enough that he pitches forward, his hold loosening as his body covers mine on the ground. I twist, spinning out of his hold, and immediately straighten and knee him in the chin.

His head snaps back, and before he can recover I slam my foot into his groin. It isn't a sanctioned kickboxing move, but the douche deserved it.

Kiaro keels over, red faced and cupping his crotch. I give him the same double tap I gave Jules, one punch to the temple followed by another to the chin, and he's out for the count.

I stand over him, my breathing ragged as much from the match as it is from the desire to give this guy another kick to the nuts, but I manage to restrain myself.

The crowd is going crazy, and I look up to catch Becks' eye. He's calmed enough that no one is holding him back anymore, but his chest is heaving, and his hair is standing up every which way. There's a wild spark in his eyes that makes him look unfamiliar to me in that moment. He blinks and his eyes go slitted like they are in his dragon form, and then another blink and they're back to normal.

I may be physically okay, but Becks doesn't look like he's doing all that well mentally.

Forcing my gaze away from Becks, I trudge toward the cage door, which opens for me when I near. Some guys who I assume are friends of Kiaro brush past me to grab him and haul him from the cage. I don't linger, and wearily walk back to the locker rooms, realizing that I won't be able to stop fighting until I either win this whole thing or end up like Kiaro or Jules, knocked out cold and lying on the bloodied concrete.

More matches happen over the next hour, and I listen to the roar of the crowd and the winners being announced with detachment, just trying to keep myself in the same headspace. Jules wins her next match, which probably saves her from elimination, but means she doesn't have to fight again because her loss to me took her out of the running for overall winner. I'm a little envious she doesn't have to fight anymore. I'm exhausted.

I get looks from my fellow competitors who are still in the competition, but I can't interpret what they mean. Perhaps they're simply confused why I'm still here. I'm easily the smallest one left.

The next and last round of fights start, and as I wait for my name to be called, the aches and pains and stiffness from the first two rounds start settling in my joints. They're holding only one match at a time now, and slowly the room empties until it's just me and another guy, a white-haired teal-eyed fae named Titus who isn't exactly friendly but hasn't been openly hostile either, so that makes him cool in my book. He has a cut on his forehead from his last match that won't stop weeping blood, but honestly it makes him intimidating, so the look could work for him.

The game master's voice booms beyond the closed door as he starts to announce the next match. Talon's name is announced, and the crowd starts cheering. I straighten, waiting to hear who he's paired against. There aren't many of us left. My heart jumps to my throat when my name rings out across the warehouse.

I walk woodenly toward the door, each step heavier than the last.

"He's going to favor his left ribs," Titus says, startling me.

I glance over at him with my hand on the doorknob, my gaze catching on part of his tattoo that winds over his shoulder from his back. From the quick look I got at it earlier the image that spans his entire back is of a tree with twisting vines and flowers. It's so large that parts of the design curl over his shoulder and onto the tops of his arms.

"I caught the end of his last match up," he says, drawing my attention back to his bright eyes. "He took a hit pretty hard. Good luck."

"Thanks," I say, and then push through the door to find Talon hanging back, waiting for me, and I catch a faint bruise on his left ribs just where Titus said it would be.

Talon is tall and muscular. Not in the same way Becks is, but something tells me he's just as powerful, with or without magic. A ball of lead settles in my gut. I don't want to fight him, and not just because he'll probably beat me. There are other more nebulous reasons too that I don't have the headspace to examine right now.

"It's me and you, Freckles," he says, and I lift my gaze to catch the grim look on his face. "Any chance I can convince you to fake a knockout, so I don't have to do it for real?"

I purse my lips before saying, "No. But I'd be willing to let you fake one, so I don't have to damage your pretty face."

A low chuckle rumbles in his chest and we start toward the

game master, both of us doing our best to ignore the chaos around us.

"I'm impressed," he says. When we reach the cage, the game master is droning on about how the winner of our match will move on to the final battle.

"Impressed that I made it this far because I'm just a small girl?" *And magicless*, I think but don't say.

He shakes his head, his blue-gray eyes never leaving mine. "No. I'm just impressed."

Unwantedly, warmth sparks in my chest. How is it that out of everyone in my life it's Talon, a relative stranger, who makes me think I don't need magic to be powerful? That I'm enough all on my own.

The cage door swings open and Talon gestures for me to go in before him, his movements almost gentlemanly. When I step into the cage I do what I've done the last two battles—I look for Becks —but when I spot him he isn't looking at me, he's glaring at Talon like he wants to gut him.

Talon takes a moment to scan the crowd as well, and as if feeling the heat from Becks' stare the two lock eyes. Becks' mouth doesn't form any words, but his eyes are telling Talon that if he hurts me he's going to pay. Talon's gaze narrows and his mouth flattens into a thin line, breaking eye contact with my best friend. His gaze lands on me just as the ten second countdown begins, and they soften.

The buzzer sounds and we both drop into defensive positions, but neither one of us moves. After several seconds tick by and nothing happens, boos start from the spectators, who are expecting a bigger show.

I should be watching Talon's body for telltale signs he's about to attack, but instead our eyes are locked.

"Fight! Fight! Fight!" the crowd starts to chant, and individual voices filter through the noise as well.

"Take her out!"

"Don't just stand there, do something!"

"You can take him, Locklyn!"

"I didn't come here to watch you two eye screw each other!"

That last comment severs the link between us, and I glance outside the cage, looking for whoever said it. As soon as our gazes disconnect, Talon comes at me, dropping low at the last moment and sweeping my legs out from under me. I hit the hard concrete with a thud but twist out of the way of Talon's follow-up punch. Popping to my feet next to him, I kick out, hitting his hip, and send him staggering back a few feet.

With my hands raised in front of me to defend my face, I bounce on the balls of my feet, a fresh wave of adrenaline surging through me.

Talon takes his time, almost lazily getting back into position. He's not smiling but there's a twinkle in his eye that tells me he wants to.

"Nicely done," he says conversationally.

I narrow my gaze. What's he playing at now?

Talon returns my glare with a look of pure innocence, which from experience means he's anything but.

I don't want to admit it, but the truth is whatever he's doing is working. I get an uncomfortable sense of being off kilter. I need to attack this match differently than the last two. Instinct tells me Talon's stamina is just as good or even better than mine, so trying to wear him out probably won't work, so it's time to change up my M.O.

I attack first, aiming kicks at his knees and ribs so that he's forced to retreat to avoid serious injury. I back Talon up to almost the bars of the cage before he blocks my last kick and then comes at me with a flurry of attacks from both his fists and feet. Some of them connect, but most don't. But the hits that I do take aren't hard. They're like blows I'd expect from a friendly sparring match, not a knockout fight.

Talon's pulling his punches.

But then again, so am I.

We go on like this for several back and forths before the crowd starts to notice neither one of us is really full-out attacking the other. The boos and catcalls start up again, and for the life of me I can't seem to block everything out like I did the last matches.

Getting distracted, I catch Becks' gaze right as Talon comes at me again, sweeping my legs out from underneath me for a second time, but I catch him on my way down and bring him with me, so we end up on the concrete floor grappling with each other.

First he has the upper hand, then I do. Our limbs tangle as we wrestle, and since neither one of us seems to be taking this fight as seriously as we should, the slide of our hands over each other ends up more intimate than aggressive. When wholly uninvited sensations start to trickle through me, I quickly and efficiently slide out of Talon's hold. We both pop to our feet and separate, staring at each other from opposite sides of the spiked cage.

Even though we haven't been going at each other in earnest, we're still slick with sweat from the exertion, and our breaths come out just shy of panting. It gives me a bit of pride to see Talon looking equally winded. But even so, we both know what we're doing isn't battling. It's closer to working out, honing our skills on one another without any intention of inflicting damage.

"Oh, and there's one thing I failed to mention at this part of the trial," the game master says, his rough voice echoing throughout the cavernous space. "From this point forward, if one of the competitors isn't unconscious when the time runs out, then both will be ineligible to win the advantage for the next trial."

A round of cheers raises from the crowd, and Talon flicks an annoyed glance at the game master. We both know he just made that rule up.

Talon and I look at each other with matching looks of resignation, and then as if an opening shot is fired we converge on each other in a flurry of fists and feet. I get a solid jab into his left ribs, which up until now I'd been avoiding, and he clips me on the chin. He knees me in the gut, and I jab him in the side of the head.

It goes on and on between us as the clock ticks down, and even though we're definitely going harder now, we're still not giving it all we've got.

The crowd is a cacophony of sound outside our cage. At one point I think I hear Becks shout, but it's drowned out by all the other noise.

"Thirty seconds remain, and it looks like we might be eliminating two of our most promising fighters of the night," the game master says.

A streak of frustration laced with indecision flashes across Talon's face. Honestly, I don't mind getting eliminated by a draw. At this point neither one of us is going to get eliminated from this Chaos trial. I didn't think I'd get this far, and I'm so worn out that I can't possibly imagine fighting another match after this one anyway. Sitting the rest of the trial out secure in my place as a competitor that's moving on to the next round sounds pretty good to me, but from the look on Talon's face, he doesn't feel the same way. He really wants that advantage.

The crowd starts counting down with twenty seconds left and Talon and I are circling each other. When they get to ten, Talon mouths a curse and with speed he hasn't used on me up until now, he fakes a jab that I dance away from and then somehow he's behind me, one arm wrapped around my chest, rendering my arms useless and securing my body against his.

"I'm sorry about this, Freckles," he says, his breath tickling my ear, and then his free hand slips to the side of my face, almost cradling my head.

I never see the hit or feel the impact, but before I know it my vision goes black.

Sixteen

"I THINK SHE'S COMING TO!" someone shouts, and the sound ricochets in my head like a spiked ball. Even though my eyes are already closed, I squeeze them tighter.

"Lock, hey, how are you feeling?" That voice belongs to Becks, and when I crack my eyelids his face is hovering over mine.

I glance to the side and realize I'm laid out on the ground in the locker room with Becks crouched next to me and several other faces hovering behind him, Shayla and her boyfriend, Owen, and another couple of his dragon shifter friends.

"Lock," he prompts, and my gaze drifts back to him. There's a deep groove between his brows and his eyes look tired.

"Yeah," I croak, my voice rough. I try to sit up and the world spins. "Whoa," I say, and almost tip over, but Becks puts an arm around me and helps me back to a seated position.

"Take it slow," he urges, and I wince. The lights are too bright and the muffled voices coming from behind the door make my ears ring.

"What happened?" I ask while rubbing my eyes.

Becks doesn't respond so I drop my hands and glance over at him. A muscle in his jaw jumps and I swear I can hear his teeth grinding. His eyes go slitted, he shudders, and then a shock of scales flash down his arm before disappearing again.

Whoa. Becks never has issues holding back his shift. He must be furious.

I rack my brain, trying to remember what happened. I was fighting with Talon in the cage, we traded blows, but nothing serious. I may have a few bruises from it tomorrow, but I've been injured worse during sparring at the gym. The time was about to end and then . . . nothing.

"I've got it from here," Becks says to the strangers in the room, and with nods and a few polite words to me about being glad that I'm okay they filter out. "Talon knocked you out," Becks finally grits out once we are alone.

"What? He did?" My mind is a little muddled and I'm light and sound sensitive, but it reminds me more of when I accidentally took too much of my mom's herbal meds for sleeping and woke up the next day with something akin to a hangover. I probe my head with my fingers, but don't come across any sore areas.

"Are you sure?" I ask, and Becks gives me a look like I'm stupid that makes me bristle.

I'm not an idiot. I've been knocked unconscious before. It doesn't happen often, but occasionally things go a little too far in sparring and someone gets hurt. This doesn't feel like that.

"I watched you go unconscious in his arms after he punched you in the temple," Becks says bluntly. The scent of smoke and ash starts to taint the air.

"Huh." I can't think of any other explanation, so I guess he did knock me out. Weird that I don't remember and can't find a sore spot.

With Becks' assistance, I get to my feet. When I sway a little, Becks wraps an arm around my back to steady me. Clamping his hand on my opposite hip, he anchors me against his side. I can't say I mind the contact at all, at least until I remember how sweaty and gross I am.

"So who won?" I ask as I squirm away from his hold.

Becks' nostrils flare, telling me who won before the name even leaves his mouth. "Talon."

"At least I lost to the winner," I say with a shrug as I look for my clothes, which I find neatly folded on a nearby chair.

"Are you kidding?" Becks asks, disgust heavy in his voice. "That's all you're going to say about it?"

"It's not like he jumped me in an alley or anything." I sit down to pull my socks and shoes back on, and then stand with the small bundle of clothes tucked under my arm. "It was a match. He won."

Honestly, I didn't feel too bad, and now that the second trial is over, euphoria that I'd made it through to the next round of Chaos is starting to bubble up inside.

"I don't care if it was the bloody World Cup he was competing for, he still shouldn't have hurt you."

Am I happy Talon knocked me out in our match? No. But I don't hold it against him. Clearly Becks does.

"Let's go," I say, not having the energy to argue with my friend. It's been a long night. All I want right now is to soak in a warm Epsom salt bath. The fuzziness in my head has mostly dissipated, but my muscle and joint soreness hasn't.

Becks clamps his mouth shut and nods.

I'm not two steps out of the room when I hear, "Hey, are you all right?"

When I look over, Talon, who's changed back into his clothes, pushes himself off the wall next to the room and starts toward me. He was obviously waiting for me. I don't get to answer him though. Becks is up in his face before I get a chance to.

"What are you doing here?" he growls.

Talon tries to move around Becks, but Becks isn't having it and blocks him.

A flash of frustration passes over Talon's features. "Look, I'm just checking on Locklyn," he explains. The use of my name rather than Freckles sounds weird to me.

"You don't get to do that after you're the one who hurt her," Becks says, and Talon visibly flinches.

I grab Becks' bicep and try to tug him away from Talon, but Becks is a brick wall and doesn't budge.

"Becks, it's fine," I say, still tugging on his arm.

His head snaps in my direction. "The hell it is."

His slitted pupils are back, and I have a bad feeling that if I don't deescalate the situation soon, a fight is going to break out. And there have already been too many of those for one night.

I sigh, weariness seeping into my bones. "I'm leaving."

Turning, I walk in the other direction, hoping Becks will follow. My body is tense until I hear the slap of Becks' shoes against the concrete floor a few seconds later as he jogs to catch up with me. Without a word he drops an arm over my shoulder, something he does on occasion, and it always makes butterflies flap in my stomach when he does. But tonight I don't fool myself into thinking it's anything more than what it is: a message to Talon to stay away from me.

THE NEXT MORNING my chin is a lovely shade of green and a purple smudge is starting to grow high on my cheek. Interestingly, I don't have any bruising on my temple where Talon knocked me out. It's surprisingly easy to explain away my injuries the next day to my parents. Their eyes bulge when they see me, but I tell them I sparred at the gym, they nod, and that's the end of it.

Part of me hates how easy it's been to lie to them over Chaos and the trials, but another part of me is glad about it. I mollify myself by remembering that even if I want to tell the truth, I can't.

The magical gag from the first night is still in place. I know because I tested it out a time or two and the moment I start to say anything about Chaos, my throat freezes and the words won't come.

It's not until I get to school the next day that I realize the world has flipped upside-down. I don't even make it to the main entrance before classmates start to swarm me.

"Hey, Locklyn, great show last night."

"Locklyn, where did you learn to fight like that?"

"Do you think maybe sometime you can show me that two-punch move you used to put Jules down?"

My eyes bug out as students I didn't even think knew I existed come up to me, calling my name and acting like we're old friends. It's weird.

After giving my Peet's Gym information to a lower classman who said she wants to start learning some self-defense, I look up and catch Talon staring at me from the parking lot in front of the main academy building. Wearing faded jeans and a dark tee, he stands with his arms crossed over his chest as he leans up against a black sports car. He's wearing a knit cap like the first time I saw him, and strands of his dark hair curl around the front edge. The hem of his t-shirt has ridden up, exposing a sliver of skin that only gives a peek at what I now know is a washboard stomach.

I won't lie and say he doesn't look good. I try not to think too much of the way my stomach dips when our eyes connect. Even though he was the ultimate winner on yesterday, he surprisingly doesn't have a swarm of well-wishers mobbing him like I do.

He nods once, and then waves me over. My feet are moving before I realize I've made the decision to go to him. I only get a half dozen steps before I'm tackled by a blur of blonde and pink streaked hair.

"I can't believe I wasn't there last night," Ensley says, looping her arm in mine and dragging me away from Talon and back toward school.

Ensley called me late last night and wouldn't let me go to bed until I'd given her a detailed blow-by-blow of the trial. She was super disappointed to miss it and made me recount my match with Jules twice.

"It's all anyone can talk about," Ensley goes on, oblivious to how she blocked me from going to Talon, but that's just as well. "Well, it's all that the kids that *can* talk about it are doing at least. Since the gag magic prevents so many of us from openly talking about Chaos at home, I think everyone is extra excited to spill at school. But seriously, you're like, semi-famous now. How does it feel?" she asks with a grin after someone high fives me the moment we step into the building.

"Umm, weird," I answer honestly, then look up to see Becks cutting his way through the throng of students toward us. My heart skips a beat at the intensity of his gaze.

Ensley is still chatting away next to me, but I'm not listening. The world has fallen away and my focus narrows in on Becks as he nears.

When he's finally standing in front of me, I'm a little breathless. His gaze dances over my face, checking every inch of it. I did my best to cover my bruises, but from the frown on Becks' face it's clear the makeup isn't doing its job. I should have asked Ensley to glamour them away until they have a chance to fade.

"How are you doing?" he asks, his voice a little huskier than usual.

"I'm fine," I answer truthfully. A couple of bruises are nothing to worry about, nor are they new for me.

Lifting a hand, Becks runs a thumb over the discoloration on my cheekbone. His touch is gentle, reverent, and I have a sudden urge to close my eyes and lean into his palm. My lids lazily drop to half-mast as something flares in the depths of Becks' eyes.

I hold my breath, here in the middle of the academy halls with classmates passing and watching, but not caring if we have an audience or not because this moment between the two of us is too potent, too heady, too strong to be bothered by something so insignificant.

"Freckles," Talon says quietly in greeting as he walks by me, and the spell is broken.

Becks' gaze instantly shifts to Talon and darkens, his whole face souring. When Talon passes, Becks twists to glare at his retreating form the whole way down the hall until he turns the corner and disappears from view.

"I don't like that guy," Becks says unnecessarily. He was pretty clear about his dislike for Talon the night before, and even if he hadn't been, it's written so plainly on his face that I'd have to be blind not to see it.

I frown when Becks' gaze swings back to me, still darkened from thoughts of Talon. Becks never took to Talon when he started classes at Nightlark Academy a couple weeks ago, but the slight annoyance he had for him seemed to have twisted into a deep-seated hate overnight. It's clear what happened in the fighting cages tipped the scales, but unlike Becks I still don't blame Talon for what he had to do. At least not in the same way Becks does. Sure, I was annoyed he didn't just finish out the match in a draw so we'd both be ineligible for the advantage, but for whatever reason he really wants Shadow Striker and probably felt he needed the leg up on the next trial. I'm the one who really needed the advantage, but if anything I'm annoyed at myself for not giving my match with Talon my all. And that's not his fault. It's mine.

The warning bell rings, signaling we'd better get to class soon.

"See you at lunch?" Ensley asks, and I start. Between Becks and Talon I'd actually forgotten she was still standing there.

"Yeah," Becks says distractedly, twisting to look down the hallway in the direction Talon went.

"I'm off," I say with a wave to Ensley, and turn to head toward my first class.

"Wait up," Becks says and catches up with me quickly. "I'll walk you to class."

"Oh, okay." That's different.

All eyes are on Becks and me as he walks me to class. It makes me uncomfortable to suddenly have so much attention. He drops me off, and then after class lets out he's waiting for me again with his shoulder leaned up against a locker on the other side of the hall. I have no idea how he got out of class early to meet me, but Becks is a natural charmer so it's not too surprising. The rest of the day goes similarly, with Becks taking me to and picking me up from each and every class, and lunch as well. When I ask him what he's doing, he just shrugs and says he feels like it.

But Becks' sudden overly attentive behavior isn't the only weird thing about the day. The phenomenon in the parking lot with my classmates continues with creatures coming up to me at my locker, asking to sit near me in classes, and staring at me with smiles and curious eyes rather than hate-filled scowls.

Well, that's how most of the students act. I catch Jules glaring at me in the hallway between fourth and fifth period. Since I'm with Becks she doesn't say anything or make a move against me, but her stare is like a burning brand on my back as I shuffle through the crowded hallways, reminding me that I might have bested her once, but she wasn't going to let it happen again. I know Jules well enough to know she's not going to let a slight like this go unpunished. And outside the cages she still has a giant advantage over me. Magic.

By the time my last class lets out, my head is throbbing with the start of what I fear will turn into a monster headache. I'm not used to having to interact with anyone other than Ensley and Becks throughout the school day, so I'm on overload. That's at least my excuse for the temporary insanity that prompts me to slip into the underground tunnels when Becks isn't waiting for me after class. I just need a few moments to myself.

I haven't set foot in the tunnels since my run-in with Jules several weeks before, and for good reason. They're just as dangerous to me now as they were then, but desperation overrides my logic, and I can't bring myself to be sorry for it. The silence is a balm to my soul, and my headache starts to subside as the tension leaks from my muscles. Hopefully Becks will understand that I needed a few minutes to myself and won't be mad at me for not waiting for him.

I'm about halfway to my destination when an overarching sense of foreboding drips down my spine, like wax sliding down a lit candle. Turning, I strain my eyes in the low light, trying to see if anyone else is here, and then drop into a defensive pose when the crunch of rocks beneath someone's feet echoes off the walls.

With my arms up in front of me, ready to strike out, or run if need be, I wait for the attacker to show themselves, silently cursing myself for my stupidity. A shadow moves farther down the tunnel, and I swallow a scream.

"Whoa there, I come in peace," Talon says as he emerges from the darkness with his hands raised in mock surrender.

My body sags in relief, my muscles untensing as I drop my guard. "Don't you know it's rude to creep up on someone?" I ask tartly, embarrassed that I'd reacted so fearfully in the first place.

"Sorry about that." He swipes his knit hat off and runs a hand through his hair before placing it back on his head. Is Talon . . . nervous? "I saw you slip into the tunnels after class. I was hoping to talk to you without your guard dog."

"My guard dog?"

One side of Talon's mouth quirks up in a lopsided grin. "Oh, yeah. Why do you think your pal Becks has been trailing you all day if not to keep me away? If I even look in your direction he growls at me."

I roll my eyes. He's exaggerating. "Becks isn't my guard dog."

Talon chuckles, the sound vibrating off the stone enclosure and resonating in my chest. I shift, slightly uncomfortable with the shiver that trails down my spine and the goose bumps that pop out on my arms.

"You might want to tell him that," Talon says, oblivious to my internal conflict. "Whenever I see him near you, he looks about two seconds away from pissing a circle around you to claim his territory."

I scrunch my nose at the unwanted image of Becks peeing. *Ew.* I could have lived a lifetime without that imagery.

"Did you really have to go there?" I ask, and Talon's grin grows.

"You're picturing it, aren't you?"

Rather than answer, I brush past him and another round of deep laughter bursts from Talon. I tense up rather than allow another involuntary shudder to take me over again.

So I think the sound of his chuckles are a little sexy. So what? Lots of guys have attractive qualities. It doesn't mean anything.

Silent footsteps bring Talon shoulder to shoulder with me. "Seriously though," he says, his voice far more reverent than it was a moment before. "I wanted to make sure you were okay. You know, after the trials last night. I feel really bad about what went down. I hope you know I never wanted to hurt you."

I glance at him out of the corner of my eye. Most of his face is hidden in shadows, but I can make out the frown on his downcast face. He's either an extremely good actor or truly sorry. Out of nowhere I start to wonder what creature he is. I still haven't figured it out, but I suppose it doesn't really matter.

I wave a hand in the air. "You were just playing the game. It is a competition after all." I don't hold anything against Talon, so there's no need for his apologies.

He nods, looking relieved that I get it.

"Besides," I continue, "the way I figure it, now we're even."

Talon quirks a brow. "How so?"

"I was holding back last night. I basically let you win."

I expect him to scoff, but he doesn't. "I could tell," he says without boasting that he was holding back as well, because I know he was. "You're a wicked fighter. Thanks for doing me a solid," he says with a straight face.

It warms me a little that Talon recognizes my skills.

"Well, just don't expect me to bail you out a second time," I say jokingly. "It was a one-off. Shadow Striker is my meal ticket, and I don't plan on just handing it over to you."

"Freckles, with you I'm learning to expect the unexpected." His gaze connects with mine and an electric charge seems to pass between us. It's confusing.

We reach the exit to the hallway closest to the parking lot and Talon reaches in front of me to open the door for me, and then steps back to let me pass. It's a narrow space and my shoulder brushes up against his chest as I slide in front of him. I hear him take a quick breath, but when I look back he doesn't look affected in the least.

"What are you doing?" a voice bellows, and I spin to find Becks standing there, his hands clenched and the scent of smoke and ash lingering in the air.

"Becks, I was just—" I sense Talon come up behind me. Becks' eyes flare and go slitted. Reaching out, he clamps his hands on my arms and hauls me toward him.

"Take another step forward and I'll show you what it's like to fight a dragon shifter. I promise I won't go easy on you like she did last night."

"Becks!" I shove out of his embrace, glaring at him, but Becks doesn't even notice because his gaze is fastened on Talon.

When I look over at Talon I expect to see mischief in his eyes. He seems to love revving Becks up, but all I read on him is wary resignation.

"Look—" he starts, but Becks doesn't let him get any further than that before dropping a shoulder and rushing him.

"Becks, no!" I scream as my friend plows into Talon, slamming him back against the closed door we just emerged from. The wood behind Talon groans and a crack appears.

Before I can reach them, Becks buries a fist in Talon's gut that doubles him over before releasing him to step back.

"You think you can talk to her after what you did?" Becks says, his voice filled with barely contained rage.

What's happening right now? This isn't Becks. He doesn't lose it like this. Becks is the most controlled creature I know.

Talon coughs once and then rights himself, his gaze flicking to me before returning to my best friend. "I get what she means to you, so I'll let you have that one. But you need to back off. I don't want to fight you, but if you come at me again you won't like how this ends."

There aren't many students left in the halls, but the ones who are around come running to check out the commotion. I don't take my eyes off Becks or Talon to figure out who's watching.

Becks takes an aggressive step toward Talon, but Talon doesn't even flinch.

"I mean it," Talon says, and his voice has gone deadly calm.

Becks points a finger in Talon's face, inches from touching him. "You don't *talk* to her, you don't *look* at her, you don't *breathe* in her direction."

I gasp. What does he think he's doing?

Stomping forward, I stop next to the two of them as they face off against each other.

"Becks, stop!" I order, but he doesn't even acknowledge me, and that makes me furious. "You don't get to decide that for me," I say through clenched teeth, quiet enough so that my voice doesn't carry, but strong enough that I know they both hear me. "Talon was just playing the game. He wasn't trying to hurt me on purpose."

Becks' nostrils flare and he looks down at me. "All that matters is that he *did* hurt you, and for that he has to pay."

I rear back. *What is going on right now?* I've been hurt both physically and emotionally by plenty of creatures over the years. Becks was always upset about it, even furious at times, but he never reacted like this. This reaction is extreme, and bringing out a side of him I didn't even know existed.

Whatever is going on with him, I'm not going to just roll over because he's flexing his muscles. I've told Becks time and time again I need to start fighting my own battles, and if that includes standing up to him, so be it.

"Talon's my friend," I say, stretching the truth. I wouldn't actually consider him a friend, more of a reluctant acquaintance, but that doesn't roll off the tongue quite as well. "I won't have you going all macho dragon heir on him. We're in a competition. Creatures are going to get hurt. You need to deal with the fact that you can't protect me from the world."

Becks flinches like I hit him, and my heart pricks, but I force myself to stay hard.

"I won't allow this guy around you."

"It's not your choice," I snap back.

"Locklyn," he says, reaching for me, but I jerk away, and since I'm looking him straight in the eyes I can see exactly how much that hurts him.

"You're making a mistake," he says, his face hardening once again.

"Maybe, but it's my mistake to make."

Becks regards me silently, his gaze skipping over my face, and I'm not sure what he reads there.

"Fine," he finally bites out, and with a final glare at Talon he spins and stalks in the other direction, taking the scent of fire and ash with him.

"Well, Freckles, I thought saving me was a one-off?" Talon jokes from behind me, but I don't turn to look at him. Instead I watch my best friend stomp down the hall, feeling like a little part of my heart is being torn from my chest with every step he takes away from me.

I know that needed to happen, but it still hurts.

"I'll try not to make it a habit," I say absentmindedly, only barely noticing the small crowd that had gathered starting to disperse.

Talon sighs. "I know that wasn't easy for you, but he'll come around. He can't stay mad at you. He just needs some time to cool off."

The words feel hollow. Like something you tell someone to make them feel better in a situation like this, but I nod anyway, hoping he's right.

Seventeen

"MY BROTHER IS AN IDIOT," Ensley says as we lie side-by-side on her bed Saturday evening, staring up at the glow-in-the-dark stars we stuck on her ceiling when we were eight that she never bothered to take down. We put stars on Becks' ceiling as well, but he took them down ages ago.

"If you're expecting me to disagree with you, you're going to be waiting a long time," I say.

I haven't spoken to Becks since our public disagreement in the halls of Nightlark the day before, so I'm firmly in the Becks-is-an-idiot club as well, but as I turn my head to look at her I wonder what pushed her to become a member.

Ensley huffs out a frustrated breath. "He's an overbearing boar who's too stubborn to see he's ruining his life. Talking to him is like talking to a brick wall lately."

I don't disagree with that, but old habits die hard so I can't stop myself from defending him. "He has a lot going on right now. Especially with the dragon heir and council stuff."

I was hopeful when Becks finally told his sister about the arranged life-mating that she'd be able to help, but according to her she'd gotten nowhere with her parents, and Becks refuses to talk about it with her. So as of now, Shadow Striker isn't my fallback plan, it's the only plan. But things have been so up and down with Becks lately, I'm no longer confident that he'd even want to be paired with me rather than some random girl.

Flipping over on her stomach, Ensley stares at me, her green eyes probing. "Can we be honest with each other for a minute?"

My stomach drops. "What do you mean? I'm always honest with you."

The look Ensley shoots me says she doesn't believe that's true, but besides my feelings for her brother, I've never been anything but completely truthful with her, so I don't know why she's looking at me like that.

When she says, "What about the fact that you have the hots for my brother?" I'm so surprised that I jackknife to a sitting position.

"What are you talking about?" I say, my heart already beating double-time.

"Come on, Locklyn, it's been obvious for ages. I haven't brought it up because I've been waiting for you to talk to me about it. But since you haven't . . ." She splays her hands as if to say, "Here we are."

"I don't know why you would think—" I start, feeling my face reddening.

"He likes you too," she says, cutting me off and stunning me into silence.

We stare at each other for a few bloated moments. Me processing. Her waiting for me to finally spill my guts.

"Why do you think that?" I tentatively ask, and a grin spreads across her face.

Popping to her feet, she points a finger at me. "Ha! I knew it!"

I groan and cover my face with my hands. This is so embarrassing. And awkward.

"You guys should just kiss and get it over with," she says, making me groan again. "Wait, have you already kissed?"

She leans toward me, and I do my impression of a deer in headlights.

"You have?"

"No," I say quickly, while my wily friend interprets every micro expression that flits across my face.

"But you almost did," she says, a smirk curving the corners of her mouth. "When? How did it happen? I want all the deets."

"We didn't kiss, but we did have . . . a moment. At the Chaos party in Deepseat Caverns. It happened when the lights went out."

She gasps. "I was right there. How did I miss that?"

"Probably because you were occupied by a specific bandmate you've sworn up and down you're not interested in?" I answer with a smirk of my own.

She rolls her eyes. "Konan is cute, but he's just a friend. There's no spark there, ya know? I'd tell you if there were." Ensley is a beautiful girl and has guys after her all the time, yet she rarely dates. Sometimes I worry she's holding back because of me. Like she doesn't want to jump into a relationship when I'm so utterly and completely without prospects, but she holds fast to the story that she's just waiting for the right guy. "Back to you and Becks. You guys have been dancing around each other for years. Everyone sees it. The only thing I don't understand is why it hasn't happened yet."

"It's complicated."

"You don't say," she says as she plops down on the bed beside me.

"I can't talk to you about this."

"Why?" she says, looking genuinely confused.

"Because you're his *sister*. It's weird."

"Is that the reason you've been avoiding talking to me about it?"

"Well . . . pretty much."

She waves me off. "Whatever. It's not that big of a deal. Besides, I love him, and I love you. Who else would I want to see my brother with than my best friend?"

I scrunch my nose. I don't have any siblings, but if I did have a twin brother I don't think I'd want to see Ensley coupling up with him. But I guess as long as she's cool with it, I shouldn't worry about it.

"Nothing would make me happier than to see you both happy together," she stresses.

"Did you forget about the arranged life-mate issue?" I say, reminding her of the biggest hurdle. In a few months Becks will be pledged to another female and then eventually life-mated. He's been very vocal about not wanting to date or have a girlfriend in the meantime.

Ensley's face falls and anger lights her green gaze. "I have a mind to hunt down those council members and give them a piece of my mind."

"You could, but what good would that do?"

"It would make me feel better."

"But it wouldn't change Becks' situation."

"No, it wouldn't," she admits. "You know what we need to do?"

I shake my head. I truly don't or I would have done it already.

"We need to find out why the council wants Becks to mate so early. If we knew why they were pushing for it, then maybe we could change their minds."

"But how are we going to find that out? Dragon shifters are notoriously private about their internal politics." As soon as the words are out of my mouth, I remember the law text I borrowed from the Emporium.

"Or, I have a better idea," Ensley says with a grin. "We blackmail the council into holding off. Or better yet, changing that rule altogether. It's antiquated and outdated. The dragon heir should be able to pick his own life-mate."

I almost choke on nothing. "You want to blackmail some of the most powerful dragon shifters on the planet?"

She shrugs like it's no big deal. "There's little I wouldn't do for my family. And just for the record, that includes you."

I love her. "Same."

"Besides, we don't need to blackmail all of them. We only need to get one on board and then let him or her convince the rest."

"I can't believe I'm considering this."

"But you are."

I nod. "Yes, I am. It's crazy, but it might just work. You really are an evil mastermind, you know that?"

She fluffs her hair. "Yeah, I know." She takes so much pride in the title it makes me laugh.

"Okay, if we're going to brainstorm, I'm going to need sustenance."

"The energy drinks and chips are where they always are," she says, knowing exactly what I want.

"Be right back," I say, and hop off her bed and slip out of the room to hit up the extra fridge in their six-car garage, and then head to the kitchen and grab a bag of potato chips. With my arms loaded, I turn to leave the kitchen and find Becks standing in the doorway in low slung gray joggers and a black t-shirt tight around his arms, the bottom half of his dragon tattoo visible. He looks good, too good, and my mouth goes dry as he stares at me with an unreadable expression on his face.

"Becks," I say, my heart beating in my throat.

I've been in this kitchen with Becks hundreds, maybe thousands of times before, but never with the air so charged as it is now.

His gaze slides over me and I swear I feel it like a physical caress.

"I'm hanging out with Ensley," I say unnecessarily. "I just felt like a snack." I hold up the drink and chips as if he can't already see them in my hands.

"Yeah, okay," he says, and then slowly walks toward me, his gaze never leaving my face.

I should leave, I really should, but my feet are rooted in place.

He comes to a stop right in front of me, close enough that the heat coming off his body brushes against me and I can count the dark flecks in his green eyes.

"I'm feeling like something salty too," he says, and ever so slowly reaches over my shoulder to open the cabinet door behind me where they store their junk food. I shift back to give him more space until my lower spine bumps into the counter and I can't retreat any farther.

With his gaze still locked with mine, he stretches up to grab something on the top shelf, which brings him even closer.

Gah. He smells amazing.

His shirt rides up to reveal a sliver of tight abs, and then his chest brushes my shoulder before he backs away with a bag of pretzels in his hand.

My skin is tight and over-sensitized, and I can't stop myself from imagining him running his palms up my arms. I try to remind myself that I'm still mad at him, but my body doesn't seem to care.

One of us should be leaving right now, but neither of us move an inch. We just stand there staring at each other. Me with a bag of chips and an energy drink clutched to my chest, and Becks with a bag of pretzels clenched in his hand.

"I'm sorry," he says quietly. "I should have never tried to dictate who you could see or talk to." He sighs. "The beast inside just goes nuts lately when it comes to you. I'm finding it harder to control myself. I don't know why."

With his free hand, he tucks a strand of my hair behind my ear, gently trailing his knuckles down my throat before pulling away.

My mind goes completely blank. All I can concentrate on are the sensations he just brought forth with that single light touch. I lick my lower lip, my hands starting to shake with how badly I want to grab his face and bring him closer. His gaze drops to my mouth and just like in the caverns, I think that's what he wants as well.

Someone clears their throat and I start, dropping the chips and drink. The can explodes when it hits the hardwood floor, shooting sticky sugary liquid all over the floor, cabinets, and Becks' and my legs.

Becks quickly grabs some paper towels and starts mopping up the mess, and I turn to see Ensley standing with her hands on her hips. "I was checking to see if you got lost," she says with a barely contained smile that makes the corners of her mouth twitch.

"Um, no." Of course I didn't get lost. She's fully aware that I know their house as well as my own.

I pull some paper towels from the roll on the counter and drop to help Becks. We don't look at each other as we soak up the sticky mess, and when we're done he grabs his pretzels and turns to leave.

He tries to go around Ensley, but she steps in front of him, forcing him to stop. "Listen," she says in her authoritative sister voice, "we need to talk."

He cocks his head, scowling at her. "I'm sure it can wait."

She plants a hand on his chest when he tries to skirt her again. "It really can't," she says.

Over the next fifteen minutes, Ensley explains our plan to Becks, and they bicker back and forth about it. At first, Becks is furious that we'd come up with such a hairbrained and dangerous scheme, but as his sister banters with him, I watch his resolve crumble. This is the most progress I've seen Becks make with this whole arranged life-mating thing.

Finally, Ensley throws down the gauntlet. "Do you really want to pledge the rest of your life to some random creature that a group of old dudes pick out for you just because she's powerful?" she asks, and I don't miss that Becks' gaze flicks to mine before returning to his sister.

With his lips pressed into a thin line, he slowly shakes his head.

"That's what I thought," she says smugly. "Now sit your butt down and help us figure out how to dig up some dirt on the dragon council members."

Eighteen

EVEN THOUGH WE plot well into the night, we don't come up with anything concrete, but I still feel better with a semi-solid plan in place. The two key components are to dig up some dirt on at least one of the council members and figure out why they are pushing Becks to mate so early. If we can work out their motives, we might come up with a way to change their minds. And if that doesn't work we'll have the blackmail to fall back on.

Up until now Becks has always been completely respectful of dragon shifter secrecy, but the pressure of the arranged life-mating hanging over his head is too much for him, and he finally cracks. I tell them about the book I "borrowed" from the Emporium. I've already been over it from front to back and can't think of anything that will help the situation, but Becks says he's going to try to "borrow" more material to research.

Things don't exactly go back to normal between Becks and me over the next couple of weeks, but I'm starting to wonder if maybe that's not a bad thing. It's almost impossible to ignore the charged space between us whenever we are together. Becks still walks me to and from my classes, and it doesn't go unnoticed by fellow classmates. I'm no longer treated like a pariah by the general student body. Our lunch ritual has also changed. Shayla and her boyfriend,

Owen, now sit with us most days. The initial interest after the last trial also cools off to a normal amount of attention, so I'm still adjusting but not as overwhelmed throughout the day.

I haven't talked to Talon since the day Becks tried to fight him, but I sometimes catch his eye from across the hallway or courtyard at lunch. His face is usually thoughtful, and when he notices me staring back, he doesn't look away. Becks still tenses anytime he spots Talon but doesn't say or do anything. I know he's secretly pleased I haven't talked to him though, and I tell myself I'm not purposefully staying away from Talon because of Becks, but that's pretty much a lie.

The Chaos tracker has remained suspiciously quiet for almost a full two weeks. Life seems to be settling into a new normal, and if it wasn't for the lack of progress we've made in Becks' life-mating issue, I'd say I was something close to content.

Just like Mr. Brone said, I haven't been able to find any more literature about Shadow Striker, but the information he told me when I visited his shop settles my reservations about being able to use Shadow Striker safely. Even so, I'm starting to think that maybe I don't need Shadow Striker after all. What I wanted from the dagger was to get respect from other creatures and stand on my own two feet, but maybe that's something I can accomplish without magic. But every day that ticks by without getting Becks out from underneath the arranged life-mating makes me want to hold on to Shadow Striker as a backup plan.

I'm sitting next to Ensley in Elemental Chemistry when the tracker buzzes in my bag on the floor between us. We both look down at my bag and then look up at each other.

Check it, she mouths to me, but I give a quick shake of my head. It's been so long since the last trial, I let go of my anxiety around Chaos, but the moment the tracker went off it all came rushing back, making me realize I'd been lulled into a false sense of security.

The tracker buzzes again, this time louder, attracting the gazes of several other students. When it goes off a third time and the teacher turns to the class with a look of suspicion, I grab my bag and head to the door, shouting something about a bathroom emergency that makes most of the class snicker.

Whatever. I can be embarrassed about that later.

Ducking into the bathroom down the hall, I dig through my bag and yank out the tracker, which stops buzzing when I touch it. Good to know this thing is going to keep going off in the future until I check it.

On the screen is another set of coordinates and a time. Midnight. There's no date and I think that means it's tonight, which is going to suck because it's a school night. The last trial was also during the week, but not in the middle of the night. I'm going to have to sneak out, because as cool as my parents are, they're not going to be okay with me heading out so late.

I stuff the tracker back in my bag and leave the bathroom, preparing to return to class, when I spot Talon standing across the hall. He's leaning against a locker, studying what I think is his Chaos tracker in his hand. His hair flops over his forehead and there's a frown on his face. There's only the two of us in the hallway, so I can't pretend I don't see him, especially when he snaps his head up and finds me walking right by him.

"Freckles," he says, and shoves his tracker into his jeans pocket.

"Hey," I reply, stopping in front of him. I gesture toward the tracker he just put away. "Looks like we're going to be out late tonight."

He runs a hand through his hair and sighs. "Yeah."

"Not looking forward to another trial?"

He gives me a half-smile. "I'm just ready for this to all be over."

I nod like I understand, and to an extent I do. I wouldn't mind fast forwarding to the end of Chaos myself, but the way Talon said it makes me think he's talking about more than just the competition, but I don't have anything to base that on except the touch of weariness in his voice.

"Well . . . I'd better get back to class."

"Yeah," he agrees, but doesn't make a move to leave, so with an awkward wave I step away from him. I'm halfway down the hall when he calls after me. "Good luck tonight, Freckles."

I look back over my shoulder, ready to offer him the same platitudes when he adds, "And remember to watch your back," before shoving off the locker and taking off in the other direction.

A pit opens up in my stomach as I stare at his back until he rounds the corner and disappears from view. I can't help but wonder if that was a warning to watch my back against him or the other competitors. Either way it's advice I plan to heed.

Nineteen

THE CHAOS TRACKER leads us to a natural stone amphitheater nestled into the foothills of Jagged Mountain about forty minutes outside of Everton. It's a popular spot in the summer to have outdoor concerts but is mostly abandoned the rest of the year. I've never been there before, but pictures of the structure and large jutting stones around the perimeter make the area look like a sunken stadium with tiered seating in a semi-circle around a flat rock stage.

Becks, Ensley, and I spill out of Becks' truck and follow the crowd toward the stone structure ahead. There is only one way in, and we can't see much until right before we pass through the noise-canceling barrier that knocks out our cell phones.

The music blares and lights flash off the rock face of the amphitheater, making the atmosphere just as chaotic as the last two Chaos trials. Becks moves closer to me, keeping a light hand on the small of my back as the three of us weave through the crowd, looking for a chill spot to wait out the start of the trial. We finally stop off to the side with our backs to the stone.

Becks stares at the large screens set up on the stage and sprinkled throughout the perimeter of the space with a frown on his face. I want to say something to ease his concern, but what is there to say? I don't have any idea what I'm walking into any more than he does.

I had a hard time sneaking out tonight because my parents stayed up later than usual, so we only arrived a handful of minutes before midnight. We don't have to wait long until the trial starts. I'm not surprised when the music and lights cut, but I am surprised when the screens around the venue tell the Chaos competitors to follow the path out of the amphitheater. I don't know what that means until Ensley points out the bioluminescent trail that's visible now that the lights are doused.

"You've got this," she says, and then gives me a quick hug.

Becks' frown deepens when I look at him. I go to turn without saying anything, but he yanks me into his arms and gives me a hard hug.

"Give them hell," he says into my ear before releasing me, and I nod, turning quickly before I lose my nerve.

I follow the other Chaos competitors up and out of the amphitheater and along the faint blue line guiding us. It looks like glow-in-the-dark paint of some sort, and it takes us on a trail that leads up the foothills and into a sparsely wooded area. The trees get denser the longer we climb. I catch Talon's dark head in front of me, but for the most part I keep my gaze down and don't talk to anyone as we go. I can't help feeling like the other competitors are sizing me up the whole walk.

We travel for a solid fifteen minutes before the glowing line stops at a circle of torches and we all shuffle into the space and wait. As soon as the final competitor steps into the ring, mist starts to fill the area around the circle, making it hard to see beyond the torches. It doesn't pass beyond the torch line though, making it obvious it's not a natural mist, but magical in nature.

The mist and the torches that cast flickering lights around the space add an eerier touch to the already tense night. I glance around to distract myself. It's too soon in the season for the white-barked aspen trees to have leaves, so it's easy to spot the blinking red lights of the cameras that are broadcasting the trial to the spectators back at the amphitheater in the branches above and around us. I also notice a large black box suspended between the trees in the middle of the circle.

There's a light murmur in the air as some of the competitors converse with each other in hushed voices. There were over a hundred competitors who entered Chaos, sixty who battled in the cages, but there are only forty of us left now. I still don't know everyone's name, but the faces are all now familiar. Jules stands a ways off to my left, talking with a fae from our school. Titus, the white-haired fae who tried to warn me about Talon's weakness in the last trial, stands off to the side, his gaze assessing as it runs over the space and our fellow competitors. I accidentally catch the eye of Kiaro, the snake shifter who I bested in the cage. He sticks out his forked tongue and licks his lower lip and blows me a kiss. My stomach rolls and I hope that whatever we are going to be forced to do, I can keep my distance from him.

I'm looking for Talon when the robed game master appears seemingly out of thin air right outside the ring of torches. The competitors on that side move out of the way, falling silent when he steps into the space.

"The third trial will be a battle not of strength or wit, but of will," the game master announces, his voice carrying through the wooded clearing and over all the Chaos competitors.

That doesn't sound too bad. I'll take a battle of wills over magic any day. But the game master isn't finished, and his next words make my blood run cold.

"Each one of you will be compelled to do three separate tasks. Your job will be to resist that compulsion by any means necessary. Only those who can resist the compulsion will move forward in the competition."

Competitors shift uncomfortably, many of their gazes fearful. Even the vampires, who surely have an advantage during this trial, look displeased by this turn of events. Besides the obvious hesitation over having someone take away your autonomy, compulsion is illegal. Yes, it's used occasionally, but only in very specific and pre-approved situations.

For years, centuries actually, vampires were shunned out of fear of their ability to compel creatures to do things against their will. In modern society, all creatures are integrated, but if anything still holds a stigma it's vampire compulsion. It's a serious crime for someone to be found guilty of compelling another, even if the deed seems harmless, so who could they have found to break the law so openly?

As soon as the question forms in my mind, a group of figures appear in the mist, covered from head to toe in black robes similar to the game master's. And also like the game master their faces are fully concealed by both the hood of their robes and also magical means. They fan out around the perimeter, just outside the ring of torches, encircling the competitors.

Even though there's no way to see Becks, I can almost feel his concern and anxiety reaching out to me from back at the amphitheater. Or maybe it's just my imagination running away from me?

A nervous energy permeates the air. Nobody looks happy. Even Jules has the sense to look nervous. I search for Talon, finding him tucked into the shadows off to the side. His face is hard as stone and his body rigid. The way he's glaring at the game master makes me think that nothing would please him more than to be able to attack the robed figure, but Talon doesn't look nervous like the rest of us, he just looks pissed off.

As I watch him, Talon's head turns toward me and our gazes lock. I'm used to a reassuring smirk or nod from him, but I don't get that this time. Instead he just stares back at me, an empty look in his eyes that doesn't do anything to help my nerves.

"The only exception during this trial is for the winner of the last, who earned an advantage." Talon's gaze shifts back toward the game master. "That competitor will only have to fight off two compulsions rather than three."

Competitors around me start to grumble, disappointed that they hadn't won the advantage for themselves, but they quiet down when the game master makes a motion and the black box suspended in the trees above opens, dumping its contents.

Horror sinks in when I see the weapons littering the middle of the circle. My dread only grows as I start cataloging the items: knives, hatchets, bows, guns, swords, nails, hammers, rope.

I squeeze my eyes shut, cutting off my view of the plethora of weapons.

"Let the trial begin," the game master says, and then retreats from the circle, melting into the mist.

"This is insane. I'm not doing this," someone shouts, and then a tall black-haired girl runs for the edge of the circle.

She doesn't make it far. The moment she tries to pass the ring of torches, the sleeve of her shirt catches fire and instantly spreads up her arm. She screams and tries to douse the flame, but her flailing only makes the fire spread faster. My eyes widen in horror as the flames lick at her face and the girl's hair catches fire.

"Drop on the ground," I yell, as I sprint toward her when no one else moves to help.

It only takes me a few seconds to reach her, and when I do I don't hesitate tackling her to the ground and forcing her to roll. She's crying hysterically, but the fire finally goes out. When she looks up at me her cheek is black and bubbled and most of the hair has burned away from the right side of her head. Her arm from her wrist to her shoulder is badly burned as well. I can only hope that for her sake this girl is a creature who heals quickly.

"You're okay," I say, but my voice wobbles.

She nods as she cries, and as I help her to her feet the warning about not being able to self-eliminate out of Chaos rings in my mind. I'm sure I'm not the only competitor who's thinking about that right now.

"I can help her with the pain," a voice says, and when I turn, Mia, a fierce blonde vampire from Nightlark, is standing next to us.

The girl shrinks away from her in fear, but I understand where the vampire is coming from. We're all about to be compelled anyway, and the magical gag is going to prevent anyone from reporting her for compulsion. What she's offering the girl is a mercy.

I look back at the burned girl, who's shaking her head while silent tears stream down her cheeks.

"Are you sure?" I ask the burned girl. "It might be the only way you make it through this trial."

"No, no compulsion," she says, and backs away from both me and Mia, finding a tree and then sliding to the ground, slowly rocking herself.

Looking back at Mia, I say, "Thanks for offering." She just shrugs and moves to the other side of the circle.

I don't know what to think as I wait for the trial to officially begin, but I move as far away as I can from the cache of weapons sitting in the middle of the ring. I don't bother sizing up my fellow competitors. They aren't my enemies tonight. Seconds tick by and then minutes. The only sounds in the ring are the sobs of the burnt girl. And the longer we're made to wait, the stronger my anxiety grows.

After half an eternity of waiting, something slides into my mind. Like tentacles of darkness seeping in through invisible cracks and latching on to me, an unwanted entity probes the far recesses. It's as intrusive as it is unsettling, and I immediately try to throw up mental barriers to protect myself.

But how do you protect your own mind from invasion? It's not like this is something they teach us to ward against at Night-lark, but maybe it should be.

I don't know what to do, and as the seconds tick by, more and more of me gets dragged under some dark spell until the world has fallen away and the only thing I'm aware of is a whispered voice ringing in my mind, hissing to me to pick up a dagger from the pile and drive it through my own palm.

I do my best to ignore the command, to push the foreign entity out of my mind entirely, but instead I find myself striding forward and reaching for a blade on the ground in front of me. My hand shakes as my fingers wrap around the hilt of a small dagger, my knuckles white with the strength of my grip.

Part of me is completely numb as I lift the weapon, hovering the tip of the blade above my palm, but the other part of me is freaking out, completely drenched in horror. The weapon starts to lower, and no matter what I do I can't seem to move my hand out of the way or stop myself from piercing my skin.

A bead of blood wells up in the center of my palm, blooming until it spills over the sides of my hand and drips to the ground below.

The blade digs deeper, pain spasming up my arm, and I swear I hear a phantom laugh whisper through my mind.

No. This isn't how I go out of Chaos. I'm stronger than this.

Pain-filled screams and angry shouts rip through the air as other competitors battle, some losing, to fight their own compulsion, but closing my eyes I block everything out. I grit my teeth as the blade enters my hand, millimeter by millimeter, blood seeping from the wound to puddle on the stones and dirt at my feet, but I push past the pain, focusing on the part of my mind that I'm no longer in control of. The voice is whispering to drive the dagger straight through my palm, so I have until the tip of the dagger pushes through the other side of my hand to break the compulsion.

Imagining the compulsion as an intruder, I search for it, finding shadowy tendrils of the dark magic woven throughout my mind, fogging my inhibitions and manipulating my desires. The compulsion has made something inside me *want* to shove the dagger straight through my hand, to see it punch through the other side and blood flow freely. And so as the blade digs a little deeper, I don't fight the urge to stab, but instead I concentrate on the faceless vampire who is trying to bend my will to theirs.

I redirect my desires and imagine sinking the dagger through their hand instead of mine, and I'm able to pull the blade free from my hand. My hand spasms and I drop the dagger. It clatters to the ground and the spell is broken.

I don't breathe a sigh of relief, because I know I still have to beat the compulsion two more times, and that was close—too close.

Even though I didn't cut all the way through my palm, the wound in the center of my hand is still deep and bleeding profusely. I look around for help, not finding it anywhere. Each of the competitors are embroiled in their own battles. Some of them are being compelled to hurt themselves like I was, others are on the ground writhing in agony, and others are standing stock still with hollow gazes. I even catch a competitor climbing one of the thin aspen trees, high enough off the ground they'll surely hurt themselves if they fall.

There's nothing to do but stop the bleeding myself, so reaching down I rip off the bottom few inches of my shirt. It's already speckled with my blood, so it's no great loss. I've just managed to tightly wrap the material around my palm to staunch the flow when I'm hit with the second attack.

Confess, the voice in my mind hisses, and I'm overwhelmed with the urge to spout my secrets about my feelings for Becks and why I entered Chaos.

I slap a hand over my mouth to keep words from emerging, but I can feel them bubbling in the back of my throat, like magma waiting to spill over and destroy everything in its path.

Glancing up, I spot one of the red lights from the cameras. Becks, Ensley, and half my school are watching right now. I know it's just in my head, but I imagine the camera zooming in on me, waiting to hear what truth the compulsion rips from me.

How is it that the vampire was able to access my thoughts and dig up my secret about Becks? I know the general rules around compulsion, and I'd never heard it said a vampire could dig through your mind in such a way, but how else would they know about Becks and the role he played in me entering Chaos?

Confess.

My throat contracts, making phantom words I refuse to let free.

I drop to my knees, fighting even as the compulsion gets stronger and I start to *want* to spill my secrets, just like I'd wanted to skewer my own hand.

Without giving it permission, my hand slides away from my mouth. I'm two seconds away from confessing my unrequited feelings for Becks, and I can't do that. Of course it would be embarrassing for the whole school to know how I truly feel about my best friend, but worse things than humiliation have happened to me at Nightlark Academy. I can't let Becks know my truth and the depths of my emotions. He isn't ready to know, not with the arranged mating still hanging over his head. Not when things are so shaky between us.

If the words leave my mouth, my relationship with Becks will change forever, and I'm not convinced that change will be for the better.

My mouth opens, my vocal cords start to vibrate, and I do the only thing I can do in the moment. I speak my truth.

Twenty

"I HATE how weak I am. My lack of magic makes me feel less than everyone else, especially my closest friends. Sometimes I think they're only still around because they pity me. I'm scared I'll never come into my powers, and that I'll never find anyone who will accept me for who I am. And that I'll always be alone." The words rip from my throat, and I have an initial burst of relief when the compulsion releases me that's swallowed by growing horror the next moment.

I traded one confession for another, and although I didn't confess my truth about Becks, I've just given fodder to every student and bully at Nightlark Academy. I'm never going to live that admission down.

What have I done?

I look around, expecting a reaction, but the other competitors are too caught up in their own trials to pay me any mind, but I don't fool myself into believing that admission went unheard. The multiple cameras mounted in the trees ensure that the audience doesn't miss a single moment of the show we're putting on. I won't know the consequences until the trial is over and the dust has settled.

I push to my feet, my limbs shaky from the mental energy I

exerted. The piece of my shirt that's wrapped around my palm is soaked through with blood and dripping. I tear off another strip, exposing more of my midriff, and change the wrapping with shaking hands.

I've made it through two of the three tasks, but I have a sinking sensation that this third one is going to be the hardest of all. Tension knots my muscles as I look at the robed figures standing outside the torch circle, waiting to see what I'm going to be compelled to do next. I'm frayed on the inside, picked apart and jumbled and wholly unprepared for another round of compulsion.

Kiss one of the male competitors, the voice whispers in my mind.

A tangled rush of panic and desire floods my body, and I find myself scanning the competitors.

That one, the voice says when my eyes brush over Talon, and I swear I can hear humor in its tone.

No, no, not Talon. I manage to back up a step, but when the voice persists I'm moving forward in a line straight for him.

Talon looks up when I reach him. "Freckles," he says in greeting, but I can hear the strain in his voice and see it on his face. He's going through his own battle right now.

I keep my mouth sealed tightly, not trusting anything that might come out if I try to speak. Talon gazes at me quizzically and then his eyes flare, and I know he's just been given a new command. He stumbles back a step and I almost let out a sigh of relief, but then a wave of compulsion washes over me so strongly my head starts to spin, and I'm swamped with desire like I've never felt before.

I sway toward Talon, swearing I can pick up on his scent from several feet away, and he smells amazing. A spicy woodsy scent that makes me want to bury my face in his neck and inhale. I try to keep my gaze averted, but my eyes roam over him, from his dark head of hair down his muscular torso and legs and back up again, before landing on his mouth.

I lick my bottom lip and my mouth feels overly sensitive.

Talon's gaze moves to my mouth as well and a pained look sweeps over his face even as he releases a low moan. "Freckles," he says. His voice has deepened, and it runs over me like silk. "You need to stop looking at me like that."

I want to. Creator knows how badly I want to turn around and walk away right now, but I can't for the life of me make myself do it. The last two rounds of compulsion I wanted to do what I was ordered to, but this time is different. This time I *need* to. Like I'll die if I don't feel Talon's lips pressed against mine.

The air heats, or maybe it's just me, because I'm pretty sure my blood is boiling. I can't make myself stop as I take measured steps toward him. Talon's chest heaves as he sucks in a breath. He doesn't back away from me like before, but his eyes are wary as they track my movement.

Shouts of anger and pain echo in the space around us as fellow competitors fail to fight off the compulsion to do horrific things to themselves and each other, but it doesn't do anything to break the spell, and with every small step toward Talon I feel myself slip further under the control of the vampire compelling me.

Stopping with only inches separating us, I reach up and place my injured hand on Talon's chest and the other on his bicep. His muscles are rock hard under my hands, and a small tremor works its way through him.

He glances down at the makeshift bandage wrapped around my palm and frowns. My lips pulse with awareness and my breathing shallows. In the back of my mind I vaguely know I should be fighting, but I'm drowning in sensations, wave after wave crashing into me, pulling me under, and I just don't care anymore what I'm supposed to do because I know what I *want* to do.

"Locklyn," Talon whispers in a pained voice. "Don't." But he doesn't make a single move to stop me. He's as still as a statue.

Anticipation makes my body tighten. I'm so close to what I

crave, what I *need* in that moment, which is to feel the crush of his mouth against mine.

Lifting up on my toes, I bring my face closer to his, but he's so tall that he's still too far away, so I slide my hand up to his shoulder and then trail my fingers over his neck before burying them in his hair at the back of his head. The strands are as soft as I always imagined, and I play with them for a second before tugging him down toward me. His breath tickles my skin, and my eyes grow heavy.

Talon's practically vibrating with restraint as he holds himself back. A soft smile curves my mouth because I'm about to blow that restraint right out of the water.

Talon finally moves. Lifting his arm, he reaches for me with a shaky hand. The tips of his fingers brush up against my cheek. It's barely a caress but I feel it way down into my soul.

I may have never been kissed before, but I know the gist of what to do. With instinct as my guide, I tip my head to the side, lining up our mouths.

My lids slide shut. Our lips can't be more than an inch apart when a bolt of pain hits me, originating from the tips of Talon's fingers and working its way through the rest of me like an electric shock. A shouted "*STOP!*" rings through my mind and suddenly the compulsion evaporates, disappearing like a puff of smoke.

Gasping, I reel back from Talon, the reality of what I'd almost done—kiss Talon and disqualify myself from Chaos—shaking me to the core.

I stagger back several more steps, my eyes on Talon the whole time as a full-body shudder works its way through him. Clenching his fists, he drops to his knees, a look of agony bleeding into his gaze.

I go to help him, but he throws up an arm.

"Don't come any closer!" he barks, the sharpness of his voice freezing me in place.

The shadowy voice that invaded my mind has fled, but it's

clear Talon is still wrestling with his. Beads of sweat break out on Talon's forehead, and his eyes start to shadow over, darkness eating away at his muted blue irises until nothing is left but solid black orbs. I only get a flash of his black eyes before his eyelids slam down over them and he falls fully to the ground, his body twitching.

Watching him fight against the compulsion is brutal; my eyes sting as tears threaten to overflow. I want to go to Talon, to help him, but this isn't a battle I can fight for him, or even with him.

Minutes pass until a final shudder racks Talon's frame and then his muscles unclench. He takes a couple of steadying breaths before pushing to his feet. When he looks at me, his gaze is haunted.

What did they do to you?

A horn sounds, signifying the end of the trial. There's a mix of cheers and crying from the competitors.

I've passed the third trial, but at what cost?

Twenty-One

THE MOMENT I reach the amphitheater, I look for Becks, anxiousness roiling in my gut, but I can't find him anywhere in the sea of faces. As the crowd starts to clear, Ensley's somber face comes into view, and I head straight for her.

"Where's Becks?" I ask before she has a chance to say anything.

Ensley chews on her lip, looking unsure. "He took off right after the trial ended."

"Left?" I ask, having a hard time processing that. "But he drove us here."

She holds up a set of keys. "He left me these. He caught a ride back with another dragon shifter. He was a little . . . upset."

Frustration swallows me, and I suddenly have the urge to whale on a bag. "It was nothing," I say, sounding like I'm trying to convince myself as much as her.

Ensley nods. "Of course, I know that. And so does Becks. It was just . . ." Ensley clears her throat. "What we saw looked kinda intense. I know it was the compulsion, but it really seemed like you and Talon were into each other. And for a minute there . . ." Her voice trails off.

I don't need to press her because I already know what she's

going to say, and I get it. The truth is I almost gave in to the compulsion. Even though the desire was forced upon me, at the time there was nothing I've ever wanted more than to feel Talon's lips against mine, to taste him on my tongue. Even thinking about it now brings a wave of heat to my cheeks, but the important thing is that I fought the compulsion and didn't kiss Talon.

Nothing *real* happened.

But was it all compulsion? my traitorous mind asks, and I tell it to shut up. But a small part wonders. I didn't fight the compulsion to kiss Talon as hard as I had the other two. For the first two rounds of compulsion I'd retained at least a sliver of myself, but when I was compelled to kiss Talon my mind was completely and utterly taken over by the vampire. If it wasn't for the spark of pain that snapped me out of it, I probably would have done it.

But that doesn't mean anything, right? It just means that I fought harder against the first two compulsions because of self-preservation. If given the choice between stabbing yourself or kissing an attractive creature, I know which option everyone would choose. Surely that doesn't mean that some part of me truly wanted to kiss Talon, but what if that's exactly what Becks thinks?

"I know you two have stuff to figure out and work through, and that's not something you want to do until Becks is free of the arranged life-mating, but maybe just give him a little time to cool off this time."

Something inside tells me that it's not a good idea to leave Becks to his own devices right now, but I nod anyway.

Ensley's gaze fills with sadness and perhaps a touch of guilt, but I don't know why until she says, "Locklyn, about what you said back there, during the trial . . ."

My stomach drops. I completely forgot about my confession, but the dread of that admission hits me again full force. "Ensley, that wasn't—" I cut myself off. I can't lie to her now and say it wasn't true because it is. It's part of my truth that I've buried for years. A deep insecurity that I never, ever, gave voice to, but now it's out in the open.

Ensley takes my uninjured hand between both of hers and squeezes. She shakes her head. "It's not true. Becks and I don't care how much power you have. We're not your friends because we feel bad for you. We're your friends because we care about you and love you. You're family, and always will be no matter what. And you'll never be alone because you'll always have us."

I've kept myself protected for so long that I've hardened, but Ensley's words crack my shell, revealing a fleshy part of my heart that I hardly knew existed anymore. But now that it's exposed I feel raw and vulnerable, but also filled with love.

Her face in front of me becomes a little blurry as my eyes fill with tears.

"Ride or die, for life," Ensley says, tears glistening in her own eyes.

"For life," I repeat with a nod and a wobbly smile.

She takes a deep breath to steady herself and then looks down at the blooded piece of fabric wrapped around my injury. "How's your hand?"

I shrug. "It's been better," I say, playing it off, but the truth is that it throbs and is leaking blood again.

"Come on, let's get it looked at before we go." She leads me over to one of the spectators, an otter shifter who's a part-time medic and has a first aid kit in his car.

Using skin-glue he gets the cut on my palm closed and then re-wraps it with clean bandages before moving on to someone else. I'm not the only one who did harm to themselves under compulsion and he's doing his best to triage the injured competitors. A couple of the competitors are in pretty bad shape, including the black-haired girl who was burned. She was compelled to climb one of the aspen trees and jump from a limb, which she did, resulting in what looked like multiple broken bones. She was injured badly enough that her natural healing process seems to have slowed.

Some of the other competitors helped carry her back to the amphitheater, where her friends took over and whisked her away. Hopefully to a hospital.

Jules also wasn't in the best shape that last time I saw her. She was compelled to thrust a nail into her eye and is among the group of competitors who failed the trial, confirming what I always thought to be true. She is a weak-minded creature who uses her magic as a crutch. Shifters are some of the fastest healers, but she's going to be lucky if she keeps that eye. I can't find it in my heart to be sad for her though. I don't believe in karma, but I do believe in justice, and it seems to have been served tonight.

In all, another twenty-four competitors were eliminated tonight, leaving only sixteen of us to battle it out.

After getting my hand looked at, Ensley brings me home, offering to take me to a clinic to get my hand stitched properly, but I play it off as not as bad and convince her to bring me straight home instead. She drops me off on the corner, but rather than sneaking back inside to get a few hours of sleep before school in the morning, I stand where I am and watch the taillights of her car until they disappear from view.

Maybe Ensley is right, and I should give Becks some space, but instinct screams at me to do the opposite. Becks might already be home in bed, but if he's not, I think I may know where he is instead.

Quietly grabbing my bike that's chained in the alley next to our shop, I jump on it and ride through town, pulling off the street to catch a trail through the woods right after the last building. My hand throbs as my bike treks over the bumpy wooded path. It would hurt less to jump off the bike and walk it instead, but that would take too long. I'm too anxious to see if Becks is there or not.

The ride through the forest trail only takes a few minutes, but it feels like forever before the trees thin and finally open to the rock landing that Becks and I have been to so many times before.

My heart stutters when I see Becks' broad back as he sits atop the highest rock looking out over the valley. When I get up there I won't be able to see anything but darkness, but as a dragon shifter Becks' eyesight—although not as good as cat or owl shifters'—is better than mine in the low light, so he can make out some of the terrain below.

I'm sure he hears me as I park my bike and then scale the rock. His hearing is excellent and I'm not trying to sneak up on him. But other than a slight tensing of his shoulders, he doesn't react until I'm seated right next to him.

"How's your hand?" he asks without looking over.

I stare at the white wrapping, my thoughts on the shifter next to me rather than my injury.

"I hardly even feel it," I lie, and Becks finally glances at my face, giving me a look that says he knows I'm full of it.

We sit in silence for a few minutes, and it's not uncomfortable. Becks and I know each other too well to let awkwardness creep in during the quiet.

"You didn't stay after the trial," I say.

It's not a question. We both know he bolted before I made it back to the amphitheater, but Becks still shakes his head. "Yeah. Sorry about that. It was just . . ." His voice trails off, and as I study his profile I catch a muscle jump in his jaw.

"Listen, Becks, about what you saw—"

"I hate this," he says, cutting me off.

That's a broad statement. There are a million things he could hate right now. His impending betrothal, that he's the dragon heir, that I'm a Chaos competitor, that I almost gave my first kiss to Talon in front of him.

"I should be in Chaos with you, helping you, protecting you, but I'm not."

Oh, that.

He picks up a loose rock and chucks it. I lose sight of it almost the moment it leaves his hand.

"I've been holding my own. I don't need protection."

He glances at the bandaged hand resting in my lap, and I cover it with my uninjured one.

"It'll heal," is all I say, and the muscle in his jawline jumps again. I take a deep breath. "I get you don't like seeing me hurt, but—"

He turns toward me, crowding me, and the suddenness of the movement combined with his nearness steals my words.

There's a wild look in Becks' eyes I haven't seen before. "Don't like? Haven't you figured it out by now?" He runs a hand through his hair, sending strands every which way, which only adds to the out-of-control vibe he's throwing off right now. He grabs my hand, the uninjured one, his gaze beseeching, begging me to understand. "Locklyn, it's not that I just *don't like* seeing you hurt, it's that it *guts me* to see you hurt. It's not that I just *don't like* watching you struggle your way through these trials, it's that a ball of agony and dread formed and lodged in my gut the moment you crossed that line and became a competitor, and I couldn't follow you. And tonight, to hear you say you're not sure I genuinely care about you, that you feel less-than around me and that you think I pity you . . . that broke me. *Broke*. Me. And then on top of all that I had to stand there and watch you walk into another guy's arms."

He squeezes his eyes shut and a shudder runs through him, but then his lids snap back open, his green eyes brighter than they've ever been before. "It's not that I just *don't like* seeing you in someone else's arms, it's that it's *agony* for me to see you there when I know there's no one else's arms you should be in but mine."

The world freezes for two prolonged heartbeats before speeding up again.

What's happening right now? And am I ready for it?

Becks just stares at me, waiting for my reaction, but I'm overwhelmed and too stunned to say anything. He said our almost kiss had been a mistake and wouldn't happen again. Just the memory of that moment still stings like a slap in the face. The arranged life-mating is still hanging over his head, and without Shadow Striker I'm still powerless, still not good enough for him.

"What are you saying?" I finally ask, my voice small and breathless.

"I'm saying—" Irritation flashes across Becks' face, and then rather than use his words to explain he's reaching for me, dragging me toward him with one arm wrapped around my waist.

I'm practically on his lap as he palms the back of my head, tilting my face up as he slants his down and then his mouth crashes into mine.

I gasp, and Becks swallows the sound, moving his lips over mine in an unfamiliar dance that I'm quickly swept up in.

Closing my eyes, I fall into sensation, grasping Becks' biceps to keep me grounded.

Becks' kisses are passionate but not demanding, and it gives me the courage to explore, brushing my lips over his with varying degrees of pressure, from feather-like touches to soul searing connections. His hand trails from the back of my head down my neck, making me shiver. He brushes his thumb against the underside of my jaw and a low moan rumbles deep in my chest. I never knew how sensitive the skin there could be until that moment.

There's a slight tremor in his hand that intensifies when I take the kiss deeper. He starts to pull me closer, before he stops. I realize he's trying to hold back, but I can't imagine anything feeling as good as what he's doing to me right now, so I don't want him to hold back. I want him unfiltered and unfettered from duty and responsibility. I want him to give me everything he's feeling so I know his desire for me matches my own for him.

Without thinking, I nip at Becks' lower lip and the tenuous hold he has on himself snaps. With a growl, he pulls me even closer, eliminating any space between us.

He kisses me with a possessiveness I wasn't prepared for. Every glide of his mouth sends a shockwave through me, and it isn't long before I'm gasping for air, overwhelmed by a cacophony of emotions and sensations.

And just when it seems like we're at the precipice of something unknown, we break apart, both of us panting for air.

I blink as I raise my hand and press my fingers to my swollen lips. Becks' mouth looks as swollen as mine feels, and there's color dusting his cheekbones that I can make out in the moonlight.

"I'm sorry," he starts, his hold on me loosening. "I forgot myself. I shouldn't have—"

I press two fingers to his mouth, stopping his words. That was the single best moment of my life, and if he tries to take it back I may not survive.

"It was perfect," I say, and Becks releases a breath, his tense muscles relaxing.

A lazy smile grows on his face, and that combined with his disheveled hair makes him look roguish in the best possible way.

"You have no idea how long I've wanted to do that," he says, looking back down at my mouth, and my heart rate spikes.

"How long?" I ask, my gaze dropping to his plumped lips.

"Longer than I'm willing to admit," he says with a self-deprecating laugh, and then slides me off his lap.

I'm instantly disappointed with the distance. I quite liked cuddling on his lap, but I'm not bold enough to voice my preference.

"Where do we go from here?" I ask, looking at my hands. Sadness starts to darken the edges of the bliss I felt moments before. Nothing about our situation has changed in the last ten minutes, but at the same time . . . everything has.

Becks reaches across and gently takes my bandaged hand, inspecting the wrappings. A little blood has leaked through. The glue must have split while we were kissing. I should probably get it stitched.

"I don't know," he answers honestly, and my heart sinks a bit lower.

It's the truth. Unless we dig up some dirt on one of the council members soon, Becks will still be getting betrothed and then forced to life-mate with the female chosen for him. I've survived Chaos so far, making it further than anyone—even myself—expected, but it's still a longshot that I'll come out victoriously.

Becks is still the dragon heir.

I'm still as magicless as ever.

He throws his arm around me, tucking me into his side, and I go willingly, relishing his warmth in the chilly night and the butterflies that flutter in my stomach.

"About earlier tonight," Becks starts, and I tense. I'd forgotten the events that served as a catalyst for Becks' confession. "These trials are dangerous. Cage fights, compulsion . . . there is real potential for serious injury, not to mention the legality of it. I'm really worried about you." He rushes to add, "And that's not because I think of you as weak or less-than—a lot of magically powerful creatures were injured tonight. These trials are no joke."

I start to relax. This is the same argument we've had for weeks, and although I'm fatigued from going around in circles, I'm just glad he didn't bring up Talon.

"And the thing with Talon," he says, and I tense back up. "That was—"

"It was the compulsion," I spit out, feeling the need to explain myself even though I know I shouldn't have to. I didn't owe Becks an explanation before we kissed, and I don't owe him one now either.

He nods. "Yeah, I know. It's just . . ." His arm around me tightens. "I just don't get a good vibe from that guy. He's hiding something. And the way he looks at you makes me want to tear his face off."

I smile in the darkness. Talon's done nothing to deserve Becks' ire, but now that I know for certain he's into me like I'm into him, I don't mind the show of jealousy so much.

"There's nothing going on between us," I say honestly. He

can't possibly think I'm harboring feelings for another guy when I just kissed him like that. "And if it makes you feel any better, it's not like I ever plan to search him out. I'd rather keep my distance anyway."

He's silent for long enough that I turn to look at him. A muscle jumps in the side of his jaw, making me think he's stopping himself from saying something. Finally, he says, "Yeah, okay. I'll drop it. It's not like I have any hold on you right now. Not when I'm in the position I'm in myself." He starts to let go of me and I know he's not just physically retreating, he's emotionally pulling back as well, but I'm not going to let him.

Reaching up, I place a hand on his cheek, gently turning his face so that he can't help but look at me.

"I've said it before, but I'll say it again. We're going to figure it out. You're crazy if you think I'm going to stand back and watch you be mated to another female. Especially now."

Something sparks in his eyes, and I know I've drawn him back to the here and now. "You don't want to watch me with another female?"

I purse my lips. "I thought I just made that pretty clear."

Becks rubs the back of his neck, a wicked gleam in his eye that makes heat bloom in my gut. "I don't know. Maybe there's a way for you to make it clearer," he says, as he holds back a grin.

"And how do you suppose I do that?" I ask, full well knowing what he's alluding to, but enjoying his sudden teasing manner. Flirting is a whole new side of Becks I'm not used to seeing, let alone being on the receiving end of. I like it a lot.

"Hmm." The sound he makes in the back of his throat is super sexy and makes my heartbeat pick back up again.

Twisting, he grabs me around the waist, and as if I weigh nothing he settles me so I'm resting with a knee on either side of his hips. As I look down on him, he swipes his tongue over his lower lip. When his gaze fastens on my mouth, I have to swallow the sound that threatens to bubble up my throat. It's suddenly incomprehensible how I kept myself under control for so long. Now that I know what he tastes like, there's no going back for me.

Rather than waiting for Becks to make a move, this time I do the taking. Dipping my head, I press my mouth against his, and just like before, coming together in this way is nothing short of bliss.

I follow Becks' lead as he moves his mouth over mine, and when his tongue slides against the seams of my lips I open wider, letting him in. I can't stop myself from running my hands over him. I caress his biceps and dive my fingers through the soft hair at the back of his head. He trails his fingers back and forth over the exposed skin at my sides and cups a hand around the back of my neck.

This kiss is so much more than just the result of pent-up physical attraction. This kiss is everything. It's slow and decadent and makes my toes curl. It's an expression of the depths of our emotions. The depths of our desires. It's everything I never knew I needed, and I'll remember this moment for the rest of my life.

I don't know how long we stay like that, leisurely exploring each other, but when Becks pulls back and rests his forehead against mine, my lips are swollen and my eyes heavily lidded.

Rubbing a hand up and down my back soothingly, he sighs and it's part-resigned, part-contented. "Come on. Let's get you to an all-night clinic. That hand needs to be stitched. We can brainstorm what you're going to tell your parents when we get there."

My parents. I'd completely forgotten about them. Nothing like bringing up the parents to throw cold water on a romantic moment.

Dropping my head back, I sever the connection between us and groan. A few bruises were easy to explain away, especially since they looked like sparring injuries, but a knife wound in the middle of my palm is an entirely different matter.

Becks laughs at my reaction and sets me aside. Standing, he pulls me up after him. "We'll figure something out."

When we climb down from the rock to the ground, he does something he's never done before. He takes my hand. When he squeezes it, I feel a jolt all the way down to my toes. And when he looks over his shoulder at me with a carefree and contented smile, I think my heart might explode.

I don't know what tomorrow will bring, but for one night everything is perfect.

Twenty-Two

THE NEXT MORNING, things are not so perfect. After getting my hand stitched, my parents catch me sneaking back into the house only a few minutes before dawn. My mom notices my gauze-wrapped hand right away. I try to feed her the excuse Becks and I came up with, that I went out for a run because I couldn't sleep and tripped and punctured my hand on a spiked fence post when I tried to catch myself. But the excuse is weak at best and doesn't hold up to my parents' scrutiny. So when my lie falls apart, they ground me for two weeks by taking away my phone, banning me from the computer except for school related work, and informing me the only places I can go for the next weeks are our house, school, and the shop. No afterschool workouts at Peet's Gym, no hangouts with Ensley, no dinners with Becks. I want to argue, but how can I when they are justified in their actions? So I take the punishment with a somber nod and start to get ready for school.

"Can you pass the milk?" I ask my mom a little later that morning when we are sitting at the kitchen table after I've had a shower and changed into clean clothes.

Frowning, she picks up the carton and hands it to me. I make the mistake of reaching for it with my bandaged hand, and her frown deepens and her eyes well. My heart squeezes. I love my parents. I want to say something to make the situation better, to take away the wounded look on her face, but there's nothing to say to make this better. She knows I'm not telling the truth, and the truth is the one thing I can't offer her right now.

We eat the rest of our breakfast in silence, then she leaves to do some early morning work in the shop before it opens. My dad comes into the kitchen as I'm rinsing my cereal bowl, being careful not to get the fresh wrappings wet. When I look up at him, there's disappointment shining in his eyes, and I can't even blame him for it. I've been lying and feeding half-truths to them for weeks, and that isn't us. We don't lie to each other like this, but the crux of the matter is that even if I wanted to confess that I entered Chaos and put myself in danger, the magical gag would keep me from doing so.

The weight of their sadness and disapproval is crushing, wiping away any lingering joy from my night with Becks.

When I finish and turn to leave and head to Nightlark, my dad stops me.

"Are you in some sort of trouble?" he asks, his voice gruff yet filled with concern.

I don't want to lie to them anymore, but I don't have a choice.

"No, nothing like that. Everything's okay, Dad."

I can tell immediately that he doesn't buy it. "You can tell us anything, Locklyn. We'll always be on your side. If you've gotten yourself into something you can't seem to get out of, we're here to help you. I hope you know that."

My dad's reassurances hit a little too close for comfort, but he'll never have any idea how badly I want to confess to him right now. I have to swallow around the giant lump in my throat before I can talk. "Yeah, Dad, I know. I'm fine, I promise," I lie, and then force a smile I'm sure isn't very convincing.

My dad heaves a sigh. It's obvious he knows I'm hiding something. "Then I guess we'll see you directly after classes today," he says, a not-so-subtle reminder that I'm grounded.

I nod and slip by him, grabbing my backpack on the way out of the apartment.

If my morning wasn't hard enough, the stares from my classmates as I walk down the hallway to my locker later remind me of my embarrassing confession the night before. I'm tense as I wait for someone to bring it up, throwing my own insecurities in my face. My words the night before were like chum in the water, and I'm expecting the sharks to start circling any minute.

"Hey," Shayla says, coming up beside me at my locker. I flinch away from her, bracing for condemnation, but when her brows pinch at my reaction, all she asks is, "Are you all right?"

Some of the tension leaves my body when I look into her concerned hazel eyes. She's not turning on me. She's not here to ridicule me.

"Sorry. I'm just on edge this morning. But I'm all right," I say as I heft my bag over my shoulder and then shut my locker.

She smiles and nods, her delicate braids swinging gently with the movement. "I get it. Last night was intense. You had me really worried there for a few minutes. I'm glad you made it through though." She takes a step closer and lowers her voice. "And I wanted to let you know that what you said last night under compulsion . . . it was actually pretty cool."

Come again?

I look at Shayla, searching for any hint of insincerity, but her face is open and free of malice. She's serious.

"What do you mean?" I tentatively ask.

"It's just that you're not the only one that feels that way, but no one wants to admit it. I get you're probably feeling pretty exposed right now, but you should know that it was nice to hear I'm not the only one who thinks those things, is all." She shrugs almost awkwardly, and it occurs to me right then, for maybe the first time ever, that my fears and insecurities might not be unique to me, that I'm not the only one out there who struggles with self-doubt.

Shayla is a powerful panther shifter. I'm not sure what type of magic she has, but her reflexes are sharp and she's super strong. I would never have guessed she feels insecure about herself, but something I said last night resonated with her, and that blows my mind.

Before I can respond, her boyfriend, Owen, comes up next to her, throwing an arm over her shoulder. She glances up at him and smiles, and he drops a quick kiss on her lips before turning to me.

"Hey, Locklyn." He gives me a quick nod. "How's the hand?"

I blink back at him as he waits for me to respond. I don't pick up any negative vibes from Owen either. I thought for sure I'd lose the new friends I made after my confession last night, but maybe I was wrong. Wrong about my friends, and wrong about myself.

"Does it hurt?" Owen prompts when I don't say anything.

"Oh, right. My hand," I say as I shake my head to clear my thoughts. "It's not too bad. Becks took me to get it stitched up last night. They don't think I'll have permanent damage."

Ensley joins our group at the tail end of my sentence. "You saw Becks last night?" she asks, tucking a strand of her purple-streaked hair behind her ear.

My cheeks heat. Ensley tried to take me to get my hand looked at, but I turned her down. She has to think it's strange that I saw her brother last night after she dropped me off.

"Ah, yeah," I say, choosing not to elaborate. I'm not ready for her questions just yet.

I haven't seen Becks yet today, and I'm both looking forward to and also dreading our first interaction post-kiss.

What if he has doubts like before? What if he wants to ignore the whole thing happened?

Her eyes narrow and I can practically see the wheels turning in her head.

"Did you guys hear about Tenn?" Owen asks, unknowingly coming to my rescue.

We all shake our heads and Owen blows out a breath of air, his face somber. "It's bad. They found him on the edge of Woodwinds Forest. It looks like he'd been beaten."

Ensley gasps. "Is he okay?"

Owen shakes his head. "He's in a coma."

Tenn is a Chaos competitor. In fact, now that I think about it, he wasn't at the trial last night and he should have been. He made it through the last round of cage fights.

"That's not all," Owen says. "One of his buddies claims that Tenn wanted out of Chaos. That he wasn't planning on attending the trial. He left his house just before midnight last night and wouldn't have had enough time to get to Jagged Mountain in time to participate."

My eyes widen as the game master's words echo in my mind. *Once you enter Chaos, there's no way to self-eliminate.*

"Does anyone know what happened?" I ask, a sick feeling settling in my gut.

"No, but the timing is suspicious. Students are saying something happened to him because he tried to pull out of Chaos."

I let that sink in.

"This Chaos stuff is getting serious," Shayla says. "I heard from Freya that Jules actually lost her eye, and her parents are pulling her out of school because she won't tell them what happened."

"Like, for the day?" I ask.

Shayla shakes her head. "No, like for good. They're going to send her to some shifter school up north to finish out the year."

Surprisingly, I don't really get any pleasure out of hearing Jules is transferring when a month ago that would have completely made my day.

The first bell rings, letting us know we have fifteen minutes to get to class.

"Oh shoot," Shayla says. "I have to grab a book out of my locker before class. Catch you guys at lunch?"

"I'll come with," Owen says, and with a wave they're both gone.

Ensley and I turn in the other direction, my mind swirling around Tenn and what happened to him. Was it truly because he didn't show up to Chaos last night? I'd assumed the game master's warning was hollow, but what if it wasn't? What if there are real consequences to missing a trial and Tenn just paid?

But then again it could have been something else altogether. A fluke attack of some sort and the timing is just coincidental.

"Something's up with you," Ensley says, shaking me from my thoughts about Tenn and Chaos.

"What? Nothing's up," I say, and glance away. I can't look at Ensley without thinking about Becks right now, and it feels like what happened last night is written clearly across my face.

"Hmm. No, something is definitely going on with you. My best friend radar is pinging. Do you care to share with me now, or are you going to make me pull it out of you?"

When I look over at her, Ensley regards me with slitted eyes, watching my face carefully. I muster the most innocent look I can, but she's not buying it. I'm saved from having to answer when we turn the corner, and someone calls my name. When I glance back, Becks is jogging toward us. My heart starts to pound so hard I worry it's going to burst from my chest.

When he reaches us, he makes a move like he's going to pull me into his arms, but then stops himself and takes a stilted step away.

Clearing his throat, he rubs the back of his neck. "Hey. I tried to check on you this morning but couldn't get a hold of you."

Suddenly shy, I duck my head, willing my face not to start heating. "My parents didn't buy the story of me falling on a run. They confiscated my phone. I don't get it back for a couple of weeks."

Wincing, he nods. "That sucks."

I look up at him and my stomach flips. Over the last several months I might have thought I caught him staring at me a time or two with a hint of longing, but I easily talked myself out of believing it. But now Becks' emotions are reflected on his face, clear as day, and all the feelings and sensations from the night before come rushing to the surface.

"So, ah, how's the hand?"

"Better." Lifting it, I open and shut my fingers a few times as if to prove that it's in working order.

I'm very aware of Ensley's gaze ping-ponging between us. Becks has yet to even acknowledge her presence and I'm sure she thinks this interaction is kinda odd.

I clear my throat, shifting my weight from one foot to the other. "So, um . . . did you sleep well last night?"

Groan. That was such a cringy thing to say. We got home so late that he, like me, probably didn't even get any sleep. But I can't take it back now.

The corners of Becks' mouth twitch, but he manages to hold a straight face. "I had a decent night's sleep." He moves a little closer, and I'm hit with his delicious scent, vanilla with a hint of burnt cinnamon. "I had some pretty good dreams actually. How about you?"

"Me?" *What were we talking about again?*

He takes a half step forward, his voice dropping an octave and his gaze flickering to my mouth before jumping back to my eyes. "Did you have good dreams last night?"

"I, ah . . ." Did the temperature in the hall just jump a million degrees?

Reaching out, he lightly circles my bicep. He's so close I have to tilt my head back to keep eye contact. "I wanted to talk to you about . . . things."

Becks drinks in my features, looking like he's memorizing each contour and slope of my face. I've never been looked at like that before, and in that moment I fall for him a little bit more. My worries about him not being into me anymore are swept away like dust particles in the wind and I just stare back, soaking up as much of him as I can.

I swallow. "Things?"

"Yes, what *things*?" Ensley asks, and I jerk my head in her direction to see her grinning at us with a smile as wide as the Cheshire Cat.

"Yo, Becks! You ready for Saturday?" comes another voice from behind Becks.

The spell is broken, and releasing my arm Becks turns away and toward one of his vodenball teammates, Tyler, who's coming down the hall toward us.

Becks greets him with a quick nod. "Yeah. I'm ready for this weekend."

"Sweet," Tyler says and then slaps him on the back. "Wanna get in an extra practice later?"

"Yeah, sure. After classes?"

"Awesome. Let's go find Owen and see if he's in."

Tyler takes off, fully expecting Becks to follow. With one last lingering look he says, "We'll talk later," and then takes off.

I watch him stride down the hall and disappear into the sea of bodies.

"So that's it," Ensley says, and when I look at her she's still wearing that same maniacal smile. Looping her arm through mine, she drags me toward the nearest bathroom.

"That's what?" I ask, playing stupid.

She shoots me a knowing look, and after she strongarms me into the bathroom she checks the stalls to make sure we are alone. Satisfied they're clear, she turns toward me, a smirk on her face as she crosses her arms. "You and Becks totally locked lips."

I stare at her in shock, sputtering nonsensical words before regaining some sort of composure. I can't believe she just put it out there like that.

"What makes you say that?" I say, trying to keep it under

wraps, but my friend knows me too well and can see a lie coming a mile away.

"My brother didn't even know I existed back there. You guys totally kissed. Just admit it already."

My cheeks heat, and Ensley, the sly little mind reader that she is, notices and gasps. "You didn't just kiss, you full-on made out, didn't you?"

Unable to hold back any longer, I crumble.

"Okay, fine. We kissed."

The squeal Ensley releases is piercing and makes me question if she's part banshee. I cover my ears until she stops.

"Finally," she says. "I was getting so sick of watching the two of you dance around each other. It was like a bad sitcom at times."

"Hey," I protest, but Ensley keeps going.

"So tell me everything! Where was it? How did it happen? And most importantly, was it good? Everyone probably thinks Becks is a fantastic kisser, but is it bad that I'm kinda hoping he's sloppy so I can tease him about it forever?"

I scrunch my nose at her.

"Ew. It's your brother. How can you ask that?"

She waves me off. "Whatever. I'm over it, so you should be too."

I put my hands over my face. "I seriously can't talk about this with you."

Just then the warning bell rings and Ensley groans. "Horrible timing."

Awesome timing.

"Don't think you're worming your way out of this," she says with a reproachful finger pointed in my direction. "We're picking this up at lunch."

Not if I can avoid it.

I make a noncommittal sound, but the gleam in Ensley's eyes tells me she isn't going to drop this, and so I know come lunchtime I'll be spilling my guts.

Twenty-Three

THE WAYS my life has changed over the last month are hard to grasp. I used to walk the academy halls with my head down, eyes on the floor so that I wouldn't accidentally make eye contact with anyone. Now I can't get from one class to the other without someone calling my name or coming up beside me to walk through the halls. It's a lot to get used to, but I'm not complaining.

Classmates have asked to see my hand and want to know how I broke through the compulsion, but I make it through the first half of the day without anyone else bringing up my confession from the night before. No one seems to really care like I thought they would. Or if they do they keep it to themselves. So I'm not as jumpy or paranoid as I walk to meet up with Ensley for lunch, even though it's something I've been dreading all day long. But there's a good chance we won't be eating lunch alone, so I figure that will put off the inquisition for a couple more hours. Ensley is a lot of things, but I know she won't embarrass me in front of Shayla and the others.

My mind is on Becks when someone grabs my arm and pulls me into an empty room. My brain doesn't process that it's Talon until he's turning to lock the door behind us. He twists back to me, and when I look into his blue-gray eyes something inside gives a little flip, but I tell myself it's the lingering effects of the compulsion and nothing more.

"Talon, I don't—"

"You're not answering your phone," he says, and the look on his face brings me up short. I'm used to his easy smile, the teasing light in his eyes, but for the first time since I met him Talon's gaze is shuttered from me—completely blank and cold.

I lift my bandaged hand. "My parents took it away when I came home like this without a good enough excuse. I'm basically under house arrest and cut off from the world for the next couple weeks."

Talon nods and shoves his hands in his pockets. "Yeah, that tracks. My parents would probably flip too."

I knit my brow, trying to figure out what's going on here. "Did you need something?"

"You need to fail out of the next trial," Talon says without a lead up, and it's so unexpected it takes a few moments to find my words.

"Wait . . . what?"

Talon shifts uncomfortably. His gaze is lasered over my shoulder rather than my face.

"Where is this coming from?" I ask.

"The last couple of trials are going to be even more dangerous, and I think it's for the best if you safely withdraw from Chaos." He still won't look me in the eye.

Defensiveness swirls in my chest, and I cross my arms. I don't know who Talon thinks he is, but he can't make this decision for me any more than Becks, Ensley, or anyone else can.

"No." My voice rings clear in the empty room.

Talon's gaze finally settles on me. There's a storm cloud of emotion swirling in his light eyes. "Locklyn, you don't understand."

Locklyn, not Freckles.

"No, *you* don't understand," I say, cutting off whatever else he might have been about to say and taking an aggressive step forward. "You don't get to tell me what to do in Chaos. Nobody does. I made the decision to enter the competition, and if I want to purposefully tank a trial or give it my all until the very end, that will also be my decision."

Removing his hands from his pockets, he crosses his arms over his chest, mirroring my stance. His fists are clenched and a muscle jumps in his jaw.

"There are things going on here that you don't know about. I just don't want you to get hurt."

"Newsflash. Chaos has always been dangerous. There's always been a chance I could get hurt. Yesterday I did, yet I'm still here. I'm not purposefully throwing the next trial, and nothing you can say will convince me to."

His features pinch in annoyance. "Why not? It's not like you're going to win anyway, so what's the point?"

As soon as the words leave his mouth, regret flashes across his face.

I feel like I've just been hit by friendly fire. "We're done here."

I go to leave the room but Talon steps in my path. "Freckles," he starts, but I hold up a hand.

"I said we're done here."

Panic crosses his face. "Wait." When I try to step around him, he grabs my arms and hauls me into him. I press my hands against his chest to keep distance between us, but when I look up at him, unwelcome memories of the night before bombard me.

The feel of his muscles beneath my fingers.

His warm breath ghosting over my lips.

The way I craved his touch with an intensity I've never experienced before.

He reads my face with ease, and he parts his lips, his gaze dropping to my mouth.

The breath in my lungs stalls, and as he looks down at me I finally notice the dark smudges under his eyes and the ashen color of his skin. Something is going on with him, but I don't know what.

"During the last trial, they tried to compel me to kill you."

Shock vibrates from my chest outward, chasing away any lingering desires from the night before, turning the blood in my veins to slush.

Kill me.

Who would want to kill me? And why?

I sway a little on my feet, becoming a little lightheaded. Talon's grip on me tightens and he shifts closer. "Are you all right?"

My fingers start to tingle and go numb.

Kill me.

"But why?" I'm so confused.

Real concern shines in his eyes and his voice softens when he answers. "I think someone is poking for my weak spots. And they found one. You."

That sobers me. I push against Talon, and he releases me. I take a step back to clear my head.

"Why would anyone think that I'm a weak spot for you?"

Talon pulls off his knit cap and plows a hand through his hair, making the dark waves go every which way. He runs his tongue over his bottom lip while scrutinizing me, making up his mind about what he wants to say next. Finally, he lets out a long breath of air. "Probably because I helped you during the first trial and then went easy on you during the second."

My mouth quirks to the side. "Went easy on me. You knocked me out cold in that fight."

"Yes and no," he says mysteriously, and I narrow my eyes. "I used my powers to make you pass out," he explains. "I think that tipped them off to who I am and painted a target on my back, and in turn yours as well."

Used his powers? But creature magic was nullified in the cages, so how was that even possible? Is Talon so powerful that he fought the magic dampener? And tipped who off to what?

I take a long look at Talon. He isn't as antsy as he was before, but I start to wonder if I know him at all. I thought I was peeling back some of his layers, but what if everything has just been smoke and mirrors?

"What kind of creature are you?" I ask bluntly.

Talon pokes his tongue into his cheek and looks away for a second. "I can't tell you," he says.

I scoff. "Won't is different than can't."

He barks out a laugh that's devoid of real humor. "If you only knew," he says without really addressing my comment. "But I need you out of the competition so that you stay safe. I *have* to get Shadow Striker, but I don't want you to get hurt, or worse."

"Is getting the dagger for your father really that important?" I ask.

He tilts his head and shoots me a look. "I think we both know by now that I'm not looking for a kitschy gift for my dad."

I feel my eyes widen. Could Talon be after Shadow Striker for the same reason I am?

"Well then, why?" I challenge. "Explain to me why it's so important for you to get that dagger."

Talon clamps his mouth shut. I know I'm making him uncomfortable, but since it's apparently my life on the line, I need him to level with me once and for all.

With a sigh he relents. "That dagger has been in my family for generations. Someone stole it a few months back. We've been looking for it ever since. We got a lead it was in this area, so I came here to check it out. Our lead was right because it popped up as the Chaos prize. I entered the competition to get it back."

"You used to own Shadow Striker?"

"As much as any creature can own it," he says. "And I'll do whatever it takes to get it back."

I take a moment to mull over everything. Does Shadow Striker really belong to Talon, or is he lying to me? I look into his eyes and my gut says he's telling the truth, just not all of it.

"Why would someone steal the dagger just to give it away?"

A shadow crosses Talon's face, and before he even says anything I know it's going to be a lie.

He shrugs, and the movement looks too practiced. "How should I know that?"

I narrow my eyes at him. Even if he doesn't know for sure, I'll bet he has a theory, and I don't like that he won't tell me what it is. "You're not telling me everything."

Talon sighs and walks a few feet away to lean up against the wall. "None of that information really matters anyway. The important facts are that the thief knows who I am and that I'm here to get the dagger back and that they are going to try to use you against me in these last two trials. I don't want you to get hurt, least of all because of me."

He says he doesn't want me to get hurt, but I see through the layers of what he's not saying. If it's between me and that dagger, he'll pick the blade over me, letting me get hurt. I try not to be offended by that because the ugly truth is that if it came down to Talon or the blade I'd be tempted to pick the magical object over him as well.

Talon crosses his arms. His face is passive, but his eyes sharpen. "I know why you entered Chaos. And let me tell you, he's not worth it."

My stomach drops and I look away. "You don't know what you're talking about," I snap.

"Don't I?" he says, and then pushes away from the wall to stalk toward me. He only stops when he's standing right in front of me, close enough that I can see the silver flecks in his blue eyes. "Then let me tell you what I *do* know. If I had—" He snaps his mouth shut. His nostrils flare as he sucks in a breath.

If he had what? I wonder, but when he starts talking again he doesn't pick up where he left off.

"You shouldn't settle for someone who doesn't accept you for who you are. You need someone who sees you. *Really* sees you and recognizes that you are enough, *more* than enough, just the way you are. It's not magic that makes the creature powerful, it's the strength of their character and the depth of their soul, and you, Freckles, are the most powerful creature I've ever met. If that pathetic excuse for a dragon heir doesn't recognize how powerful, strong, and beautiful you are, he's not worth your time, let alone your life." His gaze skips over my face, his eyes softening. "You'd be a fool to change one thing about yourself. You're already perfect."

My breath catches and I'm frozen by his confession. No one has ever said something like that to me before. Not even Becks. My mind flutters like a hummingbird, moving far too quickly to figure out what part of that little speech to focus on first, but what keeps circulating are his last words.

You're already perfect.

I'm not perfect. Far from it, but no one really is. But that doesn't mean being called perfect just the way I am doesn't have a profound effect on me. Something shifts in my very core, but I don't know how to process that, or even if I should believe Talon. What if he's just feeding me lines to get me to abandon my quest for Shadow Striker?

I shake my head and tell myself to ignore everything Talon just said. He doesn't understand the situation or know anything about Becks and me. His words were pretty, but unreliable at best. And even so, they don't change anything. Becks still has an arranged life-mating hanging over his head. I'm not giving up that dagger.

Clearing my throat, I take a step back to get some space from the intensity of the situation. "Well, thanks for the warning about Chaos," I say. "I'll keep it in mind."

"So you'll safely fail the next trial?" he asks, his body tense.

I lick my lips and Talon's gaze flicks down before returning to my eyes. There's a bit of heat in his gaze that's too blatant to ignore.

"It means," I start as Talon hangs on my every word, "that I hear what you are saying, that someone might try to do something to me to distract you in the trials, and that I'll keep that in mind."

"Freckles—" Talon starts, but I hold a hand up.

"I said I'll keep it in mind," I say firmly. "I appreciate you telling me what you can, and now that I know I'll watch my back. But at the end of the day I don't expect you to protect me through these challenges. I can take care of myself."

After what Chaos has already put me through, I truly believe that now. I'm strong. I'm fierce. I've got this.

Talon looks frustrated with my response, but eventually he heaves a sigh and nods. "You need to know I will do whatever I have to do to get Shadow Striker. There's more at stake than you realize."

"I know," I say, truly understanding the message. He means that not only will he not be there to protect me if I need it, but that if I get in his way he'll figure out how to move me out of it.

We stand there staring at each other for several more silent moments. I'm not sure what Talon reads on my face, but looking at him now is like seeing a different person, one hardened by harsh realities I know nothing about. He doesn't look like a student to me anymore. I don't know how I didn't see it before, but even dressed in faded jeans, a t-shirt, and his signature knit cap, he looks like a warrior.

For the first time since entering Chaos it feels like I'm finally seeing Talon for what he truly is, the guy standing in the way of what I want. As much as I may be standing in Talon's way, he's standing in mine as well.

"I'd better get going," I say, gesturing toward the door. "Ensley will be looking for me." I skirt around Talon, but before I pass he stops me with a light touch on the back of my hand.

"Just for the record, Freckles, I wasn't saying that you wouldn't win because you weren't capable of doing so. In a lot of ways you're the strongest creature I've ever met, a true fighter. I said that you wouldn't win because there's no scenario where I don't win the dagger back. I have to, because failure in this situation isn't an option."

Talon looks at me like he wishes there was another way, another option, but there isn't and he's sorry for it.

His words take some of the sting out of his comment from earlier, so I nod, letting him know I accept his words for what they are, an apology.

Some of the tension leaves his face. "Will you promise to think about what I've said here?"

A strangled laugh rolls up my throat before I can squash it. As if I'll be able to think of much else.

"Yeah, I promise," I say, and then Talon follows me out into the busy hallway, where we run right into Becks.

Twenty-Four

BECKS' face darkens immediately when he recognizes who I'm with. "What's going on here?" he demands, his gaze bouncing between me and Talon.

I have nothing to feel guilty for; Talon and I were just talking, but shame still rises to the surface, freezing my tongue.

Talon stays silent, waiting for me to answer for the both of us, but when I don't say anything, Becks takes an aggressive step toward him. I slide in between them, placing my hands on Becks' chest to keep him from advancing. He stops but keeps glaring at Talon over my shoulder.

"We have a project together," I lie, the words tasting bitter in my mouth. "We needed to talk about the assignment and sync up our schedules."

I glance over my shoulder at Talon, willing him to play along. He arches a brow as he looks down at me, but he nods, shifting his attention to Becks. "That's right. For our Natural Chemistry class. We're doing a project on objects in nature and their natural attractions to each other. It's going to take a couple of late nights, but I'm sure we'll get the assignment banged out soon enough."

No. He. Didn't.

I could wrap my hands around Talon's neck right now and squeeze the life out of him and not feel even a little bad about it.

The slight scent of smoke permeates the air and Becks' temperature spikes beneath my palms.

"Welp, I'll see you tonight, Freckles," Talon says jovially, and slaps me on the back before heading down the hall. It might be my imagination, but I swear I hear his low chuckle echo off the walls as he goes.

"What happened to keeping your distance?" Becks asks, taking a step back, and I drop my hands from his chest. His brows are drawn as he watches Talon's retreating form, a frown pulling down his face.

I heave a sigh. When did my life get so complicated? Oh yeah, the minute I decided to do the bonehead thing of entering an underground competition that may or may not get me killed. That's when it got so complicated.

"Sometimes creatures are unavoidable," I say, and that's sure the truth when it comes to Talon. It seems like no matter what, he keeps stepping in my path. Only time will tell if that's a good or bad thing.

Another wave of smoky air hits me. No need to guess what Becks thinks about it. His dislike of Talon grows daily.

Some of the tightness leaves Becks' muscles, and I assume Talon must have just turned the corner behind me.

"So you have a project with him?" Becks asks, his green-eyed gaze swinging to me.

I have a choice to make here. Come clean, or keep up the lie? I should come clean, but something tells me I'm going to need the excuse.

"Yeah, but it probably won't be that big of a deal," I say, and then try to shove down the guilt and shame that starts to boil over.

"Sucks," Becks says, but then tilts his head toward the courtyard and we wander in that direction.

Ensley's grin stretches across her face when we reach our table and sit down with our lunches across from her. She's sitting alone, and that doesn't bode well. I was counting on Shayla and the others as a buffer.

"So . . . " she starts, looking back and forth between us. "How are you guys doing today?"

Giving her a funny look, Becks shrugs and then takes a bite of his burger. Ensley doesn't even bother razzing him about the meat as he chews, and that right there should have tipped him off that something is up, but instead he goes on happily munching his burger without realizing what is about to hit us.

I, on the other hand, know exactly what type of cyclone is swirling in Ensley's mind, and shoot her a look that says I'll skin her alive if she continues down this path. Seeing my glare, her smile only grows, and she winks at me.

Winks. At. Me.

"So nothing particularly eventful from the last couple of days?" she asks, her voice dripping with false innocence.

Becks dips a fry in ketchup, and I try to catch his eye, but he's too focused on his food to notice. "Besides Chaos, nothing really to report."

No. Abort, Becks. *Abort*.

"Speaking of Chaos, you booked it before Locklyn even got back from her trial. I haven't gotten the chance to ask you about that yet. You weren't home when I got in last night."

Becks finally has the sense to look a little uncomfortable, but he just shrugs again. "Just some stuff I was working through. I needed to get out of there to clear my head." He finally flicks his gaze toward me, but it's too late now. Ensley laid her snare and her brother walked right into it.

"But you and Lock must have met up again last night, right? She said you took her to get her hand stitched. She wouldn't let me take her after the trial, by the way." Ensley leans forward and plops her chin on her palm like she's settling in for a long story.

I need a new best friend.

"Ensley," I warn, holding my knife like a dagger and hoping she gets the point, but she just chuckles at my weak threat.

Becks looks at me and then back at Ensley, finally catching on that she knows what happened between us. Or at least knows something. Pink appears high on his cheeks, which somehow makes him look both adorable and incredibly attractive at the same time.

"I don't know what you're talking about," he says, and then shoves the last bit of the burger in his mouth and chews slowly, keeping his mouth busy so that he doesn't have to say anything else.

I twist in my seat, scanning the courtyard for Shayla and Owen, or anyone who usually sits with us. I'd even welcome Leo's pushy company right now. Anything to keep Ensley from prying.

"Oh come on, Becks. I've been watching you two tiptoe around this for ages. It couldn't be more obvious that you both are hot for each other."

My jaw literally falls open. Becks freezes.

Ensley bursts out laughing. "This is just too good. You guys should see your faces right now."

"We're no longer friends," I say, more than half meaning it, but Ensley just snorts another laugh.

"You love me."

I do, but this is too much. I'm going to kill her for this later.

"Ensley," I grit out. "I already told you this topic wasn't open for public discussion."

Becks looks back and forth between Ensley and me. "You two have been talking about this?"

"Yes," Ensley says at exactly the same time I say, "No."

Becks rubs a hand over his face. "I cannot be having this conversation with you," he says to his sister.

"Me either," I say, and push back from my seat. Lunch is only half over, and I've hardly touched my food, but if I don't get out of here in the next two seconds my face is going to catch fire.

"Locklyn, wait," Ensley calls as I head to dump what's left of my food.

Chair legs scrape against the stone floor behind me as someone gets to their feet. I hear Becks say, "Stay put. You've done enough."

I scurry from the courtyard, feeling like hundreds of eyes are staring at me. A prickle of awareness makes the fine hairs on the back of my neck stand on end, and so I know Becks is following me. He catches up to me as soon as I push through the doors that lead back into the hallway. Without saying a word he grabs my hand and pulls me into the first empty room he finds, which happens to be a dimly lit storage closet.

After locking the door behind us, he turns to me with a wince on his face. "I'm sorry about my sister. She has the subtlety of a wrecking ball."

I can't help the snort of laugh that comes out of me. "You'd think I'd be used to it by now. We've only been friends for a decade."

Becks barks out a half laugh then shakes his head. "It's a pity you can't choose your siblings."

"Yeah."

A single low wattage bulb lights the space. We're surrounded by school supplies and cleaning products—not the most romantic of areas—but as we stare at each other the air starts to charge.

Becks trails his fingers down my bare arm, causing a chaos of sensation to break out inside me. He continues his trek down my arm until he reaches my hand; he takes it in his own and tugs me forward until I'm close enough to rest my hand on his chest and feel his heart thumping beneath my palm. It's beating just as quickly as my own.

"I didn't want to have that conversation with her before we'd had a chance to talk," he says.

"Right, talk. We didn't really get to do much of that last night."

A grin spreads over Becks' face. "You're right. We didn't get much *talking* done."

"I meant *after*," I say, ducking my head, but Becks doesn't let me look away. Stepping even closer, he uses his fingers to tip my head back, forcing me to look up at him.

"I want to be clear with you, Locklyn. You're too important to me to be anything other than honest with."

I nod, holding my breath for what he's going to say next.

"I want to be with you. I have for a long time."

Hearing those words makes my heart soar. I've always dreamed of hearing him say that, but never thought I actually would.

"How long?" I ask, greedy for the details he wasn't willing to give me the night before.

"Years," he admits, and I'm completely blown away. How is that possible? How hadn't I seen it sooner?

"That's a long time," I say, not giving up that I've been falling for him for just as long.

"I wish I'd acted on it ages ago, but I didn't know how you felt, and I was always worried about ruining our friendship. I tried to talk myself out of how I was feeling so many times. It would have been so much easier if I didn't feel this way."

Even though I can relate to what he's saying because I have the same fears and concerns, no one wants to hear that someone tried to talk themselves out of liking you, out of wanting to be with you, that part of them wished they didn't want you the way that they do.

My face must broadcast my thoughts, because he rushes to add, "You have to know having you in my life, in whatever way possible, is so important to me that the fear of pushing you away was paralyzing."

"It's okay. I get it," I say. And I really do. It's not fair of me to be upset with Becks for something I thought at one time or another as well.

"And then I became the dragon heir," he says, weariness leaking into his tone. "I wasn't free to pursue you after that. I didn't think it would be fair to either of us because I knew ultimately a mate would be picked out for me by the council and I wouldn't have a choice in who I ended up with."

I start to pull back a little, but he anchors a hand against my lower back so I can't get far. "Then what's changed?" I ask, because all those things still hang over our heads.

A dark shadow seems to pass over his face. "The thought of losing you has been driving me insane. The Chaos trials were bad enough, but last night, when I saw you in Talon's arms—" He sucks in a deep breath and holds it before letting it back out. "I was so close to shifting right there to track down Talon and rip his head off. After you broke the last compulsion, I had to take off because I was worried I wouldn't be able to stop myself if I saw the two of you together."

I don't bother defending myself again. We've already been over this. I won't apologize for what the vampire tried to compel me to do. But a seed of something ugly wedges its way between my ribs, making me uneasy. It bothers me that what finally propelled Becks to act might not have been the depth of his feelings for me, but jealousy.

Dragon shifters have a tendency to hoard what they consider their own, and I can't help but wonder if that is what Becks is doing with me. Are his feelings true, or are they muddled by his possessive instincts?

"But you're still the dragon heir," I point out. "The council is still planning to pick your mate. So where do we go from here?"

Becks swipes a thumb over the curve of my cheek, and just like every time he touches me, it scrambles my mind a little.

"I don't know what's going to happen. As the dragon heir I'm bound in unbreakable ways. The truth is we may not be able to change the council's minds, but I don't think I could live with myself if I let you go. I want to give this, give us, a shot. I think we deserve that. Don't you?"

His words sweep my concerns right under the rug and out of sight. I want that too. I want it so badly.

"I do," I whisper, and then lick my lower lip.

His gaze falls to my mouth and heats, but he forces his eyes back up to mine and groans. "We have to leave this room right now."

Not what I was expecting him to say.

"Why?"

His eyes dip to my mouth once again and hold. He feathers the pad of his finger over my lower lip, making my breath catch. "Because if we don't, we won't be leaving for a very long time."

I cock my head. I mean, that doesn't sound too bad to me.

"You're considering it, aren't you?" he asks.

I shrug and Becks laughs, shaking his head. Much to my body's disappointment, he releases me and steps back. "Come on. Lunch is going to be over any minute. I won't be responsible for you missing any classes."

He unlocks the door but turns back to me before opening it. There's a pleat between his brows. "We need to keep this between us for now. With the exception of Ensley of course," he adds with an eye roll.

I blink up at him. "You want us to hide our relationship?"

He sighs. "I don't want word getting back to the council members. It might give them an excuse to pick my life-mate quickly."

It is a completely valid reason, yet that little seed of doubt between my ribs starts to chafe. I nod anyway, knowing that, logically, he's right.

We leave the storage closet only moments before the bell rings and students start pouring into the hallways. As Becks walks me to my next class, keeping a respectable distance between us and without holding my hand, I tell myself that once we get this mating thing taken care of, nothing will stand in our way. But rather than being ecstatic that everything I ever hoped for is finally coming true, a sour sensation lingers in my gut for the rest of the day.

Twenty-Five

MY AFTERNOON CLASSES are a complete waste of my time because my mind isn't on Elemental Chemistry or Classic Mythology. Instead of being where it should be, it keeps bouncing to Becks, and then getting dragged over to Talon. His warning to me about Chaos is front and center, but there's something nagging me. Something stuck in the back of my mind that I spend most of the afternoon trying to pry free. When I finally figure it out, it's like getting hit by a bolt of lightning, but I have to wait until I see Becks after class for confirmation.

I'm searching for him when I run into Ensley in the parking lot. She looks properly repentant, and an apology is the first thing out of her mouth.

"I shouldn't have done that at lunch. It was thoughtless and really immature. I'm so sorry."

I look back at her with an arched brow. "Did Becks tell you to say that?"

"What? No. I haven't even apologized to him. He's my brother. It's basically my job to razz him."

I cross my arms over my chest. "I'm only accepting your apology if you apologize to him too."

She grimaces. "What? No. You aren't serious?"

I don't say anything and just stare at Ensley with a straight face, and she groans. What she doesn't know is that I forgave her before she even apologized—it's what besties do—but she should still say sorry to her brother as well. And little does she know she's about to get the opportunity to do so, because I spot Becks coming up behind her.

"Fine," she pouts. "You drive a hard bargain, but I'll say something to him next time I see him."

"Say something to who?" Becks asks, and she spins toward him, a sour look on her face.

"Ensley has something she'd like to tell you," I answer with a grin.

"She does, does she?" Becks asks, a smile curving his mouth as he already suspects what's coming.

Ensley plays with her purple-streaked hair, stalling.

"You wanted to say something, sis?" Becks taunts.

Sighing, she rolls her eyes. "Oh, fine. Listen, I'm sorry for giving you and Locklyn a hard time at lunch today. Your business is your own and none of my business. But let's be honest, this is also kinda my business as well, and I'm sure I'll get all the deets from my pal Locklyn anyway, but in the future I promise to only grill you individually and privately."

"That was supposed to be an apology?" Becks asks with raised eyebrows.

Ensley smiles and shrugs. "Take it or leave it, but don't expect to hear it again."

Becks shakes his head.

That's about what I expected from Ensley. Now that's settled, I have another matter to discuss with them. Before diving into it, I do a quick look around the parking lot. No one appears to be listening, but some creatures, especially certain shifters and vampires, have very good hearing, so I let Becks and Ensley chat until more students clear out.

"Hey, Becks," I finally say, ignoring the little zing that goes through me when he looks directly at me.

Calm down, girl.

"What's up?"

"Talon's uncle . . . he's on the council, right?" I hold my breath, hoping against all hopes I remembered that right.

Becks' face darkens at just the mention of Talon, but he nods. "Yeah, why?"

Finally, something is going our way. Excitement that I wouldn't let surface earlier bubbles up, and a smile stretches my mouth as I look back at Ensley's and Becks' questioning faces.

"I know exactly how to get one of the council members on our side."

"How?" Becks asks.

"Talon owes me a favor." Or at least he will once I agree to tank the next trial like he asked me to. With Becks free of the arranged life-mating, I won't need Shadow Striker anymore. Yes, it would be nice to have magic, but if the last couple of weeks has taught me anything, it's that I'm powerful even without magic. Besides, the only confirmation I've been able to find that Shadow Striker wouldn't turn me evil or psychotic is from Mr. Brone. I've been trying to ignore it, but the unknowns about Shadow Striker make me a little uneasy.

Becks' face sours at the same time Ensley's lights up.

"Locklyn, that's genius," Ensley says, bouncing on the balls of her feet in excitement. "He lives with his uncle."

"That's what he said. And if anyone can dig up dirt on him, it will be Talon." I truly believe that. Right now, I'm holding him back, at least according to him. I have no doubt he'll go to extreme lengths to get me out of the equation.

"Why would he go against his uncle and help us?" Becks asks with a frown.

"He'll help us, I'm sure of it."

"No." Becks shakes his head. "I don't like the idea of owing that guy anything."

My smile starts to fade. "You wouldn't owe him anything. Like I said, he owes *me* a favor."

"What kind of favor?" Becks asks, his mood darkening even more.

"A big one," I answer vaguely, crossing my arms over my chest. The last thing Becks needs to know now is that Talon thinks my life is in danger. "And I don't need your permission to cash it in."

At a standstill, Becks and I glare at each other. I won't let any sort of petty jealousy or possessive instincts get in the way. This is the breakthrough we've been hoping for, he's just too stubborn to see it. I want Becks on my side right now, but I'll move forward without him. It's for his own good.

"Becks." Ensley grabs her brother's arm and shakes it. "This is huge. We haven't gotten anywhere with Operation Bring Down the Council."

Glancing at her, he arches an eyebrow. "Operation Bring Down the Council?"

"It has a nice ring to it," she says with a shrug. "But never mind that. This is worth a try. You know it is."

Becks' nostrils flare. "I don't trust him. He's hiding something."

Part of me agrees with Becks, but at the end of the day, who cares? "He might be hiding something, but what does it matter if he can help us?"

Becks' green gaze swivels to me. "If he's hiding something, how can we trust him?"

It's another solid point, but in this case I'm willing to risk it.

"Talon could go to his uncle and tell him what we are doing rather than help us," Becks goes on. "If that happens, then this whole plan goes up in smoke."

"That won't happen," I assure him. "He's going to want to help us."

Becks looks skeptical, and for good reason. He doesn't know everything.

"You have to trust me," I add.

I swallow as Becks steps closer and looks down at me with burning green eyes. "You're really willing to trust Talon with my future. With *our* future?"

My stomach drops. I hear what Becks is saying, and it's not necessarily that I trust Talon, but I trust in how badly he wants me out of his way so that he can win Chaos. I saw the desperation in his eyes earlier today when he practically begged me to fail out of the game. So yes, if there's anything I trust in, it's that.

I nod.

Becks huffs. "I don't want to be indebted to someone like him."

"Locklyn already said you wouldn't, but so what if you are? Being indebted to Talon has to be the better alternative to being life-mated to a stranger. Surely you can swallow your pride in exchange for your freedom?" Ensley says, putting everything into perspective.

I watch Becks' face as he struggles through accepting the inevitable. A bevy of emotions flick over his features: denial, anger, frustration, until finally resignation sets in. He swipes his hand down his face. "Okay, fine. When should we talk to him?"

Oh no. That won't do. "I've got it. I can talk to Talon myself."

Becks frowns, and I know where this conversation is headed. "I don't know if that's—"

"If she says she's got it, she's got it. Let our girl handle it," Ensley says before Becks can get too huffy.

"You need to trust me. I've *got* this," I say.

"It's not that I don't trust you, it's that I don't trust *him*," Becks replies.

"Well, then you need to trust that I can handle Talon."

Becks presses his lips into a hard line, and I hold my breath, hoping he lets this go. Finally, he nods. "Okay. As long as you promise not to offer him anything in return."

I lift my eyebrows at that, wondering what type of deal Becks thinks I'm going to be striking with Talon.

"Like I said, he owes me a favor, that's all."

"It must be a pretty big favor," Becks grumbles.

He has no idea.

I HAVE to wait until the next day at school to talk to Talon, because besides being under house arrest for the next two weeks, my parents have my phone and are monitoring my computer, so I don't have a way to reach out to him. Despite what I told Becks, Talon and I don't actually have any classes together—hopefully that's a little tidbit Becks doesn't figure out on his own—so I'm stuck stalking his locker the next morning, hoping to catch him before classes start. Much to my annoyance, Talon doesn't come swaggering up to his locker until moments before the final bell, so by then there's hardly any time to talk to him.

"Freckles. To what do I owe the pleasure?" he says, a flirtatious smile on his face that I recognize now for what it is. A mask.

"Lunch, meet me in the tower," I say, not bothering with the pleasantries. "I have a proposition for you."

His brows shoot up and his smile turns lazy. "A proposition? Call me intrigued."

I internally groan. Wrong use of words. "Not like that."

"Not like what?" he says with false innocence.

"I've thought about what we talked about yesterday," I say quickly, knowing we're running out of time, and this isn't the place to speak freely.

Talon sobers immediately and he steps closer, his eyes devoid of any lighthearted flirtation from before. "And . . ." he prompts.

"And meet me in the tower later so we can talk about it," I say, not letting him intimidate me. Then I turn on a heel, and just as I reach the end of the hall the final bell rings, signaling the start of the period and I groan. Another tardy.

Add it to the list.

Twenty-Six

TALON IS PACING when I climb the last step and reach the tower landing that overlooks Nightlark Academy. He stops when he spots me, and I can't help but remember the last time I was up here with Becks. I wish I'd thought of a different place for us to meet, because the tower feels like Becks' and my place. Seeing Talon in this space is weird.

We stare at each other in silence as I cross the space to reach him.

"Do you agree to fail out of the next trial?" he asks bluntly, not wasting a moment of time.

"That depends," I hedge.

"On what?"

"On you."

Arching a brow, he waits for me to elaborate.

"I need you to do something for me. If you can, then yes, I'll purposefully fail out of the next trial as soon as an opportunity presents itself."

He folds his arms over his chest, his eyes taking on a glint of suspicion. "What do you need me to do?"

I suck in a deep breath, holding it in my chest for a moment longer than necessary. Becks' warning about Talon being untrustworthy rings in my mind. Once I say the words there's no taking them back. Talon will have the power to go to his uncle and destroy Becks' chances of getting out from under this arranged life-mating. And in doing so, he'll also have the power to shatter my chances of ever truly being with Becks.

I was so sure Talon would agree to this plan, but now I'm not as confident. *Am I wrong to place this much trust in him?*

I'm sure Talon reads the hesitation on my face and body language, but he stays silent, affording me the time I need to work through my fears before making this leap of faith. But really, is there any decision to make? Besides winning Shadow Striker, which considering what Talon divulged yesterday about my life being in danger makes it even more unattainable than I realized, this is the only chance we have to free Becks—we have to take it.

"I need you to find something out about your uncle that I can use to blackmail him."

Talon's face doesn't hide his shock, but he recovers quickly and then chuckles out a half-laugh. "You must be kidding. That was a good one."

He waits for me to crack a smile or agree with him, but I remain stone-faced.

The smile slips from his face. "You're not kidding."

I shake my head, and he rubs a hand over his mouth. "Why do you need to blackmail him?"

"It doesn't matter."

"Oh, I think it matters a great deal. My Uncle Drake has influence. More than you probably even know. He's a member of the dragon council and—" Talon's eyes go wide. "That's it, isn't it? You're trying to get that dragon shifter you think you're in love with out of the arranged life-mating."

My heart rate spikes. "How do you know about the arranged life-mating?" I ask, choosing to ignore his comment about me being in love with Becks. He might be right, but it's none of his business and certainly not up for discussion right now.

Talon snorts. "You don't have to be a dragon shifter to know their business."

Just like Talon. A non-answer answer. Well, two can play that game.

"It doesn't matter what I need the blackmail for, I just need you to get it. Can you? If so, I'll do what you want me to: I'll throw the next Chaos trial and get myself expelled from the competition."

Talon considers me. His gaze turns contemplative, and I can't help feeling like I'm as transparent as glass. "Not to talk you out of anything. If this is what I have to do to get you to pull out of Chaos, I'll do it. But have you given thought to whether or not he's worth it? I have no doubt that Becks wants you. It's clear to anyone with eyes. But why go to these lengths for a guy who won't even go after what he wants?"

My face heats when he says it's clear Becks wants me. I'm not comfortable talking about my relationship with Becks to anyone just yet, least of all Talon, who enjoys baiting Becks whenever the opportunity arises, but I can't seem to keep my mouth shut about it either.

"You don't know what you're talking about. I know exactly how Becks feels about me."

Talon's eyebrows rise and he cocks his head. "Finally made a move, has he?" He rubs his jaw, a sly smile forming on his mouth. "I'll bet our performance the other night pushed him into it, didn't it? Dragon shifters are a possessive bunch."

My stomach knots when Talon pokes at the one spot I was already insecure about. My face heats, but this time it's not from embarrassment. "Shut up, Talon."

He puts his hands up like he means no harm. "Don't get me wrong, if I was in his position I would have claimed you as well. I wouldn't want to share my female with anyone either. I'm only saying it's about time." He cocks his head. "But let me guess, he's keeping you a secret."

"It's not like that."

"Isn't it though? If he really wants to be with you, why isn't he staking a claim and letting the world know."

"You know we can't go public with that life-mating hanging over our heads."

Talon makes a *tsking* sound with his tongue and I suddenly want to rip it out of his mouth. "Make no mistake. Your dragon heir has a choice. He just wants his cake and to eat it too. And you're letting him."

"I don't need to justify myself or Becks to you or anyone else. It's no one's business but our own. But now *you* have a choice to make. Will you give me what I've asked for or not?"

He stares at me hard, his gray-blue eyes drilling a hole into my forehead. I can tell that some part of him wants to say no but it has nothing to do with having scruples over digging up dirt on his uncle, and everything with proving he's right about Becks. But I'm betting that part of him won't win out in the end. Talon's too calculated and wants Shadow Striker too badly to deny me this request.

Taking a step back, he leans against the stone railing, his body going from rigid to languid before my eyes. His mood swings give me whiplash. "Fine. I'll get you what you want."

Relief is sweet as it rushes through me. "Once I have the information I need from you—"

"No," he says, cutting me off. "I won't deliver you blackmail material."

I furrow my brow. "I don't understand."

"You're reckless to believe you'd be able to blackmail my uncle into doing anything. Drake's ruthless when it comes to protecting himself. He'll bury you the moment he gets wind of the threat, and I do mean that literally."

A chill runs through me. "But you just said you'd get me what I want."

"And I will. I'll get your princeling freed from his arranged life-mating. That is, after all, what you really want, isn't it?"

It is, so I nod, feeling like I'm walking into a trap, but not knowing any way else to move.

"How are you going to do that?" I ask, starting to think that Becks might have been more right about Talon than I had wanted to believe, and that there were layers to him I haven't even begun to understand.

Talon flashes me a wolfish smile full of teeth and charm. "*That is none of your business.*"

I bristle that he's using the same argument against me that I used against him. I cross my arms over my chest. "And you just expect me to trust that this is something you can do on your own?"

He shrugs. "I expect you to realize that you don't have any other option but to trust me."

I press my lips together, agitation toward Talon growing by the second. "I won't fail out of the next trial until after you deliver."

Talon nods. "Naturally."

It can't be as easy as that. There has to be a catch, but as I stare at Talon, he's giving nothing away. All I see right now is the easygoing guy he portrays himself to be to the rest of the school. That he can switch back and forth between personas so easily should be unnerving, but if he can do what he says he can do and get Becks out from underneath the arranged life-mating, do I really care what mysteries the guy is keeping to himself?

He holds out his hand for me to take. "Do we have a deal?"

I look at his outstretched hand, knowing what he's offering me is weightier than a simple handshake, but I take it anyway.

The moment my hand slips into his, a rush of heat swamps my body, starting from the point where our hands connect and running up my arm straight to my head and then down my body. It leaves me lightheaded.

I gasp. "What was that?"

"I was just sealing our agreement."

I blink back up at him, realizing what he just did. He used magic, *vampire magic* to be exact, to create an unbreakable bond between us. If he comes through on his end of the bargain, I'll have no choice but to come through on my end. So if he gets Becks free of the life-mating, then I won't be able to pass the next trial even if I want to. The only thing that frees either of us from this arrangement is if the other person releases them.

I realize I'm still gripping Talon's hand and let go immediately, but the heat from his grip lingers.

"You just used vampire magic," I accuse, my mind trying to put together the pieces so that they make sense.

"So I did," he says.

I've seen Talon use lots of different types of magic, but never one thing that I knew only belonged to one species. But now, even though it doesn't quite feel right, I can't deny it. Talon is a vampire.

With a wink, Talon turns from me and starts toward the stairs, leaving me gawking behind him.

I PUSH the revelation of Talon's creature species out of my mind. I always knew Talon had to be something, so why not a vampire? It explains the darkness that lurks in his gaze. But something about it doesn't exactly feel right, and that nags at me.

I make it back to the table before the end of lunch, but the space is crowded with our usual gang as well as a few dragon shifter friends of Becks' that I don't really know and there isn't a spot for me. Becks spots me first and jumps up to grab an empty chair from another table and slide it next to his. I smile my thanks as I slip into the seat, and when he settles into his own chair he rests his arm against the back of mine. No one seems to notice when he picks up a piece of my hair and starts to play with it, but I'm acutely aware of the way he twirls the strands around his fingers.

"Where have you been, girl?" Shayla asks, and several heads turn in my direction, including the dragon shifters that don't usually sit with us.

Letting go of my hair, Becks reaches for a fry on his tray. I try not to be disappointed, but I can't help but wonder if he stopped because he didn't want anyone to know he was touching me.

"Oh, um, I had to catch up with Talon about a project we're working on." I really hope no one knows either of our schedules well enough to call me out on that lie. I don't have to look over at Becks to know that he's stiffened up next to me.

"Talon, eh?" Carmen, one of the dragon shifters says, and then wiggles her eyebrows at me. "I wouldn't mind having a special project with him. He is one fine creature."

"I second that," Shayla says with a laugh, and then she and Carmen high five.

"Hey," Owen says next to her, looking properly annoyed.

Giggling, Shayla plants a kiss on his cheek to mollify him. "Don't worry, babe, the mysterious bad boys don't really do it for me. Besides, I'm partial to brunettes who can light stuff on fire."

Owen grumbles under his breath but picks up Shayla's hand and kisses her palm. As they stare lovingly into each other's eyes, something in my heart tweaks. I thought I would be content with knowing Becks wants to be with me as much as I do him, but I want more. I want Becks to publicly claim me as his. I don't want to hide in the shadows. I want to stand in the daylight, free to express our feelings for each other for all to see, but we can't. I remind myself that if Talon comes through, maybe we will be able to soon.

"How did that go?" Ensley asks, leaning forward. "Is Talon prepared to do his part? His part of the project, I mean."

She and Becks knew I was going to talk to Talon. I'm surprised Becks didn't ask me about it immediately, but maybe he just forced it from his mind. He certainly wasn't happy to hear I was planning on meeting Talon alone.

I nod and smile. "We're all set. He's confident he'll be able to get his part done quickly. In fact, he wanted to take an even bigger role in the assignment than I expected."

Her eyebrows rise.

"What does that mean?" Becks asks.

"Um . . ." I glance over at Becks to see the frown on his face. How am I supposed to answer that in front of everyone? "He just pointed out that he's more familiar with the material than I am, so it might be better if he runs lead on the work."

I'm not sure if that made any sense to Ensley or Becks, but that's all I'm going to say about it until we're in private.

Becks nods and then says, "Here, eat," and pushes his plate over to me. He's already eaten a burger, but there's an untouched chicken sandwich left.

I look down at the food, touched he thought to leave me something when I know for a fact that Becks can easily put away two sandwiches on his own.

"Eat up," he encourages. "The bell's going to ring any minute."

I offer him a small smile of thanks and then dive in, sitting back to listen to the conversation bounce around the table for what's left of the lunch period.

Twenty-Seven

BETWEEN STOLEN MOMENTS WITH BECKS, anxiety over my deal with Talon, and anticipating the next Chaos trial, the next week passes quickly even though I'm only allowed to go to school and home again. The injured look on my mom's face still hasn't completely disappeared, but I think the fact that I haven't bucked against their punishment has helped me gain some ground.

It still bothers me that Becks and I can't hold hands in the hallways of Nightlark or cuddle by our lockers between classes. But Becks reaffirms his feelings for me time and time again in looks he sends my way when no one's watching, and the kisses we share in stolen moments. It's enough to hold me over, for now, but as the days tick by, I have to work harder and harder to bat away the negative voice that tells me this is all I'll ever have of Becks. That he'll never truly be mine. It certainly doesn't help that the one time I managed to corner Talon for an update, he told me to chill because he was handling it but wouldn't say more.

The Chaos tracker hasn't gone off, but with every day that passes I'm acutely aware we're getting closer to a new trial, and that Talon is running out of time. If he doesn't make good on our deal, I'm back to Shadow Striker being the only card in my deck.

I'm in the back corner of the store early Saturday morning, high on a ladder and dusting the top of an antique armoire. The person who sold it to my parents said it can transport you to another world, but really it's just an oversized piece of furniture with a much less interesting backstory. The bell above the door jingles, announcing a customer, and I'm thrilled when I turn and realize it's Becks. I scramble down the ladder to meet him, but the stormy look on his face as he walks toward me makes my smile melt into a frown.

"What's wrong?" I ask when he reaches me.

He casts a quick look around the shop, but no one else is here.

"I had a council meeting last night," he says, and a knot forms in my gut. *What now?* "They voted to abolish the rules on arranging a life-mate for the dragon heir."

My eyes widen as my heart begins to soar. This is amazing news. Talon came through. But the gloomy look on Becks' face doesn't change, and I don't understand.

"Becks, this is what we were hoping for."

He shakes his head. "It's not. They changed the law surrounding *picking* a life-mate for me, but they didn't change the timeline. I still only have until graduation to announce a betrothal, I just get to choose the person rather than them going out and finding someone for me."

"Okay, that's not exactly what we were hoping for, but it's better than before. At least now you have a choice," I say, trying to find a silver lining.

Becks' laugh is full of bitterness. "But I don't really. They still need to approve my choice."

So we're back to exactly where we started. With Becks needing to mate with a powerful female, and me not having any magic.

It hits me that I bartered away my only chance at getting that power, and I start to feel sick.

"Talon tricked you," Becks says, and I find it hard to disagree with him. He might have technically fulfilled his end of the bargain by getting Becks out of an arranged life-mating, but the obstacles between us are still there.

"I haven't pushed you on this, but will you tell me what you had to do to get this favor from him?" He's tense as he waits for me to respond. I don't see the point in not telling him anymore.

"I promised Talon that I'd fail out of the next Chaos trial," I say, and Becks' gaze instantly brightens.

"That's it?"

"That's it," I confirm, and Becks lets out a sigh of relief, his muscles unclenching before my eyes.

"Thank the Creator," he says, and pulls me into his arms, where I stand woodenly while the reality of what I've lost sets in. If the council has to approve his choice, I'll never measure up.

Becks doesn't realize what I've really given up, so it's no wonder he's not more upset. In his mind we didn't lose anything to make this minor gain. In fact, this is what Becks has wanted all along, for me to not be competing in Chaos. It's ironic that this is the thing he and Talon finally agree upon, the thing that might have given us a chance to be together.

"It's hopeless," I say into Becks' chest, my eyes welling. After everything I've done and everything I've been through, it is over. This was my last play. I'm out of ideas, and I'm now also out of a backup plan.

Becks crushes me closer. "No, don't say that. I'm not giving up. I've always seen the council as unmovable, but I don't anymore. If it's possible for Talon to get them to bend, then I can too."

I hear the confidence in his voice, but it doesn't do anything to lift my spirits.

"Hey," Becks says, loosening his hold so that he can pull back and look into my eyes. A tear slips out and treks down my face; he wipes it away with his thumb. "Don't cry, Lock. We'll figure it out. It's not over."

I bite my lip and try to pull myself back together. We've made it this far. I can't fall apart now.

Becks traces my lower lip and then frees it from my teeth. I hold my breath as he swipes his finger slowly back and forth against the underside of my mouth, loving the tingles that small touch causes to race down my spine. Taking my face between both his hands, he leans toward me and places his lips on mine, giving me an achingly soft kiss that I feel all the way to my toes.

A throat clears, and Becks and I break apart.

"So this is a thing now?"

With a gasp, I shove against Becks, stumbling away from him to find my dad standing with his arms crossed, staring down both of us with a stony-faced frown.

I've never been more mortified than I am as my dad's gaze moves from me to Becks and then back to me again.

"So. . ." my dad prompts.

I open my mouth to answer, and then shut it again, looking to Becks for help. No one knows about us except Ensley. And with the life-mating hanging over Becks' head, we haven't defined what we are. I'm not honestly sure how to answer my dad.

Becks rubs his neck, clearly as uncomfortable at having been caught by my dad as I am, but he takes the initiative and says, "Yes, sir. This is most definitely a thing."

Despite the awkward situation, a small smile slips on my face. I like hearing Becks acknowledge what we have out loud to someone other than me or his sister.

"Sir?" my dad asks, and I swear the corner of his mouth twitches. Becks has never referred to my dad as "sir" before. He usually calls my dad by his first name, Garrett.

Becks shifts nervously under my dad's intense regard, and just when I don't think it could get any worse, my mom appears. "What's going on?"

I groan, and Becks winces.

"I caught these two making out," my dad says, and I slap my hands over my heated face.

"Dad," I whine from my fingers. "We were *not* making out."

"You did?" she asks, and I drop my hands to see my mom's face light up.

"This one here says that this is a thing?" my dad adds, pointing to Becks.

She looks over at Becks. "It is?"

He nods, and a smile spreads over her face. "Well, it's about time."

I shut my eyes. *Great.* She's as bad as Ensley.

My dad clears his throat as my mom says, "Right," and then tries to plaster a serious look on her face but falls short. "Well, you realize this means we're going to have to set new rules for you, such as staying over at their house and such?"

Rather than argue, I nod. I don't need to be in any more hot water with them than I already am.

"So, how long has this been going on?" she asks.

"It's pretty new," I admit. "So can we not pick it apart right now?"

To my extreme surprise, my parents let me out of working all day in the store to hang out with Becks, reminding me that I still have almost a week before I'm completely let off my grounding.

We don't do anything particularly special. He takes me out to lunch at Sloan's, then we work out at Peet's and catch an early movie so that I can be home by eight like my parents asked. When the lights dim in the theater, Becks takes my hand and rubs his thumb back and forth over my knuckles. It's so distracting I don't catch half of the movie, but it also feels so natural. We do our best to avoid talking about anything dragon heir related, both of us seeming to want to escape reality if only just for a few hours. It feels like an almost perfect day.

Becks and I pull up to the curb in front of the store at three minutes to eight. I'm reluctant to leave him, but I don't think it's a good idea to push my parents, so we say our goodbyes and I slide from the seat of his truck. With a wave, Becks takes off and I waste another minute standing there until his taillights disappear. When they do, I turn toward our building.

The store closed two hours ago, so rather than going through it to reach our apartment above, I go around the side alley to the outdoor entrance to our home. I'm reaching for the door when it opens, startling me. I jump back a step with a sharp yelp and feel instantly silly when it's just Mr. Brone leaving our place.

"Locklyn, dear. I didn't mean to scare you," Mr. Brone says as he steps out into the alley with me.

"Don't worry about it, Mr. Bro—" I start, but then correct myself when I see the look on his face. "Kerrim."

He smiles broadly when I use his first name without having to be told. "I was just helping your parents with their new security system that I'd recommended. You can't be too careful these days. They invited me to stay for dinner and we just finished. I'm sorry you weren't able to join. They mentioned you were out on a date."

My parents are talking about my love life? How embarrassing. I'm going to have to let them know not to spread the news around though. I don't want the dragon council finding out about us.

"I was with my friend Becks," I say, neither confirming nor denying it was a date. "So which one of them cooked? Mom or Dad?" I ask, hoping to move the topic away from me.

He laughs because he's aware what a wretched cook my dad is. "Your mother. It was delicious. In fact, we made sure to leave you a slice of your favorite cake."

Yes. "I love her carrot cake. She hasn't made it in ages."

Even though I ate a full meal with Becks, and candy during the movie, my stomach still grumbles at the thought of Mom's famous carrot cake. It's dense and perfectly moist, with the lightest cream cheese frosting you've ever had. I'm glad they left me some because I know my dad can finish off almost the whole thing himself.

"Then it seems it's your lucky day," Mr. Brone says with a polite smile.

"It sure does," I say and then turn toward the door, ready to race up the steps and claim that last slice of cake, when Mr. Brone asks politely, "How did your project go?"

"Oh. You mean about Shadow Striker?" I ask and he nods. "You know I actually took your advice and decided to drop it after all."

"Really?" he asks, with a tilt of his head. "You seemed so determined to stick with that topic. What changed your mind?"

I shrug. "I hit a dead end. I guess it just wasn't meant to be."

"Hmm," Mr. Brone says, his cordial smile slipping just a little. "Well, the Emporium's library is always open to you if you need it for research."

Guilt sours my gut when I remember that I still haven't returned the *Dragon Shifter Law* book I took from his library the last time I was there, and I make a mental note to take it back after I'm no longer grounded.

With a wave, Mr. Brone leaves and then I shoot up the stairs, going straight for the kitchen. The slice of carrot cake is waiting for me in the center of the table. After pouring myself a large glass of milk, I grab a fork and dig in. I'm on my second bite when my mom enters the kitchen, and seeing me, she sits down at the table with me.

"Like it?" she asks.

"Delicious," I say after swallowing. "Seriously my favorite dessert on the planet. You should consider selling these to customers."

She laughs at that because the idea of selling cake in a high-end antique shop is somewhat ridiculous. "I'm glad to hear you still like it. How was your day with Becks?" she asks with a twinkle in her eye.

"Good," I say, and duck my head to hide my telling smile.

"I've been telling your father for ages that you two would be so cute together. I'm glad it finally happened."

"Mom," I complain, fully embarrassed now.

"What?" she asks, her face full of innocence.

I shake my head. "I saw Mr. Brone on the way in. Can you please at least keep the news between our family, at least for now."

"Why ever so?"

I don't want them to know about Becks' life-mating. That's his business, and if they find out he has to get betrothed in the next month and a half, they're going to flip. But there is more than one reason why I don't want our status circulating.

"Well, for one thing I don't know that it's going to work out between us," I tell her honestly, my gaze unfocused on the half-eaten slice of cake in front of me. Confessing that out loud really makes it feel real, and my appetite starts to dim.

She frowns. "Why do you say that?"

I shrug. "We're just so different. He has a lot of pressure not to be with a girl like me."

"A girl like you?" she asks with a furrowed brow.

"Yeah, Mom, you know. . . . Becks is the dragon heir and I'm just . . ." I sigh. I don't mean to beat myself up, but the facts are the facts. Magically speaking, I'm not on Becks' level. And no matter what Becks says or what we want, that's going to matter in the end.

"You're just a kind, intelligent, and beautiful young girl any boy would be lucky to have," my mom finishes for me when I fall silent.

I force myself to give her a smile of thanks for the compliments. I do believe that is what my parents see when they look at me, but they just don't get it.

"I'm also magicless, Mom, and it's no secret Becks is going to end up with a powerful female."

My mom frowns. "Haven't we always taught you a creature's worth is measured by far more than the level of their magic? What use is a powerful creature who's lacking in character?"

She's right, that is what I was raised to believe. My parents never seemed fazed by my lack of magic. When the doctors came back and said that my magic must just be so small that it's not registering, they didn't even look surprised. Their support really helped me over the years, but in a weird way it also made it harder to talk to them about my insecurities. They just don't get what it's like to be magicless in a supernatural world. It's lonely.

"Maybe you should tell the dragon council that," I say with a self-deprecating laugh.

"Maybe I will," she says, a fierce look sharpening her features. I'm familiar with that look. It's the one that says, "Someone hurt my baby girl and I'm going to make them wish they were never born." My mother might be petite, but she's a force to be reckoned with. I'd like to think I got some of my fierceness from her.

"Please don't," I say, half worried she's serious. I don't need to be coddled by my parents any more than I need to be by Becks or Ensley. "Let Becks and me work it out. If we can't, we were never meant to be together anyway."

I say that to keep my mom from doing anything rash, but the truth of that statement stabs me in the chest, stealing my breath.

Rather than finish the rest of the cake, I push it to the middle of the table and tell my mom I'm full. There's sadness in her gaze as I get to my feet, but she doesn't press the issue anymore. She tells me she loves me, and I say it back. It might seem like a small thing to most, but I find a deep sense of comfort in our relationship, because no matter what happens, I know that will always be true.

The rest of the weekend passes slowly. Becks doesn't stop by again, and Monday morning Talon is waiting for me with his shoulder pressed up against my locker when I arrive at school.

"I filled my end of the bargain, Freckles. I got your princeling out of an arranged mating. It's time for you to make good on our deal."

I scoff and nudge him out of the way, and when I open my locker I proceed to shove books in harder than necessary. I had all weekend to stew on what Talon did, and I feel played. Sure, he got Becks out of an arranged life-mating, but he's still under the council's thumb, so Talon didn't actually do much to help our situation, and he knows it.

I wait until I've loaded my bag with the books I need to slam my locker and face Talon.

"You know the council will never agree to let me be with Becks," I hiss only loud enough for him to hear.

Talon shrugs, a lazy smile on his face that I want to smack off. "Then it looks like you are going to find out one way or another exactly how important you are to him."

"How can you be so cruel?" I ask, my voice hitching. I hung all my hopes on Talon, and he let me down.

Something softens in his gaze as he sighs. "It was the best I could do. The council has their reasons for wanting Becks mated sooner rather than later. Even if my uncle could have been persuaded, the other members wouldn't have budged. The ball's back in your princeling's court now."

I shake my head. "He doesn't have a choice." Despite Becks' confidence this past weekend that we'd find a way to be together, I don't see how it's going to all work out. And now I've lost my backup plan.

"We've been over this. There's always a choice."

When I look down, he uses two fingers under my chin to tip my face back up toward him. "Don't you realize that you often have to fight for the things most worth having?" Reaching forward, he pushes a strand of hair behind my ear, and for some reason I let him. "You're worth fighting for."

I blink up at him, feeling raw and exposed.

"I know you've been fighting for your princeling, but has he really been fighting for you?"

"Yes," I say, coming to Becks' defense, but as Talon stares down at me I can tell he doesn't believe that.

Talon's gaze flicks over my shoulder. Straightening, he steps back. "And that's my cue," he says, and then abruptly turns and walks away, blending into the hallway traffic right away.

"Was that Talon talking to you?" Becks says behind me, and when I turn he and Ensley are standing there.

I nod. "I was just giving him a piece of my mind."

A muscle in Becks' jaw jumps. "Good. I always knew we couldn't trust him."

"At least the situation isn't quite as dire as before," Ensley says, trying to stay positive, but winces when she sees the look on my face.

"I'll figure something out," Becks says, and I can only hope he's right, because I already played my ace and lost.

Twenty-Eight

A BUZZING NOISE wakes me up in the middle of the night. I'm disoriented as I slap around my nightstand, searching blindly for the light switch on my table lamp. By the time I get it turned on I'm more awake and know exactly what woke me up.

Sliding from my bed, I rush over to my backpack and pull out the Chaos tracker. Sure enough, a set of coordinates are flashing on the screen as well as the words, "One Hour." I go to reach for my computer before I remember I don't have it or my phone. My grounding is officially over tomorrow, but how am I supposed to know where I'm going, or even get a ride there without my computer or phone?

Panic starts to set in when I think of Tenn. Something happened to him because he skipped a Chaos trial. He's still in a coma, and they aren't sure if he is ever going to wake. If I don't figure out where this next trial is and how to get there, that could be me.

Moving quickly, I throw on a pair of jeans and a t-shirt, not even really paying attention to what I grab. I shove my feet in tennis shoes and then look out my window. I know my parents are keeping my computer and phone in the store below, but Mr. Brone just helped them install an alarm on our front door so I can't sneak out that way. Becks and Ensley live too far away to get there in time on foot, so my only chance is to go out the window and then get into the shop from the outside. I know the keycode that will unlock the store door from the street. I just need to get down there. Once I have my phone, I can call Becks and he'll come and get me. I just hope the trial location isn't far, or else I'll run out of time.

I close my eyes, not believing what I'm about to do, and I wish, not for the first time, I wasn't magically gagged. If I could, I would wake my parents and tell them everything. Sure, they'd be furious, but I know they'd help me if they understood the consequences.

Shoving the Chaos tracker in my pocket, I open my window and look down. It's a two-story drop, and my only way to the ground without breaking something is to scale the drainpipe running next to my window. It's not something I've ever tried before, but I don't have a choice now.

I maneuver so that I'm sitting in the window with my feet dangling out over the ground. The drainpipe is only a few feet away, so without thinking too hard about it, I grab the metal pipe and swing onto the wall, anchoring my feet against the textured stones to keep from sliding. The stitches in my hand pull as I grasp the pipe. My feet have a tentative purchase at best as I start to slowly descend. Hand-over-hand, I descend the stone wall, my shoes slipping every now and then, forcing me to dangle by my grip on the pipe. At one point, the bandage wrapped around my still-healing hand snags on a jagged piece of the pipe, and I have to rip it free, exposing some of the stitches.

When I finally plant my feet on the ground, I'm shaking from the effort, and sweat plasters the fine hairs around my face to my cheeks and brow. Now that I've made it out of my room, I still need to figure out how to get into the store without waking my parents. It feels like there's a ticking clock hanging over my head, each second clanging loudly in my ears, letting me know I'm getting closer to missing the trial and facing whatever conse-quences may come.

I pull out the Chaos tracker and see that it's counting down. I only have thirty-four minutes left to get to the location.

Panic swells in my chest, threatening to pull me under, but I bat it away. I made it through three Chaos trials on my own, or at least mostly on my own. I'm not going to miss this one even though I have no choice but to throw it. Rushing over to the store door, I quickly key in the unlock code, but rather than flashing green and disengaging, the light on the panel turns red.

No! No no no no.

A sinking feeling settles low in my gut when I realize that my parents must have recently reset the code without telling me. I rack my brain trying to think of what they might have switched it to. I try their anniversary, all of our birthdays, even the name of our first dog, but the same red light appears every time.

An engine revs in the distance and I spin, ready to defend myself. I haven't missed the trial start yet, but now that I can't get into the shop I know it's only a matter of time. I check the Chaos tracker. Twenty-nine minutes. Are they coming for me already?

A motorcycle curves around the bend in the distance, its sleek chrome pieces flashing in the moonlight as the rider expertly maneuvers down the street, the engine piercing the stillness of the night.

I can feel the blood pumping through my veins as it nears and then skids to a stop almost directly in front of me. The rider is dressed all in black and his head is covered by a shaded helmet.

My body is primed to run, but just before I spin and take off, the rider reaches behind him and grabs an extra helmet, tossing it to me. I catch it before it hits me in the chest, confused at what's happening.

"Get on," the rider orders, but my feet are cemented to the ground.

I'm ready to drop the helmet and run when the rider yanks off his helmet and I catch a familiar scowl.

Talon.

"What are you doing here?"

"Isn't it obvious?" he asks.

"Not really."

"You're still grounded, right?"

I nod.

"Thought so. I knew you wouldn't have a way to know where the next trial is or get there. Bad things happen to the competitors who don't show up."

"So you came to get me?" I'm just so shocked that he thought to get me, let alone drove all the way over here, that I'm stating the obvious.

"Yes, now get on."

"But . . . why?"

He throws his head back and groans, and then pulls out his Chaos tracker and checks the time. "The next trial is a twenty-three-minute ride away. We only have another twenty-seven minutes. Do you really want to stand out here and have a discussion about this?"

Shoving the helmet on my head, I rush to the bike, throwing a leg over the seat. A zing of awareness runs through me when I lean forward and wrap my arms around Talon's waist, but I brush it off as nerves as he hits the gas and takes off.

I've never been on a motorcycle before, but it makes me think of flying. At least the way Talon drives it feels that way. I don't try to check the speedometer over his shoulder to see how fast we're going as we zip through the streets, passing the few cars out at this time of night.

I can't hear much with the helmet on besides the buzz of the engine and the wind whipping by. There's a stretch of winding road up ahead, and Talon doesn't bother slowing to take the turns. The bike tilts to the side as we careen around the first curve and with a *yip* I tighten my hold around Talon, bringing the front of my body completely flush against the back of his. If I fly off this piece of metal, I'm taking him with me.

I can only breathe easier once we hit straight road again. "This is crazy," I mumble to myself. "He's going to kill the both of us before Chaos gets the chance."

I hear a chuckle. "Don't worry. I've been riding almost as long as I've been walking."

Eep. There must be some sort of microphone system in the helmets so we can hear each other.

"Oh, ah. That's good to know." Now that we're past the curves, I try loosening my hold on him, but as soon as I relax my grip Talon hits the gas and I have to clamp back around him to keep from jolting back.

"You did that on purpose," I accuse.

Rather than answer, Talon makes some sort of noncommittal sound. We fall silent as we slice through the night, the wind whipping my hair behind me as the darkened landscape passes by in a blur. I don't dare loosen my grip around Talon's waist another time, but as his nearness starts to get to me, I start counting down the minutes to distract myself.

"We're almost there," Talon announces as we speed past a red sedan.

I nod even though he can't see me, and then less than two minutes later Talon pulls us into the gravel parking lot of what looks like an old, abandoned building that foliage has almost completely taken over. The structure would almost be beautiful if it weren't so creepy. It looks like the plants covering it are trying to swallow the structure whole.

I recognize the small purple blooms that dot along the ivy creeping up the cobblestone walls: shade ivy, a highly poisonous plant that shoots spores into the air and whose vines have three-inch thorns. Inhaling the spores will cause hallucinations, but they only shoot spores when they are burned or encounter fire, so we should be safe.

Talon slows to a stop near the smattering of cars parked along the grounds in front of the building and then cuts the engine. A handful of competitors loiter in front of the arched building entrance. This is nothing like any of the other trials. There are a few spectators, but for the most part there are only other bleary-eyed competitors with us, waiting for the trial to begin.

I don't realize I'm still holding tight on to Talon until he places his hand over where mine are clasped around his waist and says, "It's safe to let go now."

I immediately rear back, almost losing my balance and toppling from the bike.

How embarrassing.

Scrambling off the seat, I yank the helmet off and hand it to him. His gaze goes from my face to my hair, and I self-consciously reach back to find a matted mess.

Fantastic.

As I finger-comb the mess, he flips open the top box behind the seat and pulls something out. "Here," he says as he offers me a small black ring.

"A hair tie?"

The corner of his mouth quirks, and it's charming enough that for a moment I forget how angry I am at him. "You didn't think you were the first girl I've had on the back of my ride, did you?"

And I'm back to being annoyed.

Rolling my eyes, I snatch the hair tie and twist my matted hair up into a bun on the top of my head.

"Let me look at this," he says, snatching my hand when I'm done.

The bandage wrapped around my injured palm is ripped, and one of the remaining stitches has popped. That's just great. I was supposed to get them removed tomorrow. At least it's healed enough that it's not bleeding. Reaching back into his box, Talon pulls out a roll of gauze and starts re-dressing my hand, expertly covering the healing wound.

"Thank you," I say quietly as Talon looks up from my hand. As much as I want to be angry with Talon right now, I know I owe him.

"It's no big deal. You should get someone to look at those stitches tomorrow," he says as he ties off the gauze.

"Not just for that. For coming to get me tonight. I don't want to think what would have happened if you hadn't shown up." A shiver runs through me when I realize just how close I was to missing this trial.

"I told you I don't want to see you get hurt," Talon says, his gaze connecting with mine, and a different type of shiver works through me. "Besides, I'm sure your princeling would have come and saved you if he wasn't snoring away in his castle right now."

I cock my head. "You know you could have just called him and told him about the trial. He would have come to get me."

A wicked smile kicks up the corner of Talon's mouth. "And miss the feeling of you holding on to me for dear life? Never."

My stomach flips and I have to turn away. I can deal with a grumpy Talon, even a dark and mysterious one, but I'm not too proud to admit this flirty one is the one I need to stay away from.

All of a sudden red lights illuminate the building in front of us, making it glow like it's on fire. Talon and I exchange a look and then head for the front entrance where the other competitors are waiting. Even as we make our way there, a sleek silver convertible comes barreling around the corner and then skids to a stop just feet from Talon and me.

The door swings open and Titus, the fae who gave me fighting tips during the cage fight trial, pours out of the car wearing only a pair of sleep pants and sandals. His back tattoo is on full display and his light hair is spiked in different directions. His cheeks are flushed, but a look of relief settles on his face when he sees the trial hasn't officially started yet.

"Cutting it a bit close, aren't we?" Talon asks.

Titus bares his teeth. "I wasn't expecting that blasted tracker to go off in the middle of the night. I'm a deep sleeper."

Talon's gaze drifts to a mark on Titus's neck that looks suspiciously like a hickey. "Deep sleeper, you say?" he asks with raised eyebrows.

Titus scowls back at Talon, but in fairness it does look like his disheveled hair could have been from someone running their fingers through it, so I have to swallow the giggle that wants to creep up my throat.

I sober as we join the other competitors. There's no loud music or flashing lights tonight. No cheering spectators. No revelry of any kind. It's just our small group of remaining competitors waiting outside of a creepy dilapidated structure drenched in red.

Nope, nothing ominous about this setting at all.

It's strange to think that Becks and Ensley probably won't even know about the trial until it's over. Perhaps that's for the best though. Watching me put myself in harm's way has been undeniably hard on Becks. By the time he learns of the trial, it will most likely be done, and then I'll be out of Chaos, exactly what he's been hoping for since the moment I crossed that yellow start line.

As we wait for something to happen, I do a head count and realize there are only fifteen of us. Someone is missing, but I can't figure out who. Talon's shrewd gaze moves over the others, and I think he notices as well, but before I can ask him if he knows who isn't here a horn blares and an explosion of smoke detonates in front of the group. When the smoke clears, the game master stands before us in his usual hooded red robes.

"Welcome to the fourth Chaos trial. Congratulations for making it this far in the competition. After making it through the cavern maze, triumphing over your fellow competitors in hand-to-hand combat, and overcoming compulsion, you might be feeling somewhat invincible right now, but be warned that these final two trials are more dangerous and challenging than the ones before."

I don't doubt the game master. I squeeze my aching hand, reminding myself that the dangers of Chaos are very real. My mission tonight is simple: fail out as soon as it's safely possible to do so. I don't like that I'm giving up on Shadow Striker, especially since Becks' and my relationship is far from sanctioned by the council, but I'd be lying if I said part of me isn't a little relieved to know this will be my last trial.

"Tonight's trial will challenge your wits," the game master says. His hood swivels as he takes each of us in even as his face is obscured to us. "You will enter the asylum as a group."

Asylum? I didn't think this trial could get any creepier. I was wrong.

"The rooms inside have clues you must decipher to find the safe route out of the building. There is more than one path to make it through the rooms and out of the building, but if you fail to decode a clue correctly, there will be consequences. If you fail to make it out of a room in a timely manner, there will also be consequences."

It might be my imagination, but it sounded like the game master said that with a touch of anticipation that makes the hairs on the back of my neck stand on end.

"You will have until sunrise to make it out of the building and to the gazebo in the back gardens. If you are still trapped in the asylum and haven't reached the gazebo when the sun crests the horizon in an hour and forty-two minutes, you will be disqualified. Those who do escape, however, will move on to the fifth and final trial."

Trapped. Escape. I don't love how he put that. Especially since in order to fail out I'm going to have to wait out my time in the scary asylum. He needs to stop talking because everything he says just makes this night even worse.

"It will take a keen and intelligent mind to make it through the rooms of the asylum. Look around," he commands, and our gazes start to roam. "You might think the person next to you is your friend but they're not. They're what's standing in the way of your victory."

I glance at Talon, expecting him to be glaring at me since he's made it clear that's how he sees me, but instead he's sizing up everyone else. The hard look on his face as he assesses each of the other competitors is chilling, reminding me that Talon has a dark side I've only seen glimpses of.

"But," the game master continues, "not every challenge awaiting you in the asylum can be completed on your own, so choose your allies, and your enemies, wisely. This trial will not be broadcast to spectators as the others have been. You are allowed to help, or *hinder*, your fellow competitors at your discretion."

Well, my plan is to stay put the moment I enter the building, so I won't need to worry about finding allies or watching my back for enemies. At least there's a silver lining.

"Once the doors seal behind you, they won't reopen until after sunrise. The only way out of the asylum . . . is through. Let the trial begin."

With a flourish, the game master disappears in a plume of smoke. When it clears, the asylum's double doors are standing open, welcoming us inside.

As a group we all shuffle into the building. When the last person crosses the threshold, the doors slam behind us.

Twenty-Nine

SWALLOWING to wet my suddenly dry throat, I assess the space. We're in some sort of two-story foyer lit by red faelight sconces and a rickety chandelier hanging in the middle. The same foliage that covers the exterior has made its way inside, and even though the spores on the shade ivy have to be activated with heat, I steer clear of them.

From our position in the foyer there are four possible directions to go. There are closed doors to the right, left, and in front of us, and a curved stairway that leads to a landing on the second floor. I suppose from here we're meant to decide which direction to go, but if this is a trial of wits, then there must be a way to determine the right path.

I wander around the foyer, looking for a safe spot to run out the clock.

"Sabine's not here," I hear a competitor say to another.

Sabine. The wolf shifter from another school. That's who's missing.

"I hope she's okay," the other says, a fae named Raven with two-inch gauges in her ears and a dark braid that reaches her waist.

The first competitor, Caden, a gorilla shifter with short black hair and muscles for days, shakes his head. "After what happened to that other guy who didn't show to the last trial, it's stupid to miss this one."

"She probably didn't do it on purpose," Raven says. "It's not like any of us were prepared to be woken in the middle of the night."

"Like it matters whether or not it was intentional or not. She's going to pay the price regardless."

"Hey," yells Kiaro, the snake shifter I fought in the cages, "shut up and help figure out which way to go. When we get out, you two can braid each other's hair and gossip all you want."

They grumble under their breaths but break apart and start to search for clues. Kiaro catches my eye and sticks his forked tongue out, wiggling it suggestively. I turn away and run into Titus, who's inspecting one of the faelight sconces.

"Whoa," he says when my hands land on his bare chest to steady myself.

Stepping back quickly, I mumble an apology and he waves me off.

"No problem. Just watch your step."

My eyes catch on the parts of his tattoo curling over his shoulders. The swirls of veins and deliberately placed flowers are quite beautiful, delicate, yet somehow still masculine, and if it wasn't completely weird I'd ask him to turn around so I can check out the rest of it. But instead I ask if the tattoo means anything, thinking of how Becks got his dragon tattoo after being named dragon heir.

Titus looks down at me, his mouth a hard line, "Yes," he says, and then turns and walks away.

I suppose that was a rather personal question, so I don't take the dismissal to heart as I head to the corner of the foyer to get out of the way of the other competitors. Standing with my arm's crossed, I watch the other competitors scour the room for clues and come up empty.

"We're wasting time," Kiaro says from the middle of the foyer, drawing everyone's attention. "We just need to split into groups and try the different rooms."

"You want to leave this up to chance?" Raven scoffs, and Kiaro rounds on her.

"Do you want to waste an hour searching one room? If so, be my guest. That will be one less competitor I have to go up against in the final trial."

The room dissolves quickly into an argument about picking doors at random and continuing to look for clues.

"The game master said there's more than one path through the building," Titus says, raising his voice above the arguments. "As much as I hate to agree with the snake shifter, we've already lost ten minutes here. We have to start moving."

"Whatever," Damon, a tall and lanky vampire says. "I don't care what the game master said. I don't trust any of you anyway. I'm going on my own." Before anyone can stop him, he yanks open one of the doors on the ground floor and we all freeze.

I can't see anything in the adjoining room. It's pitch black. Damon pauses, but then gathers his courage and enters. He's swallowed by unnatural darkness almost immediately, but after several moments when nothing happens, two more competitors take off after him.

I look for Talon, waiting to see what he's going to do, and find him on the stairs, not even paying attention to what's going on as he inspects the sconces. The ones running up the stairs are all a little crooked. Talon straightens one and then moves on to the next. I take a step toward him, curious about what he's doing when someone shouts, "What is that?"

When I look over my shoulder, black mist is trickling out of the open doorway Damon and the other competitors went through. It brushes up against the toe of Raven's shoe and then latches on, clinging to her as it snakes its way up her body.

She yelps when she moves away but the mist doesn't disengage from her. Everyone else quickly backs away from her and the growing mist as she frantically tries to shake or wipe it off her, but it keeps creeping up her body until tendrils of smoke wrap around her limbs, torso, and neck.

My heart leaps into my chest when the sinister black substance reaches her face, and she lets out a scream of agony and drops to her knees. She swipes furiously at her eyes, wailing that she can't see. When she stops rubbing her face and looks up, her eyes are completely white, and I gasp. My heart speeds up and I'm torn between going to help her or backing away.

"Someone help," she begs, but no one moves.

Suddenly, the blackness starts pouring out of the open doorway, heading straight for us. I'm frozen for a moment as the competitors split and bolt for the other doors, desperate to escape the blinding mist.

There's no way I'm waiting out this trial in the foyer anymore. Forcing myself to move, I start toward the nearest door, the one on the other side of the foyer, when someone grabs my hand and jerks me in the other direction.

"Talon," I yell, as he pulls me up the stairs behind him.

"You don't want to go that way," he warns.

"How do you know?"

"Look!" He points toward the wall as we zip up the steps. All the sconces are straightened and the faelight has changed from red to purple, revealing arrows painted on the wall that point up to the second floor.

Shock runs through me. He figured it out while the rest of us were waiting to see what happened to the first few competitors.

Reaching the landing, Talon grabs the knob and throws open the door, pulling me in after him. The room we pour into is full of books, shelves and shelves of dusty tomes from floor to ceiling, and covered with shade ivy. It looks like the books haven't been touched in decades.

A scream from somewhere below pierces my ears. Talon and I twist around in time to watch three bodies barrel in after us: Titus,

Kiaro, and Stryder, a dragon shifter who graduated from Nightlark the year before. The black mist crawls up the stairs behind them.

"Shut the door," Talon yells, and Titus slams it shut. Immediately, any noise from below is cut off. The only sound filling the room is our own ragged breathing. Hopefully that means the door is barrier enough to keep the mist at bay.

We regard each other warily as we catch our breaths. This might not be the grouping any of us would have chosen, but it's the one we're stuck with now.

Talon checks his watch. "We're twenty minutes down. Let's get working," he says, and we fan out.

There's only one door that leads out of the room, but we quickly find it locked.

"We must be looking for a key of some sort," I say, and a moment later Stryder comes across a small, locked chest.

Talon immediately snatches it from him and tries to break it open, but it doesn't so much as dent.

"The lock needs four numbers," Titus says, after coming forward to inspect it.

"Check the books," I say, and start carefully pulling books down to inspect them, doing my best to avoid the shade ivy's thorns.

The guys join the search, and after less than a minute I pluck a thick book from the shelf and there's a number written on the wall behind it. "You guys, look."

"Keep checking," Talon orders. "We need three more numbers."

"And then we need their order too," I remind him.

"We'll cross that bridge when we come to it."

Stryder pulls a book from the shelf and then yelps and jumps back. When I look over my shoulder he's revealed a hole in the wall that a rat is crawling out of. Kiaro curses, and I jerk my attention to him to see he's uncovered another hole that spiders the size of my fist are scampering out of.

"Wait!" I shout, searching through the pile of books at my feet for the one that revealed the number. I remember it was a burgundy leather cover and find it quickly. "It's a copy of the Ancients. Look for more of them on the shelves."

Talon finds one and there's another number behind it. Stryker, Titus, Talon, and I look for the remaining two copies while Kiaro is busy stomping the spiders, which is honestly fine with me. I don't want those hairy little beasts getting anywhere close to me. It's only a few minutes before we've revealed all four numbers.

"We have to check the books for clues on the order," Talon says, and I start flipping through the burgundy copy I first pulled. It only takes me a few seconds to realize I don't have the full copy, it's only a volume of part of the Ancients. I ask Talon for the one he found and see that he has another copy.

"They're different volumes," I say, getting all the guys' attention. "The one I pulled is volume three. Talon's is volume one. That must be the order of the numbers."

"You're right," Titus says and then goes over to the chest and asks for the numbers in order. When we give them to him he puts them in the lock, and it springs open to reveal a key inside.

We did it! We figured out how to get out of another room.

"Give me that," Kiaro says, and snatches the key from Titus. He jams it in the lock and the knob turns.

The rat Stryder released skitters across the wall near his head, spooking him, and he immediately shoots a stream of fire at it.

"No!" I yell, but it's too late.

Stryder fried whatever creepy crawly spooked him, but he also charred a bit of the shade ivy. There's a visible plume of spores hanging in the air around him. Talon's the closest and tries to twist out of the way, but coughs when he inhales some of the spores. Stryder, who got a faceful of the spores, falls to the ground batting at his clothes like they are on fire, shouting for us to put it out.

Before I have a chance to react, Kiaro slams his fist into Stryder's face, knocking him out cold, and then spins toward Talon with his arm raised.

"Try it, and I'll break your hand and every finger," Talon warns, and Kiaro sneers at him.

"I don't know how much of that you inhaled, but if you slow me down I'll put you out just as easily," he says, and then walks into the next room without a backward glance.

Titus looks into the next room with weary eyes, and then turns to Talon and me. "Come on. We'd better keep going. Who knows how many of these little hellscapes we have to get through to get out of this place."

He slips through to the next room, and rather than following right after, I wait for Talon to near.

"Are you okay?" I ask, trying to catch his eye.

"I'm fine," he says, but the next step he takes he has to steady himself on the wall.

"Are you two coming?" Kiaro calls from the next room.

"Yeah," I yell then lower my voice to hiss at Talon. "You're not fine."

His eyes are glassy. He shakes his head as if trying to clear his now hazy mind.

"I'll make it through. I can't fail this trial," he says as he grits his teeth. But I easily see the spark of vulnerability and fear he's trying to hide. He knows he's in trouble, but he's not going to stop until he reaches his goal.

"Come on," I say, pulling him forward. "I'll get you through the rooms."

I can't believe I have to endure this entire trial for nothing. When this is done, Talon is going to owe me another huge favor.

Thirty

WE MAKE it through the next three rooms with varying degrees of difficulty. In one room we have to use light and dark magic to activate a secret compartment in the wall that reveals a riddle we have to solve in order to figure out which of two doors to go through. Thank goodness Titus is good with riddles; the rest of us had no clue how to solve it. For the most part, Talon seems okay after we make it through the first room, but every once in a while he jerks away from something that isn't there or stares at nothing for too long.

The next room after the light and dark magic room has a giant puzzle in the middle with missing pieces scattered throughout the space. Kiaro and I search for the pieces while Talon and Titus work on solving the puzzle. We must take too long like the game master warned us against doing, because halfway through solving the puzzle the room starts to fill up with freezing water. The water gets all the way up to our hips before we complete the puzzle, which reveals the location of the key we need to get out of the room.

The next room is like an icebox, literally. Clues to figure out a keycode to open the exit door are frozen in the middle of ice blocks. Stryder's fire magic would have been really handy, but since he's not with us we use brute force and body heat, which after being drenched in the previous room I don't have much of, to get to the clues. By the time we pull the clue cards out of the ice and decipher what turns out to be a cryptogram, I'm shivering badly, and the tips of my fingers are a little blue. Titus's bare chest is tinted blue as well, and it takes Kiaro three tries to punch in the correct code because he's shaking so badly he keeps hitting the wrong numbers.

When we pour into the next room, it's filled floor to ceiling with some sort of fog or mist. I wave my hand in front of me to try to clear some of it, but it doesn't do much.

"It's been an hour and twenty-three minutes," Titus announces, which means we only have roughly twenty minutes until sunrise. That's not a lot of time and who knows how many more rooms we'll need to make it through before we can escape the asylum.

It's difficult to see more than a couple feet in front of us, and so we cautiously explore the parameters of the new room. I have a hard time concentrating on much because violent shudders keep racking my body, but I do find a door. It's flat with no handles and looks like it slides into the wall like a pocket door rather than swings open.

Moving around the mist-filled room is disorienting. I lose sight of the guys more than once. Kiaro calls out that he's found a pedestal with a mirror on it that swivels and tilts, and soon after Titus announces that he's found another. I continue to check the walls and find the Chaos emblem painted on one of them. I turn to call out and announce what I've discovered, but my legs don't seem to be working properly and I stumble, face-planting into Talon's chest.

Talon's hands quickly clamp down on my arms to steady me.

"You're a block of ice," he says. Wrapping his arms behind me, he hauls me closer.

When I look up at him, he stares down at me with a frown.

At each room, I considered just waiting the rest of the trial out, but then I'd catch Kiaro watching Talon closely with a calculated gleam in his eye and I knew Talon would never make it through the next room without me. Talon has been trying to hide it, but his symptoms are getting worse. He's talked to himself more than once, and his gaze goes in and out of focus. But the effects of the shade ivy spores seem to come and go, and I can tell by looking into his clear gray-blue eyes that he's having a moment of lucidity.

"You're not much better. How are you not shivering?" I ask.

"The cold doesn't bother me much," he answers as he begins to run his hands up and down my back, trying to warm me. Unfortunately, it doesn't help much. Talon is just as wet and cold as I am, so my shivering just gets worse.

"How about you two stop trying to feel each other up and help us out?" Kiaro says, appearing out of the mist.

"Chill out," Talon snaps. "I could hear her teeth chattering from the other side of the room. She's practically hypothermic."

"So are all of us. Titus is half-naked, and snake shifters aren't exactly known to like the cold, so I'm not living my best life over here either. She needs to suck it up like the rest of us."

"Just give her a minute."

"We don't have a minute," Kiaro barks, but then melts back into the fog to keep looking for clues.

I sigh. He's a jerk, but he's not wrong. I try to pull out of Talon's arms, but he holds me tighter.

"Ignore the snake shifter. You won't be good to anyone if you can't stop shivering."

I should really step back, but Talon's embrace is actually starting to warm me up, so I can't make myself move. I'm not just cold, I'm exhausted as well. Giving up, I press my ear to his chest and close my eyes. His heartbeat drums steadily beneath my cheek.

Suddenly, heat starts to pour into me from Talon's hands on my back. I gasp, and pulling back slightly, I tilt my face up to look at him. "What are you doing?"

"Making sure I get you back to your princeling with all your fingers and toes intact," he says, and I go rigid.

Becks would freak if he saw me in Talon's arms like this, but then I remember this trial isn't being broadcasted and relax. This isn't anything. It's just Talon trying to help me warm up. It's nothing Becks needs to know about.

But even so, a speck of guilt lodges in my chest.

I don't know what kind of magic Talon is using to warm me up. I've heard of fire-welding shifters being able to create and transfer heat into another creature, but never a vampire. I'm too spent to pick it over though. All I care is that whatever he's doing, it feels amazing.

It takes less than a minute for me to stop shivering, and when he releases me I can finally feel all my fingers and toes again.

"Thanks," I say, and force myself to look into his eyes. There's some emotion simmering below the surface of his gaze, but I can't put my finger on what it is.

"I found something else," Titus announces, cutting off anything Talon was about to say.

"Me too," I call, remembering the Chaos emblem I forgot to tell them about when I stumbled into Talon.

We all meet in the middle of the room. Titus holds up a Chaos coin, exactly like the ones we looked for in the first trial with the emblem stamped into it. I tell them about the Chaos symbol on the wall and the door I found, and Kiaro lets us know he came across two more pedestals with mirrors, so four in total. All the mirrors are attached to a base but can be twisted and angled in different directions. That has to mean something.

"Where did you find the coin?" Talon asks, and Titus answers that it was lying on the ground. We split up, Titus and Talon looking for more coins, and Kiaro and I trying to figure out where they go.

I come across a pedestal and take my time inspecting it. The mirror up top has an ornate gilded frame. There are crystals and flowers etched into the wood, and it swivels and turns just like Kiaro reported. Next, I drop down to inspect the pedestal it sits on, which is a long thin column also painted gold with the mirror perched on top and a wider base. It's when I get to the bottom that I notice the coin shaped indent.

"I think I found where the coin goes," I call out, and Titus shows up first.

"I found another coin," he says, and then Talon and Kiaro appear.

"I found two as well," Talon says, but then he jerks back and swipes at something only he can see on his shoulder.

Unease grows in my gut, but I do my best to ignore it.

"Someone give me a coin," I say, and Titus drops one into my palm. Bending down, I place it in the indent, and it fits perfectly. The moment the coin settles in its slot, a laser shoots down from the ceiling, hitting the top corner of the mirror and bouncing off in the opposite direction.

"Each pedestal needs a coin," I say, and Talon and Titus take off to place them.

Soon, there are four different-colored laser beams shooting toward the mirrors and bouncing off in different directions, but now what?

"Did you guys see this?" Titus asks as he looks at one of the mirrors, and we all move closer to see what he's talking about.

Very faintly in the mirror's reflection is a light purple design, the color matching the laser reflecting off of it. Three interconnected swirls.

"Isn't that one of the symbols on the Chaos emblem?" I ask, and Kiaro jets off to another mirror.

"There's another symbol here. A starburst."

"That matches the emblem. Let's see if the other two match as well."

Sure enough, the last two mirrors have a zigzag and two interconnected circles.

"Quick, point them at the Chaos emblem on the wall," I say, getting an idea.

I have to go to the wall and direct their angles because they can't see the emblem through the heavy fog, but eventually we manage to get three out of the four lasers hitting their respective symbol.

I'm trying to direct Talon, who's working on the last symbol of the starburst, when I hear Kiaro tell him he's useless and to shove off.

The shade ivy spores are definitely affecting Talon, and for his sake I hope this trial is almost over or he's not going to make it.

It only takes a few adjustments to get the last laser pointed in the right direction, and when it connects to its symbol, the light in the room changes to purple and the emblem glows. There's a grinding noise and Titus calls out that the door is opening. I quickly join the rest of them and together we watch the door slide open. Some of the mist clears from the room, and light from whatever is beyond shines in, giving us a little more visibility. I don't see anything much past the door except a white hallway, but that's new. Each room so far has dumped us into a new room.

Titus looks down at his watch. "Eight minutes. We gotta go," he says, and then takes off.

Kiaro starts to follow him, but then Talon shouts and starts backing up, swinging wildly at the fog around him.

"Talon!" I call, and try to go to him, but I can't get close without getting hit as he fights an imaginary foe.

I'm trying to decide what to do when the purple light goes out. I swing around to see that Kiaro has moved one of the mirrors so that the laser is no longer properly aligned, and then a thump tells me that the door has slid closed again.

"What are you doing?"

Kiaros' gaze is fixed on a thrashing Talon when he says, "Bettering my chances for a win," and then flies at him, tackling him to the ground.

Talon tries to fight him off, but he's also fighting imaginary demons in his mind and can't fend off Kiaro's fury of punches.

"Kiaro, stop!" I scream.

Running over, I try to pry him off an almost defenseless Talon, who's now hardly moving under the onslaught of Kiaro's attacks.

With a growl, Kiaro swings toward me, abandoning Talon to his temporary madness. He comes to his feet, and I back up, apprehensive of the unhinged look in his eye.

"I'll deal with him in a minute. You and I have unfinished business."

"This is stupid. We're running out of time. Just tilt the mirror back and leave."

"Oh, I intend to. But not before I get a taste," he says, and then lunges at me. But I'm ready for him and twist out of the way before he can touch me.

He licks his lips with his split tongue, and I have to suppress a shudder. He truly is vile.

"I'm going to enjoy this," he says with a lecherous grin, and then springs at me again. I spin out of the way a second time, already familiar with his moves from the time we faced off in the cages. But unlike the time we faced off in the cage, Kiaro can now use his magic. The third time he makes a move at me, the ground below my feet shakes and I lose my footing and go down.

I pop to my feet, but Kiaro is already on me, all hands as his fingers skate over my body. With a scream I rear up, headbutting Kiaro right in the middle of his face, breaking his nose. He falls back with a roar, cupping his face, and I scramble to my feet, trying to figure out what to do next.

I chance a glance at Talon, but it's hard to see him through the mist. I think he's unconscious in the corner of the room. I don't know how to get us both safely out of this room and away from Kiaro.

Kiaro lumbers to his feet, throwing obscenities and curses at me the whole time.

"No more playing around," he says when he faces me, the lower half of his face covered with the blood from his broken nose.

He gathers his power and fear shoots through me when I realize what he's about to do. There's nothing I can do to stop him before he shifts into a snake. But Kiaro doesn't turn into just any snake. He shifts into a giant, white-scaled anaconda.

I back away from his coiled body, my muscles going weak with fear.

Snakes. I can't handle snakes, especially ones big enough to swallow me whole.

My back hits the wall and I look for somewhere to flee, but there's nowhere to go.

I've moved far enough away from Kiaro that I can't see him through the mist anymore, which is a mistake, because now I don't know where he is, even though I can hear his slithering over the floor.

I have to move. I can't just stand here and offer myself up as prey. I don't know where Kiaro is, but I think I hear movement to the left, so I jut to the right. I only make it two steps before Kiaro flies at me, his body cutting through the mist and then winding around my legs.

He takes me down easily, but I'm not giving up. We're close to one of the pedestals so I grab the thin column and drag myself forward a few feet. But it doesn't help. Kiaro just manages to wrap more of his lean body around my own. Letting go of the pedestal, I try to squirm out of his hold, punching his scaled body that's twisted around my legs and midsection, but Kiaro just squeezes until I'm sure he's going to crack a rib.

I cry out; the snake hisses, and I swear Kiaro is laughing at me, and that makes me furious. I'm done with creatures treating me like I'm weaker than them.

Reaching up, I grab the pedestal again. They're secured to the ground, but I pull with all my might, yelling out my anger and frustration, and the top-heavy pedestal teeters. Kiaro must realize what I'm doing because he quickly uncoils.

That's right. This pedestal comes down and none of us are getting out of this room.

Before he has a chance to stop me, I give it another yank and the whole thing tips over, the mirror shattering on impact. Kiaro makes a furious hissing sound and darts at me before I can reach for a piece of the glass.

Throwing my hands up, I catch his triangle head before he can put his mouth over my face. I try to reach for a piece of broken glass to defend myself, but I can't let go of Kiaro without leaving myself vulnerable.

Hands suddenly appear out of nowhere and close around Kiaro's narrow skull.

Talon.

Black shadows seep out of Talon's palms, sink into Kiaro's head, and the next moment the giant snake goes limp.

Talon drops Kiaro and falls to his knees.

"Are you hurt?" he asks, his gaze half-lidded as it runs over me. He's fighting to stay present.

I do a quick assessment. I'm sore, but I don't think anything's broken, so I shake my head at him.

"Is he. . . ?"

"Not dead. I just knocked him out the same way I knocked you out in the cage. He'll be fine in an hour or so," he says, and then his eyes cloud over.

Before he can fall back into the hallucination, I grab his face, holding it between my hands, and force him to look at me. "It's in your head, Talon. There's no one here but you and me."

His gaze clears again, and he nods then looks at the broken mirror. "How are we going to get out of here?"

I search the mirror shards on the ground. Finding a large one, I grab it and stand. "We still have a chance. We only need to get that door open. Go to the emblem and direct me," I say, holding up the piece of glass until I find the laser. I'm not sure if this will work with the mirror broken, but it's worth a try.

It takes us a couple precious minutes to get the angle right, but eventually we get the laser pointed back at the wall. The purple light appears, and the door reopens. "Go," I tell him, and he stumbles toward the door.

I calculate the distance from the door to where I am, and I think I can make it. No way am I waiting in this room alone with Kiaro. I don't want to be anywhere near the psycho when he wakes.

Dropping the mirror shard, I sprint toward the door, squeezing through it right before it snaps shut.

I lean up against the hallway wall and close my eyes, giving my heart a moment to recover. When I open them again, Talon is resting against the wall across from me, his gaze glazed, but he's conscious at least.

There's a door at the end of the hallway that we both move toward. When I reach it and turn the knob, it swings open easily, revealing the overgrown garden behind the asylum.

We did it.

But the sky has already started to change from a dark blue-black to a deep purple, and even lighter on the horizon line. How much time before sunrise? Minutes? Seconds?

We can make it. We just need to get to the gazebo in the middle of the garden. I can even see the roof from where we're standing. It can't be more than a hundred yards away.

"Come on, Talon, we're almost there. We gotta go." But when I look back at him he's sliding to the ground.

Reaching down, I manage to get him on his feet by urging him to loop an arm around my neck. I go to move forward, but no matter how hard I try I can't make myself step out of the building.

At first I think we're stuck in a magical trap of some sort, but then I realize what it is—the unbreakable bond Talon put on me when we made our agreement. My body won't let me move any farther because I agreed to fail out of this trial, and if I keep moving forward I'll pass and move on to the next trial. But Talon can't make it to that gazebo on his own. The only way he's passing this trial and moving on to the next is with me.

I let out a growl of frustration and twist toward Talon. Propping him up against the wall the best I can, I drape his arms over my shoulders to keep him upright. His head lolls forward as he only just holds on to consciousness.

"Talon, you have to free me from the bond so that I can help you finish the trial."

He mumbles something I can't quite hear, and so I lean in. "Talon, say you release me from our bond or else we both will be disqualified from Chaos," I try again.

With effort he shakes his head. "No. You'll get hurt," he all but slurs.

"Then I guess you're okay letting Shadow Striker go to Titus or whoever else wins Chaos, because you're not making it to that finish line without me."

Talon's eyes flare before drooping again. "Can't . . . lose."

"Well that's what's about to happen. The sun is going to be up any minute now."

Anxiety claws at my chest when Talon groans and tips his head back against the wall and then lets his eyes slide shut again.

Part of me wants to drop it, to wait these final moments out and let Talon deal with the consequences, but I know if he were in his right mind he'd be fighting tooth and nail to get to that gazebo. Talon and I are friends, or maybe not friends exactly, but this whole ordeal has bonded us in some way. I can't just let this be the end for him.

Or you, a small voice inside whispers.

"Talon," I say, trying to shake him fully awake, but that doesn't work because it's super hard to shake someone you're also trying to hold up, so I slap his cheek. His face scrunches like he's trying to figure out what just happened, then his eyes open and focus on me.

"I need you to pull yourself together."

"Okay, okay. I'm awake. No more slappy-slappy."

"Release me from the bond," I order.

A lazy smile kicks up the corners of his mouth. "You're even cuter when you're feisty."

You've got to be kidding me. Now he's hitting on me?

"I love your freckles, Freckles. I wanna kiss each one of them."

I ignore the way my face heats. "Yes, I know I'm just adorable, but you need to do as I say. Now!"

When his eyes start drifting shut again, I give him another slap and they pop back open.

"Ouch."

"*Talon*," I warn.

"Okay, okay, bossy. I release you."

I don't feel any different, but I don't waste any time pulling a half-conscious Talon toward the door. I hold my breath as I step forward, but this time I pass over the threshold with ease.

Yes! It worked!

But we're not out of the woods yet. We still need to get to that gazebo before the sun crests the horizon.

"Come on," I say to Talon, who isn't really paying attention to me.

His body weight on me is heavy as I practically drag him through the overgrown garden as the sky lightens overhead.

"A little help would be appreciated," I grumble after we almost go down when I snag my foot on a root.

When the gazebo comes into view, I keep my eyes fixed on the peeling white paint as we get closer and closer. Titus is standing there already, and he stiffens when he sees us struggling to reach the steps. It looks like there are three other competitors with him, but I don't waste time worrying about who they are as I channel all my focus and strength to hauling Talon to that finish line.

I look up when we are about twenty feet away and notice the clock hanging in the middle of the gazebo. There are only eight seconds left.

"Drop him and run," Titus shouts.

For a split second, I consider it. With Talon out of the picture I'd have a much better chance of winning Shadow Striker, but I can't do it. It's not who I am. So digging deep for whatever well-spring of strength I still have, I force Talon and myself into a stumble-jog as the final seconds drain away.

Thirty-One

I DON'T EVEN BOTHER TRYING to scale the last two steps that lead to the gazebo platform. Instead I pitch us forward and we land in a heap on the rotting boards. Our bodies have only just connected with the floor when the buzzer goes off, signaling the end of the fourth trial.

We made it.

Next to me, Talon jerks and twitches, his face skewed into a mirror of horror. We may have made it in time, but Talon is still in the midst of his trial, and I don't know what to do for him now.

Dropping to his knees next to us, Titus puts his hands on either side of Talon's face. His palms start to glow like Ensley's do when she's glamouring me.

"What are you doing?"

"Healing him from the shade ivy," he says, his face strained with concentration.

"Healing him? You could have done that at any time?"

"It would hardly have made sense for me to aid my biggest competition," he says with his gaze still on Talon.

I gape at him. He has a point, but still.

"There," Titus says, and sits back on his heels.

Talon has stopped moving and his face is lax. The next

moment he groans and then opens his eyes, his gaze fully alert. He pops to his feet so quickly I scramble out of his way before pushing to my feet as well.

"What happened?" he demands, his head on a swivel as he takes Titus and me in, and then the rest of his surroundings.

"Despite being in a shade ivy fog, you just made it through the fourth trial," Titus says. And then adds as he tips his head in my direction: "Thanks to her."

Talon's stormy gaze lasers in on me. "How?"

"I dragged you across the finish line."

His nostrils flare and I can tell he realizes that means I'm still in Chaos as well. A muscle jumps in his jaw as he tries to rein in his emotions, but after a pause he finally grits out, "Thank you."

"Any time. Except let's not make that a habit, okay. You're really heavy."

Talon huffs out a half-laugh and shakes his head before tipping it skyward. "What am I going to do with you?" he groans.

"What happened back there? Why did the door shut behind me? And where is Kiaro?" Titus asks, looking out into the garden.

At the mention of the snake shifter, Talon's face goes dark. He must remember at least a little of what happened.

"He moved the mirror on purpose to trap us inside. He went after Talon . . . and then me."

I don't have to be looking at him to feel the tension rolling off Talon.

Titus' gaze goes to Talon. I'm sure he notices the dried blood and bruises on his face even though they're already starting to fade.

"So you guys took him out." He shakes his head. "I'd like to say I'm surprised to hear that happened, but I'm not. What an idiot to go up against the both of you. You're a formidable team."

"Oh no, we're not a team," I quickly say, but Talon remains silent.

Titus arches an eyebrow. "Could have fooled me."

Damon, the vampire who first walked into the black room,

walks up to us. One of his eyes is completely white, probably blinded by that mist, and he's cradling his arm. The only other two competitors, Chase, a muscled dragon shifter, and Vivian, a redheaded fae, stand a little ways behind him. "Do you think we can take off now? I gotta get this checked out."

I look to the west and the sun hangs just above the horizon line. "The game master said the trial is done at sunrise, so I don't see why not," I say.

As a group we leave the gazebo and make our way through the gardens toward the front of the asylum. The building looks no less creepy in the morning light than it did under the moonlight. The plants crawling up the sides still look like they are trying to eat the structure, and in the better lighting I can see the cracks running like veins through the stucco and stacked stones. I shudder. It's a miracle the walls didn't cave in around us while we were in there.

"We have to talk," Talon says as we're rounding the corner of the building.

"About?"

"About what to do now that you're still in the competition. This complicates things."

I sigh. "I'm not going to apologize. If it wasn't—"

"I know," he says, cutting me off. "I'm more grateful for what you did than you'll probably ever realize. But we've created a situation that has to be dealt with."

I hear my name being yelled, and when I look over Becks is running toward me. He scoops me up in his arms the instant he reaches me, crushing me to his chest, and I freeze. It's the most public affection he's shown me since we confessed our feelings for each other, and it's not that I don't like it, it's just that I'm not used to it.

"Thank the Creator you're okay," he says. Leaning over, he buries his face in my neck as a shudder runs through him.

"It's okay. I'm all right," I say, trying to soothe him.

"You don't understand," he says, finally pulling back so I can look him in the eyes. "They found one of the other competitors an hour ago on the side of the road, beaten almost beyond recognition. She's in the hospital now and they aren't sure she's going to make it."

Sabine.

"I knew you didn't have a phone or a computer, a way to call me for a ride. I thought . . ."

I know what he thought. He thought I hadn't made it either and I'd ended up like Sabine.

I shake my head, an image of myself lying broken and bloodied on the ground rising up in my mind's eye. I wasn't Sabine, but I almost was. "No. I made it here all right."

"How *did* you get here?" he asks, and my gaze tracks over his shoulder to Talon, who's waiting off to the side with his hands shoved in his pockets.

Becks twists to see what I'm looking at and then he tenses. A growl rumbles up in his chest.

"Talon knew I didn't have my phone too, so he swung by to get me. If it wasn't for him I'd be in a hospital bed next to Sabine right now, or worse."

He sucks in a deep breath then lets it out slowly. The fight drains out of him as he realizes the truth, that if Talon hadn't come to get me I could be dead right now. His arms slide away from me, and as he turns to walk toward Talon he grabs my hand and pulls me with him.

Becks' hand wrapped around my own causes warmth to bubble up in my chest. The other competitors and handful of friends who showed up have almost completely cleared out, so there aren't many others around, but holding Becks' hand in public still makes a zing go through me. It reminds me of what I want with him. What I've been fighting for. To be given a chance to be his and him be mine out in the open for the whole world to see.

We stop in front of Talon, whose gaze drops to our clasped

hands before bouncing back up to our faces. I think a flicker of something crosses his face, but it happens so fast I can't be sure. He lets a lazy smile curve his mouth. "Here to thank me for looking after your girl?"

I snort. "Right. Let's not forget who got who through that house of horrors," I say with a pointed look.

His gaze drifts to me and I swear there's a bit of smolder in his eyes that I absolutely do not react to even a little. "I delivered you back to your princeling with all your fingers and toes like I said I would, didn't I?"

"That's overselling it a bit."

He shrugs, and Becks' hand tightens around mine.

Clearing my throat, I drop the subject.

"The important thing is that Locklyn made it through this last trial in one piece. So yes, I owe you thanks," Becks says, and it looks like every word tastes sour in his mouth, but he still gets them out.

Talon assesses Becks for a long moment, but eventually dips his head in acceptance and it makes me feel a bit lighter. Maybe there's some common ground the two of them can find after all.

Becks sighs and looks down at me. "I'm just glad this night-mare is finally over, and we can move on with our lives."

I lock up, and Becks notices right away.

"What is it?" he demands.

I glance at Talon, and he arches a brow at me as if to say, "Are you going to tell him, or should I?"

"Lock," Becks presses.

"Well, about that." I suck my bottom lip into my mouth and bite down. It draws Becks' attention and distracts him for a second, but then he gives his head a small shake, his gaze moving to my eyes and holding as he waits. "So there were some extenuating circumstances during this trial, and so I kinda sorta maybe didn't actually fail out like I was supposed to."

His eyes grow. "Are you saying you passed the trial? You have to compete in the next one?"

I bite my bottom lip again and nod, but this time it doesn't distract him.

He rounds on Talon. "You let her do this? Why? That was your one stipulation."

"I didn't really have much of a choice in the matter." He looks over at me. "Without her help I would have failed, and that's not an option."

"The hell it isn't!" Becks explodes. "I thought you cared about her. At least enough to make sure she doesn't die in this idiotic competition."

Talon presses his lips together, not commenting one way or another whether he cares about me. I want to not be bothered that he doesn't answer, but I kind of am. And that, in and of itself, annoys me.

Becks looks like he's gearing up to really lay into Talon, when a commotion at the front of the asylum draws all of our attention. When I look over, Stryder stumbles out of the building, yelling something about shadow beasts as two creatures run up to meet him. I think one is his sister, another dragon shifter, but I don't recognize the other.

Becks lets go of my hand the moment he sees his fellow dragon shifters. I won't lie to myself and pretend it doesn't sting.

"I'm done here," I say with an edge to my voice that I'm sure both guys don't miss. "I need to get home and try to sneak back into my bedroom before my parents find me gone and ground me for two years rather than just two weeks." I start off toward where Becks' truck and Talon's bike are parked.

"Want another ride, Freckles?" Talon says, but before I can answer Becks speaks up.

"I'm taking her home."

That's what I was planning anyway, but I'm almost annoyed enough at Becks to consider jumping on the back of Talon's bike. But not quite.

Talon ignores Becks and waits for me to answer, but I shake my head. "No, I'm good."

Talon just shrugs like he doesn't care either way. I know he only asked to nettle Becks and I wish he'd stop doing that. He's only making the situation between the three of us that much harder, which I'm sure he's aware of and even more sure that he doesn't care.

He reaches for his helmet but pauses before putting it on. "We're going to need to talk," he tells me, and a low growl emanates from Becks.

"You guys have nothing to talk about anymore," Becks says.

"That's where you're wrong," Talon says, finally looking serious. "Because like it or not, the only way we're both making it through that next trial is together."

I can tell Becks hates how intertwined Talon and I are in this competition, but it's not something I can help at this point.

"If it makes you feel better, come with her if you want. As long as you can put your ego aside for a minute. I don't have time to put up with you growling or shooting fireballs to try to prove to Locklyn you're the alpha male in the room. This is serious." His gaze shifts to me and his eyes are as hard as granite. "There are things about Chaos that you don't know. Things I was hoping I wouldn't have to tell you, but now that we're both in the finals, it's too dangerous to keep you in the dark. Meet at my house after school today."

He waits until I nod, and then throws on his helmet. After revving his engine he takes off, leaving a cloud of dust in his wake.

"That's what you rode here on?" Becks asks when the noise from Talon's engine has faded.

It irritates me that's what he's concerned with right now. "Yeah, so what?" I say, then yank open his truck door and haul myself into the cab.

Becks rounds the front of his truck and then climbs in behind the wheel. I can practically hear his teeth grinding as he cranks the engine and throws the vehicle into reverse.

"I'm coming with you to that meeting this afternoon."

"Sure, whatever," I say, sitting in silence until a wave of boldness overtakes me. "You know other girls might find this whole jealous boyfriend thing hot, but it's a real turnoff for me. Especially when you're not even really my boyfriend."

Becks snaps his head toward me and I catch the mixture of hurt and anger on his face before he turns back to watch the road. I tell myself not to care. I'm hurt and angry too.

"That's not fair," he says, his jaw clenching.

"Which part?"

"All of it. You know I can't control our situation."

"That's debatable."

His gaze shifts back to me, his brows low over his eyes. "And I can't help that I don't like seeing the two of you together."

"You know what I don't like? I don't like how fast you dropped my hand back there at the first sight of another dragon shifter."

Becks at least has the decency to look guilty. "That wasn't what you think."

I laugh and the sound is bitter, even to my own ears. "It's exactly what I think it is. You don't want anyone to know about us. You want to hide our relationship. You're ashamed of me."

Panic crosses Becks' face. "No, Locklyn, it's not like that at all. I don't want to hide anything. If I could I'd march right into Nightlark Academy holding your hand, letting the whole school know who you belong to."

We pull up in front of my parents' store. I don't know how I'm going to get back inside without them knowing, but right now I'm too worked up to really care. So what if my parents ground me for the rest of my life?

"Then why don't we?" I challenge.

"It's complicated. You know that."

I do, but my feelings aren't just hurt anymore, they're wounded and bleeding out. Maybe it isn't fair of me to ask Becks to stand by our relationship, to stand by me, but that's what I'm doing anyway. I'm tired of feeling less-than. If Becks isn't going to stand up for me, I have to do it for myself.

Opening the door, I glance back at him before getting out. The look on his face is torn, and my instinct is to say something to soothe him, but I'm done with all that. I've always been willing to fight for us, but if Becks isn't, then there's truly no hope for us.

"Then I'll uncomplicate the situation for you. I'm done," I say, and then jump out of the truck, slamming the door behind me and walking away from him, my heart shredding a little more with every step.

Thirty-Two

"YOU LOOK AWFUL," Ensley says when she slides up next to me in the hall as I'm on my way to first period.

"Thanks," I answer sarcastically, but she's not wrong.

After climbing back up the drainpipe to sneak into my room, I didn't have a chance to shower this morning and so my greasy hair is piled on top of my head in a knot. I barely paid attention when I was throwing on clothes and only realized when I got to school that the shirt I'm wearing has a stain on the front, and the jeans I chose are from last summer and too short. The redness of my eyes and the dark smudges under them complete the look.

I don't look at her, but I can feel Ensley silently assessing me until she finally says, "Why do you look so sad? Everyone is buzzing about you making it to the finals. You now have a one in six chance of winning, but even if you don't you're already a legend. You should be on cloud nine."

I steal a glance at her out of the corner of my eye and she appears genuinely confused. "Have you seen Becks this morning?"

She shakes her head. "He was already gone when I got up. I just assumed he had an early morning practice. Why, what happened?"

"He picked me up from the trial. Someone must have texted

him the location, and we got in another fight." I look over at her and lower my voice so we can't be overheard. "I think we broke up. Or at least however you can break up before you're ever really together."

She gasps. "No you didn't."

I nod, snapping my mouth shut because tears are starting to well in my eyes.

Grabbing my arm, Ensley yanks me into an empty room and demands I tell her everything, and so I do.

"Oh, Locklyn," she says when I stop talking. "I'm so sorry. But you have to know Becks adores you."

I look away from her to keep tears from spilling over. "Even if he does, that may not be enough. It may not have ever been enough. There's just so much against us." I glance back at her, sure my heart is shining from my eyes. "I'm not sure we ever even had a chance to begin with. Maybe I just built this all up in my mind to be something it's not."

She's shaking her head before I even finish talking. "No. Don't say that. It isn't true. What you and Becks have is real."

"You're just saying that because you love both of us."

"I'm not," she says forcefully. "Anyone who cares to look can plainly see what's there between you two. You two just fit together."

"I don't know. I just don't feel . . ." *Cherished. Pursued. Wanted.* I sigh. "Everything is just so messed up right now. Becks and I have been off since the news of his arranged mating came down and Chaos started. I don't know how to get back to being us."

She tilts her head. "But you don't really want to go back to where you were before anyway. Right? Your relationship with Becks is evolving."

"It feels like we spend half our time fighting. We never used to do that before."

"That's not unexpected since you both are under a considerable amount of stress right now. You have to admit the last month and change hasn't exactly been typical. There have been some pretty big speed bumps."

I sigh. She's not wrong.

"Change can be hard," she continues. "But some things are worth it. Don't you think you two are worth it?"

"I do." But I'm not convinced Becks does. At least not anymore. "I don't know, Ens. Maybe this is just it for us. We gave it a try and it didn't work." My heart screams at me to shut up even as the words come out of my mouth.

Ensley sighs. "I think you just need a little time right now. And I think Becks needs some time as well. Boys are slow. We can't expect them to be as quick on their feet as we are," she says with a grin that makes me laugh. "You know Becks. He overthinks everything. Give him a chance to catch up."

I make a noncommittal noise in the back of my throat, and Ensley gives me an encouraging smile. I guess only time will tell what happens between Becks and me, but in the meantime I should probably put my energy toward Chaos anyway now that I'm stuck seeing it through. The competition seems determined to take its pound of flesh from each competitor, and I'm starting to worry that it's going to try to take a lot more than that from me.

I MANAGE to avoid Becks for the entire day, and after two bus rides and a long walk I make it to Talon's house on my own. He lives with his uncle, Drake Brayden, in Crested Heights, a gated community on the west side of Everton. The homes here can't really be considered houses. They look more like mini palaces and castles, each on their own sprawling multiacre lot. Once I make it past the gate guard at the base of the neighborhood—at least Talon remembered to give him my name—it's another ten-minute hike up a steep hill to his uncle's mini castle. My body is already worn and exhausted from lack of sleep and the physical and emotional stress of the trial the night before, so by the time I find myself in front of his door I'm mentally cursing Talon for making me come here. Couldn't we have just met in the academy library or something?

To my left and right, stone dragons flank the ten-foot black double-door. When I raise my hand to knock I half-expect a butler in a suit to answer. What I don't expect is for Drake Brayden himself to open the door.

With black hair and steel-gray eyes there's a faint resemblance to Talon, but the similarities stop there. Standing at least six seven, Drake is broad chested with a full beard and wearing an imposing frown. He's a large man—then again, most dragon shifters are—but as he stands looking down his nose at me he seems even more so. I'm not ashamed to admit, at least to myself, that I'm intimidated. Talon's warning about how ruthless his uncle is comes back to me, and I'm suddenly very glad he handled Drake himself.

Drake doesn't move, blocking the entrance with one hand on the door. He cants his head, and I realize he's waiting for me to say something.

"Oh, sorry. I'm here to see Talon." I didn't mean to, but it comes out a little like a question instead of a statement.

"Are you now?" he asks, not cracking a smile or moving an inch.

"Yes. We're working on a project together," I say, using the same excuse I gave Becks a couple weeks back, and Drake's eyes narrow. Shoot, maybe Talon told him something else. I shouldn't have said that. "We go to school together. I'm Lock—"

"I'm very aware who you are," he says, taking me aback.

"You are?" I ask, confused.

Drake's gaze travels over my shoulder and I twist to see Titus come up behind me.

"Titus. What are you doing here?"

His gaze bounces from me to Drake and back again. "Probably the same thing as you. I was summoned by Talon."

Just then the second double door opens, and I can finally see past Drake and into the two-story grand foyer. To say it's opulent would be an understatement. There's a sculpture of a fire-breathing dragon in the middle of the room that's at least ten feet high, and beyond that a double curved stairway leads to the second floor. Everything is decorated in shades of black and gray with hints of gold.

After opening the door, Talon steps forward, casual as usual in dark jeans and a long-sleeved shirt. His hair is damp like he might have just gotten out of the shower, and his feet are bare. There's no denying he looks good, but I quickly acknowledge it and move on. I've always thought Talon was attractive, but I don't miss the dark circles under his eyes as he invites us in.

Talon doesn't hold my attention too long because Drake stares me down as I pass him, his gaze stormy and hostile. Does he know I was going to try to blackmail him? The look on his face says he does; there's a real possibility Talon told him.

I avert my gaze, pretending to be interested in the gaudy dragon statue, but Drake's stare makes the fine hairs on the back of my neck stick up.

"This way," Talon says, waving Titus and me to follow him without so much as acknowledging his uncle.

I sneak a peek over my shoulder as we follow Talon up the stairs and find Drake's gaze still trailing me, just as dark as it was before. A chill races down my spine, and I'm relieved as soon as we are in the hallway and out of view.

I come even with Talon and hiss quietly, "Does he know?"

"Does who know what?" Talon asks, looking down on me.

"Your uncle. Does he know about the thing that we had planned?"

"No. Why?"

"Because it looked like he'd like nothing more than to

barbecue me back there. And he knew who I was when he opened the door."

Talon's eyebrows lift at that. "Interesting," is all he says before falling silent again. His nonchalance makes me want to wring his neck, but instead I just clench my fists and follow him through the maze that is Drake Brayden's home.

I lose count of the turns we take before Talon finally opens a door and gestures for us to enter what looks to be a combination of a home library and old fashion game room. I feel like I've stepped back a century in time. The room is ringed with floor-to-ceiling bookshelves, and in the center there are chess and backgammon tables, and a seating area set up in front of an unlit fireplace.

Titus quickly surveys the space and then turns to Talon, crossing his arms over his chest. "Okay. We're here. Care to let us know why?"

"Maybe I'm just looking to make new friends," Talon says, and I roll my eyes. He had more friends on his first day at Nightlark than I could hope to have in my entire life.

Titus shoots him an annoyed look. "We know this has something to do with Chaos. Are you looking for an alliance or something? Because if so, it's a little late. We're headed into the last trial, which means it's every creature for him, or herself," he finishes, tipping his head in my direction.

I smile, appreciative of the acknowledgement.

"No offense, because I like you both," Titus goes on, "but as far as I'm concerned, you two are the enemy."

Talon opens his mouth to respond when the game room door opens, and Drake appears. "I found two more of your guests," he says, and then Becks and Ensley enter the room.

Becks' gaze finds me immediately, and when our eyes connect my heart rate kicks up and something twists in my chest. He looks as miserable as I feel, and I both wish we were alone right now and am grateful that we aren't.

"Thanks," Talon says, a clear dismissal to his uncle.

Drake scowls at his nephew, and then eyes Becks and me, where we're standing at least five feet apart. There's a calculating gleam in his eye that starts to make me nervous when he doesn't turn and leave.

"I've got it from here," Talon says, prompting his uncle to leave us alone.

Drake's nostrils flare in annoyance, but he finally leaves, closing the door after him.

That was weird.

"Why didn't you invite your parents over as well?" Talon asks Becks, eyeing Ensley with a look of frustration.

"We're not here for you. We're here for her," Becks says, nodding toward me.

Ensley crosses her arms over her chest. "Like it or not we're a package deal. That's how this friendship works."

Talon shakes his head but doesn't complain anymore.

When Titus introduces himself to Becks and Ensley, I don't miss the appreciative way his teal gaze travels up and down Ensley, or the way her eyes light up when it does. Neither does Becks, who steps forward and offers Titus his hand to break up whatever is going on between the white-haired fae and his sister.

After introductions are over, Talon tells us all to take a seat on the couch and chairs around the unlit fireplace. Becks and I take opposite sides of the same couch. I don't look in his direction, but I feel his gaze brush over me like a warm summer breeze. I have to bite my lip to keep myself from sneaking a peek.

Talon stands at the mantel with the rest of us seated around him. His gaze trips from Becks and me as he reads our body language, and a smirk lifts one corner of his mouth. "Trouble in paradise?"

"Quit stalling, Talon," Becks says. "Why are we here?"

The smirk melts off Talon's face and then he purposefully looks away from Becks and Ensley to focus on Titus and me.

"Chaos isn't what you think it is. I thought I could do this on my own, but I was wrong. I need your help, and I realize if I'm going to get it I have to let you in on some of the truth."

"*Some* of the truth?" Titus asks with a raised brow.

"As much of it as I can," he answers, and then proceeds to tell everyone the same story he told me when he came into my parents' store about Shadow Striker and the Vampire King.

When he's done, the room goes silent. Titus looks thoughtful and Ensley is on the verge of tears, which I get. That story is just as heartbreaking the second time I hear it as the first. Becks looks unconvinced.

"Are you trying to get us to believe the Chaos prize is a real artifact with the magical ability to give creatures powers?" He huffs out a half-laugh. "Only a fool would believe that."

I duck my head. *Umm. Ouch.*

"You can believe whatever you want," Talon says to him. "I'm only concerned with what these two believe," he says, indicating Titus and me.

Titus leans back in the brown leather wingback chair he's sitting in, looking just as unconvinced as Becks. "Why should we believe this dagger is some fabled artifact from an Ancient I've never heard of?"

I keep my mouth shut because I already know what Talon is going to say, and sure enough he explains what he already confessed to me about how Shadow Striker has been in his family for years and was stolen.

"Why would someone steal the dagger just to turn around and give it away?" Becks asks.

That was my thought exactly when Talon told me, but at the time he wouldn't give me any more information. I study him now, wondering if he's ready to let go of more of his secrets.

Talon rolls his tongue in his mouth. I'm sure there's something he doesn't want to tell us, but he's coming to the realization he's going to have to in order to get Titus and my cooperation.

Finally he says, "We think someone stole Shadow Striker to activate it."

I sit up straighter. Now this is information I haven't already heard.

Becks leans forward. "Activate it? What does that mean?"

"If the dagger is linked to a specific creature, its powers can't be used by another until it's been activated again. Only one creature can use Shadow Striker's powers at a time. And that creature is linked to the blade. When the Vampire King wielded the dagger so many millennia ago, it was linked to him, so no one else could use its powers. We think the thief knows what needs to be done to sever the connection between the dagger and the creature it's currently linked to, and that's what Chaos is really about, activating Shadow Striker."

"So you think Shadow Striker is still linked to the old Vampire King?" I ask, finally speaking up. Surely the Vampire King from the Ancient is long since dead, but maybe that doesn't matter.

Talon hesitates before answering. "My family hasn't had the dagger forever, so we can't say what happened to it before it came into our possession. But it has to be linked to someone if they need Chaos to activate it. Otherwise they'd already be using it, not making it the prize."

The way Talon talks about this mysterious "we" makes it sound like some sort of underground spy organization or something.

"Who's we?" Becks asks, and Talon presses his lips together in a hard line.

"My family and I, mostly," he says, not giving a straight answer.

"Do you have any idea who the thief is?" Titus asks.

"We have some leads," he hedges. "And before you ask, I've already tried to take out the game master. He's protected by some sort of shield magic. I can't get within three feet of him."

Titus leans back and crosses his arms over his chest. "So you want us to help you get back a family heirloom? No offense, but why should we care who has the dagger?"

"There's a prophecy about the Shadow Striker," Talon says, looking annoyed he has to give up more secrets. "Real end of the world stuff if it falls into the wrong hands."

"Easy solution," Titus says. "I'll just give you the dagger after I win it."

Ensley snorts. "Just like that, you'd hand over a powerful artifact that could give you unlimited powers?"

Titus looks over at her and shrugs. "I'm powerful enough. I don't need it."

"Then why did you even enter Chaos?" she asks. "For funsies?"

He smiles back at her and winks. "For the glory."

She purses her lips, but I'm not fooled. There's interest in her gaze.

"That won't help," Talon cuts in. "If you win Chaos, then the dagger will be linked to you."

Titus shrugs. "So what?"

"*So what* is that if you win Chaos, the dagger will be bonded to you, and whoever stole it isn't just going to let you keep it. The wielder of the dagger is vulnerable before they use it for the first time. If the dagger can be used against the one it's bonded to before they use it to obtain any powers, then the bond will transfer immediately."

"And when you say *used against* . . ." I ask.

"I mean kill," Talon says, looking me straight in the eye. "So if one of you wins Chaos, whoever stole the dagger in the first place is going to kill you to bond to the blade themselves, which will probably set off an apocalypse, but I guess that won't really be an issue for you because you'll already be dead and won't care."

Becks curses under his breath and some color drains from Titus' face.

"You're telling the truth about this?" Ensley asks. Her face has gone ashen as well.

Talon nods.

"So you want us to help you win the final trial so the thief will kill you instead of us?" I ask, not believing for a minute that Talon's as altruistic as that.

A wicked grin spreads on Talon's face. "They can try."

I roll my eyes. "Wow. Conceited much?"

"The best I can figure is that they are banking that a weaker competitor wins, one they can easily get the dagger from. But when I have Shadow Striker back, no one is taking it from me again," he says with conviction, and I just shake my head.

"This is nuts," Ensley says, leaning forward in her seat. "So to recap, you're saying that the Ancient about Shadow Striker that you just told us is real and that someone stole a dagger made by demons from your family and is using an underground competition to activate it so that they can trigger some apocalyptic prophecy that ends the world? Is that the gist of it?"

Talon flicks his tongue against his canine tooth, his patience with us running thin. "More or less."

"What if you're just feeding us a story to get us out of your way?" Titus asks with a look of suspicion on his face.

"There's a way for you to tell if I'm telling the truth," Talon says with a pointed look at Titus.

Titus' brows shoot up. "How do you know about that?"

"I know a lot by looking at someone," he answers, and for a brief second his gaze flicks to me before returning to Titus.

"What are you talking about?" Becks demands.

Talon just looks at Titus, who blows out a breath of air with a huff. "I'm a truth reader," he says, and it's my turn to raise my brows.

Truth readers are fae who have the power to detect lies. It's an old magic that is very rare these days. I'm starting to believe Titus when he says he isn't interested in Shadow Striker's abilities. He must be an extremely powerful fae.

"If you know that about me, you know how powerful I am. I can take care of myself if I win."

"Test these words," Talon says, urging Titus to use his truth reading abilities.

Getting to his feet, Titus places a hand over Talon's heart, and after a moment it starts to glow with silver faelight.

"I know exactly how powerful you are," Talon says, his stare unwavering as he looks back at Titus. "But I'm more powerful."

Titus sucks a quick breath through his nose.

"Everything I've told you about Shadow Striker is true," Talon goes on. "If I don't get it back, all our lives are in danger."

Titus removes his hand from Talon's chest, the light fading from his palm. They stand face-to-face and I hold my breath, waiting to see what is going to happen next.

"Well," Becks prompts.

Still looking at Talon, Titus says, "Tell me what we need to do."

Thirty-Three

I'M SO SCREWED. Forget winning Chaos, once Titus verifies Talon is telling the truth any secret hopes I still have of winning Shadow Striker and using its powers instantly die. But Talon doesn't stop with his revelations; the floodgates have opened, and Talon explains that in order to activate Shadow Striker competitors have to have their strengths tested to be found worthy of the dagger—specifically their physical, mental, intellectual, and magical strengths. That means that the next trial is a test of magical powers, of which I have none.

Titus and Ensley send me pitying gazes when that bomb is dropped, but Becks shoots to his feet.

"Locklyn will be defenseless," he says, his eyes going wild.

"Which is one of the reasons I wanted her out of the competition before now," Talon grinds out.

"If I'd failed the last trial you wouldn't be here," I snap back.

"I know," Talon says. Plowing a hand through his hair, he turns toward the mantel, giving us all his back.

"It's all right, Locklyn," Titus says. "We'll make sure you make it through okay."

And then it dawns on me . . . the only reason I'm even part of this discussion. "I'm only here so that when you and Titus come up with a plan, I'm around to agree to stay out of the way," I accuse Talon.

Talon turns toward me, his face unreadable. "I want you to stick close to me," he says, not contradicting me, but he's not done talking. "There's a chance the trial will be skewed in your favor. If I'm right about all of this, now that you've made it this far they want you to win."

"Because they see me as the easiest to kill?" I say, and he nods.

That's offensive, but fair.

I cross my arms over my chest and slump back into the couch. "Oh, this just keeps getting better."

Becks starts to pace. Tendrils of smoke wisp from him as he walks back and forth.

"Don't you dare shift. Some of the books in this library are worth more than you," Talon warns.

Becks glares at him but stops pacing and turns to me. "You won't go to the last trial. You'll skip it."

"I can't. You know what happened to the other competitors who didn't show up to a Chaos trial."

Becks sits down on the couch next to me, curving his body toward me. "I'll stay with you night and day and make sure nothing happens to you when the time comes."

"That won't work," Talon cuts in. "Once we entered Chaos we entered into a magical agreement to see it through. It's not that someone inflicted those injuries on the competitors who failed to show up. Their injuries are magical, and you won't be able to fight that off. She has to be there or the same thing that happened to them will happen to her. There's no way around it. She has to compete."

Becks' gaze snaps to Talon, his eyes burning with intensity. "How do you know that?"

"Because I know that's true about the dagger's activation. Haven't you heard anything I've said? Chaos is just a cover. And here's your proof."

Talon lifts his shirt and drags down his jeans to expose some of his hipbone. I start to look away until I realize what he's showing us. On his hip, right below where his pants sit, is the circular brand of the Chaos emblem.

"That mark on the flyers and the coins, that's not a Chaos symbol," he says. "It's the Shadow Striker emblem."

"You branded yourself?" I ask in shock.

He shakes his head. "Not exactly. It's kind of a family thing. That doesn't matter though. What you need to understand is that the cross symbolizes the dagger. The inner circle represents the first trial that's meant to thin the herd. And then the four symbols in each of the quadrants stand for one of the trials of strength I mentioned before. Three swirls for physical strength, zigzag for intellectual strength, the two overlapping circles for mental strength, and then the six-pointed starburst for magical strength."

He lets go of his shirt and tugs up his pants, covering the mark, and then shoves his hands into his pockets. "Who knows if Chaos was really ever more than an urban legend. The thief or thieves who stole Shadow Striker are just using the games as a disguise. And I know the rules of an activation competition. Once it begins, you can't opt out."

The room falls silent as everything sinks in. This is such a mess. I'm glad Talon is finally telling us the truth, but if he'd only been honest sooner, this all could have been avoided.

Becks stands and walks to Talon. I hold my breath, half expecting that Becks is going to throw a punch, but instead he asks, "Do I have your promise that you'll protect her?"

Talon doesn't even hesitate before answering. "With my life."

Becks sucks in a lungful of air and then slowly lets it out. "Okay. Then let's come up with a game plan."

We spend the next two hours going back and forth, brainstorming what might be in store for us during the last trial. It feels like a waste of time though. Besides the fact that it will center around magic and be dangerous, there's no telling what the game master will throw at us.

"Should we bring any of the other competitors into this alliance?" Titus asks, and I'm surprised none of us have thought to bring this up sooner.

Talon shakes his head. "No. I don't trust them."

"Do you even know them?" I ask. I mean I don't, but if everyone was on the same page, that would certainly make all of this easier.

Talon rattles off the names of the remaining competitors as well as some random facts about each. I raise my eyebrows. He's done his homework.

"I don't want to bring anyone else into this. If I wasn't backed into a corner, I never even would have brought all of you in."

"Geez, thanks," I say.

He shrugs. "It's just the truth."

I don't know how I feel about that. That Talon is only admitting to the truth when he's forced to. What other secrets is he keeping? My guess is a lot.

"It's getting late. I gotta go," Titus says as he gets to his feet and stretches. "We may not know how everything is going to play out, but at least we know we have each other's backs when it all goes down. That seems like the best we can hope for at this point."

Talon doesn't look pleased with that, but he nods in agreement.

I check the time on my phone and realize it's already past eight. I missed two texts from my parents and quickly shoot one back letting them know I'll be home soon. I just got my phone back that morning, I don't want to give them an excuse to take it away again.

"Need a ride?" Ensley asks me, and without meaning to my gaze goes to Becks, who's talking to Talon. "He drove his truck over," she says, correctly reading my face.

I nod. "Yeah, a ride would be great." It's not that I'm avoiding Becks, but our argument is still fresh. I need time right now to figure things out. Besides, with the last Chaos trial looming, what's going on between us needs to take a back seat anyway.

We tell the guys, who are now talking in a circle about who knows what, that we're taking off, and then head out. After only two wrong turns, Ensley and I make it back to the foyer. It's not until we have descended the staircase that Ensley realizes she left her purse back in the game room.

She groans. "This place is a maze. I'll go get it, but if I don't make it back in ten minutes, send a search party."

"You got it," I say on a laugh, and she takes off, jogging back up the stairs.

With nothing else to do while I wait, I inspect the giant dragon statue in the middle of the foyer. It's carved from some sort of black stone, and as I move closer I realize just how macabre the scene is. The dragon is standing on the bones of various animals and creatures, crushing vampire skulls beneath its feet. Bits of flesh are in between its teeth as it throws its head back in a silent roar.

Creature species are always jockeying for top position, boasting that they're superior and more powerful to others, and the message is clear that the artist considers dragon shifters at the top of the proverbial food chain.

"Majestic, isn't he?"

I start and twist to face Drake. His gaze drifts from the dragon statue to me, his eyes as cold and lifeless as shards of onyx.

I take a step back, not wanting to be any closer to this powerful shifter than I need to be. I don't trust him, and the hard look on his face as he studies me says that I'm wise not to.

"It's nice to finally meet the girl who all the fuss has been about."

"Excuse me?" What is he talking about?

His mouth curves into a smile that's lacking any real warmth. "Oh yes. We know all about you and your little friendship with our heir. A troublesome issue over the last few years that I'm confident will be resolved shortly."

My heart starts to pound.

"What are you getting at?" I ask, well aware he's trying to bait me, but not able to control my physical reaction.

His gaze skates down my body and back up again in an assessment that leaves me feeling like spiders are crawling over my skin. "Perhaps I misjudged you. I took you as naïve, not stupid."

I've had just about enough of this guy. Yes, he might be a super powerful dragon shifter, but if I've learned anything in the last several weeks it's that I don't have to sit back and take it anymore.

"I get that you have an issue with Becks' and my friendship, but you and whoever else has a problem with it are just going to have to learn to live with it because I'm not going away."

Rather than anger, amusement seeps into Drake's gaze. "How entertaining you think Becks' life-mate will put up with his crush on another female. The minute we find a suitable partner for him, your days in his life are numbered."

My stomach sours, but I do my best to keep Drake from knowing he's getting to me. "Becks was granted the authority to choose his own mate."

He tilts his head, looking at me like I'm the biggest idiot he's ever seen. "Simply an illusion of choice orchestrated by the council."

This shifter is absolutely villainous.

I grit my teeth, furious with the dragon shifter and the whole council for the control they have over Becks' life. "Why are you doing this to him?"

"*Doing* this to him?" His eyebrows raise in feigned surprise. "Why, my girl, we are saving him. At first his friendship with you seemed to be little more than an embarrassment, one we assumed he'd grow out of, but when reports started coming in about the growing infatuation between the two of you, well, drastic measures had to be taken."

Ensley's words from earlier in the day drift back to me.

"Anyone who cares to look can plainly see what's there between you two."

The air feels trapped in my lungs, and as the pieces click together I start to get lightheaded. "That's why you're forcing him to mate so soon? To keep him away from *me*?"

He tilts his head, a false mask of pity sliding over his face. "Did you really think we'd let our heir degrade himself with a magicless creature?"

The blood drains from my face. This is all my fault. Or maybe not my fault exactly, but because of me.

"You can't do this."

"It's already been done."

"Well, undo it," I snap.

"Why in the world would we be motivated to do that?" There's a cunning sharpness in his gaze that reminds me of a predator who has cornered his prey and is anticipating devouring it.

"Would the council change their minds if I wasn't in the picture anymore?"

"Hmm. That's an interesting proposition."

It's in that moment that I realize Drake is just as ruthless as Talon said he was. This is what Drake and the council wanted all along, to get me out of Becks' life, one way or another. And he's smart enough to know that I'd do just about anything for Becks, including take myself out of his life.

I lock down my emotions, forcing myself to go hard rather than to fall apart, not willing to give him a shred more than he's already taken from me.

"Got it!" Ensley calls, and when I look over she's descending the stairs.

The smile on her face slips when she sees me standing with Talon's uncle. Even though I'm doing my best to keep myself under control, she knows me too well not to see my distress.

Her eyes narrow as she glances back and forth between us. "Creepy statue."

"It's a three-hundred-year-old work of art. Practically price-less," Drake says, and Ensley snorts.

"Could have fooled me," she says, and Drake's face scrunches like he just smelled something rancid.

She reaches into her purse and pulls out a small notebook and pen. Scribbles something on a piece of paper. She rips the page out and then hands it to Drake.

He takes it with a frown. "What is this?"

"The number of our interior designer. Looks like you need some help freshening up this place. It's giving off serious dated dungeon vibes. You can do better."

She doesn't wait for Drake to respond before grabbing my arm and hauling me toward the front door. I hear paper being ripped into pieces, but don't look over my shoulder. I've seen enough of Drake to last me a lifetime. I just want to get the heck out of this mansion and never look back.

Thirty-Four

I MAY NEVER WANT to see Drake Brayden's face again, but I still find myself loitering outside his business office the next day, pacing back and forth trying to make myself go inside the building and confront him. I wish I didn't have to see him face-to-face, but I don't have his number and wasn't about to ask Talon for it, so stalking him at his place of work was the only way I could think to have a conversation.

I was up most of the night before, tossing and turning, knowing what needed to be done but not wanting to admit it to myself. When the sun finally rose this morning I came to terms with what I have to do, but that doesn't mean it's easy to make myself do it.

I've been pacing for over a half hour when Drake shoves through the door and heads to his car. I force myself to hurry over to him before he can get in and drive off.

"I'll do it," I say, and Drake turns to face me. If he's surprised to see me, he doesn't show it.

"Do what?" he asks with a mild expression.

What a jerk. He's going to make me spell it out.

"I'll make a clean break from Becks and promise to never have a romantic relationship with him. And in exchange you will get the council to back off about this life-mate stuff. And when the time comes he'll be able to choose who he wants to be with without council interference."

He lifts his eyebrows. "You really think I'm going to agree to that."

I nod. "I don't just think, I know. Do you want to know how I know?"

He tilts his head as he regards me. "Enlighten me."

"I know that you're going to agree to this because you all are so scared of Becks picking someone magicless to mate with that you'll go to extremes to stop him. And I also know you're going to take this deal because it's the only way to keep me out of his life for good."

Drake's gaze turns calculating. "I'm comfortable with the current situation. Once he's mated in the fall, that will solve the issue."

"Do you really want to find out what happens if Becks is forced to choose between me and his duties as the dragon heir? Because chances are he'll choose to life-mate like you want him to —we both know how duty bound he is—but there's always a small chance he won't. And it's that small chance that has you scared."

I'm not bluffing. I can tell by how aggressively Drake has come at me that he's worried Becks will go against them. But I'm not willing to give up Becks forever for anything less than his guaranteed freedom of choice. He deserves to choose his own life-mate, even if that's never going to be me.

I stand my ground, waiting to see what Drake will do.

"Okay," he finally says. "I agree to those terms."

I nod, feeling an overwhelming sense of relief, but also a deep, aching pain in my chest.

"But you need to understand that you can't just tell him you don't want to be with him. That's not good enough. You have to do something to convince him there will *never* be a chance between you." Drake takes a step closer to me, crowding me to hit home his point. "You have to crush him."

I suck in a quick breath of air and my stomach roils. There's only one thing I can think of that will convince Becks I don't want to be with him anymore, but there'll be no coming back from this. Becks will never know why I've done this and might hate me forever for it. If I go through with this, it will truly be the end of us. And not just us as a couple, but our friendship as well. He'll see it as a betrayal and will probably never trust me again.

My heart screams at me, but I shove it in a box and bury it deep. I've committed to this path and now it's time to see it through.

"Got it. If you come through on your end, Becks and I will be through, forever."

"I NEED A FAVOR."

Talon looks over at me as I keep pace with him in the hall at school the next day. I've received three text messages from Becks that he needs to talk to me. Each message sounds more urgent than the one before. I've ignored them all and gone to great lengths to avoid him at school this morning. There was a council meeting last night, so I already know what he's going to tell me. The council has had a change of heart and decided they won't require him to find a life-mate by graduation, nor choose or approve his future life-mate. He thinks this fixes everything between us. He has no idea I have to crush his heart before he can have a chance to give me the news.

"No," Talon says, and keeps walking.

"What do you mean *no*?" I ask, taken aback.

He arches a brow at me. "I'm pretty sure you're aware what that word means."

I put a hand on his arm, stopping him, and he looks down at me impatiently.

"You owe me."

He barks out a laugh. "How do you figure?"

I start ticking off reasons on my fingers. "You wouldn't have made it through the last trial without me. I agreed to stay out of the way during the final trial. I'm going to do whatever I can to help you win Chaos. Should I go on?"

He sighs. "What do you want this time? Let me guess: you need help getting back together with your princeling?"

"The opposite. I need you to pretend to be dating me, so he knows we are over."

Shock registers on Talon's face but is wiped away quickly. "Giving up on him so soon?"

If he only knew.

"You can look at it that way."

Talon's gaze turns assessing. "No, that's not it. You're being forced to do this. Or feel like you have to."

My heart jumps into my throat. Is he a frickin' mind reader?

"It doesn't matter the reason. I just need to make it clear to Becks that we're over, and the only way he's going to believe me is if he thinks I've moved on."

Talon crosses his arms over his chest. "And you want to use me to make that point."

"He's already insecure about our friendship, so if I show him we're together, he'll believe it."

Taking my arm gently, Talon guides me to the side, out of any hallway traffic. "Freckles, you don't want to do this."

"You're right, I don't. But I'm not doing it for me. I'm doing it for him."

His eyebrows rise in question, but I refuse to tell him anything else.

"Are you going to help me or not?" I ask.

"I should say no."

I really didn't think this was going to be that hard of a sell. "I don't understand why you're not jumping at the idea. You always seemed to find great pleasure in sticking it to Becks or rubbing things in his face."

"This is different."

"How so?"

Talon takes a step forward, crowding me. My breath catches when his eyes roam over my face, and he raises a hand to tuck a strand of hair behind my ear. The pad of his finger rings the shell of my ear before he drops his hand, sending a shiver down my spine.

"Fine. I'll do it," he says rather than answer my question.

"Good," I say, swallowing to wet my throat and taking a step away from him. "We'll do it at lunch."

"Do it?" he says with a smirk, and I roll my eyes.

"I mean make it clear we're like a *thing* now, or whatever."

He leans a shoulder up against the wall, looking way too relaxed for the situation. "And how do you want us to do that?"

"We can meet up beforehand and walk into the courtyard holding hands or something."

He chuckles. "And you think that will convince your princeling you've moved on?"

I cross my arms over my chest, annoyed at his mocking tone. "Well, then, what do you suggest?"

He smirks. "The hand holding is a good start, but if you want this to work, if you want him to *believe* it, we have to go further than some innocent hand holding."

I swallow. "You want us to kiss in front of him?"

He shrugs. "It will certainly make a statement."

My stomach flips, and I'm not sure if it's because I know what it will do to Becks to see me kiss someone else or from the thought of kissing Talon.

No, I tell myself, *it's just because I know what seeing Becks kiss someone else would do to me and I don't want to hurt Becks like that.*

Kissing Talon is going to shred Becks' heart—along with mine —but as much as I hate to admit it, he's right. It's what needs to be done.

I straighten my resolve and my spine and look Talon dead in the eye. "Fine. We'll kiss."

Surprise flashes in his eyes. He didn't expect me to agree to that. But he recovers quickly. "With tongue?"

"Don't push it," I growl, and he chuckles.

"Okay, Freckles, you have yourself a deal." He holds his hand out for me to shake, and when he wraps his fingers around mine, a little zing of awareness shoots up my arm. "I'll see you at lunch," he says, and then takes off to class.

Numbness starts to set in, and I watch his retreating form with one thought in mind. What have I gotten myself into?

TALON and I never discussed exactly where we would meet, so I'm stuck hiding in the science room, looking through the narrow rectangular window to avoid Becks while I search for Talon. I haven't spotted either of them, but my biggest concern is running into Becks too soon.

Finally, *finally,* Talon swaggers past. I spring out of the room, almost barreling into him, but rather than looking off guard he just stares down at me.

"Change your mind yet?"

I shake my head. "No. Now take my hand so we can walk through that door like a couple."

"So bossy," he says, but slides his hand into mine, and then with a tug pulls me closer. When I give him a questioning look, he says, "Any girlfriend of mine wouldn't want to be so far away from me."

"Let me guess. Because you're so irresistible."

He smiles down at me. "You said it, not me."

I'm jittery as we push through the doors and walk into the courtyard, hand-in-hand. The first thing I do is scan for Becks, my head on a swivel.

Talon squeezes my hand and leans over. "Perhaps be a little less obvious," he says. "Our classmates are watching. Focus on me."

Sure enough, when I take a moment to notice, the majority of the students are staring at us. I know it was my idea for this to be so public, but I hate the attention. It makes me want to melt into the floor to escape their prying glances, but the point of all of this is to be seen.

"Locklyn," comes a surprised voice, halting me. When I look up, Shayla stands in front of us, a tray loaded with food in her hands.

"Hey," I say and give her an awkward little wave with my free hand.

"Shayla, right?" Talon says, and her wide-eyed gaze shifts to him and she nods. "Nice to meet you. I'm Talon."

"Oh, I know who you are," she says, and then looks back at me and blinks. "So like . . . this is . . . a thing?"

"Uhh, kinda?" I say.

Talon wraps an arm around my waist and tugs me to his side. "You betcha," he says and then plants a kiss on my head. How cheesy. I have to smother the urge to swat him away. "It took me a while to wear my little love muffin down, but she finally caved."

Love muffin?

Heat rises to my cheeks. I'm going to kill him for this later.

The look on Shayla's face would be hilarious if I weren't so embarrassed. "O-kay," she says, taking a step back and eyeing us with either confusion or revulsion. I can't tell which. "Are you guys eating with us today?" It looks like she's not sure if she wants us to or not.

"I think I'm just going to eat with Talon."

"Sure. I guess I'll see you later," she says, and then flees.

That was bad.

"Talon," I grit out. "That was too much."

"Was it?" he chuckles as his arm disappears from my waist and he turns to face me. "Isn't that how devoted boyfriends are supposed to act?"

"I'm going to make you pay for that later."

He lifts his hands up in surrender. "Hey, I'm just doing what you asked of me."

I shoot him a look, but he misses it because his gaze shifts to the side. The smirk melts off his face and he steps closer, bringing a hand to my hip. The light touch causes something in me to stir.

Brushing the hair off my shoulder, he curves his body forward to whisper in my ear. "He just showed up."

My heartbeat picks up and I look over and catch Becks walking toward our usual table in the corner. He hasn't seen us yet, but when he gets there he says something and then Shayla points in our direction.

I quickly avert my gaze and focus on Talon. "It's time."

Stepping into his space, I slide my hands up Talon's chest and then drape them around his neck. His arms loop around me, bringing me almost flush up against his body.

It's now or never.

I look up into his stormy eyes, terrified. I think I'm going to be sick.

"Freckles," Talon says with a frown. "I know I goaded you into it, but we don't have to do this. I didn't actually think you'd want to go through with it when I suggested it."

I lick my lips and his gaze flicks to my mouth before returning to my eyes.

"We do," I say. "You were right before. It won't be convincing otherwise."

His gaze searches mine. "You do this and it can't be undone," he says quietly, giving me another chance to change my mind. "Your princeling won't forgive this. There's no going back."

The box I shoved my heart into starts to rattle, so I slap a padlock on it so it doesn't burst open and ignore it the best I can.

"Kiss me," I command. "And make it convincing."

Thirty-Five

TALON ONLY HESITATES a second before dipping his head. My eyes slide closed, and I wait to feel the press of his mouth against mine, but it doesn't come. His breath brushes against my lips, making them tingle.

I crack my lids to find his face lined up with mine, his mouth a hair's breadth away. "Talon, what are you doing?" I whisper, and my lower lip brushes against his, sending a shock through my body.

He shifts his head, his nose gliding over my cheek. My eyes slide closed again of their own accord, and I go lightheaded. His lips graze the shell of my ear, making a shiver run down my spine.

"The first time we kiss, Freckles, it won't be to make another guy jealous. It'll be because we can't live another second without tasting each other's lips. I'm a patient creature. I can wait."

Wait. What?

"Lock?"

Becks' voice breaks me out of my daze, and I rear back from Talon so quickly I almost trip over my own feet. Only Talon's arms still locked around me keep me from falling. I try to pull away from him, but he holds tight and gives me a look, which is the only thing that keeps me from blowing our lie before we've even had a chance to spin it.

Still within the cage of Talon's arms, I glance at Becks, and what I read on his face almost breaks me.

Disbelief. Hurt. Betrayal.

"What's going on here?" he asks, and I know he's hoping that his eyes are playing tricks on him, that there's some reasonable explanation for why I'm in Talon's arms. And I know that because if the situation were reversed, that's what I'd be hoping for too.

Talon chuckles, and Becks visibly bristles. "I didn't think I'd need to spell this out to you. I wouldn't have had a chance with her if you didn't pass. Thanks for that."

I smother a gasp and Becks clenches one fist, the dragon tattoo on his left arm rippling when his muscles bunch. His gaze tracks back and forth between the both of us, and he shakes his head. "No. I don't believe it."

He looks so angry yet so broken that I can't stay silent anymore.

"Becks," I say, tugging free from Talon. When I take a step toward Becks, he takes one back and a sharp pain shoots through my chest. "It's—" I can't say it's not true, because he has to believe it is. There's nothing I can offer Becks in this moment. "I'm so sorry."

Becks makes a strangled noise that I think's supposed to be a laugh, but just sounds like bitterness.

"No. I'm the one that's sorry," he spits at me before turning to stride out of the courtyard.

A pit opens up in my stomach.

It's done. I've lost him.

But he's free.

I'm still staring at the swinging doors when Ensley runs into view. She glances over her shoulder, shooting me a wounded look right before she disappears after her brother.

When I look back at Talon, he's holding his Chaos tracker and wearing a somber expression.

"It's time," he says. "This ends tonight."

THE LAST TRIAL is just outside of town in the ruins of the original settlement. Everton was founded over three hundred years ago and was becoming a bustling village when most of it burned down. When they rebuilt the town, they decided to go to higher ground, but the ruins of the original settlement still exist. They're open to the public during the day, and at night it's a notorious spot for secret parties or couple hook-ups. We went there on a class field trip in middle school, but since I'm not a partier and have never had a boyfriend, I haven't been back since.

I'm holding my phone hours later, trying to decide who to call or text for a ride. The original plan was for Ensley to drive me to the last trial. I've already cleared a sleepover at her house tonight, promising my parents Becks is gone for the evening, but after the stunt I pulled with Talon at lunch earlier today, I'm not even sure if my best friend *is* my best friend anymore. Talon's number is still programmed into my phone, and I'm sure he will take me if I ask, but the thought of being on the back of his bike again after what he said to me earlier today makes me feel a certain type of way.

The first time we kiss, Freckles, it won't be to make another guy jealous. It'll be because we can't live another second without tasting each other's lips.

Talon's words ring as clearly in my ears now as when he said them. And just like then, I don't know what to think about them. My mind is a confusing mess of contradictions and I only know one thing for sure: Becks and I are over.

Something squeezes painfully in my chest, and I rub the spot, convinced I'll carry this pain with me for the rest of my life.

My phone buzzes and I start, almost dropping it. When I look at the screen there's a text from Ensley.

"I'll be there in ten minutes. Meet me out front."

My cowardice rears its head and I consider messaging her back that I already have a ride but stop myself. I can't tell Ensley the truth, but I owe it to her to at least face her.

Ten minutes later, Ensley pulls up as I'm waiting outside with a backpack of overnight clothes and toiletries to sell the sleepover to my parents. I scramble into the car. Ensley isn't looking at me as she pulls away from the curb, and I can't help but think the red and black streaks in her hair match her mood right now.

"Do you know where you're going?" I ask, and she nods.

We drive for five minutes in silence before she breaks.

"What are you thinking?"

When I don't answer her, she glances over at me with fire in her eyes before turning her attention back to the road.

What do I say to her? "It's complicated."

She barks out a bitter laugh. "That's where you're wrong. The dragon council called a special meeting last night. They let Becks out of the life-mating all together. He isn't under a time limit anymore and they won't have any say over who he picks as his life-mate in the future. It will be completely up to Becks who he's with."

"I know," I say as I hunch in my seat, feeling about an inch tall.

"I've never seen him so excited. He couldn't wait to tell you the news. Because he wanted to be with you for real and publicly. But then he had to watch you in Talon's arms—" Ensley cuts herself off and her brow scrunches. "Wait . . . you knew?" She glances over at me again, pinning me with her stare. "How?"

Oh shoot. That was a mistake. I should have acted surprised at the news. I wasn't thinking. "Umm. I overheard some dragon shifters talking about it in the hallway this afternoon."

"No, you didn't," she says, calling me out. "And do you want to know how I know you didn't," she asks. I'm about to shake my head, but she goes on anyway. "I know you didn't overhear anyone talking about it because the only ones who know about it are the council members and my family. They're going to make an official announcement about it tomorrow because Becks wanted to tell you about it himself first."

"It must have been leaked," I say, trying desperately to hold on to my lie, but Ensley knows me too well.

"Locklyn, what did you do?"

I know I shouldn't, but the whole story comes spilling out of me. About Drake Brayden, our deal, Talon. I don't finish until we've already turned onto the dirt road that leads to the ruins.

"You can't tell any of this to Becks, ever," I say, hoping I don't regret everything I just told her.

Ensley stays silent until she pulls into a spot on the side of the road; the small parking lot is already full. She shifts the car into park and then turns it off before facing me.

"You have to tell him," she says.

I shake my head, ignoring the noises of the creatures walking by us and heading toward the ruins outside the car. "I can't, Ens. If I do, the council will take away his freedom again. He'll be mated by the end of summer."

"This is Becks' decision as much as it is yours."

"But that's the point. If I go back on my word, it won't be Becks' decision anymore."

"This isn't your fault. You have to know that. This is the council's doing. The blame lies at their feet."

I clench my fists. "I know the dragon council is a group of bastards, but if it wasn't for me they never would have put pressure on him to mate so early. That's just facts. If I have to pay the price to get him out of it, so be it."

"Locklyn, you're not the only one who's suffering. He loves you." It couldn't have hurt more if she'd stabbed me with a rusty knife. "What happened in the courtyard at lunch today, he was completely blindsided by that. It gutted him."

"He'll get over me." *But will I ever get over him?*

"Maybe, maybe not."

"I did this for him. Don't take that away from me, or him," I plead, and Ensley starts chewing her bottom lip.

"I don't know. This doesn't feel right."

"I know. I'm gutted too. But this is what had to happen to get him out from underneath the council's control."

"There has to be another way."

"We've spent weeks trying to find another way and there isn't. We both know that."

Ensley leans her head back against the rest and groans. "Why did he have to be named heir?"

"I don't know," I say, even though it's a rhetorical question.

Ensley sighs. "Come on, we've got to get you to the ruins. Let's just get through this last trial and put Chaos behind us, then we can try to figure something out."

I don't think there's any fixing this situation, but I still give her a small smile, and nod anyway.

Ensley's about to open her door when I ask, "Is he coming?"

She looks back at me, her eyes softening in understanding. "You might have stomped on his heart today, but you still mean the world to him. He wouldn't miss it."

I let out a sigh of relief. It's probably not fair, but even just knowing that he's going to be here tonight gives me strength.

"All right. I'm ready. Let's get this competition over with so we can all move on with our lives."

Thirty-Six

JUST LIKE THE OTHER TRIALS, the area around the ruins is cloaked so the lights and sounds can't be heard until we pass through the invisible barrier. The atmosphere once inside the barrier reminds me of the first trial in Deepseat Caverns. Spectators are spread around the space, dancing and laughing. It feels like a party rather than a potential fight for my life.

I get stopped repeatedly on my way to where the other competitors are waiting on the edge of the ruins by creatures who want to wish me luck or let me know they're rooting for me. It's a surreal experience. Five weeks ago, when I walked into the caverns, these creatures didn't know who I was and wouldn't have given me a second look as I passed. Now I can't seem to make it twenty feet without someone stopping me. Somehow along the way I earned their respect and admiration, but for what? Making it through a competition? It all seems so hollow and unimportant. I'm still the same magicless creature I was all those weeks ago.

I never deserved the scorn I received from creatures like Jules or the other bullies at Nightlark. But on the same note I don't deserve all the fuss that's being made over me now either.

I'm suddenly weary. Weary of this competition. Weary of

trying to fix everything in my life. Weary of all the energy I've put into trying to become someone other than who I really am.

I'm just me, and it's about time for me to understand that's enough.

I can't stop myself from looking for Becks, but I don't spot him anywhere, and soon enough I reach the other competitors. There's a small platform that Titus and the other three competitors I don't know well are standing on, but Talon is missing.

Before I step up to join the others, Ensley gives me a hug and tells me to be careful. I assure her I will, and then jump up onto the stage with the others. Titus gives me a chin nod, but the other competitors, Damon, Vivian, and Chase, just stare at me with calculated eyes. Despite the revelry going on, none of us are jovial. We know this last trial is going to be a fight, and we're all trying to mentally prepare for the battle.

I turn away from the spectators and survey the ruins, which are empty. The game master must have something in place to keep creatures from venturing into that area. Plants grow up between the cobblestone of what's left of the road that used to run down the middle of the settlement. The hollowed-out shells of shops and homes stand on either side. At the end of the road is what used to be a small cathedral. It was made of stone, so it's the most preserved of all the structures in the old settlement. From here I can see a slight glow emanating from within, but the rest of the ruins are dark and lifeless.

"Hey, Freckles, you ready?"

I turn, ignoring the flash of heat that shoots through my body when I find Talon standing casually next to me with his hands shoved in the pockets of his dark jeans.

I lower my voice. "Ready to run and hide behind you and Titus?"

He smiles, and I hate that it makes my stomach flip. "Good. You are."

It's just jitters, I tell myself. But I know it's a lie. Whether I like it or not, what happened between us today has changed things. He can act as nonchalant as he wants now, but that doesn't erase the fact that he spoke to me like a kiss between us was not only inevitable but would also mean something.

I shake off thoughts of what happened in the courtyard at lunch to focus on the here and now. Talon, Titus, and I have a loose plan for tonight, but that doesn't mean a number of things can't, and won't, go wrong, especially since I'm at such a disadvantage during this trial. But I'm not really worried about the other competitors, I'm worried about the mysterious game master who seems to be pulling all the strings from behind the scenes. If Talon is right, he's going to try to kill someone tonight, and if I'm not careful that creature will be me.

"Running a little late, don't you think?" I ask, looking at my watch and seeing it's mere minutes before the trial is scheduled to start.

Talon surveys the rowdy crowd, his face blanked of emotion. "I was trying to check out the ruins before the trial started. The whole area is warded and encased in a magical barrier. I couldn't get through. I think he's making sure once the trial starts no one can interfere."

"Do you really think this is going to be a fair fight?"

He shakes his head. "Not for one second."

A horn blasts and then the game master appears atop the closest ruin in a cloud of smoke. A toxic mix of fear and hatred rises in my chest toward the hooded figure for all the pain he's inflicted for his own selfish desires. I can't wait to see Talon beat him at his own game and claim the dagger back for his family.

The game master starts droning on about what an accomplishment it is for the six of us to have made it this far and how the winner will go down in infamy. It's all shallow words, a front for the deception he's running. I'm only half listening as I wait for him to lay out the rules of the last trial when my gaze snags on a familiar blond head.

Becks is standing off to the side, watching with his arms crossed over his chest. The moment my gaze connects with his I visibly jolt. Talon must notice, because the next thing I know he's leaning over to whisper in my ear.

"Do you need me to put on another show? Because I'm willing and available."

The blasé tone in his voice makes me bristle. Regardless of how necessary it was to break things off for good with Becks, feelings were still involved. Specifically Becks' and mine.

Becks' gaze narrows when Talon leans closer, and his face darkens, but he doesn't break eye contact.

"Careful, Freckles. Keep staring at your princeling like that and he might start to doubt the sincerity of our fake relationship."

He's right, but I can't look away.

"Now for the rules of this last trial," the game master says, and I'm finally able to tear my gaze from Becks.

The game master is angled toward the competitors now, his face a blurred shadow beneath his hood. "This is a battle of magical strength," he says, confirming Talon's theories. My stomach roils. Part of me was hoping Talon would be wrong about this trial and everything else, but it looks like he isn't. I catch Titus's attention flick toward Talon before he looks away. "One at a time you'll each be directed to a starting location in the ruins," the game master continues. "When the horn blares again, a free-for-all battle will begin. Your objective is to use your powers to take out your fellow competitors and then make your way to the cathedral at the end of the street. The competitor who makes it to the ruin first and captures the Blade of Power will be our Chaos champion."

Reaching into the folds of his clothes, he pulls out Shadow Striker. Talon stiffens next to me, his face as hard as stone and his eyes lasered in on the wavy bladed dagger. The game master's face is obscured but I'd bet money he's grinning back at us right now. A low growl comes from Talon's throat, and he starts forward, but I grab his arm and he halts. His muscles bunch beneath my hand, but he doesn't try to take another step.

"One other thing. I've hidden two magical objects somewhere in the ruins. Find one, and you'll find you have an advantage in this trial."

My interest piques with that news. I don't have magic, but maybe I can get a leg up by finding one of those objects. At least then I won't be as much of a liability for Talon and Titus.

But the game master isn't done. "In order to keep the location of each competitor secret until the trial begins, the ruins will be cloaked. They'll enter one at a time and follow the lights to their location. Good luck to each of you."

In another smoke explosion, the game master and Shadow Striker disappear; the area around the ruins goes dark and opaque, like the shadows have solidified. The competitors all glance at each other, waiting to see who's going to go first.

Titus steps forward. "I'll head in," he says, and doesn't wait for anyone to stop him and agree before jumping off the platform and walking right toward the ruins. The blackness swallows him immediately.

"Locklyn will go next," Talon says for me, and gives me a little nudge forward.

"I will?"

Talon leans over and pretends to kiss my cheek, but really whispers, "I want you to go between me and Titus in case our locations are close to each other." He pauses. "Good luck, love muffin," he says loud enough for those closest to us to hear, earning some scowls from the remaining competitors who now, no doubt, know that we're working together.

Grumbling under my breath I start for the end of the platform. Right before I step down I look for Becks, but he's gone. My heart drops. I just wanted to see him one more time. Just in case something goes horribly wrong.

My nerves start to take over as I walk the few short steps to the barrier. I push against it with my hand, but it doesn't let me through. I try it a couple more times and finally my hand sinks through. I can only assume it won't let a competitor in until the one before is hidden.

Taking a deep breath, I step forward and I'm on the other side by the time my foot touches the ground. There's a lighted purple path on the cracked cobblestone road leading forward. I follow the path about halfway down the street and then into one of the structures on the right. I have to duck and move vines out of the way to get inside the ruin, where I find the glowing purple circle I'm assuming I'm meant to stand in. Taking a deep breath, I enter the circle and wait as one by one the other competitors are led to their starting spots.

An eternity passes while I wait. Every minute that ticks away, my nerves fray a little more. I cast my gaze around the space to distract myself, learning every nook and cranny of the ruin. I miss it on my first sweep, but the second time I glance over the stones on the wall I notice a round indentation in one of the rocks. It's dark in the ruin. The roof is missing, but a tree has grown in the middle of the room and the branches cover a lot of the sky, blocking the moonlight. But when I look hard enough, I realize what it is: the Chaos, or rather Shadow Striker, emblem.

Is that where one of the magical objects is hidden?

I won't know until I look, but I have to wait for the trial to begin before I leave the purple circle. The moment the horn blasts, signaling all the competitors are in place and the trial has started, I rush over to the stone with the emblem and immediately notice there's no mortar around it. Reaching forward, I yank the stone free. Sitting in the now empty space is a gold cuff. I pull it out and fasten it around my wrist and forearm. And then . . .

Nothing happens.

Is it a dud or something? Hopefully its powers will show themselves sooner rather than later.

Shouts sound from outside the crumbling walls of the ruin.

I'm trying to decide if I should join the fray or hunker down for as long as I can, when a body comes crashing through the entrance and smashes into the tree trunk in the middle of the room.

Titus scrambles to his feet and looks wildly at me. "Oh good, it's you. Stay out of Chase's path if you can. He has super strong wind magic."

"He just blasted you in here?" I ask with wide eyes, and Titus nods. "Are you okay?"

"Yeah, I'm fine, but we'd better get out of here before someone comes looking for us."

With Titus going first to shield me, we leave the ruin. The rest of the competitors are battling it out in the middle of the street. Talon's back is to us as he holds off both Damon and Chase. With his arms moving rapidly, it looks like he's pulling shadows from around him and then flinging them at the pair. It's not a power I've ever seen before, and I'm awestruck for a moment.

"Stay down and out of the fray the best you can," Titus says, and then runs for Vivian, who's sneaking up on Talon while he's distracted with the other two.

She looks like she's getting ready to throw some sort of faelight ball of energy at Talon, but Titus swipes his leg out, taking her down before she can. They grapple on the ground, rolling a few times, until Titus comes out on top. Covering her eyes with his hands, he blasts her with white faelight, temporarily blinding her. She screams in outrage, trying to buck him off, but it's no use. Titus knows how to use his body and his magic in a fight, and I'm suddenly relieved I don't have to go up against him.

Titus jumps off Vivian, but even blinded she tries to get to her feet.

"You're out," he yells at her, "stay down."

"Never," she screams, and rushes him, but he easily sidesteps and then slams his fist against her temple, knocking her out. He peers down at her with a look of regret, but then shakes his head and takes off.

A roar of cheers fills the air. I look in the direction of the crowd, but the blackness is still doming the ruins, making it impossible to see the world beyond. The game master must have cameras hidden around here like he did before.

"Watch out!" someone screams, and I look up just in time to see a ball of fire whiz toward my face.

It's coming too fast. I throw up my arms in a feeble attempt to protect myself. Just before the fire reaches me it hits an invisible barrier and explodes, leaving me unscathed.

I look down at the cuff in shock, realizing it very well might have just saved my life.

When I glance up, Talon is sprinting toward me with a look of relief on his face. I see Chase behind him, running for cover. I guess wind magic isn't the only creature power Chase has.

Titus is farther down the road battling Damon, giving Talon and me a temporary reprieve.

"That blast was meant for me. Are you all right?" he asks, skidding to a halt in front of me. His eyes run from my head down to my toes and back up again in a quick sweep for injuries.

"Yeah, I'm fine. Thanks to this," I say, holding up the cuff.

"You found one of the magical objects?"

I nod. "It was in the ruin."

"That's convenient," he says with a hint of suspicion.

"It is. But it just saved me from being barbecued, so I don't think I care."

"Good point." He checks over his shoulder and then says, "I'm going after that shifter. Stay behind me." I nod and we take off, rounding the back of one of the ruins. "He's over there," Talon says, pointing ahead.

I don't see anyone or any movement though. "Are you sure?"

"Yeah. I can see his magical aura."

"You can see that?" He nods, and I'm so confused. That's a fae trait, not a vampire one.

"Come on," he says and takes off.

I do what I can to keep up with him as he sprints ahead. He rounds a corner and I quickly follow, almost running into Talon's back because he's stopped short.

Sure enough, Chase is there. Sweat dampens his brow and his eyes are wild. "Stay back!" he warns, holding something up in front of him.

I get a quick look at it before Talon shoves me behind him. It's an enhancer. Another one of the magical objects the game master hid in the ruins. It's shaped like a horseshoe, with four different gems that amplify a creature's natural magic embedded into the metal. Enhancers are very rare and very expensive. I've only ever seen one in a museum.

"I'm giving you a chance to bow out on your own terms," Chase says, and Talon chuckles darkly.

"That's not going to happen."

"I'll use it. I will."

"Then do it," Talon says as he shifts his stance. I know what he's doing. He's getting ready to charge the dragon shifter.

I peek around Talon, and Chase's gaze tracks to me and then shifts back to Talon. "I don't want to hurt her," he says. "I know she's close with our heir. But I will if I have to."

The mention of Becks makes my heart squeeze.

"This is a lot of talk and not a lot of action," Talon says, sounding deceptively bored.

"I have to win this competition. You don't know what this will mean—"

Talon jolts forward in the middle of Chase's sentence, moving so quickly he almost blurs, taking him off guard. Ducking, Talon plows into Chase's gut, sending him flying back onto the cobblestone street.

Chase lands hard, cracking his head against the stones. Sitting up, he touches the back of his head and his fingers come away coated in red. He tries to push to his feet, but Talon is already on him, delivering an uppercut followed by a cross to his temple that puts him out.

"Where's the enhancer?" I say, searching the stones around Chase but not seeing it anywhere.

"There," Talon says, pointing down the street to near where Titus and Damon are still trading magical blows.

Titus shoots a ball of white faelight at Damon, but he doesn't have time to dodge the streak of dark shadow magic that Damon fires off and takes a hit to the shoulder. When Titus falls backward from the hit, Damon advances on him, but then his gaze catches on the enhancer.

Oh no.

Talon and I take off, but Damon is closer and scoops it up. Immediately, he shoots shadows at Titus that cocoon him in a ball of darkness. I can hear Titus shouting from within the blackness, but I don't know what to do about it.

Talon doesn't hesitate, and matching shadows whip from his palms and shoot toward Damon, squeezing him like a vise, but with the enhancer he's too strong and quickly breaks free. Turning on Talon, he blasts him with a stream of dark magic. It hits Talon in the chest and sends him sailing right into me. We go down in a pile of limbs and roll until we come to a stop with me on top.

"Are you okay?" Talon asks, but before I can even nod Damon follows up with another blast.

I lift my arm to shield us, praying the cuff works like it did before, and it does because right before the magic hits us it explodes. When we look up, Damon hasn't waited to see if he finished us off. He's going for Titus again, who has broken free of his shadow cage and is flinging white faelight at the vampire.

Damon dodges the attacks, and then suddenly Titus falls to his knees, grabbing his head, his mouth open in a silent scream.

Horror washes through me. "What's he doing to him?"

"Compulsion," Talon says grimly, and I gasp, remembering what it was like to be under vampire compulsion. Titus is mentally strong. If he wasn't, he wouldn't have passed the compulsion trial, but he can't hope to break free while Damon has that enhancer.

Titus' back arches and he lets out a pain-filled bellow.

"He's hurting him," I cry, and Talon and I scramble to our feet.

Damon slowly walks toward Titus, his face expressionless, almost vacant.

"We've got to get that enhancer away from him."

"But how?"

Talon glances down at the cuff around my wrist, and I can read the indecision in his eyes. I can also guess what he's thinking.

"Let's do it," I say. "I'll distract him, and when he attacks me, come in behind him and get that enhancer."

He presses his lips together, not liking that plan, but we both know it's solid.

"He can't hurt me with this on," I remind him.

"We don't know that for sure."

"I'm willing to take the chance."

Finally he nods. "I'll loop around the other side. Wait about ten seconds and then get his attention."

Talon sprints away, blending into the ruins' shadows in moments. I cringe as I have to watch Titus go through whatever hellish torture Damon is putting him through. I've just counted out ten seconds when Titus' body goes limp, and he falls to the cobblestones.

"No!" I scream, and Damon's head whips toward me. Shadows ring him as he lifts his hands to launch an attack, shooting his dark magic right at me.

I lift my arm to thwart the attack and the magic explodes before it reaches me.

Damon's face skews with confusion until his gaze drops to my forearm, then understanding dawns.

"That's not going to protect you," he says, taking determined steps forward. "I can best you without using magic."

I stand my ground, loosening up my stance in case this comes down to a physical fight. Part of me is even hoping that it does because hand-to-hand combat is one of my strengths, but I don't get the chance before Talon appears seemingly out of nowhere and tackles Damon.

The pair hit the ground, and the first thing Talon does is rip the enhancer from Damon's hand and chuck it off to the side.

I don't wait to watch the battle but rather rush over to Titus. He's face down on the cobblestones, and when I flip him and try to wake him, it doesn't work. His chest rises and falls though, so at least I know he's still alive.

"Come on. This isn't over yet," Talon calls to me, and when I look over he's standing over an unconscious Damon. His hair is a little mussed, and he swipes at a trickle of blood on his lower lip, but he doesn't even look winded. The enhancer is now in his hand, and considering how powerful Talon already is, I can only imagine that he's virtually unstoppable now. I'm unsure if that gives me comfort or fills me with worry, but I don't have time to analyze my own feelings right now.

With one final look at Titus and the bodies of the other competitors scattered around the ruins, I get up and join him.

Talon is tense as we rush toward the crumbled cathedral that's glowing at the end of the cobblestone street. Even though the other Chaos competitors have been defeated, Talon's gaze is bright and alert as he scans the shadows, the enhancer clenched in one fist.

I stop when we reach the entrance to the ruin. A foreboding feeling crawls up my spine, leaving goose bumps in its wake. I don't know why, but I don't want to go in there.

Talon brushes back a curtain of vines and starts to duck under them, stopping halfway when he realizes I'm not following him.

"Go on without me," I say. "You don't need me to claim the dagger."

He shakes his head. "Something doesn't feel right. I'm not about to let you out of my sight."

I can't disagree with Talon when I have the same instinct that something is off. Part of me screams not to go into that ruin, but the only way to end this living nightmare is in front of us. It's time we end this, and in truth I want to do that together, so rather than dig in my heels I follow him into the ruin.

The first thing I notice when we enter the cathedral is Shadow Striker, placed on a pedestal within a ring of white light at the back of the ruin. It sits there so innocently, representing everything I thought I needed—but no longer want. If Chaos was good for anything, it taught me I'm enough just as I am. If anyone can't accept me for my lack of magic, then that's their problem, not mine.

I follow Talon as he takes careful steps forward until he's standing right in front of the blade. He's close enough that all he has to do is reach out and take it and the dagger will be his, but he hesitates.

"What's wrong?"

"It's too easy," he says, and I choke on a laugh.

"Too easy? Do you not remember what we did to get here?"

He glances over at me, a frown on his face. "Yeah, maybe you're right."

He reaches for it, but when his hand breaches the ring of light the floor beneath our feet vibrates. Talon's eyes go wide, and he tries to snatch the blade, but his hand passes right through it as the floor gives way, and then we're falling.

Thirty-Seven

I COME to coughing and find myself lying on an uneven stone floor covered in stone dust and small bits of debris. There's a clanging noise that makes my head feel like it's going to split open as I force myself to sit up. The air is thick with a haze of dust, but as it starts to clear I realize we dropped into a pocket under the cathedral, a cave that's probably been beneath the ruin all along. Maybe a catacomb of some sort? I can just make out the edges of the crumbled floor we fell through. The opening is probably ten or twelve feet above, so it wasn't too far of a drop. Besides the sore spot on the back of my skull and a monster headache, I think I'm okay.

I push to my feet and turn toward the noise, spotting Talon in a large cage, the enhancer lying uselessly on the ground beside him. He's repeatedly kicking one of the bars, trying to bend it.

With a gasp, I rush over to him. "What happened?"

"That wasn't the dagger, just another hologram. The floor must have been rigged to cave in when someone tried to take it." He looks around his cage, searching for a weak point. "I fell directly into this cage. When I hit the ground the top slammed shut, sealing me inside."

I have so many questions. Where are we? Why are we down

here? But right now none of that is important. I need to get Talon out of this cage, and we need to get out of here.

"We have to get you out of there."

"The cage is blocking my magic, and the bars are too thick to bend. We need a key or a way to break the lock."

I immediately start searching for something to break the lock when a voice comes from behind me.

"You have no idea how long I've been waiting for this moment."

I spin around in time to see the game master step out from the shadows.

"I'm guessing this is what you are looking for," he says, pulling Shadow Striker from the folds of his robes.

"That doesn't belong to you," Talon yells, kicking the bars to show his frustration.

"And you think it belongs to *you*?" the game master asks. Talon just glares back at him.

"Who are you?" I demand, quickly scanning the area for something I can use as a weapon. There are rocks I could use, but that's about it.

There's a promising one about the size of my fist on the ground to my left that I'm about to go for when the game master says, "I suppose it is time for that reveal."

He reaches up and grasps the hood of his robe, pulling it back to finally reveal himself.

A gasp echoes throughout the chamber, and I don't immediately realize it's from me.

"Mr. Brone?" I ask, the rock all but completely forgotten as I stare back at him.

The aging hawk shifter shrugs out of the red robes. His face is as familiar to me as a beloved uncle yet standing in front of me with a sharp gleam in his eye, he almost looks like a stranger—one I don't want anything to do with.

"Kerrim," he corrects me.

"You know him?" Talon asks.

I glance over at Talon, my mind spinning. "He owns the Emporium. He's been a family friend for years." I focus back on Mr. Brone—*Kerrim*. "It was you all along? You stole Shadow Striker? You set up Chaos?"

He nods, his gaze assessing, cold. I've never seen him look at me like that before.

I shake my head. "I don't understand."

"I promise you will soon."

I don't know what possible reason he could have for stealing Shadow Striker and creating this scenario to activate the magical artifact. Mr. Brone is just a middle-aged antiquities dealer. What use could he have for Shadow Striker's powers?

But just because I don't understand doesn't mean I shouldn't be wary. He's obviously not the creature I've grown to know, so in an instant he goes from Mr. Brone to Kerrim in my mind.

"What do you want from us?" I ask, my voice growing hard.

"From him, nothing," Kerrim says, gesturing toward Talon. "But from you, I want the world. Or rather a very specific world."

"Leave her alone," Talon yells, slamming his palm against the cage bars. "This is between us. It has nothing to do with her."

"Oh, my boy," Kerrim says, glancing at Talon. "You are so very wrong about that. This is *all* because of her. It always has been. In fact, I'm a bit surprised you haven't already figured that out."

The blood leaches from my face, no doubt turning me white as a sheet. My fingers start to tingle, and my toes go numb.

Because of *me*? What's he talking about?

"You see, Locklyn, I put a great deal of effort into making sure at the end of Chaos it was you standing here in front of me, ready to claim the prize."

I shake my head, my mind frantically trying to make sense of what is happening. It's like someone spilled a jigsaw puzzle in front of me and expects me to put it together without seeing the picture the pieces are supposed to create. "No, I don't see anything. You couldn't have even known I would enter Chaos, let alone win it."

Kerrim tips his head, a sly smile curving his lips. "Who do you think tipped the dragon council off about the growing affection between you and your friend Becks?"

The breath catches in my lungs, and it's a beat before I'm able to speak. "Why would you do that?" I ask, my voice hardly louder than a whisper.

"Because I knew without presenting creature magic they'd never allow the two of you to be together. They provided you the perfect motivation to enter Chaos."

My eyes widen. That lines up with what Drake revealed. That they'd been told of how close Becks and I had become, which is what prompted them to push up the timeline on his arranged life-mating.

But something doesn't quite make sense. "Shadow Striker's powers were never publicly divulged, so you didn't even know that I knew about Shadow Striker when Chaos started."

"Didn't I though?"

"What? How?"

"Your parents reached out to me saying that their daughter had been approached by someone looking for it. They gave me the whole story you were told. I had a plan to introduce it to you myself, but just like that—" He snaps his fingers. "I didn't even need to. Someone had oh so helpfully already planted the idea in your head."

He looks at Talon. "Oh yes, I knew exactly who you were the moment you stepped into town. Hiding the scope of your magical abilities during the trials was completely needless, but it was amusing watching you try."

A muscle jumps in Talon's jaw. "If you knew who I was, why didn't you just kill me? Why let me enter Chaos at all?"

"I certainly considered it, but my plans shifted after the first trial when you came to her aid. Thank you for that, by the way. I was worried when that wolf shifter stole her coin. It was very convenient that you had an extra for her. I couldn't have planned that better myself," he says with a smug smile.

"And then in the second trial when you both refused to fight each other, it was obvious some sort of bond had formed," Kerrim goes on as Talon glares daggers at him. "It was clear you didn't want any real harm to come to her, which played into my ultimate goals quite nicely. So why would I kill you when you became my biggest ally throughout these trials? I should thank you for that. She may never have made it to this point without you."

Talon remains silent, but I swear I can hear his teeth grinding against one another.

"You had him compelled to kill me during the third trial," I say. "If he hadn't been able to fight the compulsion, I wouldn't be standing here right now."

Kerrim chuckles. "I was simply testing the limits of his affection for you. Did you know that he's actually the one that stopped you from kissing him? If he hadn't shocked you with his powers, I think you would have given in to that compulsion. That was, admittedly, a tactical error on my part. I assumed you'd fight that compulsion a little harder considering your affection for the dragon heir." He shrugs. "But no matter, the important thing is that you were never in any real danger, and the whole point was to push the both of you even closer. Which worked beautifully. The thought of you dying was what really made him aware of his growing connection to you."

A low growl comes out of Talon, a very "shifter" sound I haven't heard from him before.

Kerrim raises his eyebrows in amusement. "Do you deny that wasn't what happened?"

"I tried to get her to drop out of the trials after you pulled that stunt," he grinds out.

"Yet here she is," Kerrim says with a chuckle. "Did you think I wouldn't be clever enough to devise a plan to motivate her through the following trial as well? As soon as that dragon shifter used his fire magic, I used my wind powers to push the spores in your direction and keep them away from her. Again, your affection for each other won out because she made it through that trial by trying to get *you* through it."

Talon's nostrils flare in annoyance when he realizes how we were played.

Kerrim's gaze swings back to me. "Although, I'll admit I was a bit concerned when I found out you'd ditched your dragon heir for greener pastures. I worried your motivation for winning the dagger had waned, so I had to monitor this trial a bit more closely than the last few. And good thing I did, because it looks like he was able to convince you to abandon the prize." Shaking his head in disappointment, Kerrim makes a *tsking* sound with his tongue. "I didn't expect you to be swayed by a handsome face. Your dragon shifter must have been crushed. But no matter, I took precautions." He waves his hand to indicate Talon and the cage he's trapped in.

"If you wanted me to activate Shadow Striker so badly, why did you discourage me from looking into it when I came to the Emporium?"

He cocks his head, giving me a look that says he expected me to put together those pieces myself and is disappointed that I haven't.

"Because it only piqued my interest more," I say, when I realize why he did that.

He gives me a condescending nod that makes me want to throw something at him. "The best way to get a teenager to do something is by telling them not to do it. Speaking of that visit, did you enjoy the book you borrowed?"

I snap my mouth shut. I'd returned to the Emporium last week to finally return the *Dragon Shifter Law* book I'd taken. I checked for another but couldn't find anything. Had he had the foresight to plant that book there, so I'd know how bound Becks really is? From what he's already told me, I wouldn't put it past him. But

I've heard enough about all of that. It's time for Kerrim to get to the point.

"Why do you need *me* to activate Shadow Striker? Is it because you think I'll be easy to kill? Because you can try, but I promise you I won't be as easy to take down as you think. I've been underestimated my whole life."

If I didn't know any better, I'd say Kerrim looked offended. "Kill you? Why ever would you think that?"

"Why else would you want me to activate the dagger than to kill me so you can take it for yourself?"

"Oh no. That's not what I want at all. I won't need to kill you to use Shadow Striker."

Surprised, I look over at Talon, but the crease between his brows says he's just as lost as I am.

"No, there's a very specific reason why I need *you* to activate the dagger." Kerrim takes a step forward and some softness enters his gaze, making him look like the creature I thought I knew, throwing me off. "You're special, Locklyn. I knew it almost the first time I met you. Do you remember how old you were then?"

I think back, confused. "Maybe ten or eleven?"

"Twelve, to be precise, years past when creatures usually come into their magic. But there you were, completely powerless and utterly one of a kind, at least in our world."

"What's that supposed to mean?"

"I'm sure you've always wondered why you never came into your creature magic."

I keep tightlipped. It doesn't matter if I say anything though. The answer is obvious.

"Of course you have," he says almost gently. "It must have been so hard for you not knowing what type of creature you are when all along there has been a simple explanation for it."

Despite everything, I find myself hanging on his every word, and I hate myself a little for it.

"The reason you never developed creature magic is because you aren't actually a creature at all."

I blink back at him. "Of course I'm a creature. What else would I be?"

He shakes his head. "No, my dear. You're not. You're a human."

Human?

"I can see by the look upon your face you're unfamiliar with the term."

"No. That's not possible," Talon says from his cage, and Kerrim glances over at him.

"You had to have at least suspected," he says. "I'm sure you can't detect any magical aura on her."

Talon shakes his head. "There's no way. The gateways have been closed for hundreds of years. We made sure of it."

"Yet here she is," he says, waving his hand toward me.

"What's a human?" I ask, looking between them both.

"An excellent question," Kerrim says. Turning his back to Talon, he takes a step in my direction, and I'm too numb for the warning bells to sound. "You see our world isn't the only one out there. There's a whole world full of beings that exist without magic, and that's where you're from."

I laugh. I can't help it. I'm beyond strung out and what he's saying is insane.

"Oh, I understand now. You're crazy."

He shakes his head. "No. I'm determined, meticulous, and patient. I've been searching for the dagger for decades. And ever since the moment I realized just what you are I've been planning for these trials to activate Shadow Striker. Lining up the pieces so you wouldn't only enter the competition but make it to this point. I'm not insane, I'm brilliant, but because our world only values might, I've been overlooked and shoved aside my entire life. Not anymore."

"Okay, so let's pretend I believe that I'm a being from a

completely different world. One without any magic at all. Who cares? Why does that even matter?"

"It matters a great deal, because once you're bonded to Shadow Striker, the dagger will open a pathway, a portal so to speak, to that magicless world. And when I bring the dagger there, I won't just be another creature among the rest, I'll be a god."

That's the moment I know that whether Kerrim is telling the truth or not, he's most definitely insane.

"If this different world is free of creatures with magic, then the dagger won't be of any use to you there."

"That's where you are wrong. When the dagger crosses into the human world, its powers will be unleashed. It won't need to be activated. It won't be bonded to any one being. I can do with it what I please."

"You're foolish if you think you can control Shadow Striker," Talon speaks up.

"That's rich, coming from you," Kerrim snaps.

"The dagger isn't meant for that world. It's too powerful there," Talon tries again, but his protests fall on deaf ears.

"Now that you know the facts," Kerrim says, completely ignoring Talon, "the time has come." He lifts the blade, holding it out to me. "Take the dagger, Locklyn."

I quickly back away. "I'm not *touching* that thing."

Kerrim's lips purse. "I've spent almost an entire lifetime orchestrating this moment. Let me assure you, before this night is out you *will* activate this dagger."

I shake my head. "I won't."

"We'll see about that."

There's an ominous note to his voice that adds to my unease. Kerrim takes out his phone, taps the screen a few times, and then hands it over to me. "I didn't want it to come to this, but you've left me no choice."

I reluctantly take it from him, and then put a few feet of distance between us before looking at it. What's on the screen makes my heart sink. It's a video feed of my parents sleeping in their bed.

"How do you have this, and why are you showing it to me?" With a sickening feeling, I remember when he came over to help my parents install a new security system. Did he plant cameras in our apartment at the same time? He's obviously skilled with electronics. All the trials except one have been broadcasted, and from what I can tell, he's not working with anyone else. And what else might he have done in our apartment while he was there? It's not as if my parents wouldn't have left him alone. He's an old friend.

"I've had a long time to prepare. Take the dagger, Locklyn, or I'll release a gas into your home that will kill both of your parents."

Fury rises up inside. I trusted him. My parents trusted him, and now he's threatening their lives?

"Or rather, your adoptive parents," he adds with a smirk.

It doesn't matter if what he said about me being a human rather than a creature is true or not. My mom and dad are my parents. *Period.* Losing them would kill me. I'd never recover from it, especially if there were something I could have done to prevent it.

Kerrim holds the dagger out again. "Activate the dagger so I can leave this world and you can go back to your life. It won't cost you anything."

"Freckles, don't do this," Talon says, and when I look over at him the grave look on his face makes my stomach roil. "You don't know everything."

"Shut up," Kerrim snaps, but Talon ignores him, his gaze never wavering from mine.

"I'm bonded to Shadow Striker. If you activate the dagger, it will kill me."

Shock vibrates throughout me, and I freeze. My body goes hot, then cold, then numb.

This whole time Talon has been bonded to Shadow Striker? How did I not know?

As the shock fades, it's replaced by clarity, and as if a veil has been lifted, everything about Talon starts to make a sick sort of sense. How his magic never seemed to fit into a specific creature species. The real reason he was always so secretive. Why he's been almost desperate to win Chaos.

The truth has been staring me in the face since the beginning, but I was just too blind to see it.

"Kill you?"

Talon nods. "Shadow Striker can only be tethered to a single being at once. If the bond is severed because it's been activated by someone else, it will kill the other creature. If you take that dagger its magic will transfer from me to you, and I won't survive."

I stare back at Talon, desperate for him to tell me he's lying, because now I'm faced with an impossible choice: kill Talon or let my parents die.

I don't know what to say. I don't know what to do.

"I'm sorry," he says, and I can see the apology shining from his blue-gray eyes.

"Why didn't you tell me? Don't you trust me?"

"That wasn't it. Some secrets aren't mine to tell."

"But this one is."

"Not really."

Not really? What does that even mean? If not his secret to tell, then whose?

"I know what I'm asking you isn't fair, but you can't activate that dagger."

"Don't listen to him," Kerrim cuts in. "He's just trying to save his own skin. What's one life in exchange for the lives of your parents?"

Talon grasps the bars of the cage, his gaze boring into me. "It's not just one life. If he brings Shadow Striker into the human world, the dagger's powers will multiply. He'll be unstoppable. It won't just be my life you're ending, but the lives of millions, maybe billions of beings like you."

"If you don't, your parents won't live to see another day," Kerrim growls, his face contorting into the picture of rage. "And after I've killed them, I'll go after Becks, then your friends, and anyone else you've ever cared for. I've been in your life for years. I've been watching and studying, learning your weaknesses along with your strengths. I know exactly who means something to you, and I will destroy them to get what I want."

"You wouldn't . . ." But looking at Kerrim I'm not so sure. I might have known him for a good part of my life, might have even had affection toward him, but right now I don't recognize the creature in front of me.

"I'm not evil, but you have no idea the depths I will go to see this through."

Tears stream down my face. Whatever I decide to do, someone dies.

There has to be another way.

"My patience is running thin. Perhaps I need to make an example of your parents before you believe me."

"No!" I shout, holding up my hands to stop him from doing something rash. I take a step forward, bringing me within an arm's length of Kerrim and the dagger.

"Then are you ready to do what needs to be done?"

I look over at Talon through a veil of tears. "I'm so sorry. I don't have a choice."

I expect his face to harden, for him to toss insults or scream at me, but instead his gaze softens. He looks resigned when he says, "I understand, Freckles. Do what you have to do."

With a nod, I look back at Kerrim, my hand shaking as it nears Shadow Striker. There's a feverish look in Kerrim's dark eyes as his gaze laser focuses on my hand as I reach for the dagger.

Good. That's exactly where I want his attention.

Still reaching for the dagger with one hand, I snap the other out and snatch the key ring off his belt loop that I spotted the moment he shed his robes. Turning, I go to toss the keys to Talon, but as I'm about to throw them Kerrim plows into me from behind, taking me down. The keys arc through the air, and I lose sight of them as I hit the ground.

"You stupid, stupid girl," he says, and slams a fist into my kidney. "I'll kill everyone you ever loved, taking pleasure in every death."

He's completely and utterly unhinged. I manage to flip onto my back, but he crouches over me, unrelenting in his onslaught, using both fists to hit any fleshy parts of me that he can reach. I'm trained for situations like this and how to get out of them, but Kerrim's wrath seems to be giving him superpowers and I can't squirm free or get a hit in. All I can do is protect my face against his onslaught.

"Hang on, Freckles. I've almost got the keys," Talon yells, and Kerrim's head snaps up.

While he's distracted, I reach out blindly, patting the ground for a rock or something to smash into his face. I don't even register what my hand comes in contact with until my fingers close over it and I've swung out. At the last moment, Kerrim rears back and the object in my hand slices harmlessly through his shirt.

I start to strike again, but the look in Kerrim's eyes makes me pause. Pure glee radiates from his face as he stares at my hand. When I look down, horror fills me, because clenched in my fist is Shadow Striker.

Thirty-Eight

I DROP the dagger and scramble to my feet, spinning toward Talon and freezing when I find him standing just outside the open door of the cage, staring back at me with the keys I tossed still in his hand.

"Freckles?" He tries to take a step, but staggers.

I jolt forward, reaching him just as his knees give out. Helping him to the ground, I prop him up against the cage's bars.

No no no. This can't be happening.

But then I can feel it happening. Shadow Striker's magic starts to pull from Talon and transfer to me. I can even see silver and gold tendrils weaving through the air between us, and I can't deny what's happening. The dagger is bonding with me and killing Talon.

"Talon, no. I didn't mean to. It was an accident. I don't know what to do."

Lifting a hand, he places two fingers over my mouth, stopping my rambling. "Get Shadow Striker. Take it to my uncle and tell him what happened. He'll bring you to my family. They'll know what to do."

I look over to where I dropped the dagger and my breath catches. An expanding ball of light and energy hangs in the air above Shadow Striker. Kerrim has forgotten about Talon and me completely, his gaze stuck on the growing brightness that I can only assume is the portal to the human world.

"Don't let him go through," Talon says, and I can tell that every word costs him. "Get the dagger and run."

My mind can't wrap around the thought of just abandoning Talon, so I hesitate. I'm about to spring into action when there's a boom overhead and the ground beneath us shakes. It happens again, and I jerk my gaze up as dirt and debris rain down upon us.

Kerrim takes a step back from the portal that's now almost large enough for a creature to fit through, and looks up at the sky. I do the same, but I can't make out anything past the shadowed dome encasing the ruins.

There's another boom as it seems like the shadows above are dissipating. I can see stars through the barrier. One last boom, the shadows overhead shatter, and a scaled and winged beast breaks through.

Becks.

From his position in the sky, it only takes Becks a moment to locate us. He dives, splaying his wings to slow his fall before he drops into the space, stirring up a cyclone of dirt.

I've only seen Becks in his dragon form a handful of times, but each one of them I've been in awe of his size and strength, as well as beauty. In dragon form, Becks is roughly twelve feet high, and his wingspan is double that. His scales are iridescent teal; he has two black horns that curve back from the sides of his head, and spikes that run down his spine and tail. His talons are easily eight inches long and lethally sharp.

For the first time since Talon and I fell through the floor, I start to feel hopeful.

Slapping his tail against the ground, Becks swings his body toward me. He starts to take a step forward, but behind him I notice Kerrim snatch Shadow Striker from the ground and start toward the portal.

"Becks, don't let him get through the portal," I yell, jumping to my feet.

Becks has no idea what's happened here tonight. Kerrim would never have broadcasted all of this, but even so he doesn't hesitate, spinning toward the game master and shooting a stream of fire directly in his path.

Kerrim hits the ground, avoiding the deadly flames, but pops up quickly. At first I think he's going to shift and fly through the portal, but then I realize that he'd have to drop the dagger to do so. Magical objects won't transform with a shift.

Becks rounds on Kerrim, swiping at him with his claws until he backs away from the portal. Kerrim tries to fight back, even going as far as to try to strike at Becks with the dagger, but he's no match for the powerful dragon shifter with almost impenetrable scales. Even so, Kerrim's attempts are enough to keep Becks busy, if not enough to actually get the upper hand.

Talon coughs at my feet. When I look down, his breathing is ragged, and his face is pallid underneath his usual tan skin. Even as I stand above him, I can feel the magic from the dagger draining him and filling me.

He's dying. I know he is. And it's all my doing.

I fall to my knees next to him, confident that Becks can hold off Kerrim on his own.

"I'm so sorry." A tear falls from my eye and trickles down my cheek, falling on his chest.

He lifts a hand and wipes away the track of wetness it left behind. "Get me through the portal," he says, his voice weak and soft.

"The portal?"

"I need to be separated from the dagger so I can heal. Get me through that portal and let it close behind me."

"Talon, if I do that you'll be trapped in a different realm."

"If you don't, I'll be dead in minutes."

Swallowing the knot in my throat, I nod. I don't let myself

think about what I'm doing as I slip my arm around him and help him to his feet. The first few steps are wobbly, but then we get the hang of it. Somewhere behind us, Kerrim hurls insults at Becks as we shuffle toward the glowing circle that's now at least ten or eleven feet wide, if not more. When we near the portal, the world beyond becomes visible through a translucent shimmering veil.

At first glance it doesn't look any different than ours. On the other side of the portal is a grassy field ringed by trees in the distance. I'm not an expert, but it looks like regular maples and oaks. The night sky overhead is dotted with stars, just like our world. There's nothing particularly frightening or alien about it, but I'm still scared to cross through until Talon tenses up next to me. When I look over, it's obvious he's in pain. He's biting his lower lip to keep from shouting out, but his muscles shake. The thin silver and gold strands connecting us pulsate, brightening with each beat, sucking away more of Talon's energy, his life, every moment that passes.

I'll only be gone for a minute. Once I go through, I'll come right back, I tell myself as I gather my courage.

I take another step forward and something detonates, hitting Talon and me from the side and throwing us through the air and into a wall of rock. For the second time this evening, I hit my head, and then crumple to the ground. Talon groans next to me and I force my eyes open. My vision is hazy, and when it clears I spot Becks and Kerrim battling each other in the middle of the cave.

It's clear Becks is struggling, but my foggy brain can't make sense of it at first. Becks is one of the most powerful shifters alive, yet he's getting pushed back by Kerrim's attacks. But then I notice the objects in Kerrim's hands. In one fist he grips Shadow Striker, and in the other he holds another enhancer, identical to the one still lying useless in the cage Talon was trapped in. As a hawk shifter, he has an affinity for wind, and he keeps sending massive gusts of air at Becks, which keeps him at bay.

I realize too late what Kerrim is doing. I try to pop to my feet, but the world goes sideways, and I put a hand on the wall to steady myself. Closing my eyes, I swallow down a wave of nausea, but I force them open again in time to watch my worst nightmare.

With a yell of fury, Kerrim sends a wind power blast at Becks' chest. He tries to block it with one of his wings, but the force of the hit sends him sailing backward right into and through the portal.

"No!" I scream, and Kerrim's head whips in my direction.

He's standing right in front of the portal, dagger in hand. There's nothing to stop him from walking right through to the human world.

"It didn't have to be this way," he says. He then takes two steps and disappears into the glowing ring that I just watched him push Becks through. The moment he passes through with Shadow Striker, the portal starts to shrink.

I take off, my steps unsteady. I can see Becks in the rapidly shrinking portal. He's shifted back into his non-dragon form and his back is to me. I scream his name and I hobble forward.

Becks' head swings in my direction, his gaze filled with confusion.

The portal is hardly big enough for a creature, no more than a three-foot ring. I'm too far away and I'm not moving fast enough. I won't get there in time.

"Get out of there before the portal closes," I yell, and he turns toward me and starts running.

I almost cry in relief. *He's going to make it*, I tell myself, but when he's just feet from the portal Kerrim appears behind him almost as if out of thin air. He raises Shadow Striker over his head preparing to strike.

"Behind you!" I scream in warning, but it's too late.

I stumble forward as the portal contracts to the size of a basketball, watching in horror as the blade punches through Becks' chest. His eyes widen in shock, and the last thing I see before the light ring collapses is him mouthing my name as a trickle of blood leaks from the corner of his mouth.

I fall to my knees in the exact spot that the portal opened, digging my nails into the dirt beneath me, my mind and body numbed from shock.

No. *No no no.* That did not just happen. Becks did not just get stabbed. He's not trapped in another world.

No, it didn't happen. Becks is safe. Becks is okay. Becks is here.

I repeat the lies over and over in my head as if that will make it true.

A hand lands on my shoulder and I jolt, scrambling back, but when I look up Talon's standing above me, pity and regret in his gaze. He still looks weak, but some of his coloring has returned, and he was able to get over here without my assistance. There also aren't any more silver or gold threads connecting the two of us.

That's when it really sinks in. Kerrim took Shadow Striker to the human world, exactly what we were trying to prevent him from doing, but it separated Talon from the blade, saving his life.

"Freckles, I'm so sorry," he says, sounding almost like he understands what I've just lost.

"We have to go after him."

Talon shakes his head, but I won't accept that Becks is lost forever.

I get to my feet, and when I wobble Talon steadies me. I pull out of his grasp, his touch reminding me of how I betrayed Becks, about how even thinking I had chosen Talon over him he found a way to reach me, and now he was in another world and might never know the truth.

I was never with Talon. I've always loved Becks.

"You said there were gateways. Gateways that had been sealed. We'll open one and go after him."

"Freckles—"

"Don't call me that," I snap, and Talon flinches.

"I never meant for this to happen."

I hold up my hand, stopping his apologies. I can't hear them right now. "After everything, after the lies you told and the ways you deceived me time and time again over the last several weeks, you owe me."

Talon looks at me like he wants to pull me into his arms, but he wisely keeps them at his side. "Frec—Locklyn, even if we could get to the human world, we wouldn't even know where to start looking for him. That world is as big as ours. He could be anywhere."

"That's not true," I say, my mind snagging on something I saw through the portal. A sign in the distance. A map with the name of the location written above it. "I saw a sign through the portal. I know exactly where to look," I say, my confidence growing.

I can fix this. We can go to the human world, find Becks, and bring him home.

If he's still alive, my mind whispers, and a sharp pain pierces my chest as if I were the one stabbed.

I take a shaky breath and push doubt aside. Becks is strong. He's alive. I won't believe otherwise.

"Where?" Talon asks with a frown.

I look him straight in the eye, remembering the words from the sign exactly how they were written, in big, bold, white block letters on a green background.

"Central Park."

Dear friend,

   Thank you for reading! If you enjoyed this book, please take a few moments to rate and review it so that others might decide to read my books. Thank you!

~ Julie

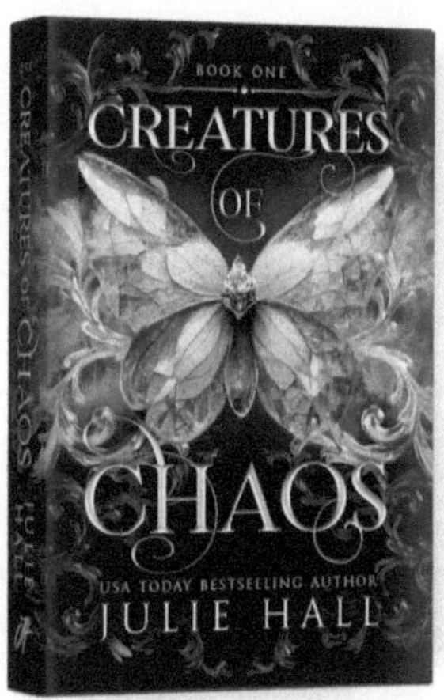

http://Review.CreaturesOfChaosBook.com

Acknowledgments

I couldn't do what I do without the love and support of my amazing husband, Lucas. I would have thrown in the writing towel long ago if he hadn't been there to carry me through more than one rough spot. He's also the design genius behind 'Creatures of Chaos,' making it my most visually stunning book yet.

A special thanks to my good friend and fellow author, Leia Stone. Without her, I might not have made it through this book with my sanity fully intact. I'm so blessed to have someone like her in my corner.

I feel incredibly fortunate to have collaborated with an outstanding editorial team on this book. Working with Wendy, Lee, and Janelle was an absolute pleasure. The dedication and hard work each of them put into this project has undeniably strengthened the book.

Maria and K.D.'s covers are to die for! I'm so proud to have their stunning designs showcasing the books in this series.

This book owes much of its special charm to the beautiful illustrations contributed by Irene, Damien, Camille, and Lyubov. Their exceptional talents brought the characters to life in a truly remarkable way.

Thanks to Andra, Brit, Erin, and Heidi for stepping in and helping me polish Creatures of Chaos. I'm truly humbled that they were willing to volunteer as tributes. They're the best readers and friends an author could hope for!

Kelly, my PA, is an angel for keeping things moving behind the scenes. I'd truly be lost without her and I'm so thankful for her support.

And finally, no thanks to my furbabies, Coco and Moose, who did everything they could throughout my writing days to distract me with their cuteness as they begged for cuddles and food (not usually in that order). You both are the worst, in the best way possible and I love you for it.

Julie Hall is a *USA Today* bestselling, multiple award-winning author. Before diving into the world of publishing, she was publicist and marketer for Sony, Summit Entertainment, Paramount, The Weinstein Company, and the National Geographic Channel.

Now, she crafts addictive action-packed fantasy stories that leave readers with epic book hangovers. Julie's books have been translated to four languages and won or were finalists in over 20 national and international awards.

Julie currently lives in Colorado with her four favorite people–her husband, daughter, and two fur babies.

Website:
JulieHallAuthor.com

Join the Fan Club:
facebook.com/groups/juliehall

Get exclusive updates by email:
JulieHallAuthor.com/newsletter

Let's Connect:

amazon.com/author/julieghall

facebook.com/JulieHallAuthor

instagram.com/Julie.Hall.Author

tiktok.com/@juliehallauthor

goodreads.com/JulieHallAuthor

youtube.com/JulieHallAuthor

Books by Julie Hall

Fallen Legacies Series

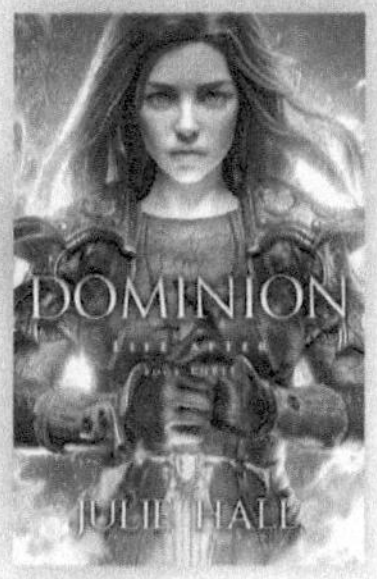

Life After Series

Shadow Angel Series

www.JulieHallAuthor.com